The Twice Lost

SARAH PORTER

HOUGHTON MIFFLIN HARCOURT
BOSTON NEW YORK

The text of this book is set in 11.5-point LTC Deepdene OT

The Library of Congress has cataloged the hardcover edition as follows:
Porter, Sarah—
The twice list / Sarah Porter.
p. cm.
Sequel to: Waking storms.
Summary: When humans declare war on mermaids, Luce swims to San Francisco Bay where
she finds a group of "twice lost" girls, lost once when trauma turned them into mermaids and
again when they defied mermaid law, and unites them into an army under her leadership.
[1. Mermaids—Fiction. 2. Supernatural—Fiction. 3. Interpersonal relations—Fiction.
4. War—Fiction. 5. San Francisco Bay Area (Calif.)—Fiction.] I. Title.
PZ7.P8303Twi 2013
2013003918

ISBN: 978-0-547-48252-1 hardcover
ISBN: 978-0-547-48255-2 paperback

Manufactured in the United States of America
DOC 10 9 8 7 6 5 4 3 2
4500667304

Joining Together

I wanted to ask if you would go talk to them. To the other mermaids around the bay." Luce hesitated; it seemed so presumptuous. "Ask them if they'd like to join us for training tonight."

"You mean—if they'll promise not to kill humans in exchange for learning what you can do?" Yuan thought about it. "You even want me to ask the crazy ones?"

"If . . . if that's okay with you. I mean . . ." Luce tried to shake off her embarrassment. "I think we're going to need as many mermaids working with us as we can get. If we're really going to stop the humans . . ."

"So you're not just talking about teaching everyone? You're talking about . . ."

"About asking them to *really* join us. Yeah." Luce considered the question, then straightened herself. "Please tell them that General Luce is inviting them to join the Twice Lost Army."

For my mother, Betsy Hart Porter,

with love

When the world is sick, can't no one be well,

But I dreamt we was all beautiful and strong.

A Silver Mt. Zion, "God Bless Our Dead Marines"

1

The Tank

"Hello," the young man in the lab coat purred into a round speaker, his hands fidgeting. Ripples of azure light reflected on his cheeks. "Are you awake?" There was no response. He stood with a few other stiff-backed men, among them the nation's secretary of defense, in a room divided in half by a wall of thick—and perfectly soundproof—glass. Behind the glass was something that resembled the kind of fake habitat found in a zoo, like an enclosure for keeping penguins or seals. Bubbling salt water filled most of the tank to a depth of about five feet, but on the right there was an artificial shore of baby blue cement sloping down into the water. That was where the resemblance to a zoo display ended, though. A giant flat-screen television blazed high on the wall above the tank's deep end, playing what appeared to be a reality show about rich teenagers. Flouncy pink satin cushions were heaped along the shore just above the waterline, and a large white dresser decorated with golden scrolls perched on a ledge at the back. Various electronic gadgets were scattered on the cement, but beyond the clutter the tank gave no sign of being inhabited. "You have a very important visitor today, so . . . your full cooperation . . ."

The crowd behind him shifted impatiently, and the young

man flinched as if he could feel their disapproval pricking his skin. "Getting on with it! I'm going to be turning on your microphone so you can talk to these men. But I have to warn you . . ." Far back in the tank something sky blue and pearlescent flicked up for a moment from behind a pile of cushions. For a second the young man's voice grated to a halt, and he stared urgently before he mastered himself enough to keep going. "We've programmed the computer to recognize any hint of singing. If you try anything, it will send out an electric shock automatically. A pretty severe one. All right? I'd like you to be on . . ." There was that blue flash again, and a trace of rippling gold. "On . . . your best behavior, please." He turned to look at the secretary of defense and offered a tight, ingratiating smile. Then he flicked a switch in a small control panel set into the glass beside the speaker. "Please meet the United States secretary of defense. Secretary Moreland?"

Moreland leaned toward the glass, an odd expression rippling over his heavy reddish face with its sagging jowls. His white hair shone like meringue above his gleaming pate. "Anais," he snapped, then waited, scowling, for a reply. It didn't come. "I'd suggest you get your damned tail over here. You're our little mermaid now."

The sky blue tail rose above the water again, twitching irritably. Pinkish iridescence shone on its scales, and the cushions stirred as a golden head shifted up into view. Dreamy azure eyes turned to gaze through the glass. Several of the men stepped forward as if involuntarily, and others visibly braced themselves. She shook herself, and her inhuman beauty came at them like a living wave. Moreland's smirk tightened, and his upper lip jerked sharply higher to expose his perfect teeth. "Hello, there."

"Hi." She examined Moreland's crisp, expensive suit with a trace of approval. "Are you really important?"

It was hard to tell if Moreland was leering or snarling in response. "Oh, I'd say so."

"Then I only want to talk to *you*." She scanned the other men disdainfully. "Having all these people staring at me makes me feel so shy!"

She didn't look shy, but Moreland nodded almost indulgently. He made a quick motion to the young man in the lab coat, who hurried to tap at the control panel, cutting off Anais's sound. "Do you mind, gentlemen?" Moreland asked.

"We can observe through the monitors in the next room?" the lab-coated man asked anxiously. "She is—I mean I am her primary handler, and I should know—"

"Oh, I don't think so." Moreland's lip hiked up again. "I don't think you should observe. I'd like to allow *her*"—he cocked his head toward the tank, where Anais, piqued at not being able to hear what they were saying, was now swimming toward the glass—"a chance to confide in me. Privately."

"But—of course you're aware, Mr. Secretary, that she's suffered some very serious trauma. Those mermaids she was living with, all . . ."

"A fragile flower," Moreland agreed, grinning horribly. "I'll use my most delicate touch."

The young lab-coated man didn't look particularly reassured, but he still nodded. "The blue switch controls sound going into her side. The red cuts her off over here. Given the precautions we've taken, though—"

"Thank you, Mr. . . ."

"Hackett. Charles."

"Thank you, Mr. Hackett. I'll let you know when I need your assistance."

Anais was tapping, though inaudibly, on her side of the glass. She was supporting herself in the deepest water with a slight circulating motion of her fins so that her face and shoulders floated just above the surface. Her hair rippled and shone around her, and she looked sulky and eager. Hackett gave her a coy little smile and a wave as he turned to leave. "Even *without* any singing," one of the men observed as they walked to the door, "she's still remarkably . . ."

"Remarkably?" one of his companions asked archly, eyebrows raised.

"Compelling, I would say."

"I'd use a different term, frankly."

Secretary Moreland didn't watch them go. Instead he was staring fixedly into Anais's blue eyes, though the look on his face didn't exactly suggest attraction. It was somewhere between caressing and murderous, and a smirk kept tweaking his lips. Once everyone was gone he reached to flip the sound back on, still keeping his gaze locked on Anais's face. "Better now, tadpole?"

Anais pouted. Her lips were slick with strawberry pink gloss. "You have a problem."

"I'd say there are some other—you really can't call them people—some other nasty animals who have much bigger problems these days. You should be very, very thankful that we're taking such good care of you. When you could be in the same mess as your little killing-machine friends . . ."

Anais shrugged impatiently, sending a quick surge through the water around her. Her hair lapped at her shoulders. She was wearing a sparkly, sky blue tank top that matched her tail almost perfectly, and diamond studs sparked in her ears. "I don't care about that! Charlie told me about that boat of yours that got trashed."

"Charlie?"

"Mr. Hackett. He said there was a big wave that came out of nowhere and, like, *totaled* the boat with your guys on it, after . . ." Anais suddenly seemed a bit uncomfortable. "After . . . I surrendered. I knew you'd want to *talk* to one of us, if we just acted nicer. And—"

"That wave didn't come out of nowhere, I think, tadpole. You shouldn't assume that Mr. Hackett's information is entirely reliable."

"That's what I'm trying to *tell* you!" Anais was getting exasperated. "I just didn't want to tell . . . Mr. Hackett because I didn't think he could really do anything. I figured it all out. You can go and kill mermaids without the *singing* stopping you now. Right? But you don't have any way to stop her from bashing your guys with those waves. You *have* to kill her. Soon! Like, right now she's the only one who knows how to do that, but she'll probably start teaching everybody else, and then you won't be able to get rid of mermaids anymore at *all* . . ."

Secretary Moreland was clearly trying to keep his expression steady, but it wasn't working. Tiny spasms of excitement bent his features and shimmered in his eyes. "So you're claiming you know the mermaid who committed the assault on the Special Ops boat?" He paused for a moment, assessing. "Several of our men were killed. This isn't something we take at all lightly. You wouldn't want to be anything less than perfectly candid on the subject."

"Of course I know her. We had to kick her out of the tribe because all she did was cause *problems,* but then she wouldn't stop hanging around . . ." Anais's tail was swishing faster now, its pink iridescence flashing candied reflections on the glass.

Moreland looked disappointed. "So she wouldn't consider you a friend? Try to find you?"

"No way! She knows I see right through her. Though she did keep trying to get me to pay *attention* to her."

Moreland nodded. The sparks in his eyes seemed agitated. "I *see*. But you'll tell me all about her, won't you? I'd suggest you start now."

Anais leaned back from the glass with a motion that suggested someone settling into an armchair, although there was nothing but water around her, and smiled slyly. Her fins lightly stroked across the tank's blue cement floor. "That depends."

"*Does* it? On what?"

"On you letting me out of here!" Anais shook her head, golden rays of hair swinging with the movement. "I mean, I know my parents must have left me a *ton* of money. And the house! And there's a pool, and I could get our servants to come back, and—"

"Tadpole, tadpole . . ." Moreland shook his head, and his smile was much softer, much more slippery, than before. "You haven't thought this through."

"I totally have! I—"

"You aren't *human*, little tail. Not remotely."

"So?"

"So the law doesn't apply to you. Not one teeny bit. And that's including due process and inheritance law. Legally you don't exist. There's no provision in the law for leaving a house to a precious little monster . . ."

This clearly hadn't occurred to Anais before. Her eyes widened in dismay and her mouth opened onto a round darkness that seemed to threaten the unleashing of terrible music. Moreland grinned stonily and raised his eyebrows at her. She paused and glanced around her tank, then shut her mouth again.

"Exactly," he hissed. Anais scowled. "But you don't like this troublemaker mermaid, do you? She absolutely deserves to die, doesn't she?"

Anais was still sulking. "Of course she deserves it!"

"So maybe helping us track her down would be worth your time anyway. I promise you we'll tear her guts right out. Maybe we'll even take our time doing it. Remember, legal protections don't apply to her either, and we're very, very annoyed with her."

Anais cocked her head, brazenly intrigued. "You *should* be. She's a bitch, and she's really nuts. And just, like, *weird*."

"Tell me her name." Moreland's voice was suddenly rough.

"Luce." Anais spat it out.

A shadow passed through his pale eyes. "Luce. I believe I've heard her mentioned before. And what about her . . . *human* name? Do you know that much?"

"Will you at least show me *pictures*? Once you kill her?"

"Oh, certainly. Probably even video. We'll watch it together. It will be my great pleasure. Virtue should always be rewarded." Aqua light from the tank gleamed on Moreland's wet teeth as he spoke.

"Lucette . . ." Anais visibly struggled to remember. "She said it . . . No, *Catarina* said it once when they were fighting. Lucette Kip . . . No. Lucette Korchak?"

"A very good beginning, Anais." Moreland smiled. "You know, at first I wasn't sure your information was reliable. But I'm beginning to think we can come to an understanding after all."

"What about Sedna? Will you at least make sure you kill her, too? And Dana, and Violet."

"Sedna was the leader of the group you identified? In southern Alaska?"

"Yeah. She—"

"Ah, but that's why I didn't think we could trust you, my dear. We couldn't find any trace of mermaids anywhere near the location you described to us. Unless you can do better, I'm afraid I won't be able to show you video of Sedna's dismemberment."

"I told you the truth." Anais's pout tightened moodily, and her head tipped sideways. "I bet Luce got there first. I bet she *warned* them."

Moreland nodded, a bit curtly. "Very possibly. I need you to understand something, Anais. It won't be easy, and it won't happen anytime soon. But if you help us enough, I might eventually see my way to . . . encouraging special consideration of your case. Maybe a judge could be persuaded that you deserve your inheritance after all, in view of your services to your country."

Anais mulled this, her blue fins rippling irritably. Then her face changed completely. All at once she beamed with gentle innocence. "Of *course* I'll help. It isn't safe for anyone to have Luce swimming around out there! She'll just kill so *many* of your men if no one stops her!"

"Quite so." Moreland's tongue slid across his bluish teeth, and his eyes widened with a fake sincerity that almost equaled Anais's, except that his smile kept twisting into a leer. Every tiny disturbance of the water sent greenish light crawling across his stiff white hair. "We're very grateful for your patriotism. Now, did . . . Lucette ever mention the name Dorian to you? Dorian Hurst?"

"Who?" Anais asked. Her confusion looked genuine enough.

Moreland was disappointed again, but Anais suddenly leaned forward in excitement. "Wait, wait, wait! A guy? You're saying that Luce was seeing a *human guy*? That is so sick!" She squealed with laughter. "And she thought she was supposed to be queen!

Oh, I can't wait to tell . . ." Anais's laughter faltered abruptly, and she looked down.

Moreland observed her for a long moment. His gray eyes were covetous, cold. "Oh, but there's no one left to tell, is there, tadpole? The abominations who would have liked to hear your gossip about Lucette and her human boyfriend are all dead." He gazed at her with something that might have almost passed for compassion. "We destroyed every last one of them in front of you. And even as we speak the teams are out there, hunting down other groups of your kind."

"I didn't *want* to be a mermaid!" Anais snarled. "I never wanted to! They're not my kind! I loved being human. Everything was so *perfect* . . ."

Moreland considered this. "You didn't want to be a mermaid. Were you somehow changed against your will?"

"Of course I was!" Anais was staring down, plainly on the verge of tears. Maybe they were even real.

The secretary of defense didn't look convinced. "Then who changed you?"

"Luce did it." It came out in a sullen whimper. "She *forced* me, but I . . ."

"That's *very* sad." Moreland stared at Anais for a few more moments. Now that she wasn't looking at him, he examined her stunning form with a mixture of hungry fascination and naked loathing. "Well, then, it's a very fortunate thing that you're living with humans again, isn't it? You can talk to us. Now, what you said before, about this Luce . . ."

2

Southward

How long had she been lost in the same rhythm? Weeks, she thought, although her sense of time was blurred. She kept swimming south. Always hugging the coastline, always rippling through waters that shifted from tints of olive to milky jade to tarnished silver, and continually gusting out a long cry like moaning wind: an alarm-song. Luce checked any caves she noticed, but there were inevitably ones she missed, with entrances below the depth where she was swimming or sometimes deliberately concealed behind thick fans of seaweed. As the human population rose along the coast, the local mermaids made greater efforts to keep themselves sheltered from discovery. That was why Luce kept the airy half-song constantly whistling from her throat: she might not see them, but they would almost certainly hear her. And if they did—if they respected the timahk at all, at least—they would rush out to see who she was, and if she needed help.

Then she could tell them. Clusters of unfamiliar faces would gather around her in the water. Sometimes Luce would have to blink, to rub her eyes, to stop herself from seeing different faces shining like movie projections on their wavering bodies. If she didn't concentrate, she'd start to see Nausicaa, Miriam, Rachel,

Catarina, even—horribly—Dorian . . . But maybe it didn't matter who she saw as long as she remembered to say the right words. "The humans know about us. Soldiers massacred my old tribe, up in Alaska. Singing to them won't work; they have helmets that block out our songs. And somehow they can find our caves.

"You have to move to new territory. Make sure it's secret and remote, and stay as hidden as you can. And whatever you do, don't sink any ships. If you do they'll know you're nearby and start hunting you . . ."

Luce was too numb to do much besides repeat the same message. Her voice was urgent, sad, and still distorted and airy with the windy song that never completely died away in her chest. She barely registered their reactions: disbelief or terror or even misplaced fury, as if the coming horror was somehow Luce's fault. She didn't care. She had to breathe out her warning to as many mermaids as she could. Once the words had left her, she was done. Empty. Like a tunnel charged with wind, the only thing inside her was movement.

At least, she was empty until she found the next tribe.

Where was she now? Canada somewhere? Or had she already reached the coast of Washington? Luce didn't ask. The tribe she'd just called to come out to her—it must have been the seventh or eighth after Sedna's—heard her out quietly, even gently. They seemed to understand that she was caught in some toxic dream, that the words had to finish hissing out of her before anything else could happen.

Luce was already flexing her aching tail, ready to pulse onward. A hand caught her arm, and dark blond hair waved in the corner of her eye. *Dorian? Is that . . .*

"We know." The mermaid holding on to her had an unusually

sensitive, open face; Luce felt a flutter of unaccustomed hope at the thought that this was their queen. She'd take good care of the girls with her. "We've already heard what's happening."

Mermaids had said all kinds of wild and desperate things to Luce along her journey, but nothing until now had quite caught her attention. This time she looked up and truly saw the queen in front of her in a way that she hadn't observed anyone for some time. Her expression was sorrowful, and now Luce realized that the mermaids surrounding her all looked heart-shocked, anxious and pale.

"You . . ."

"We *know*. Listen . . . the tribe south of us got slaughtered two nights ago. Three of them escaped and made it up here, but they were out when it happened, so they didn't see anything besides the bodies. We weren't sure if maybe it was just that one tribe, and this is the first we've heard about *how* the humans are doing it, about the helmets—"

"It's not just that tribe!" Luce was gasping, and she felt an urge to get away. Waking from the trance of her journey meant feeling more horror and heartbreak than she could stand. "Please . . . you have to hide."

"And we might know who you are, too, I think. Queen Luce? We've heard . . ."

The other problem with stopping like this was that it gave her time to notice how utterly crushed, how nauseous and heavy she felt. Her body felt like lead, bizarrely cold and molten at the same time. Each word she spoke seemed to cost her more effort than the one before. But the fact that this strange girl recognized her—even more, the fact that she addressed Luce as *queen*—might mean that Luce was getting closer to finding the friend she needed most in the world.

"Nausicaa?" Luce barely breathed. "When?"

"When was she here, you mean? A few months ago." The blond queen said it in a sympathetic voice that showed she knew this would be unwelcome news. "But she talked about you a lot, Luce. She told us to expect you."

That didn't make any sense. "She . . ."

"She said she thought you'd be coming this way sometime. And that we should help you." A pause. "You look like you could use a good rest. We'll get you some food first, though."

"No!" She had to keep going. The hideous truth was just sinking in: the tribe south of this one was already dead. She hadn't been fast enough.

"I *promise* we'll follow your advice, Queen Luce. Okay? But you could sleep while we scout for a new place to live." She examined Luce, gently critical. "You look like you might be getting sick."

Luce's whole body writhed as if she were snarled in a net. It was far more effort than she needed to pull her arm away. "No! I have to . . . There are other tribes. I can't just stop."

"You have to rest *sometime*, though."

Luce couldn't understand the icy thrumming of her heart, her clenching stomach, the utter physical terror that possessed her, as if she'd found herself in a closing trap. These mermaids were warm and sincere; they genuinely wanted to help her, look after her. She gazed around the circle, watching their growing perplexity in the face of her panic. "I . . . don't mean to be rude. I'm sorry. But I have to . . ." Their eyes looked like the unseeing orbs in the faces of the dead girls heaped in her old cave; Luce remembered a head split open so that its staring blue eyes were much too far apart. Talking was simply too hard for her. She had only enough words left inside her to keep repeating her warning.

She gave up trying to explain and dived away. She couldn't suppress her fright, and she lashed her tail as if she were being chased, though she knew that her fear had nothing to do with reality. But she was so tired. For days now she'd only slept in occasional snatches, her sleep so shaken and wrung out by nightmares that it hardly felt like rest at all. The lozenges of glow in front of her might be only refracted moonlight or they might be shining fish. The rocks were pitching in a way that made them hard to distinguish from the waves, and she could feel her body weaving.

"Dorian," Luce said to herself. His name was just a sickness, a taunting noise that kept appearing on her lips. She spat to clear it away. He'd forgotten her; he was probably kissing Zoe right now, staring at her with adoration the same way he'd once stared at Luce.

And somewhere men in a locker room might be taking off their complicated black helmets, peeling off slick rubber suits, laughing about that night's kills. Of course, mermaids had laughed about killing humans too, but knowing that didn't make Luce any less determined to protect her own kind. They were the lost girls, the ones the humans didn't want. They were all so broken that Luce couldn't bear the idea of their breaking again. She imagined fragments of porcelain, stars made of blood on a cold marble floor. Once they died they shifted back into human form; there would be childish feet and legs where their gleaming tails had been . . .

She had a vague idea of stopping to scavenge for shellfish then realized that if she ate she wouldn't be able to keep the food down.

The thought of all the tribes she had to warn kept her moving. And moving was the only thing that kept her alive.

* * *

It was late afternoon, a cool, pearly day with the scent of wild-flowers sweetening the breeze. The blackness she saw everywhere, Luce realized, had to be coming from inside her. She lashed her tail recklessly, straining to keep her eyes open, to keep seeing the curved winglike shapes of daylight that flared above her head, to sustain the wind-toned song pouring through her mouth. The light on the waves above her seemed to be blinking out, though. Streaks and coils of pitch darkness appeared scrawled on the surface of the water, as if it were a page where someone was drawing in thick black ink. *Strange,* Luce thought. She must be starting to see things that weren't there.

How long had it been since she'd darted away from that last tribe? A few hours? Longer?

Maybe she really did need to find somewhere to sleep, but this wasn't a good place for it. She'd swung farther out to sea to avoid what looked like a fairly large town with too many boats crisscrossing its waters, and now there was a long row of water-front houses tucked among the spruce trees. Their windows flashed silvery daylight at her like some kind of signal, and voices carried faintly through the water. Now and then unsuspecting sailboats flew by overhead, and Luce heard people laughing.

To Luce's relief, the shore grew somewhat wilder, the houses a bit scarcer, and soon there were patches of low cliff and zigzag-ging rocks that might offer her somewhere to rest. There were still too many boats around, though, for her to risk sleeping on a beach, even a sheltered one. It would have to be a cave. She swam deeper, searching under the waterline for a dark entrance, but the first cave she found was entirely submerged. To sleep, she needed a place where she could keep her tail in the water but her head above the surface. Nothing looked right.

She drove herself, trying to go faster, but she barely seemed to be making any progress at all. Sometimes she caught herself going limp, simply wavering according to the lift and fall of the water. Twilight was coming, and Luce skimmed the low cliffs with an increasing sense of urgency, though there were more houses again. Then up ahead she saw something promising: a dip, a shadow in the rock, just below the dark stained line that marked the lowest tide. As she came closer she knew it was definitely a cave, and from what she could see of its entrance the roof appeared to curve upward inside, probably rising enough that there would be a crucial pocket of air: an ideal mermaids' home. Gratefully Luce swirled closer, energy surging into her muscles at the prospect of finally collapsing into sleep.

Then the smell hit her. It blasted into her nose, her mouth, and she was gagging, her whole body curving backwards as she fought to pull out of the momentum that was carrying her toward the cave. Blood and decay; the sickly, musty stink of death. Even as she floated in the middle of the water Luce started sobbing at the realization: this was where the murdered tribe had lived. The cave was full of their torn bodies, just the way her own old cave had been. She pulled away through fouled waves, choking and crying. Her stomach heaved repeatedly, but it was so empty that instead of vomiting she only tasted a single sour mouthful of bile. If only she'd realized sooner that the humans were coming after them, if only she'd pushed herself harder, swum faster down the coast, maybe she could have reached this tribe in time.

Luce's whole body screamed in protest as she drove herself farther out to sea again. She had to get away from here, as far away as she possibly could, no matter how dizzy she felt. She swam on and on, but it was hard to tell if she was still traveling forward or simply drifting in the current. Her tail thrashed awkwardly, its muscles seizing with cramps. How much longer could she keep going like this? The darkness in her head was getting thicker. Now the windows above were shining golden rectangles scattered across a forest like thick blue smoke.

Or maybe the smoke was coming from inside her, too. She was still seeing a line of trees and houses in the dimness, but from the weight pressing in on her she was vaguely aware that she wasn't at the ocean's surface anymore but many fathoms below. The houses were far away, but she could still see a crowd of people dancing on a front lawn—was that a lawn?—that sloped down into nothingness. She could see the people, in fact, as if they were very close. Dorian was there, waltzing with a girl whose hair spread out into a kind of floating globe of pink lace, singing a song about the ghosts of lost sailors. The dancers seemed to have their own internal light, but everything else was dark. They weren't actually on a lawn, though; like her they were suspended in some uncertain middle depth, a half-place inhabited by dreams.

Suddenly the pink-haired girl was no more than a yard away, staring at Luce over her shoulder. She wore a complicated dress of pale lace that frothed up her neck. Dorian had lied, Luce thought, when he'd said Zoe wasn't especially beautiful. She was snow-colored, glinting, splendid, but also hard to see clearly . . .

Dreamily Luce reminded herself to hate Zoe. But it seemed like too much trouble.

"Luce?" Zoe said. "Isn't there something you're supposed to be doing? Something important?"

Probably, Luce thought. She couldn't speak.

"Then why are you drowning?"

That's a good question, Luce thought. She didn't have an answer.

Certainly she was very deep under water now. Too deep, even for a mermaid. But her body didn't seem to be interested in swimming anymore.

Zoe turned to go back to her dancing, and Dorian reached for her with an exaggeratedly formal grace. Then, with no warning, Zoe swung back around and punched Luce hard in the gut, driving her fist up and in so that Luce gagged and doubled. The fist kept plowing into her stomach, forcing her rapidly up through the water . . .

Luce opened her eyes wide—when had they closed?—and found that her body was draped over something crimson, slick, and fleshy. Whatever it was, it was shooting upward through gray-black water. It was carrying her toward the surface, but apparently not because it wanted to. It began to shake and thrash, and Luce tumbled into watery space. Her body was so cramped and weak that she could barely control her movements anymore, but she could still look around at the flashing swarm of animals on all sides.

There were dozens of them. Hundreds. Rocketing shapes, dark in the distance but blood-red where they came close to her, all propelling themselves toward the air Luce needed so desperately. Winglike triangles flapped at one end of each tubular crimson body while at the other end tentacles looped and pulsed. Squids, Luce realized, though some of them were almost as big as she was. A huge one was hurtling toward her, and Luce instinctively threw her arms around it and held on. It was speeding upward so quickly that by the time it managed to shake her free the terrible weight of the water was lessening noticeably. Luce began to feel a slight tremor of hope.

Did she *want* to live, then? The questioned ached inside her, and Luce ignored it, flinging her body a few yards to one side to grab for the next squid. She could barely swim, and she knew she didn't have enough air left in her lungs to form even one whispering note, much less to sing the powerful song that controlled the water. But if she could ride enough of the squids toward the surface, she might still be saved from drowning.

The squid turned on her. In an instant Luce was caught in a kind of living net made of two long tentacles that bound her back and shoulders, squeezing her like sticky, raspy fronds. Its shorter arms pawed her, exploring her skin as if it couldn't quite make out what she was. But even as it grappled with her, the squid was heading toward the surface. Luce tensed against her own urge to fight as the tentacles dragged her closer to the thing's thick body, as a kind of pale fleshy tube approached her face. In the center of that tube, Luce realized, there was a hooked black beak like a parrot's, and it was opening.

Luce gritted her teeth, twisting her face as far away from it as she could. A bite wouldn't kill her. Drowning would. As long as the pressure of the water kept getting lighter, it would be stupid to fight back. The black beak came at her cheek, and Luce fought down a scream as her skin broke and pain shot through her face. The surface wasn't all that far away now, and adrenaline raced through her until she trembled. Her empty lungs were burning, and Luce couldn't stop herself from inhaling any longer. Salt water raked down her throat and penetrated her lungs like a mass of frozen nails. Luce's hands twisted through the web of sucker-covered arms, digging for the squid's globular eyes. She could feel two slippery balls under her fingers, and she braced herself to claw at them.

The squid bit in again, tearing Luce's right ear this time, then abruptly flung her away. She gagged and gasped in rolling space, then felt something brush across one flailing hand.

Wind.

Her head was finally free of the water, and she was coughing desperately, water spitting out of her. It felt like her chest was full of cold fists punching their way up through her throat so that she choked and choked again. Even now that the wind caressed her face, she was retching too hard to breathe.

Then at last enough of the water was out, and Luce managed a lungful of air. On all sides of her huge crimson squids whipped past, their feeder tentacles swinging out to grab fish that were then pulled in toward their snapping beaks, just the way she had been. A stray tentacle groped at her back for a moment, then curled away. The squids were frenzied by the hunt, and as Luce inhaled again and again she realized that, even if mermaids weren't their preferred prey, it would probably still be a good idea to get away from them.

Besides, she was bleeding. It was never safe to stay in the open ocean when there was blood in the water. She looked and saw the dark line of the coast framed by a scatter of stars. Now that oxygen was flowing through her body again she felt a little stronger. Slowly, tentatively, Luce began to sing to the water, though her throat rasped with pain. A soft current came in response to her song. It wasn't very strong, but it was enough that she was now heading toward the shore.

It was horrible to see how flat that shoreline was, how houses still dotted the woods. She'd have the same problem she'd had before, Luce realized: there was no chance of finding a decent cave or even a craggy stretch where she wouldn't have to worry about humans finding her. She knew she couldn't keep traveling any farther. It wouldn't be long before she would lose consciousness again and sink helplessly.

It had been an extremely close call, after all. Just how close was starting to become clear. Only the wildest luck had made that first squid slam into her and knock her back into awareness. She wouldn't be that lucky a second time.

Then Luce saw something ahead and interrupted her own song as she moaned aloud from pure relief. There were no caves, but there *was* a long, low dock stretched out above the beach in a shallow cove. She could swim under it and sleep hidden from the humans, even as they ran along the planks above. Luce crooned to the water again, urging it on, and soon there was sand stirred up by her dragging tail. She slipped under the dock and pressed her unhurt cheek gratefully against the shore. Blood trickled into her mouth.

Darkness filled the world beyond, but it was no match for the darkness inside her.

*   *   *

Her sleep was utter oblivion. Dark and heavy and for once dream-less. She woke to feel a beam of sun lancing between the planks and straight onto her eyelids; she woke to feel something—a hand?—carefully touching her shoulder.

A hand. Luce told herself not to panic. Low waves sloshed at her back as she very slowly opened her eyes and lifted herself. The hand jerked back, and Luce heard a quick intake of breath. Luce turned enough to see a little girl, maybe seven years old, kneeling on the sand and staring at her. The girl wore an oversized red windbreaker, and the cuffs of a gray sweater bulged out around her wrists.

Without even thinking about it, Luce smiled at her. "Don't tell anyone I'm here," Luce whispered. "Okay?"

She might have to get away fast, of course. Luce flexed her body, trying to assess her strength; she felt sick and faint and achy, but she hoped she could still outrace most human boats if it came to that.

The girl stared at her silently for a few moments, pushing back loops of light brown hair. "I won't," she whispered back, then hesitated. "Um, are you real?"

For some reason that made Luce laugh, though she stifled it almost instantly. The laugh sounded harsh, maybe even bitter. The girl looked dismayed, and Luce felt a bit sorry. "Well, I'm real to myself anyway," she told her gently. "Does that count?"

Luce stretched again, velvet sand against her sore belly, and noticed that it was the first time she'd felt *real* in weeks. The feeling was painful, and she wished she could go back to sleep.

The girl considered the question but didn't answer it. "You got hurt?"

Luce reached up reflexively, touching the throbbing spot at the side of her head. A triangle of flesh almost an inch deep had been ripped from the side of her right ear, but the cuts in her cheek didn't feel too bad. Even without looking, she could tell that her stomach was badly bruised where the first squid had crashed into her; that would slow her down. Luce's physical injuries were the least of her damage, really, but they were all the girl could see. "A squid bit me. I'll be okay."

"Are you hungry?" The girl was digging in the pocket of her windbreaker, pulling out half a candy bar.

Luce stared at her, suddenly horribly sad. The mermaids had killed so many humans without caring at all. This little girl had no idea what kind of creature she was offering to feed. "I am hungry," Luce said softly. "Thank you. But . . . I don't think I can eat that. It's not mermaid food."

The wind curling over her cheeks was warm and soft. It was a beautiful spring day.

It was also the first time she'd been aware of *beauty* since Dorian had abandoned her, since she'd found the bodies . . .

"What *do* you eat?"

"Shellfish, mostly. Some kinds of seaweed are good."

"Wait here." The girl ran off, and Luce watched her wading out along a sandbar down the beach. She was bending low, gathering mussels. The prospect of food hit Luce with stabbing intensity. Now that she thought about it, she wasn't sure how long it had been since she'd had anything to eat. Two days?

Footsteps thumped along the planks above Luce's head. She tensed, but it wasn't likely that anyone would notice her: by contrast with the brilliant day outside, the shadow covering Luce was very dark. She could see two colored shapes through the gaps between the slats, then she watched them emerge onto the dock. A man and a woman. Sun flashed in their windblown hair as they adjusted life jackets. They were talking about how they couldn't find one of the paddles for their canoe.

It had been crazy to fall asleep here, but she hadn't had much choice. The waters spreading out around the dock were shallow, Luce realized, and the sunlight was bright and piercing. If she swam away, anyone who happened to be looking in the right direction would see her clearly. But maybe it didn't matter anymore. The FBI knew about the mermaids; soldiers were hunting them down. It was simply too late for secrecy to do them any good. Why shouldn't *all* the humans know the truth, then?

The girl was scampering back, a heap of mussels balanced on her outspread hands. A few of them fell as she ran.

"What are you doing, Chrissy?" The woman on the dock was calling to the little girl.

"Playing," the girl said defensively. It sounded like a lie.

"You know you shouldn't pick the mussels if you're not going to eat them."

"I'll put them back in the water. I'm just moving them over here . . ."

The couple on the dock had finally found the paddle, and they were lowering their canoe into the water. Luce found herself gazing after them with emotions she couldn't sort out: a strange kind of sorrowful envy. As long as Dorian had kept pressuring her to turn human again, she'd been convinced she didn't want to, but now that it was too late, now that Dorian didn't care anymore, was she sure she'd made the right decision? Not that turning human had actually been an option . . .

Chrissy dropped the mussels in a clattering heap at Luce's elbow, and Luce smiled at her with genuine gratitude. "Thank you so much. I'm not . . . feeling very well." She glanced nervously toward the canoe. It was just pulling away, and the couple was chatting about what the best picnic spot would be. Being this close to strange humans felt almost as dreamlike and peculiar to Luce as the hallucinations that had overcome her as she'd lost consciousness the night before.

"Why aren't you eating?"

"I will. As soon as they're gone." Cracking the mussels would be noisy; Luce was nervous about trying it at all. Then hunger jabbed through her again, and she decided she didn't care who heard her. She smacked one on the dock's stone foundation then gobbled it too quickly. Another, then another.

Chrissy watched her while she ate, clearly fascinated. "You're so *pretty*. Even with bites in your face."

Luce didn't feel like smiling anymore. "That's just because of magic, Chrissy. How pretty I am." The adoring shine of those warm brown eyes made Luce sad. "You shouldn't take magic things too seriously, okay?"

"Why?"

"Because magic can trick you. You shouldn't let it." After all, Dorian hadn't. He'd called her enchanted beauty "freakish." That was all she was to him.

"You're not trying to trick me," Chrissy murmured uncertainly.

"No," Luce agreed. Lying under this dock, looking at this child striped by sunlight, it was horrible to remember how she'd helped her tribe sink ships before. Luce knew she was partly responsible for the deaths of girls just like the one sitting beside her now. Dorian's little sister had been about this age. Luce smiled warmly at Chrissy, and her smile felt like a scar. "But that's because . . ." Luce wasn't sure what to say. Chrissy obviously admired her, but Luce wished she wouldn't; she gazed at Luce, her expression somewhere between hopeful and apprehensive. Luce sighed. "Because we're friends." Chrissy beamed.

Luce knew she'd rested for too long. It was time to be moving on again. She had to warn the next tribe, and the next, before they were killed. The responsibility was all hers.

Did she even care that there was another group of people, maybe half a dozen this time, already getting out of their cars and heading for the dock?

3

The Video

It was lucky that Zoe lived so far away. Even if she started driving right after school let out—and sometimes she did—Dorian would have at least an hour to sit on the beach alone without Zoe catching him at it. He didn't see any reason to mention it either. It wasn't like he'd even glimpsed Luce since the day they'd broken up, since she'd refused to drown him and left him dripping on the shore. He always sat in that exact spot now. It was funny, in a sick kind of way, to realize how much he still resented Luce for *not* murdering him. Maybe he should have been grateful. But it was hard not to think that, if she'd only loved him more, she would have gone through with it.

He was pretty sure Luce had left the area. If she hadn't, wouldn't she have come to look for him at least once? One time he'd even rowed to the shallow cave where she used to take him, just in case, although getting there and back in the rowboat took a full day of exhausting effort. It was dangerous, he knew, to steer such a small boat through the rough seas. But it wasn't like he could do any of the things he might have tried with a human girl, like calling or sending an e-mail.

And even if he could call Luce, what would he say to her?

That he was sorry; that he was still in love with her? They'd only have the exact same problems as before. It was ridiculous to think the two of them could have a future together.

His phone let out a burst of percussion and Dorian jumped. Just for a fraction of a second he was possessed by an irrational fantasy: that she'd somehow turned human again, that she missed him too . . .

It was his friend Steve, already talking as Dorian answered. ". . . got to come over! You are not going to *believe* this!"

Dorian groaned inside, but he kept his voice calm. "Believe what?"

"You're the mermaid guy, right? There's this video. It's *got* to be fake, but—"

"You mean on the Internet?"

"What do you think? But, dude, she's got short hair. Just like that one you used to draw all the time. She looks so *real*."

Dorian was already on his feet. His knees were trembling.

"Dorian? Are you—"

"I'll be right there."

"It's *got* to be fake, but it really looks . . ." There was something strange in Steve's voice, Dorian thought; it was a little too soft, too floaty.

"I'll be right there, okay? Ten . . . ten minutes."

Then he was sprinting, the gray road and tattered spruce trees veering around him, billows of mist parting around his face.

There were a lot of mermaids out there, Dorian knew. He'd met a few of them personally, and some of them besides Luce must have short hair. But this particular mermaid was also reckless enough to let herself be filmed . . . His heart surged and his stomach cramped, but he kept running at top speed all the way back to the village, his sweat instantly turning clammy in the fog. Then he was dashing up the low wooden steps and his outstretched hand slapped hard against Steve's door.

He had to knock a few times, more and more loudly, rocking with impatience. "Okay . . ." Steve finally called from inside, and shuffling steps approached. The door swung open and Dorian looked in, across the living room and down a hallway and through another open door. A sliver of the computer in Steve's room was visible. Even that partial glimpse was enough to set Dorian's heart thudding quicker than it had from his run. Steve's face had a stunned, foggy look to it. The rims of his eyes were red, and he didn't even say hello as he caught Dorian by the elbow and hauled him down the corridor. As they got closer to the computer screen, the video stopped.

Steve's hand was already reaching out hungrily to hit *Replay* as he skidded into his chair. Dorian stood behind him.

The video started normally enough. A few people jostling around on a dock, laughing, taping one another, and then turning the camera toward a pair of seals lounging on a sandbar off to the right. A little girl in a red windbreaker came wandering into view on the beach below. She kept looking back over her shoulder, obviously watching something, maybe under the dock, that the adults hadn't noticed.

Then, off-camera, a woman screamed, and for half a second the camera lurched madly as she grabbed for it. There was a flash of blinding sun as the lens veered skyward. Voices were crying out: "My God! Nick, look!" and "What on earth . . ."

The camera swung sharply, pointing down into the shallow water, and Dorian's insides wrenched at the sight of the silvery jade green tail whipping ten feet below the surface, the jagged dark hair. He heard himself crying out involuntarily, but Steve didn't seem to notice. He was staring too hard at the image, at the rippling grace of the mermaid's movements. But, Dorian thought, mermaids could usually swim much faster than that. Was she showing herself on purpose?

Incredibly, she broke the surface twenty yards out, right in a diamond-bright patch of reflected sun. Dorian wanted to shout at her, to tell her not to be so crazy.

Incredibly, she glanced back. Straight at the camera. She hesitated for a moment, almost as if she wanted to say something but felt too shy. And then Dorian saw something dark on the right side of her shining face, and his chest tightened as he realized that it was almost certainly dried blood.

Was she swimming so slowly because she was injured? That still wouldn't explain why she'd done something so utterly perverse, though, coming so close to a human town and swimming right where people could see her.

Just as Dorian finished wondering that, Luce dived. Only a quick green smear showed under the low waves, then she vanished from the image. The camera went on staring blankly at the water for a minute. The people on the dock were absolutely silent, and Dorian realized he was crying. He hoped Steve wouldn't turn around and see.

"It's totally fake," Steve muttered huskily. "Right?"

Dorian realized that he didn't have to worry about his friend looking around at him. Steve was crying too, just as if *he* was the one who'd loved her.

The video was titled "Mermaid sighting? May 28th." Just one day ago, Dorian realized shakily. Where *was* she?

It had already been viewed nearly a million times, and there was Steve's hand snaking helplessly to hit *Play* again. *Luce*, Dorian thought, *Luce, how could you?* She'd always been so worried that humans would find out mermaids existed, and there she was blowing their cover herself. What conceivable reason could she have for doing that? The seals lounged, people laughed, the little girl in the red windbreaker looked at *something* with terrible longing on her face . . . Then the flash of sun and she was on the screen again. *Luce*.

It was her, it was her; there was no way it *wasn't* her. Rippling, rising, glancing. Hesitating and then turning away again. She was too small for him to quite make it out, but it looked like something had happened to her ear. This time Dorian thought her movements definitely seemed like she was very tired. Maybe even sick.

"Where . . ." Dorian said. Steve didn't seem to hear him, and Dorian rapped on his shoulder. "Steve? Does it say *where* she is?"

"Oh . . ." His voice was even more distorted by crying now. Dorian heard him gulping. "In the comments. They say it was outside Grayshore, Washington."

Washington. Dorian was hit by a nauseating surge of disappointment. She didn't care about him at all anymore or she never would have gone so far away. Unless . . . It seemed crazy to think it, but maybe she'd let those people video her because she'd hoped that *he* would see it? When she glanced back over her shoulder that way, was she looking through the camera's lens in an effort to meet his eyes?

She was about to say something, Dorian felt sure. Was it his name?

The picture on the screen showed empty, sun-blinking water and a line of wooded coast to the left. Then it went black. *Replay.*

He was starting to feel precarious, and he wished he was sitting down, but Steve had the only chair.

Of course, the FBI already knew mermaids were out there. Dorian had told Luce that himself several months ago. But he was pretty sure Luce's worst fears hadn't come to pass. FBI agent Ben Ellison had told him that the authorities "were still reviewing the options." As long as the feds weren't actually trying to exterminate the mermaids, why would Luce risk provoking them?

There she was again, looking back as if she could see him watching her. Dorian leaned closer to the screen, trying to make out the look on her face. He was desperate for any sign that would tell him what she'd been thinking in those moments, but she was too small, too distant. All he could tell was that she was hurt and unsmiling. If he could get to Anchorage, get on a plane, somehow drive from Seattle to the coast . . .

She'd be long gone, of course. She already was.

The screen showed nothing but water dropping into sudden blackness.

"It has to be fake," Steve said again. His voice was murky and unconvinced, and he still wouldn't look around "Right?"

"Of course it's fake," Dorian snarled, too roughly. "How the hell could that be real?"

"I thought maybe *you'd* believe it . . . since you kept drawing her . . ."

Her. What did Steve mean by that? "Crissake, Steve. I was drawing a *comic book*. Like, it was imaginary?"

"The one you used to draw, though . . . She *really* looked like . . ."

Irrationally he'd started hating Steve a little for coming this close to the truth. Dorian forced himself to stay calm. "Not so much," he said coldly. "Just the hair."

His phone was ringing again. Dorian had a good idea who might be calling.

Replay.

"Steve?" No response. "Steve, I'm going to take off, okay?" Dorian felt a little bad for lying now. He wiped his sleeve across his face.

"Oh—sure. See you later." Dorian wondered how many times Steve would watch Luce swim through sunlit water before he got tired of it. But Luce was supposed to be *his*, even if all he had left of her was memories. No one else was allowed to watch her this way, to see just how beautiful she was.

Once Dorian was out on the street he stared around in a daze. Gray mist curled between the small wooden houses, and at the bottom of the street he could see the iron-colored shimmer of the small harbor, the dock where he'd sprawled face-down, his body leaning toward the water to kiss Luce goodbye after she'd brought him home late at night. It took him a while to pull himself to-gether, walk down to a lonely spot on the beach again, and call Ben Ellison back.

* * *

"It's *her*."

"I'm assuming you're referring to the video? It's Luce, you mean?" Why did Ben Ellison's surprise sound so phony? "But, Dorian, it's hard to see much detail. Are you certain?" His doubt sounded phony, too.

"Yeah I'm *certain*. Why would she do that? She was always

worrying, like if humans really knew the mermaids were out there they'd come after them and wipe them out."

Even Ellison's silence sounded wrong now. It was taut and strange, and it took him too long to reply. "Well, Dorian, I was hoping *you* would have some insight. Into what she might be trying to accomplish through this."

"Why would I know anything? You didn't even know that was Luce."

"She matches your description." This time Ellison's response came too fast rather than too slowly. "Quite well. It did occur to me that she might be . . . your friend."

"I bet she doesn't think of me as a friend anymore." Dorian heard how bitter he sounded.

"You know her very well, though, Dorian." This time the voice on the phone had an odd touch of gentleness to it. "Of course, there's something about this video that strikes anyone—anyone with any real knowledge of the situation—immediately."

"It looks like she's *hurt*."

"It does, yes." A pause. "But that's not what I meant. She doesn't sing."

Dorian had trouble understanding where this was coming from. Of *course* Luce didn't sing. "Why would she?"

"This is the first, the very first, publicly available evidence for the existence of mermaids. It shows a mermaid clearly stopping and looking back at a group of people. There's no question that she's aware of them. And then she goes peacefully on her way. No singing, no enchantment, and nobody winds up drowned." Ellison almost sounded impatient now.

"So?"

"So if you were attempting to convince people that mermaids are simply beautiful, harmless girls—girls who just happen to have tails—then allowing this video to get out would be a very good move. In terms of public relations."

"But I've told you! Luce doesn't even *believe* in killing people! She wouldn't . . ." *She wouldn't even kill me,* Dorian thought glumly. *Not even when I was pushing her to do it.*

"Naturally, though, she's aware that other mermaids don't share her ideas about the supreme value of human life." There was something in Ellison's voice that confused Dorian. He sounded prickly and on edge. Ellison was usually very steady, calm even when he was insulted.

"Well, sure. But there's no *way* Luce would have sung to those people! Another mermaid would, maybe, but . . ." He was so agitated, Dorian realized, that he'd completely missed what Ellison was implying. Suddenly he understood. "You think she let them tape her on *purpose*? To convince everyone that mermaids don't go around killing?"

"I think it's quite clear that this was a deliberate maneuver, yes. The way she comes to the surface and looks back at the camera . . . There's no other reasonable explanation."

"Luce wouldn't think like that." Dorian couldn't imagine that Luce would be so calculating. "She acts kind of crazy sometimes, like she's stupid brave, but *public relations*? That's just not what she's like." It sounded lame, even to him. But he felt sure. Whatever the explanation was for Luce's behavior, it wasn't what Ellison thought.

"People are enthralled. Simply by watching this clip." Ellison sounded like he was complaining about it.

"I know," Dorian snapped.

"Infatuated."

"I *know*." Was *that* what Steve was? Infatuated?

"And this mermaid . . . Luce . . . she knew that they would be."

"No. No, she didn't." Dorian thought about it. "She knew her face was magic, but that just made her uncomfortable. Luce is pretty shy. It wasn't something she ever *tried* to use."

Something in Ellison's silence made it clear that he didn't believe a word Dorian was saying. "You see, Dorian? You have valuable insights to offer after all." There was a distinct edge of sarcasm to the words.

"You think I'm full of shit, though." Dorian was curt.

"I think you're still trying, in whatever ways you can think of, to protect her. It's understandable enough, given what we can see of her, but . . ."

Dorian felt even more annoyed. It sounded like Ellison thought he'd only loved Luce for her beauty and gracefulness, that he'd simply been out of his mind, addled by enchantment like all the idiots who were sitting in front of their computers now, gaping slack-jawed at that clip. *It wasn't like that with us*, Dorian wanted to say. *I actually knew her. It's different.* "I'm just telling you what she's like. You don't know anything about her."

"I know what I can see." Ellison gave a strained laugh. "Dorian . . ."

"Yeah?"

"How could you stand it?"

She didn't do it for public relations, Dorian thought. *She did it for me!* But he didn't think he could say that to anyone.

By now, he was sure, Zoe must be staring at the same video. She'd see Luce rise, and turn, and look into her eyes.

4

Red Tide

The brilliant sun, the stunned human faces, the camera's black glass eye were all fixed on her. Luce's first impression was that everything in the world was staring straight at her; she cringed, anxiety prickling through her aching body. Swimming hurt so much that she'd surfaced to get a grip on the pain before pushing herself onward again. Then she'd stopped where she was for a second, struck motionless by a sudden insane hope. If she talked to these people on the dock, then could they somehow get a message to her father? At least let him know she was alive?

She didn't even know where her father was now, though. And starting a conversation with strange humans would only lead to problems. The sunlight on the water was so bright that Luce's outstretched arms appeared to be sleeved in fire. She shook her body and dived, forcing herself to move faster in spite of the pain.

They'd definitely been pointing that camera at her. Maybe she should feel guilty about that; it was an outrageous violation of the secrecy the mermaids guarded so carefully. But if the government already wanted them dead, well, maybe it was time *everyone* knew. The humans should know that mermaids were their own daughters, the girls they'd driven away.

Maybe *that* was what she should have done when she'd seen them filming her.

Explain.

Tell them the whole story.

Luce kept wearily on. After a while she remembered to sing again, disguising her voice so that it sounded almost like wind. Calling. She couldn't go quickly at all, and she needed to rise to the surface for air much more frequently than she normally would. The day passed without her covering nearly as much distance as she thought she should have. She found a secluded beach, slept a few hours and ate a little. She didn't want to risk passing out while she was swimming again. Then she forged on just as dawn was breaking.

Luce felt different than she had for the past few weeks, suddenly awake and aware, her pain sharply defined. The world stared back into her eyes. The coast was wilder again, and Luce began to search for caves, singing her alarm-call all the while. It looked like promising territory.

She was skimming twenty yards below the surface through a green zone thick with seaweed when she saw tiny diving shapes, still very far ahead of her, their arms stretching out as they swam. Luce wanted to hurry to greet them, but the bruises on her stomach throbbed with every flick of her tail. If only she were well, she could have been with them in moments instead of drifting sluggishly forward like this. It looked like they were ducking into a cave, one after the other. Their bodies showed jet black against the gold-green dawn shining down behind them.

A cloud passed, and the water dimmed. The figures only looked blacker than before. Luce paused where she was and watched as a mermaid eddied in place for a moment. Her tail looked too short,

Luce thought. Then as Luce watched the tail spread wide, split in two, bent in a way that was much too angular, and kicked what she'd thought were fins . . . The diver vanished. Luce tried to stay calm. Most human divers were harmless, weren't they?

At that moment mermaid song began to blast and warble through the water, strongly audible even from behind rocky walls. It didn't begin slowly and seductively. Instead it was harsh, brittle, and panicked, coming from several throats at once. Luce felt the shock of that terrified song racing through her and lashed her tail, trying to reach them. There must be a dozen soldiers in their cave, maybe more, all armed with those guns that shot silver blades. She'd have to do her best to fight, any way she could; she'd send the water crashing against them, batter them unconscious before they could kill . . .

But before she'd gone a dozen yards the songs had turned into screams. Half a dozen screams, more, loud at first then fading toward silence like a loud chord struck on a piano and left to decay.

Then there were only two voices Luce could pick out. Then one. And she was still so far away, still fighting the seizing muscles of her tail, still straining as her heart smacked at her ribs.

That final screaming voice was harsh and furious, and it wouldn't stop. Luce was getting closer now, curtains of seaweed brushing around her torso. They must have their weapons trained on that screaming mermaid, Luce thought in confusion. Why hadn't they already shot her? Were they *torturing* her?

Luce hovered at the mouth of the cave, sick with dread. The rock bent and she couldn't see what was going on; she huddled back into the seaweed. She was so outnumbered. If she was going to rescue the girl in there she needed to have some kind of plan;

anything would be better than a crazed dash into the center of a massacre!

"You better shut *up* now! Goddamned tail. You think you can just swish your fins at us and we'll melt? That crap doesn't *work* on us. We know too much about you. We know what you *do*." It was a man's voice, buzzing and distorted by some kind of electrical mouthpiece.

The mermaid screamed again, and Luce heard a smack.

"Shut up and answer our questions like a good tail, and *maybe* we'll let you swim out of here, okay? But we can't hear you. You'll have to write with this. Know how to write?"

The scream had faded to a rhythmic wheeze. At least, Luce thought, they probably weren't hurting her now, but they'd be ready to shoot her at any second. If Luce rushed in to rescue her she'd probably only guarantee the girl's death. If she did nothing, though . . .

"I . . . Look, I *can* write, okay? Just stop . . ."

Luce could taste the seeping blood. She could see red corruption staining the water in long slow curls.

"Stupid tail. Remember we can't *hear* you. Look. We're looking for one of you in particular. *This* one. You know this one? She was heading this way."

What was the man *talking* about? One in particular? Why? Luce froze, her bewilderment darkening into dread.

"A . . . What? A *photo*? But that looks like . . ." the mermaid began. Her voice was piercing, startled.

Another *smack*. "What did I tell you about writing?"

There were a few seconds of near silence: just a faint moaning and the surge of the sea around Luce's ears.

"You haven't seen her? You *sure* about that? She's called Luce. The one we're looking for. You know Luce?"

There was another silence, this time broken by a few rough sobs. Luce had the feeling the girl had noticed the face of a murdered friend among the dead.

Had the mermaids in that cave died because these men were hunting for *her*? But why would they care about her at all? She'd thrown their boat into a cliff when those soldiers fired at her back in Alaska, of course, but . . .

How did they know her name?

"What do you mean, you've only heard about her? She got away from us up north, killed a few of our guys, and now she's causing us *more* trouble. We're not too happy about that, all right? If you help us find her . . ."

Another silence. Luce's dread thickened, knotted like slimy ropes. Was there any chance they'd let the girl go? It didn't seem likely. Luce started to slide into the bloody water oozing from the cave. She turned a corner and saw a crowd of black legs on a stone floor. Men stood chest-deep in crimson water.

She had one advantage, Luce realized. Only one. The same protective helmets that blocked out the mermaids' songs . . .

"Is that a fact? You won't help us catch *Queen* Luce? Well, then . . ."

Luce's song was already rising, calling the water. The soldiers couldn't hear it, of course. They didn't notice anything as the first note soared up around them. But a few seconds later they *could* feel their legs suddenly yanked out from under them by currents like twisting snakes. Luce's song split into several violent notes all curling in different directions, and soldiers in slick rubber suits shot through the black air, waving in space, and bashed into the walls.

Coils of blood-bright water chased them, gripped them, threw them again. Their bodies collided with the corpses of the mermaids they'd killed, already back in human form. Most of the soldiers had dropped their guns, but a few still held on. Luce couldn't stop singing then, not while they might still shoot, and in desperation she hurled her voice up the scale.

Even as they swung, shouting through the cave's darkness, one of them had seen her. His gun was up, and he was trying to aim. Luce focused on the water gripping him until he was buffeted face-first again the ceiling. The heavy gun finally flung free, whipping into a girl's severed arm before it tumbled down into the water.

The *living* mermaid had to be here somewhere, spinning through this chaos of crimson water and electric screams and black thrashing limbs . . .

Luce didn't mean to kill the soldiers, just stun or hurt them enough that she and the other mermaid — *there* she was, clinging to a rock in the corner, blood-slicked, flurried by waves — could get away. But she couldn't keep her song going at such a frenzied pitch forever, and at least one man still clutched his gun like a baby against his chest, both arms wrapping it close.

Luce's voice flung higher, sharpening into a scream, and dashed him headlong into the jagged wall.

There was a loud crack. He fell limp into the water, and Luce could see that the angle of his head was very wrong.

She hadn't *wanted* to kill him. Her voice died away in anguish, and bodies plummeted into crimson foam. Luce fought through the pounding rain of half-conscious men. There wasn't much time before they recovered, at least enough to dive for their guns again.

The mermaid in the corner was wheezing out a kind of low, rhythmic shriek. When Luce grabbed her wrist under the water she only clung harder to her rock, then swung at Luce with her tail. Luce dodged, splashing up through the surface, and crashed right into a black-suited diver, who made a bleary grab for her throat. He just missed her, then lost his balance and flailed in the crimson froth.

"Are you insane? We've got to get *out* of here!" Luce shouted at the blood-drenched mermaid. Every moment of delay could be one too many.

The girl stared around as if she couldn't tell where the voice was coming from, still wheezing shrilly. She was so spattered with gore that the faint glow of her skin came through like moonlight through ruby glass. Luce grasped her by the arm and pulled, and this time the shocked mermaid folded passively toward the water, letting Luce drag her away.

They were flowing toward the entrance, weaving through crashing legs, through divers who swept below them as they reached for their scattered guns. The strange mermaid suddenly lunged to one side, tugging Luce with her, and a shining silver blade flashed past just where Luce's head had been. It clanged into the stones, the water trembling with the sound. Luce tried to spiral her tail to drive herself at full speed, but the water was so crowded with bodies both living and dead that her movements were blocked by jumbled flesh.

Then it was the other mermaid who was picking up speed, towing Luce out through the fouled water and into crashing gray. Whorls of golden dawn spread out above them, leaping with the heave of the sea. Luce's injured stomach clenched with pain as the other mermaid jerked on her arm, urging her to *move*, and from the corner of her eye Luce saw a few of the sleek black figures already after them. She was holding the other mermaid back, Luce realized, going much too slowly. Her whole body spasmed from pain as she forced herself into a burst of speed.

Beside her the other mermaid bucked and screamed. Luce glanced over at her in terror, but she was still alive, gritting her teeth as the blood sheeted off her light brown skin.

Away. They were getting away, the human divers drifting somewhere behind them. They were heading deeper, dipping around a bend. Far above Luce saw the black oblong shape of a boat silhouetted against rippling greenish light. The other mermaid was whirling forward in her panic, and Luce couldn't stand the pain of going at this speed anymore. She tried to pull her arm free. The stranger was safe now, or as safe as she could be. It would definitely be better for her to go on without Luce.

Since Luce was the one they were after, in *particular* . . .

Since they'd just *seen* her, and they'd know she couldn't be all that far away, and she'd probably killed at least one of them moments before . . .

"Come *on!*" the girl beside her barked, her voice distorted from the water. "I know a . . . It's close . . ."

A hiding place? Luce made herself keep going, and in a few moments they were at a narrow crevice in the rock. Luce reared back. They were far below the surface, and she'd exhausted too much of her air by dashing so quickly. The crevice looked dark and ominous, and Luce felt sure they'd only get stuck in there and drown.

"Come on, already!" The other mermaid darted into the ragged shadow, and after a moment Luce followed her.

It went upward, and at first it was so narrow that her tail thrashed against the rock. Luce had no trouble seeing in the darkness, but she knew it was utterly lightless. Now and then the fins of the mermaid ahead swished against her face.

Then the crack began to widen and a subtle wash of light refracted through the water. They kept squirming upward, and Luce heard the stranger inhale a few seconds before her own head broke free of the surface. They were in a narrow span of water, smooth as black glass. The crevice kept twisting upward before it ended in a shard of daylight at least a hundred feet above them.

There was no real beach in here, but there were outcroppings and natural shelves where they could at least rest for a while. Luce saw that the other girl's left fin was sliced by a three-inch gash at its bottom edge, both sections writhing as if they were trying to hold each other. That was why she'd screamed, then. Her face was still taut with pain, her forehead furrowed. She was close to Luce's age, and she looked at her roughly.

"Are you who I think you are?" the girl asked.

Maybe her tribe had met Nausicaa too. Nausicaa must have talked about Luce all the way down the coast, bizarre as that seemed.

"I'm Luce."

"Yeah. That *wild* business you pulled with the water. I should have guessed right away, but I was too . . ." She paused, breathing hard, obviously struggling for self-control. "Luce. My God. Did you hear what they *said?*"

Luce nodded. "I'm so *sorry.* I didn't know. I thought they were just murdering any mermaids they could find, but if they were looking for me, and that's why . . . your tribe . . ."

"What did you do to get those creeps in that huge of an uproar? They said something . . ."

"They didn't say the *whole* thing," Luce snarled. "They massacred my old tribe. Everyone. Then they were shooting at me. They made it sound like I just attacked them out of nowhere!"

"You did that water thing to them?"

"I smashed their boat into a cliff. Back in Alaska. I was just trying to stop them, really, but I guess a few of them died? But I don't know . . . I can't understand how they knew who I *was*, or my name, or . . ."

Actually, there *was* one obvious explanation for how they might have gotten their information. Luce just didn't want to believe it. There was someone who could easily give the authorities the name of the mermaid who knew how to control the water with her singing. *She sent a giant wave at your boat? Oh yeah, that was definitely Luce. She's the only one who could have done that!* More than that, he could show them very good drawings of her.

He could also confirm her identity after some people just happened to tape a mermaid. *She was heading this way*, the soldier had said.

The girl's eyes were wide, and she was biting her lip. Luce wavered, all the blood rushing away from her head and leaving a stripped, nightmarish shore behind it. Could Dorian really have done that to her?

"I'd heard about you and the whole water-cannon act. You're getting to be kind of legendary, for sure. But you've really got enough power to pick up a boat and crack it in half?" The girl laughed, too wildly, then choked on her own laughter. Her face kept bunching strangely.

Luce gaped at her. She was overwhelmed by the hideous things she'd just realized. "It . . . works better when I'm really upset. I couldn't always . . ."

"Oh, I think you're going to get *sufficient opportunities* to be upset!" Suddenly the girl's poise crumbled completely, and her face deformed like smashed clay. Sobs racked her, and she doubled and gasped. Luce wasn't sure what to do at first—the girl seemed too tough and confident to want to be held.

Then Luce didn't care anymore. She swam over and hugged the weeping mermaid, resting her head on the same rock. Luce didn't know why *she* couldn't cry now. She definitely had enough reasons to. She'd never felt so cold, so utterly poisoned inside. She'd thought that abandoning her would be enough of a betrayal for Dorian, but apparently he'd only be satisfied with getting her murdered. *That* was what humans were like; *that* was what happened if you trusted one of them.

Why hadn't she wanted to kill them, again?

The strange girl's sobs grew only more violent.

Luce listened to her and thought with icy loathing of the boy she'd once loved so completely. *He* was responsible for this.

* * *

It was at least an hour before the strange girl cried herself out. "Queen Luce? We're going to have to get moving."

"I know," Luce said. *Another* tribe had died because she'd come too late. And after what had happened that morning the divers would be more determined than ever to catch her, and they'd go on killing all the mermaids along her route.

Far from saving them, she'd only ensured their deaths.

"Where are you going, anyway?"

"South. I was trying to warn everyone, but now . . ." Luce shook herself. "I never asked your name?"

"Oh, right. Where are your manners? There we were escaping from a complete bloodbath, and you didn't give me a proper chance to introduce myself!" There was still an edge of hysteria in the stranger's voice that made her annoyance sound more serious than she'd probably meant it to. "J'aime."

"Gem?"

"No. Like *Jem*. Je-aime. It's French for 'I love'."

Luce looked up at J'aime. Even without peering into the cloud of dark shimmer around the other mermaid's head Luce was suddenly sure that whoever had hurt J'aime enough to change her into a mermaid hadn't been her parents. Not if they'd given her a name like that.

Just like it hadn't been Luce's parents who'd driven her to the point of losing her humanity. Her father still loved her, Luce knew.

That, Luce thought bleakly, was why she didn't want to kill humans. Why she *still* didn't want to. She didn't even want to kill those black-suited divers who were hunting her and all the other mermaids they could find.

If she did they might leave daughters behind. Girls who'd only wind up like her and . . .

"Hi, J'aime."

"You said they killed your tribe, too?" J'aime's voice was suddenly much softer.

"Yes. My ex-tribe, really. But the divers just slaughtered everybody, and ships weren't even going anywhere *nearby* anymore, so it wasn't like, like really self-defense or . . ."

"Did you *see* it happen?" J'aime's eyes were wide in the dimness. Luce knew she was seeing unspeakable things all over again; that, no matter how long she lived, she'd never completely stop seeing them.

"I . . . just found the bodies." Horrible as that was, Luce understood that it was much worse for J'aime.

"And it's because of those helmets? Why we can't just drown them?"

"Yes."

"*You* can still kill them, though!" J'aime gave a hacking laugh that showed how close she was to sobbing again, but her voice turned crisp and assertive as she went on talking. "Thank God one of us can! But damn, you're going to be one busy girl, Luce. You'll have to kill them for everybody! Smash the *hell* out of their boats! I'm gonna have to come with you just so I can watch those creeps get what they deserve. After they cut Maya's *throat* like that . . ."

"J'aime . . ." Luce didn't know how to break the news to her, but she realized she was sick of hiding her real feelings. The time for that was long past. "I'm sorry. I won't kill anyone. Not unless they're about to kill one of us and there's really no other way. I'm not about to murder people for *revenge*, though."

J'aime stared at her. "You *have* to! You won't after . . ."

Luce tried to think of a way to explain it. "It doesn't *help*, J'aime. Mermaids have been killing humans for thousands of years, and it hasn't helped anything. It's just making them go insane wanting to murder us! And besides . . . weren't there any humans you loved?"

J'aime was glowering at her. "Sure. My parents. My grandma. They're *dead*. So whether I loved them is no longer particularly relevant, okay?"

"But anyone we kill could be the only person some other girl loves, and then she could wind up . . . in foster care, or with someone a lot worse."

"Those helmet guys are out to kill *all* of us! They blasted those spear things at everyone; they spilled their *guts*—"

"I know that." Luce's head was starting to wobble again, and her face felt hot and heavy. J'aime's fury made her want to weep and scream and hide all at once.

"You *will* kill them! I don't care what kind of queen . . . If I have to make you do it myself, every last one of them is going to die for that!"

"No." Luce braced herself as J'aime glared at her. "J'aime, look, however many of those divers we kill, they'll just send more of them after us, okay? If I thought I could save the mermaids that way I'd do it, but I know it won't work!"

"Yeah?" J'aime spat it out. Her raw hatred hurt Luce more than anything that had happened that morning. "What will? 'Cause if you won't get out there and dispose of the problem, that's going to be a lot of dead mermaids who you did *nothing* for!"

"We'll . . . have to think of something different. Some other way." Luce knew how pathetic that must sound and stared up at the fragment of blue daylight far above.

"Like *what?*"

"I don't know." Admitting that made Luce wonder if it would be better for everyone if she was dead. If the soldiers wanted her in particular, maybe they'd stop once she was killed?

J'aime shook her head. "I heard you were some kind of great queen. But you're just sad. All that power—like who's ever even *seen* that?—and you won't do one thing to help." She turned to go, her torn violet tail snaking awkwardly in the deep water.

"Be really careful, J'aime, please? Keep hidden."

"Great advice. You stay away from the rest of the tribes out here, okay? If you're not willing to do anything *positive*, you'll just get them killed."

"But . . . someone has to warn them, J'aime!"

"I'm on it."

J'aime was gone.

She had a point. And even with her sliced tail she could go faster than Luce now, anyway.

But if Luce was really that useless, so marked and hunted that she'd do more harm than good even by spreading the alarm, then . . .

Then what reason was there for her to live at all?

Someday, dearest Luce, I will find you again . . . The voice in her head was Nausicaa's, and Luce tensed for a moment before the bright blue patch in the dimness above melted in her tears.

"Nausicaa, *please*," Luce said out loud. "Please find me soon."

Why do you think I left you, Luce? Nausicaa retorted. She hadn't said those words in real life, though. Why could Luce hear them so clearly? *I can only find you once you learn for yourself where you are.*

5

Little Girls

On a path high above the ocean a man was walking. His hair was shorn within half an inch of his scalp, stubble covered his face, and a backpack thudded on his shoulders. He walked as if he were in a hurry, but then he would stop, sometimes for several minutes, as if he was searching for something in the long silvery grass. At first the path looked down on a harbor where sea lions sprawled, but after a while it bent back and ascended still higher over open sea. Tall cliffs plunged to knife-sharp rocks and the tumbling slopes of enormous waves.

It had happened somewhere around here. The man half expected a spike of cold anger to let him know when he was passing the exact spot, but all he could feel was the cool spring wind and the feverish determination crowding his thoughts.

He might go to prison for this, of course. Even if they bought his story—and there was no reason to think they would—the law didn't make allowances for the kind of justice he had in mind. But that was okay with him. It wasn't like he had anything better planned for the rest of his life. Luce was probably lost to him for good.

After another mile the dusk was dotted with golden squares

and oblongs. Shining windows stood out against the blue evening and glowed through the spruce trees on the hillside behind while to the right a rolling silver-blue meadow dropped abruptly down into the waves.

Almost there, now. His heartbeat clattered in his chest like a handful of coins dropped on a hard floor. He climbed the steps up to the back door of a small brown house.

Through a gap in the curtains he could see a grubby pea green kitchen. A patch of bare wood showed where the floor's linoleum had split and peeled away. Two heavy sock-clad feet were resting on the wood, but that was all the man could make out. It was enough, though.

He knocked. No response. Maybe the jerk had passed out. He knocked louder, sharper, making the loose windowpanes clack in their frames.

A moan, a shuffling noise, a fan of golden light where the door swung open. Eyes on his, blank and bleary. Definitely drunk. "You got a problem?"

"I got a whole *bunch* of them, as it happens, Peter."

There was a long pause, a few panting breaths. Then recognition landed like a stone. The man on the outside step couldn't help grinning as he watched his brother reeling back into the kitchen, too scared and shocked to muster a response at first. After another uncertain moment it came. "You're *dead*."

"Tell me about it. But I'm not half as dead as I used to be, brother. Shoulda seen me a couple months ago."

"Andrew. You're *not* . . . Christ, man, how did . . ."

"Gonna ask me in?"

"Oh. Yeah. Good to . . . good to see you. Didn't think I'd ever . . ."

Andrew Korchak stepped into the house. It was almost too easy. He shut the door at his back and locked it then dropped his backpack. "Got anything to eat?"

"There are . . . I've got some cans in the cupboard. Go ahead and help yourself. Whatever you want. Andrew, how did . . ." Peter's eyes suddenly turned skittish as if there was something in the room he hoped his brother wouldn't notice. His body was bloated and saggy, and a web of broken blood vessels reddened his face. A half-empty bottle sat on the table.

Andrew Korchak didn't move to get the food he'd asked for. Instead he paused in the center of the kitchen, slowly and deliberately looking around. He kept on examining the room, walking back and forth, his face carefully composed into a look of mystification.

"Something missing here, Peter? Feels like you moved some things around."

"It's about like when you left." A pause. "Want a drink? It's got to be a hell of a story. How you *got* here and everything." Peter moved to sit back down at the kitchen table, but once he was sitting he didn't look comfortable.

"Oh, I'm all right. But thanks. Or maybe someone? Isn't somebody else supposed to be here?" Andrew was still peering around, down the dim little hallway, into the corners.

Peter's face was just getting redder. He stared down, obviously straining to pull himself together. "I . . . You mean Luce? About that. I got some bad news."

"I guess it is Luce I'm missing here, isn't it? Yeah. How's my little girl doing? Is she out with friends?"

"Andrew. About that. It's a terrible thing . . . I don't know how to break it to you, but . . ."

"She ain't been doing good in school, or something? I'll straighten her out."

"She . . . Andrew, sorry, Luce passed on. To a better worl— She just . . . she got in with a bad crowd, drugs and everything, and she wound up going over the cliff. Got ruled a suicide. I'm real sorry."

Andrew stopped searching the kitchen and paced over to his brother's sagging figure. For a long moment he simply stood over him, too close, staring down into Peter's worried eyes. "Well. That is bad news, Peter. My sweet little Luce a suicide."

Peter slumped a little deeper with what looked like relief. "I didn't know how to break it to you," he agreed.

"I can see it would be a hard thing to say. But you manned right up and told me the truth. I appreciate that."

Peter was nodding eagerly. "Had to do it."

"Yeah. Now it's my turn. I've got some even worse news I need to tell you. I'm afraid it's gonna hurt." Andrew was standing even closer to his brother. His arms were swinging lightly.

"I . . . What news?"

"Luce didn't die."

A swarm of conflicting expressions buzzed through Peter's face. At first they were mostly variations on confusion, but as he felt his body heaving out of the chair and crashing backwards onto the floor, there was a lot more terror in the mix. Then Andrew was on top of him, knee on Peter's chest, fists slamming down into his rubbery cheeks. Andrew punched again, feeling a few teeth break, while Peter's heavy body flopped and grunted below him. It would have been more satisfying if only Peter had done a better job of defending himself. He tried to swing at Andrew's head, but his blows were limp and disjointed, slapping like damp frogs.

It should have been a great moment, Andrew knew, making his creep of a brother pay for what he'd done to Luce. He'd been looking forward to it. But somehow in practice it came as a disappointment. His revenge felt as mushy and pathetic as his brother's doughy flesh jiggling under his knuckles. Andrew hit Peter again, harder, hoping that savagery would help cancel out the disgust he felt. The bridge of Peter's nose snapped.

In fact, Andrew felt more like vomiting than anything.

He stopped punching and stayed where he was for a minute, half kneeling on his brother's chest, staring around the room. He'd faked looking for Luce before, but now he searched for her in earnest, desperately wishing she'd walk out of the shadows—*walk out, on legs, the way a young girl ought to do*—and gently pull him to his feet again. Peter was gasping, struggling uselessly. Andrew toyed with the idea of strangling him. He'd pretty much planned on it. He didn't doubt that his brother deserved to die, and he didn't care at all about the consequences. It was just . . .

It was just too sad.

Killing Peter would be too sad, too senseless.

"I should rip your throat out," Andrew said to the twitching mass under his knee, but his voice didn't have much conviction. "I should throw your dirtbag of a corpse off the same damn cliff where you left my little girl after you tried to *rape* her. I should . . ." There was a rivulet of blood dribbling from Peter's swollen lips, pooling on the green linoleum. At least, Andrew thought, he'd accomplished *that* much before punking out.

Andrew got up heavily, walked to the cabinets, and picked out a can of chili. He started poking through the drawers for a can opener. Behind him Peter made slobbery noises and spat out his teeth. Andrew didn't bother turning around.

"Andrew . . ." The tone wasn't what Andrew would have expected. It was high and soft.

Andrew still didn't look back. "Yeah?"

"She's . . . really alive? Luce is really . . . she's really alive? You're not *shitting* me?"

"I just saw her. About four-five weeks ago, now." He dumped the chili into a pot and fired up a burner, flicking the match into the sink. "She was a lot less dead than I am, for sure."

The slobbery noise got louder. "Where the hell *is* she, then?" Peter's voice kept getting higher, whinier. "Little girl just *ran* off and made me think . . . Didn't even call. Is she coming home?"

"Is that what you call this dump? I'd bleed you like a pig before I'd let you get anywhere near her, Peter. No damn way you'll ever see her again. You don't even deserve a chance to *apologize* to her, you hear me?" He wasn't about to explain *why* Luce wasn't coming back. It was enough to know that the words hurt Peter more than the beating did.

Even without turning to look Andrew knew his brother was sobbing on the floor. He stood at the window eating his chili from the pan and watching the distant roil of the waves. A film of Peter's blood clung to his knuckles, sticky and red.

Luce was out there. Somewhere. But how was he supposed to find her?

* * *

He slept in Luce's old bed that night in her tiny room with books heaped on the dresser and postcards from cities they'd traveled to together tacked around the bed. High on the wall were two photos: a snapshot of Alyssa holding a three-year-old Luce on her lap, a big white sunhat casting a slanting shadow across both their faces. The photo next to it was much more recent, an official school portrait that Andrew guessed had been taken not long after his boat wrecked. In it Luce appeared unsmiling and scared, her eyes wide and otherworldly, wearing a navy sweater that was getting too small for her. She looked lovely and horribly vulnerable, and he ached to hold her and tell her that everything would somehow be okay.

Alyssa was dead. That was understandable, *natural*, even if it ripped his heart to think about it. But the way he'd lost Luce, on the other hand . . . that was too surreal, too impossible. There was just no coming to terms with something that made so little sense.

He woke up to a silent house. Peter must have actually gone in to work, then, even with his busted face. Everyone would just figure he'd had a nasty fall while he was drunk. Apart from the endless hiss of the waves there was no sound at all. After a minute Andrew pulled himself out of bed, stretched and moaned. If he wasn't going to kill Peter, then he also wasn't going to be spending the next twenty years locked up. Looked like he'd have to think of something *else* to do, if rotting in prison was off the table.

He'd clear out after breakfast. Leave Peter a note and never come back. For all he knew Luce could be anywhere along the continent's west coast, so there was no reason to stay put.

The photos of Luce and Alyssa almost hummed to him; he could feel their nearness, hear a wisp of their mingled voices. He pulled both pictures off the wall and slipped them into his backpack, then got dressed in the old clothes people on the islands had been kind enough to give him when he'd shown up wrapped in filthy sealskins. They'd been awfully good to him, the mad, tattered castaway who'd insisted at first—until he got his head together, anyway—that he'd been brought there by his daughter, Luce, and that she was a mermaid.

Andrew stumbled out into the kitchen to make himself a cup of coffee, stepping over the blotch of crusted blood on the linoleum. He'd been knocking through the cupboards for a few minutes before he noticed the dark silhouette floating on the door's sunlit curtain. Somebody was standing there, dead still, watching him through the gap. Andrew swung around and saw a sliver of a tan-skinned, thickset man, his neat silver hair like a glaze in the pale daylight.

Once the man saw Andrew looking he knocked as if he'd just arrived. But Andrew was sure the guy had been standing there for a while.

"Yeah? Help you with something?" Andrew didn't try to keep the annoyance out of his voice as he opened the door.

"Peter Korchak?" The man on the step had warm, sympathetic brown eyes, but his mouth was tense.

"That would be my brother, actually. Want me to tell him you were looking for him?"

"Your *brother*." The tan-skinned man stared for a moment as if he weren't sure whether or not to believe it. "And your name is?"

"You're the one on the *outside* of the door. That means you might want to think about introducing yourself before you go asking *me* anything."

In reply the man folded back his coat. His badge gleamed in the pallid day. "Ben Ellison. FBI."

"All right." That didn't make too much sense unless Peter had gone and turned criminal. But there it was. "And I'm Andrew."

Ben Ellison made a conspicuous effort to stay calm. "Do you have any identification?"

"No." Andrew stared for a second. "Peter can vouch for me, I guess, if you've got some reason you need to know. What's your business here?"

"My understanding is that Andrew Korchak was lost at sea. More than two years ago. But if that's really who you are . . ."

"That's who I am. I didn't stay lost, is all." He felt tired, and even though he'd washed his hand the night before, he suddenly noticed lines of dried blood still clinging in the grooves of his knuckles. "What's your business?"

"Then I expect you would know who this is?"

A photo. Zoomed in until it was very close and grainy so that it only showed her face glancing back over her shoulder. The background was bright and blurry, but it looked like shining water. Her cheek was marred, and Andrew's breath caught as he noticed the notch torn from her ear. "Where did you get this?"

"So you do recognize her?"

Andrew couldn't stand it. He pivoted on his heel and walked to the counter, leaning with his head hanging down, his shoulders heaving. He'd failed to protect Luce again. And for some reason this FBI bastard was asking questions about her, and that might mean . . .

"Mr. Korchak?"

That might mean he knew . . .

"This photo was taken just a few days ago. I'd like to discuss the situation with you, Mr. Korchak, if that would be all right." Ben Ellison stepped over the threshold and approached. The kettle was whistling out a piercing, horrible note.

"What do you want with her? Look, whatever you're thinking . . . Luce is still a little girl . . ." His arms were crossed on the counter, leaning heavily, but he was painfully aware that Ben Ellison must have noticed how he was shaking.

"You know, you don't seem at all surprised. To find out that Luce is still alive."

Oh. Right. He was supposed to think that Luce had killed herself. It was too late to pretend, though. "I knew she wasn't dead, is why."

There was a pause. Andrew looked up to watch Ben Ellison's face, to observe the thoughts churning just behind his eyes. The guy seemed pretty smart, actually. "And would knowing Luce is alive be somehow connected? To the fact that you didn't stay lost?"

It was a strange line of reasoning, unless this Ben Ellison knew a lot more than he ought to. "Knowing she's alive? It's connected to the fact that I saw her a few weeks back. She wasn't banged up like that then, though."

"But I imagine there were *other* changes in her that you might have noticed," Ben Ellison said. His tone was sardonic, but there was another suggestion in his voice at the same time, a definite hungry sharpness. Was it envy?

"What do you *want* with her?" Andrew's heart was racing and his knees wavered, but even so he was starting to feel some humor in the situation. Whether your kid got caught swilling vodka in a cemetery or shoplifting or turning into a mermaid, it was all the same. You *still* had to talk to the cops.

Ben Ellison hesitated. "I'd like to help her. I'm afraid it might not be possible, but—"

"Help her how?" Andrew found himself feeling defensive suddenly. "Far as I can see my girl is doing pretty good, considering."

"She's wanted for murder."

"She's *what?*"

"Arguably it was self-defense."

"This is garbage. She's only . . . she's a kid. A *good* kid."

"Given her current situation, it's unlikely that constitutional protections apply, and I doubt anyone will go out of their way to interpret the law in her favor. After all, she technically isn't even . . ."

"Isn't even what?" Andrew snapped.

"Human. She isn't human. Not at the present time." They were staring fiercely at each other, the kettle still shrieking behind them. "Of course you aren't surprised to hear this, either."

"Who cares? Whatever kind of . . . whatever she looks like now, she's still my *daughter*, and she's still a . . . barely more than a child, really. A juvenile, anyhow. Look. If somebody was trying to hurt her—"

"Can you contact her? Do you know where she's going? That photo was taken off the coast of Washington, and at the time she was heading south. She was seen the next day not far from the Oregon border."

"And if I did know that, you think I would *tell* you?"

"There are quite a number of people who are determined to catch her, and they'll shoot her on sight." Ben Ellison paused to let that sink in. "If you have some way to communicate with her, you'd be well advised to urge her to surrender before that happens. And if I'm involved in the process, I promise I'll do whatever I can to ensure her safety."

"Was it your people who tore up her ear like that? If you did . . ."

"That wasn't us." Ben Ellison was looking toward the window now, then abruptly he walked to the stove and snapped the kettle off. His expression was morose. "Mr. Korchak, the fact is that I think Luce has been . . . unfairly singled out. But she's also been behaving in a way that is guaranteed to attract negative attention when she should be doing whatever she can to keep a low profile. That video, for example."

"What video?"

"Check the Internet. Search for 'mermaid.' You might be the last person in America who *hasn't* seen it."

Andrew considered that. Things were starting to make a bit more sense. "So she's in some video. But then how did you know it was her? You see a mermaid, you don't go and spontaneously say, 'Oh, I bet it's that Lucette Korchak girl who everybody thought jumped off a cliff up in Pittley.'"

Ben Ellison wasn't looking at him. He kept his eyes pointed at the sea.

"Somebody rat her out, Ben? Who've you got?"

No reply.

No reply in a way that told Andrew Korchak exactly what the situation was: not only was there an informer, but it was someone this FBI guy didn't trust. Someone who was lying up a storm, talking all kinds of smack. Firing off ridiculous accusations, like . . .

"Who you all think Luce *murdered*, anyhow?"

"Five men, actually, in total. Special operations." Ellison sounded remote, maybe sad.

"A fourteen—fifteen-year-old girl? You think she's some kind of goddamned ninja?"

"She's not technically *a girl* at all any longer. As we've discussed. And there's no question at all that she can be dangerous." Ellison looked away from the sea long enough to gaze bleakly into Andrew's eyes. "The prevailing opinion is that she—and all the creatures like her—are nothing but monsters. Regardless of the fact that they were human at one time. I realize this isn't something a parent wants to hear about his child, of course."

"The 'prevailing' opinion," Andrew growled.

"Yes."

"Does that mean it's the one prevailing in your head? 'Cause if it is, that just shows how damned ignorant you are."

"I'm . . . suspending judgment. About all of them, but about Luce in particular. Clearly there have been situations where she's made a deliberate choice *not* to kill, and where I'd imagine the temptation must have been intense." Ben Ellison's voice was grim and drowsy.

"You said . . . those special operations guys . . . it was self-defense." *Maybe they'd forced Luce to kill,* Andrew thought. *Maybe.*

"They were firing spear guns at her, in fact. And they will again."

"Can't blame the girl for that! If she was just trying to survive—"

"Mr. Korchak . . . I'm afraid it's worse than that. You say you've seen Luce quite recently. How much did she tell you about her life after she changed form?"

Not much, Andrew thought. "Enough."

"She was a member of a particularly vicious mermaid tribe. It's possible that she's had a change of heart since that time, but it's extremely likely that she was at least complicit in far more deaths than the ones I've told you about."

"Like . . ."

"Hundreds. Probably hundreds. More. One ship last year had almost nine hundred passengers on board when it sank. And Luce was there. That I know for certain."

"Luce wouldn't . . . No way I'll believe . . ."

"Tell her to turn herself in, Mr. Korchak. It's the best I can do for her. Special Ops are out to avenge their own. If I'm there first, there's a chance I can get her into some form of safe custody before anyone blasts her to ribbons."

"Don't you *talk* about my girl like that! My God, after everything she's been through . . . me and her mom both gone, my loser brother beating her and— You're talking about just slashing up a teenage girl like it means *nothing*."

"I'm trying to prevent precisely that from happening. I sincerely want to help her. Luce rescued someone I care about, and I don't believe she deserves . . . Can you find her?"

"I *want* to find her. She fished me off that island where I was stranded, but then she just zoomed off and vanished."

"And? Do you know where to look for her?"

Andrew groaned. He was doing his best not to break down, but it kept getting harder. "I've got no clue where to even start."

6

Dead Zones

Now that J'aime had taken over the mission Luce had assigned herself, there wasn't the same desperate need to rush south as quickly as possible.

But now that she understood how hunted she truly was, there was an acute need for stealth. The black-suited divers probably knew that mermaids tended to cling to the coasts and that they needed air periodically as they swam. Slipping her head out of the water anywhere near the shore would be wildly risky; she'd have to travel uncomfortably far out to sea. Luce didn't even want to think about how impossible it would be to find anywhere she could sleep.

For a whole day she lingered in J'aime's narrow hiding place, letting her damaged body start to mend itself, singing low, melting songs to that piece of broken sky high above her. It was the first time in weeks she'd stayed so still and let herself succumb to everything she felt in the quiet. Her song curled around fragments of Dorian's voice: *If you want to kill me for this, you can. I won't sing back.* He'd given her a chance to stop him before he'd started trying to make sure the divers disposed of *her.* Maybe he'd decided only one of them could continue to live.

And already so many other mermaids had been slaughtered because of what Dorian had done. Girls lay in rotting heaps deep in their caves while the one in particular Dorian wanted dead somehow lived on, carrying the images of the lost with her. Dreamily Luce pictured herself trailed by ghostly faces, all glowing like jellyfish, all warping with the loft of the waves . . .

Was she sorry, then, that she *hadn't* drowned him? She'd come so close; she'd forced herself to stop just in time.

But no, she couldn't regret it. He'd wanted her to kill him, even tried to manipulate her into it, and the only vengeance left to her, feeble and fragile as it was, was to make him live with the knowledge that she was living, too.

* * *

Luce slept for many hours that night, awkwardly balanced against the cave's wall on a rocky shelf that wasn't really long enough for her body. She woke with the heavy conviction that she had to keep heading south no matter the danger. As far as she could tell, Nausicaa had passed this way, and finding her friend was the only real hope she had left at this point. Together maybe they could come up with a plan: some way to stop the slaughter of the mermaids. Maybe even some way to make peace with the humans, as impossible as that seemed. After all, any mermaids who survived these massacres would only hate humans more than ever. The idea that she of all people might somehow manage to persuade them to stop killing, well . . .

It was preposterous. But it was the only idea she had.

Luce set out again at dawn. Swimming was still painful, but the ache in her bruised midriff was starting to dull a bit and her torn ear barely hurt anymore. Risky as it was she paused at a beach and ate as many shellfish as she could manage, constantly scanning the golden waves for any hint of a black boat with silent engines. Then she went on, sweeping at least half a mile from the shore. She didn't know what kinds of predators she might encounter out here, but she had a feeling they couldn't be as dangerous as humans firing razor-sharp blades. And at least animal predators wouldn't be hunting specifically for her.

Still, she kept a close watch for any creature that appeared too big or too hungry. It was strange, though: she didn't see anything big at all. In fact, as she went on there weren't even any fish, apart from some jellyfish and unusually thick smears of bright green algae when she surfaced. It didn't make sense. Luce paused, breathing, wondering why the sea was so oddly empty. There weren't even any birds.

And, Luce thought, the water felt a little different on her skin, though not in any way she could identify. It didn't feel like fresh water, but it definitely felt wrong, almost sticky. Or somehow *slow*. Somehow breathless, sad, inert. The morning sun swayed in brilliant flags along the water's surface, and Luce felt overwhelmed by solitude so immense that it crowded the sky.

Except for, far in the distance, a single dark boat. Luce couldn't hear an engine.

It was too far away for her to guess if it was the same as the boats that were hunting mermaids, but even so her heart went cold, its rhythm fast and light and whispery. She dived, hurtling deeper than she would ever normally choose to swim, so deep that the water's gray weight squeezed in on her and the light deadened into a hard slate dusk. She could see the seafloor from here; it must be relatively shallow.

The seafloor looked all wrong. Bone white, with nothing moving, with none of the usual grades and variations of color.

Her instincts told her not to go any deeper than she was already. The pressure was too much, and she'd be too far from the air. Instead she needed to concentrate on going as far as she could at a depth where the boat couldn't find her.

Luce went down, her better judgment screaming in protest. But there was clearly something very wrong here. The sea had never looked so forlorn. She had to know what was happening here, to understand . . .

There! Something was moving. Luce's pulse quickened with hope until she saw the limp, lifeless way it drifted. It was something pale, spindly, and complicated, skimming over a plain made of impossibly spiny, whitish stones. A large crab, Luce realized after a second, but it was clearly dead. Its splintered claws trailed over the weird stones of the seabed, clacking softly.

No. It *couldn't* be. Those things she'd thought were stones . . .

Dead crabs. Many thousands of them lay packed together in all directions for as far as Luce could see, heaped and askew, their jointed limbs slopped across one another's shells. Matted weeds; decayed fish; rotting, fluctuating ribbons that were once gigantic worms. All of them were thickly covered in fuzzy, whitish slime, a carpet of disease.

What *was* this place? What kind of world allowed such a sweeping destruction of life? Luce reeled in place, her body lurching through the water, her tail suddenly lashing senselessly. Horror choked her; she felt crushed and airless.

She needed to slip back to the surface for a breath. As deep as she was now, she ought to swim up soon. *Go, Lucette!* Instead she stayed where she was, staring mesmerized at the field of unmoving animals, jagged shells, and bacteria. A transparent creature floated by her, looking like a feathery scrap of silk torn from a ballerina's dress. Countless tiny lacy filaments sprouted from its sides; it should have been wonderfully beautiful. But it was turning brownish, and it draped on the current with sickening indifference.

Go on, Lucette! Now! Her lungs were starting to burn, but that was just for lack of oxygen. Wasn't it? Or was the water here poisoned somehow? She tensed herself, forcing her tail to spiral purposefully again, to carry her *up* . . .

But hadn't she heard something about this, once? Hadn't *someone*—Luce couldn't even stand to think his name anymore—hadn't someone she once knew told her that there were ocean areas near the shores where almost every living thing was dying? That there were only a handful of species that could survive in them, because the water was starved . . .

Starved of oxygen. She remembered now. All those creatures had suffocated. That must be why the water *felt* so wrong. Humans had done this, too, Luce remembered; it had something to do with all the extra fertilizer pouring into the ocean from farms.

The water's weight began to shift off her body and green wands of sunlight reached her. She was speeding upward now, constantly imagining that, wherever she surfaced, the boat would be waiting for her. Could they find her with radar? In a place with so much death, it would only make sense if she died too. Her lungs ached, longing for air, but for another few minutes Luce lingered ten yards below the surface, her gaze searching the green-glass surface above for any hint of an impending shadow. There was nothing up there, only the twisting light pleated by the waves, but still she couldn't calm the panic that throbbed through her body. The instant she broke through into the air they'd rush in from nowhere, and glinting steel would cut the water so fast that she would only know it was there when she felt her body splitting wide . . .

At last she rocketed upward, appalled by the wind on her face, and heaved in one quick breath before diving again to hover in watery space. Her heart punched at her chest. She knew she was being ridiculous; there was nothing up there. But after what she'd seen of her own tribe and J'aime's, after seeing that field of death at the bottom of the sea, the whole world seemed jagged with menace.

No, Luce told herself. She couldn't go through her whole journey this way. She might be killed at any time but there were more important things to worry about. She floated where she was a little longer, then deliberately flicked her tail and broke the surface, looking around at the serene golden light and breathing slowly. A few lifeless fish skimmed past, pale bellies winking at the morning sky.

If she was in a dead zone, then it was time to search for a living one.

7

Favors

"Hello, Dorian." Ben Ellison smiled up at him from a bench at the back of the town's tiny cemetery. Although Dorian still felt some resentment over the conversation they'd had about that video of Luce, he smiled back. Ben Ellison was probably the only adult who actually cared about him now that his parents were dead, and in spite of himself Dorian had come to regard him as, maybe not a substitute father, but something like a favored uncle. "It's been too long. How are you?"

"I'm okay." Dorian settled onto the bench beside him. The cemetery was at the top of a hill, and views of the harbor winked between the trees. A toy boat moldered in the grass of a nearby grave; probably a fisherman was buried there. "You said on the phone you had some news?" Dorian felt a spike of tension in his stomach as he asked that—maybe they'd found Luce; maybe they knew where she was.

"I do, yes. I'm hoping you'll think it's good news." Ellison's thick brown hands were unsettled, squeezing and releasing a tissue. Dorian began to get the impression that, behind his smiling warmth, the guy was really worried. "How would you like to go back to Chicago? You can re-enroll at your old high school in the fall. Everything's set. All you have to do is agree."

This was the last thing Dorian had expected. "Chicago? But . . ."

"Theo Margulies. You told me once that he's been your best friend since first grade."

"Yeah, he is. But what—"

"I talked to Theo's mother. She's agreed to take you in until college. You'll be living with your friend, and you'll get your old life back, at least to the extent possible." The warm brown eyes flashed apprehensively as Ellison inspected Dorian's face. Dorian couldn't imagine what the problem was. "I truly hope you'll say yes, Dorian."

Ben Ellison did genuinely like him, Dorian knew. But he was still FBI, and Dorian didn't think the FBI usually got involved in looking for foster homes for orphaned teenagers. "Why do you *care?*"

"I thought it would be better for you. Staying here, so near where the *Dear Melissa* crashed, can't be easy. Luckily I was able to make arrangements with the lawyer in charge of your parents' estate to cover your expenses." Ben Ellison was looking straight at Dorian, but he was doing it too deliberately, Dorian thought. He was making too much of a display of *not* having anything to hide.

"I don't really want to go back, though," Dorian said. Testing him. He watched Ben Ellison's broad brown face, saw the nervous lights flare in his eyes. "I mean, you know, there's my band here now. And there's Zoe."

"And a pair of guardians who you know quite well are dying to be rid of you. And a tremendous number of painful memories."

Suddenly insight leaped into Dorian's mind, and he knew

why Ben Ellison was so eager to ship him back to Chicago. He wanted to get him away from the ocean. If that was the idea, well, then Chicago was about the best you could do. Dorian looked up at the older man so sharply that the thought passed between them more loudly than a shout: *This is about Luce, isn't it? This is to make sure I won't see her again.*

"She isn't even *around* anymore," Dorian objected. His voice was throaty. There was no need to say who "she" meant.

Unless maybe *that* was what Ellison was hiding? Maybe Luce was back, or they'd seen her traveling north, or . . .

"I know she isn't," Ben Ellison agreed, then hesitated. Dorian was still glaring at him, his blood quickened by the suspicion that Ellison was lying to him. "But Dorian, hasn't it occurred to you that . . ."

"That *what?*"

"That, as someone whose association with mermaids has been established beyond all question, in the eyes of the government you're . . . a dubious quantity, at best."

Dorian was confused. "It's not like— I don't have any association with them *now*. It's not like any of the mermaids who are living up here would try to see me or anything. The ones who even *knew* about me are all gone."

"That doesn't matter." Ellison's tone was suddenly dismissive.

"I mean— What are you saying?"

"As long as you're living near the ocean you'll be regarded as a potential problem, Dorian. There's no way to *prove* you won't have any more contact with mermaids while you're here, and . . . I'd prefer if that wasn't the case. There are certain individuals whose interest I'd rather you didn't attract."

"What individuals?"

Ellison shrugged off the question. "I'd like them to forget about you. If you're far from the sea, back at your old school and keeping your head down, they might decide you're no longer germane to their concerns."

Dorian stared at him, thinking this over. "Thanks, I guess. You're trying to protect me?"

"Of course I am. As usual. Not that you ever make it easy, Dorian. Or particularly pleasant."

Dorian grinned a little unsteadily at that. "I still don't want to go back, though."

"And not because of Zoe, I'd imagine. Dorian, Luce won't be returning here. I'm quite certain about that. Don't waste your time waiting for her."

"I do actually *love* Zoe," Dorian snapped.

"And yet it wasn't so long ago that you told me you were still in love with Luce. And you expressed that sentiment through some fairly dramatic behavior." Ben Ellison was referring to the time he'd found Dorian dripping wet on the beach, after he'd broken up with Luce, after he'd tried to get her to drown him, after she'd vanished . . . Dorian glowered. So what if he *was* still in love with her? That wasn't anybody's business but his. Even Zoe didn't need to know what he saw when he closed his eyes.

Dorian decided to change the subject. "Why don't you think Luce will come back here, anyway?"

He'd asked the question casually enough, but its effect was immediate. Ben Ellison grimaced and looked away, cheeks flushing and mouth tight. Dorian stared at him, perplexed. If he didn't know better, he'd think Ellison was ashamed of something.

"Luce is very far south of here by now. That video was shot in

Washington, and that was over a week ago. And she was clearly heading down the coast." Ellison seemed to be keeping his voice as flat as possible.

"So? She could still turn around."

"Dorian . . ." Now it was Ellison's turn to change the subject. "Go back to Chicago. I've done everything I can to make it an attractive option for you."

"I don't want to leave here, Mr. Ellison."

"I assume you know how unreasonable you're being?"

"And why would I care if some government assholes think I'm talking to mermaids, anyway? I wouldn't be doing anything wrong. It's not like hanging out with mermaids is against the *law* or anything."

For a long moment they stared at each other. Dorian watched shadows shifting and twisting in the brown depths of Ellison's gaze, watched his lips compress with irritation and—Dorian felt more certain of it now—embarrassment. But that wouldn't make any sense, unless . . .

Unless Luce's darkest fears had come to pass. Dorian forgot about the cemetery around him, envisioning Luce terrified, hunted, dashing through towering waves.

"Dorian . . ." Ben Ellison sighed. Whatever Dorian had seen darting inside his eyes was hidden again; the older man just seemed world-weary, impatient, tired out by trying to reason with the irrational adolescent sitting across from him. "It might be."

Dorian's thoughts were so far away that he was confused. "What might be what?"

"Talking to mermaids. It might become illegal. There's no applicable law now because there's no official recognition that mermaids so much as exist, but that will probably change soon. And if it does, it would not be in your interest to set yourself up as an object of suspicion."

"Are you guys starting a *war* on them?"

"I've told you before. There hasn't been any decision made yet about how to deal with the mermaids, beyond warning ships away from areas where there are signs of—"

"Is that why you're so sure Luce won't come back here?" Dorian's tone was rising. "Did—I mean—did you start *killing* . . ."

"No, Dorian. Of course not." Ellison's voice was tense and—Dorian thought—utterly false. Like the guy was too ashamed to even do a good job lying.

No wonder Luce looked so hurt and exhausted in that video. Dorian didn't know when he'd stood up. His legs wavered, and for the first time in months the sky and ground began to seem destabilized, as if they were possessed by the rise and fall of the ocean. "If you—if anyone—hurts her, I'll—"

"You seem to be going on the assumption that I can control what happens. I can't. I'll do what I can for Luce if I get the opportunity, but the situation is probably out of my hands."

"I don't care if you can control it! If someone—if the government does anything to hurt her—when she's the one who wants to *stop* the mermaids from killing—I'll . . ."

Ben Ellison didn't say anything, though his face was tight and sorrowful. He didn't need to. Dorian could supply the questions himself. *You'll do what, Dorian? Try to kill me? Or maybe you'll go and fight on the side of the mermaids. Is that it? Even though they murdered your whole family and almost all of them would be delighted to murder you?*

Leaf-shadows fluttered on Ellison's sad brown face. "Why don't you sit back down, Dorian?"

"No." Maybe the trouble Luce was in wasn't really Ellison's fault, but Dorian couldn't make himself care. Luce was far away, desperate and alone, and anything he could do would be completely stupid and useless.

"I'm sorry. I can understand that you must feel frustrated at not having any way to help her. I wish you'd realize that I'm almost as helpless as you are, and that the situation is very difficult for me as well."

"You won't even tell me the truth!" Dorian snarled. "You pretend we're friends, and meanwhile you're working for people who want to kill my girlfriend, and you're *helping* them."

She's not your girlfriend anymore. Ben Ellison didn't have to say that out loud either. *It was your choice. You broke her heart, you let her go, all of your own free will.*

"You have no idea of the position I'm in now, Dorian. There are people involved in this . . . investigation . . . who are almost crazed by what we've uncovered. And they have vastly more power than I do. The most I can do is to try to inject some logic into the discussion. Some restraint."

"Restraint?" Dorian was staring around at the trees, their leaves still fresh and moist and pale green in the golden sunlight. Wild, sweet wind curled around his face, but the lovely day seemed impossibly cumbersome. His every tiny movement was weighted with futility.

"I can remind everyone that these were once human girls. Children. And that's what I keep doing." Ellison's voice was very gentle now. "It's exhausting, though. And I definitely don't need the distraction of worrying about you in addition. In any case you can't improve anything for Luce by staying here. You do know that?"

He knew it. The bright leaves waved like hands trying to brush him away. "Is Luce even alive?"

"As far as I know, yes. She hasn't been spotted in some days, though."

"You wouldn't lie to me about that?"

"I wouldn't lie about that. I—" Ellison paused as if he was about to say something he shouldn't. "I promise I'll let you know. If I hear that Luce has been captured or killed."

It seemed impossible that they were even having this conversation. Dorian realized his cheeks were wet.

"Now will you agree to go back to Chicago? Dorian? I'm truly acting in your best interest. I don't want you in the middle of this."

"I'll . . ." Dorian sighed. "I'll think about it. Okay? But I really don't think I can leave Zoe."

* * *

Back in the frilly room Lindy had given him Dorian sat cross-legged on the bed. The room still didn't feel like it was really his, but at least he'd gotten used to it. *Captured or killed.* He opened his laptop, trying not to cry. If they captured Luce, what would they do to her?

"*Mermaid sighting,*" Dorian typed. The video had over sixty million views now. Then—like some kind of sick ritual—the seals lounged, and the little girl in the red windbreaker wandered down the beach, turning back to stare at something under the dock. Someone screamed. The camera lurched, the sun flashed. Then a voice cried, "My God! Nick, look!"

And Luce rippled out across the screen, her lambent movements clear in the shallow, shining water. *Captured or killed.* That hadn't happened yet, or if it had Ben Ellison didn't know about it, assuming he was telling the truth. But it could happen any day now, any second.

Even if the mermaids would let Dorian join the war on their side, what was he going to do? Head out into the Pacific in an inner tube? And they would all hate him anyway. Even Luce probably hated him now. Maybe that was contempt in her eyes as she turned to glance back over her shoulder and hesitated, clearly on the verge of saying *something*.

The screen went black. *Replay.*

"Dorian?" Zoe's voice came out high, broken. Somehow she'd come in without him hearing her, and she'd already seen the screen. Dorian looked up at her standing a foot inside his door, pink hair trailing around her devastated face. "Wow, that's a really amazing video, isn't it? And that mermaid is just so *hot*. You'd totally do her, right?" He saw her glance sharply at the tears striping his cheeks and look off.

Dorian closed the laptop. "I think they're *hunting* her, Zoe. Ben Ellison said some shit that really sounded like—I don't know, like the government is after her."

Zoe shrugged. "Well, yeah. What did you think they were *going* to do?"

"You can't expect me not to care about that! Think about how *scared* she must be. And she's hurt, and she's definitely not swimming right."

"Dorian," Zoe groaned. "The girl is a killer, all right? I for one am relieved to know that our government is committed to protecting its citizens from, whatever, these little bitch-ass, psychotic Ariels."

Dorian didn't think she meant it. Her round hazel-green eyes still looked shocked and staring; she was lashing out from jealousy and pain. But even so . . ."You know if anyone's ever going to *stop* the mermaids from killing, it's going to be Luce!"

"She's basically Charles Manson with green glitter on his ass."

"She wants to *change* things! Zoe, just because I was in love with her before, that doesn't mean—"

"You're *still* in love with her!" Zoe yelled. She was biting her lip, her body tense and twisted, the toe of one paint-spattered combat boot grinding at the carpet. "You're probably fantasizing about her whenever you're messing around with me, and you think you're doing me some big fucking favor."

Dorian sighed. "I love you, okay? Can you *stop* now?"

Zoe glowered at him, but her body was starting to droop and her voice seemed tired. "You don't love me. Not the right way, not the way I love you, not—"

"Ben Ellison's trying to get me to go back to Chicago, and I said no because of you! You think I *want* to stay here?"

"I guess you don't have any real reason to stay anymore." Zoe's black-clad arms moved up, almost as if she was stretching, but then they stopped in front of her face. Her pale hands gripped at her messy pink-blond hair. "It sucked so bad when I wanted you and you kept ignoring me. But having you hurts even worse."

"Zoe, we're *together* now—"

"You think you're helping me by staying here, but you're not. You're just fucking me up. Just because you won't admit stuff doesn't mean I don't *know*." She lowered her arms. "Get lost. Go to Chicago. But tell me the truth first." Her face was pink and swollen, but she wasn't crying. Dorian was. His back shuddered with every breath.

"Jesus, Zoe."

"Tell me the truth and we'll stay friends. *Close* friends. If you don't I don't ever want to talk to you again." She came closer and rested her hands on his shoulders. Her mouth suddenly twisted into a plaintive smile. "Are you in love with Luce?'

"Yeah," Dorian barely whispered. He was staring at the bed. Zoe reached with one hand and coaxed his head up, making him look into her eyes. "I'm not lying that I love you, Zoe. A lot. But yeah. I am."

Zoe kissed his forehead. Her pink hair brushed his face, striping the room in front of him. "Then I hope they don't kill her."

8

Golden Gate

That evening Luce stared across the ocean at the lights of what looked like a good-sized town. Rows of golden windows and streetlights tangled like vines through the dusk, and there were a few bonfires out on the shore. Things hadn't gone so well the last time she'd slept under a dock, but even so Luce realized that the margins of human towns were the safest places for her now. Those divers would probably be searching any caves they could find along the waterline, any secluded coves: the kinds of places mermaids usually lived. They'd be a lot less likely to come waving their huge black guns through clusters of people laughing and toasting marshmallows out on the beach.

She swept closer, keeping under the water as much as she could. There was some kind of boat club up ahead, with ranks of yachts parked along neat piers. She slipped below and found a quiet spot on the shore, a ceiling of planks only a foot above her, beer bottles and rusty chains scattered on the sand. She could hear human voices nearby; it sounded there was a small party going on, with soft, delicate music. Luce slept for a long time, and no one disturbed her.

Being so close to human habitations made her self-conscious

about her nakedness. Normally clothes weren't something she thought about at all, but now when she found a tattered black bikini top wadded on the shore, she smoothed it out and tied it on.

This was the best way she could travel, Luce realized: swimming as far from shore and as deep as she could manage during the day, sleeping under docks at night. For the next week or more she kept going like that, surprised to find herself enjoying the water and even her own solitude. Human towns used to make her so nervous; now Luce realized that she liked hearing people talking or laughing around her. It was oddly comforting. It almost made her feel the way she had as a little girl, drifting off to sleep in the back of her father's van while chatter and music softened the night's harsh edges.

Listening to the ordinary happiness of strangers, she could almost forget that the divers were after her. That the mermaids were still being slaughtered.

* * *

The coast turned wilder, full of cliffs and twisty inlets and beaches closed in by pinnacles of rock tufted with wildflowers. Even from a distance Luce could hear children squealing as they played in the water and the roar of motorcycles swooping along the winding roads. The town where she found shelter that night was small, but its gardens were so thick with flowers that even the dimness under the docks breathed with their perfume. And there were many more living things around her now: seals and sea lions sprawled on sandbars with their spotted bellies exposed, fins flashed in the water, and so many hawks wheeled above that they almost seemed to be gears turning in an immense blue clock. Whenever she swam near the seafloor tall anemones pulsed their wispy fronds in the current

and enormous sea stars spread their radial arms. The animals crowding the bottom all seemed to have invented new and fantastical
sunset colors for themselves: they came in peach-speckled lilacs,
rose-spined saffrons, peculiar moody pinks. Luce could barely feel
worried in this outpouring of vibrant beauty.

Light wings of fog settled over the water as Luce swam on the
next morning. She began to wonder if the black-suited divers had
given up searching for her. After all, there had been no sign of them
for days. Maybe she could try to find other mermaids and ask them
for news without inflicting danger on them. Luce was wondering
this as the green house-dotted cliffs to her left rolled back, disappearing completely behind hovering cloud-fronds, and something
huge and airy and geometric loomed above the mist. It looked so
familiar, but for a fraction of a second Luce couldn't place it. Its
two metal peaks were dully red, high and elegantly curved.

Then she recognized it. It was the Golden Gate Bridge.

Luce could hardly believe it. She'd swum all the way to San
Francisco. She remembered it from when she'd briefly lived there
with her father: a dreamlike city with, Luce recalled, a lot of run-
down and half-abandoned areas along the waterfront. She could
remember slipping with her father through a gap in a chainlink
fence to explore a cavernous building with soaring walls of milky
glass panes; it had once been used for building ships, he'd told her.
She remembered the rusting hulks of forgotten boats, an inlet mys-
teriously heaped with dozens of barnacle-crusted shopping carts
where herons perched. All around the network of bays tucked behind the Golden Gate there were places like that, he'd told her,
partly wild and partly ruined.

Luce couldn't help grinning to herself as she realized what
was in front of her.

For a mermaid in desperate trouble, this city was the perfect hideout.

* * *

For the rest of the day Luce lurked under the dock of what looked like an unused vacation home near a town she guessed was Sausalito. Sailboats swept nearby, voices shrieked with laughter. Even if she was careful to keep well below the surface, it was clear that staying in San Francisco Bay meant that she could go out only at night. But it was hard to keep calm as she waited for the darkness that would free her to go exploring. She needed somewhere sheltered and lonely without too many boats around, and especially she needed to find someplace with a reasonable supply of shellfish. Hunger needled at her, sharp and insistent.

Even more unbearable than hunger was a new idea that kept intruding on her mind, no matter how many times Luce told herself she was being irrational. She couldn't help imagining Nausicaa's greenish bronze face looking up in warm surprise, her wild black hair cascading back from her face as she dashed grinning through the water to pull Luce into her arms. Her friend might be somewhere in the bays in front of her. Luce wouldn't have to explain anything because Nausicaa would already know; she wouldn't have to think about the horrors she'd witnessed. The ancient mermaid would know exactly what they should do, and Luce would help.

At least that was the fantasy. The problem with going out to search, Luce realized, was the way she'd feel if the fantasy proved not to be true. Outside her hiding place the fog receded, and Luce could glimpse a bit of the gray mass of skyscrapers prickling upward along the far shore of the bay. An endless procession of ships heaped with neatly stacked cargo containers skimmed below the bridge and out to sea.

When night finally came it was starless, smoke black, the water crisscrossed by a thousand streaks of light thrown by the shining towers of San Francisco. Luce found a patch of oysters nearby and ate them under her dock, then headed across the bay, aiming toward the left of downtown. She thought it was somewhere over there that she'd gone exploring abandoned piers with her father. Sometimes from the corners of her eyes Luce caught distant flashes of diving shapes that looked about as big as she was: probably seals, though they seemed fast for seals. Enormous stingrays wrapped the depths in their black wings and leopard sharks ambled sleepily just below her. She didn't pay too much attention. The black water was much smoother and calmer than she was used to while overhead the reflected lights of the city formed a ceiling of prancing dots and beams of gold.

Deeper into the bay, though, the light became sparser. As she went on the darkness of the water was broken by rows of pilings like rotten teeth. She passed a pier so decayed that it slumped into the water, its wood beams gone soft as rope. There were still warehouses set back from the water, but they had a decrepit look and no light glazed their windows. Only, here and there, a street-light stood in a lonely haze of apricot-colored glow. Luce hovered fifty feet from shore with her head just above the surface, watching and listening. There was a stench of rust and pollution, and the water felt oily and warmer than she liked. Still, maybe under that pier she could make a temporary home for herself? She'd pictured somewhere wilder, but at least there didn't seem to be any people around.

No. There was one. A man was walking out on that decayed

pier, so drunk that his whole body pitched like a wave. Luce noticed the man's filthy layered overcoats; the rags around his feet; the sad, sick way he staggered. It reminded her a bit of the way her father had looked when she'd found him living as a castaway, his body swaddled in sealskins. Luce stopped where she was. The thought of her father opened like a wound in her chest, the shape of an intolerable absence. Where *was* he now? Had he recovered from all the terrible things he'd gone through?

The man swayed faster, his body doubling in the middle as if he were about to be sick. He was standing right at the pier's edge, one foot curling into empty space. Now he didn't remind Luce of her father but of her uncle Peter. Reeling, pitiful, and broken, although Luce thought furiously that he'd actually broken himself. That was how Peter had looked in the moments just before he turned vicious, smacking her or knocking her down. Her stomach tightened with disgust. Maybe that *was* Peter, homeless and stinking, wandering across the wasted margins of a beautiful city . . .

The man still hadn't straightened, but he wasn't vomiting, either. Instead he just wavered, his torso tipped precariously toward the water, one hand pawing the air in slow circles. Then he tried to step back, wobbled sharply, and pitched headlong into the bay. The splash blinked white against the darkness.

For several seconds Luce waited for him to surface. He could swim for the shore, or he could grab hold of the pilings and pull himself back up. She watched the water where he'd fallen: at first the glossy surface was rocking, but gradually it calmed until there was nothing but a scattered hoop of froth. His head should emerge from the froth at any moment, sputtering angrily.

Nothing happened. Where *was* he? Luce swam closer. There in the gray dimness under the pier she could just make out his ragged, flailing shape. His waterlogged coats splayed out around him like pinwheeling wings, but they were only dragging him farther down. He twisted randomly, as if he couldn't guess where the surface was, and Luce understood that he was drowning. His eyes bulged and his lips were moving fast, bright bubbles leaping out like silent words. There was still something he needed to say, Luce thought. For some reason she thought he was trying to tell someone how *sorry* he was. To ask for forgiveness.

Without thinking about what she was doing, Luce started singing. The water stopped dragging on the tangled coats. Instead it moved in Luce's song, and the wide wings of fabric formed a kind of cradle tugging him back toward the surface. The man gagged, thrashing in astonishment as the water shuddered with unimaginable music, carrying him *up* . . .

Up into the night air, where the enchanted water seized him in the curl of a tall wave that stood alone above the black glass surface of the bay. Luce sang a sustained note that held him there in space for a moment, his body slowly rotating as he wheezed and stretched out his hands, water spilling from his mouth and sodden clothes. She thought of teaching him a lesson by sending her song into a high spike of sound and then breaking off abruptly, letting him crash back down onto the pier so hard that his teeth would jar from their sockets. Just because she'd gone and saved his life for no good reason, that didn't mean he *deserved* any kindness from her.

Then, almost in spite of herself, Luce let the note fade slowly. The homeless man landed on the planks so lightly that there wasn't even a thud.

She was only twenty feet from him now, still glaring at him as he scrambled onto his knees and gaped at her. Of course he wasn't really Peter. He was much too old to be Peter, probably at least sixty. Just another idiotic drunk who'd destroy anything he could get his hands on, even if that meant he only wound up destroying himself.

"You're *shining* . . ." the man croaked. His hair hung in grayish clumps around his face, but his eyes were bright with longing. The cold water and the shock of almost dying, not to mention being rescued in such an unfathomable way, seemed to have sobered him up.

"*You* need to quit drinking!" Luce rasped out furiously. Her nails were digging into her palms and her tail was lashing. "I don't know why I saved you! Why did you have to go and get so *wasted*, like you don't even care what happens to you?"

Luce was too enraged to think clearly or to control the wild spasms of her tail. It kicked above the surface, sending droplets spinning out across the night. A trace of mist hung in the air, and the glow of the streetlamps floated like dandelion puffs.

"You're . . . a mermaid? And you did that to the water, didn't you? You *saved* me. You're a—"

"Well, you're a *drunk*," Luce snapped. "This is the only time I'm going to save you, okay? If you ever do that again, I swear I'll let you drown!"

"Hey," the man said. "I'm sorry. I'm so sorry. Stay and talk to me. Please."

"No!" Luce shrieked. She was already backing away.

"At least tell me your name. I want to know . . . who saved my life. You saved my life. Beautiful . . . your voice was so beautiful! I need to know . . ." He was kneeling on the pier's edge, one hand stretched helplessly toward her.

Luce didn't think that deserved a response. She'd already wasted too much time on him, she thought, and of course she shouldn't have let some human see her at all. She turned to go.

"I'm always here!" he cried out after her. Even as the water closed over her head, Luce could still hear him shouting. "I'm always here! I've come so far. I've been a stevedore, and a soldier and a ghost, but I'm here now!" Luce was still angry, but she felt the light touch of another emotion she would have preferred to ignore. Maybe there was something sweet about this old man. "Hey! Mermaid, listen up! If you ever want help with anything, you know who to ask!"

* * *

Luce kept swimming south. All at once she was overcome by weariness and shame, but she didn't know why. Of course, she'd broken the timahk again by letting a human hear her sing without killing him, even by talking to him at all, but so many things had changed that the timahk didn't seem to matter much anymore. Before she'd swum far, Luce realized why she felt so sick with herself: it hadn't been fair of her to hate that man because of what Peter had done. It wasn't his fault. That old man had never hurt her; she couldn't have any idea of what he'd gone through, the events that had left him so broken.

Why should she care, though?

The water around her seemed alive, but Luce didn't pay much attention. Something faintly luminous darted below her, torqued itself, curled upward. All at once Luce recognized what it was and reeled back, startled.

"You know this is a lousy time to be pulling that here!" a voice snapped. "*Now* you want to risk them noticing us? Don't even *think* about trying that again!"

A strange mermaid furled her pinkish gold tail in front of Luce. She was older and Asian, her long hair clouding black around the creamy golden shine of her skin.

"I . . ." Luce started, but she was too surprised to know what she should say.

" . . . just offed some homeless guy, right? Fantastic. When the bay's practically the only safe place *left!*"

"I didn't kill him," Luce said, though of course that wouldn't help. The strange mermaid glowered, disbelieving. "You . . . I actually didn't know there were other mermaids here. I'm . . ."

The girl's face softened slightly. "One of the refugees? Or were you just kicked out of your tribe? Look, I guess there's room for you, but you really can't go around *singing* like that!"

"I won't," Luce promised, but her thoughts were racing. "Are there a lot of mermaids here? It's a big tribe?"

"You *are* new here! No tribe."

"But . . ."

"No tribes, no queens. But yes, tons of mermaids. More every day now."

"Where?"

"All over the place. A bunch of them you should just kind of leave alone—they're too crazy—but you won't see them much. There are a lot of us under the old factories before Hunter's Point, though. You coming?"

She didn't wait for an answer, and Luce went swimming along beside the stranger. They skimmed between angled pilings then beside strange crenelated metal walls that stood in the water with ships docked between them. It seemed like a peculiar place for mermaids, gritty and mournful, though it had a lonely beauty of its own. "Do you know a mermaid named Nausicaa?" Luce asked at last. "I'm trying to find her."

Luce half expected the stranger to jerk back in astonishment at Nausicaa's name; she was disappointed to find that this gold-shining girl didn't react at all. "Um, I don't think I know her. But there are a lot of us out here I don't know, so maybe she's around someplace."

Maybe Nausicaa hadn't been here, then. They skimmed up for air and passed a spot where a cement-walled creek released a plume of revolting fresh water into the bay. A seal bobbed and then vanished. Then they reached salt water again and dipped under a vast ruined factory propped on a forest of upright logs. It was dark apart from a scattering of long, dimly shining forms far back in the shadows, and even though the dark didn't stop Luce from seeing, she still had trouble recognizing what was in front of her. The water lapped gently at the pilings, and stretched here and there between them was a network of what appeared to be enormous drooping webs, each web set on a slant so that one side trailed into the glossy skin of the bay. And in their webs those glowing things were *figures*, some chatting quietly to each other, the subtle gleam from their faces dabbling on the water like bits of melted star.

Then Luce understood. Of course there were no suitable caves here. Instead the mermaids had adapted, stringing up half-submerged hammocks woven from old scraps of fishing nets, plastic bags, algae-slimed ropes. Luce noticed one hammock that appeared to be made from dozens of pairs of pantyhose knotted together. They could sleep here with their tails under the water, their heads above, in the last place humans would ever think to look for them.

"New girl," the Asian mermaid announced tiredly to no one in particular. "Don't know how long she's staying."

Luce looked around the black mazelike space under its low ceiling of boards just in case Nausicaa was there somewhere. She didn't feel much hope of that anymore, but maybe . . . Condensation gleamed on the tar-smeared trunks around her. A few mermaids leaned in their nets to get a better look, though they didn't seem particularly interested. In one of the more remote hammocks Luce noticed three mermaids laughing together. One of them tipped forward as she laughed with a voice that was at once harsh and delicate, and Luce saw her red-gold hair flaring in the dimness like a match before it vanished again behind one of the pillars.

Luce's heart stopped. She couldn't let herself believe it. The mermaid beside her was still talking—something about where Luce should sleep—but Luce couldn't focus enough to make out the words. There it was again, red-gold hair suffused with its own light, and Luce was flinging herself across the water. It wasn't what she'd hoped for, but if it was true it was almost as wonderful. A long, wordless cry rushed from Luce's throat. Girls turned to stare at her in surprise as she dodged wildly around pilings. She smacked into someone and reeled away, gasping a vague apology, while red-gold light came tumbling toward the water just ahead. Bronze fins brushed Luce's shoulder. Then two moon gray eyes were staring at her, wide with disbelief, and Luce finally managed to form her outcry into a word:

"CAT! Cat, Cat, it's . . ."

"LUCE?"

There was a light splash, and shining hair radiated out through the water, rushing closer until Luce was surrounded in fiery waves. Pale hands reached up, grasping randomly at Luce's shoulders, squeezing her face, and Catarina's eyes gazed fiercely into hers.

Luce couldn't even speak at first. Her whole chest heaved with sobs as Catarina's cool fingers sank into her short hair. Then they were holding each other so tightly that Luce's ribs ached. "Lucette," Catarina was murmuring, "my Lucette, my crazy little Luce. Thank God! All this way. And after everything we've heard . . ." Catarina touched the notch in Luce's ear, then brushed her fingertips across the imperfectly healed cuts in her cheek and the white scar on her shoulder.

"Cat, I can't believe you're here! Everything's been so *terrible*." Luce breathed the words out between half-sobs, but she'd started smiling now too. She was holding someone she loved again, a friend whom she was now completely sure loved her back, and that almost made the horror and loneliness of the past weeks disappear into a cloud of warm relief.

"Where is everyone else?" Catarina leaned away to look at Luce, her eyes shining with unbearable hope. "Are they with you? Are they coming?"

Sudden dread coated Luce's insides like cold oil. She didn't know how she could begin to tell Cat what had happened. And all of it was her fault: if she'd only become queen the way Catarina wanted, the tribe might have survived. "Dana—and Violet—and a few of the little ones. They're the only ones . . ."

Luce broke off. It was too horrible to say out loud.

Catarina's lovely mouth pinched with dismay, but for some reason the eagerness in her face was still stronger. "The only ones? Luce, tell me! It's so horrible to think . . . Dana . . . Oh, but I was afraid it would be so much *worse* than that!" Luce stared at her, starting to understand. Her mouth opened but no sound would come. "Luce? That's what you're trying to tell me, isn't it? You mean those are the only ones who died?"

Luce shook her head. "No. Cat . . . No." The words came out in a croak.

"LUCE!"

"Cat . . . I mean . . . those are the only ones besides me who *might* still be alive."

9

The Twice Lost

What made it even worse was that there was no way she could tell Catarina the story privately. Other mermaids had gotten interested; they were slipping from their hammocks and flicking closer. The dim glow of their faces dotted the water on all sides. Luce stared around, and everywhere she looked another pair of eyes gleamed back at her. The soft light of their arms curled through the water. There were so *many* of them, far more than in any tribe Luce had ever seen.

"You know her, Catarina?" It was the Asian mermaid who'd led Luce there, her face a floating golden disc in that crowd of bright faces.

"Yuan! This is Luce. I told you about her."

"The one who was supposed to be queen? What happened ' the rest of your tribe, then?"

"Slaughtered." Luce breathed it out. "Those divers, with the helmets that block out our songs . . ."

It was obvious from the grim way the other mermaids looked at one another that they already knew about the divers. Luce noticed a few mermaids who were crudely bandaged, their eyes flickering with remembered terror. Refugees. Survivors. That couldn't explain what *all* these mermaids were doing here, though, could it? "How did you get away, then?" Yuan asked. "If your whole tribe was killed . . ."

"I wasn't living with them." Luce saw Catarina grimace at that, but she couldn't lie about this. "I had my own cave, down the coast. And . . ."

Yuan nodded at the white scar on Luce's shoulder. "Was that the divers?"

"Yes. They shot at me, out in the water."

Now there were too many voices, coming at her from all sides.

"Luce! What do you mean you weren't living with them? You didn't leave everyone with *Anais*!" Catarina hissed with indignation.

"Luce? She's called Luce? They—those *humans*—they said that name! They're looking for her!" one of the refugees trilled, half-panicked.

So Nausicaa almost surely hadn't come this far, Luce realized, or this strange mermaid would have heard her name before the divers reached her tribe. "The humans are hunting me," Luce admitted. "If you think it's not safe to have me here, I'll leave right now."

"They're hunting for *all* of us!" Catarina snarled imperiously. All at once her arm wrapped protectively around Luce's shoulders and her eyes flared, daring anyone to contradict her. "Having Luce here won't make any difference!"

Yuan tipped her head. "We'd better get the whole story before we decide that, Cat. Luce? Can you explain what all this is about?"

Luce stared around at everyone: dozens of mermaids who looked as if they'd come from every country in the world, the tints of their faces ranging from night dark to icy pale. Swimming away by herself would be so much easier than trying to tell this crowd of strangers everything that had happened to her. On the other hand there was Catarina gazing at her with a mixture of anger and—Luce had to admit it—feverish tenderness. Luce definitely owed her an explanation at the very least. "I'll try. I don't know where to start, though."

"Start when I left," Catarina growled. "Luce, why didn't you go back to the tribe? You were supposed to be their queen! Oh, I was so sure that once I left you would do the *right* thing, the *only* thing, and lead them."

Luce looked at her and suddenly knew that she was going to say the unsayable. "I *couldn't*, Cat. I was furious with them because of what they did to you, but . . . that wasn't the real reason. I wasn't worthy to be queen." Everyone was gaping at her; a few of them had started smiling slyly, as if they were sharing some joke Luce couldn't understand. "I broke the timahk."

There it was. Now they would drive her away, and they'd be better off with her gone.

A few mermaids had started laughing in a choked, delirious way. Catarina moaned and Yuan flashed a lopsided grin. "You don't *say.* How?"

"I saved a human. A boy." Luce wished they'd hurry up and tell her to leave. She didn't want anyone asking questions about this boy; she didn't want to confess how pathetically stupid she'd been, loving someone who'd betrayed and humiliated her and who clearly wanted her dead. And she definitely, definitely didn't want to say his name again, not as long as she lived.

"Luce!" Catarina seemed like she was about to cry. "You—oh, I needed you to be *better* than that. You were always the one, the only one who could save us. Restore our *honor* . . ."

Luce couldn't understand why, while Catarina seemed on the verge of hysterics, Yuan couldn't stop grinning as if her face was about to split open and at least half the mermaids around her had joined in that disturbing laughter. "Yeah, Catarina, this is terrible! What kind of dirty bitch would *save* a human?" Yuan sneered. Luce looked at her in total perplexity. Yuan met her gaze with a hard stare and smiled with too many teeth showing. "Just a bitch like *me*, or like Rafa, or like Imani. Nobody ever had any crazy fantasies about *us* restoring anyone's honor, right?"

Hazily Luce thought Yuan must be kidding somehow. She knew she wasn't the only mermaid in the ocean who'd violated their laws, but it couldn't be true that so *many* of these girls had failed the same way she had. Could it?

"Luce is—she was always—different from the rest of us, Yuan. She made me believe in . . ." Catarina broke off, glowering through the streaks of her tears. Luce reached out and stroked a tear away, half expecting Catarina to slap her.

She didn't, but the way the glazed shine of those gray eyes suddenly fixed on Luce's face felt worse than a blow.

"Believe in what, Cat?" Yuan's voice was silky, insinuating.

"In *purity*."

"Oh, boy. *Purity*." Yuan's face was still contorted by that sarcastic grin. "Might want to forget about that now!"

Luce impulsively pulled Catarina closer and leaned her cheek against her friend's wet face. All she could see was the fire-colored waves of Cat's hair. At least the frenzied laughter around them was finally subsiding.

"No." Catarina's voice was a blur in Luce's ear.

"Cat? Yuan's right. I'm not any more pure or honorable than

anyone. I haven't even believed in the timahk for a long time, and I broke it over and over, and then I didn't . . . do what I should have done to stop our tribe from getting killed. I did everything wrong."

Catarina moaned. "Then you're different because dishonor can't touch you. You still have your innocence, Luce! I know you do. I heard it every time you sang."

Luce didn't know what to say to that. She looked up through soft tangles of Catarina's hair to see Yuan still smiling cynically. "Guess we can't talk her out of it, then. Luce, it looks like you're just going to have to live with being Catarina's shining star, unless you decide you can't stand it and ditch. I know what it's like. My daddy used to cry and sob and say I was so pure and special that I couldn't lose my innocence no matter what, too. See, that made it okay for him to rape me."

Luce stared for a moment. "Please don't compare Catarina to him, then."

"You don't like hearing it? Why not? You love Catarina or something?" Yuan suddenly demanded; her voice was changing, turning high and strange. Luce couldn't help flinching.

"I do. I always did, ever since I met her. Even when we were fighting."

Catarina exhaled sharply and squeezed Luce tighter.

"Oh, see, but I loved my daddy, too. And the first thing I did when I changed was swim right back to our house and drown him. And my mom and my piano teacher, even though I wasn't really trying to get them. Too bad for them our house was right on the water!"

Yuan's eyes were narrowing, and her voice took on a dreamy, obsessive lilt that Luce knew all too well. But it wouldn't make any difference if someone told Yuan to let go of the past. That wasn't something you could just *decide* to do.

"Yuan?" It was a new voice, very low and gentle. Luce looked and saw a mermaid with blue-black skin and soft dark eyes; her hair was short, like Luce's, though it stood out like a halo around her head. She wore a white lace headscarf and a bikini top that appeared to be made from snow-colored lace as well, though on closer inspection it proved to have been intricately crafted from plastic grocery bags. The blue luminance of her skin reminded Luce of neon reflecting in a street lacquered by rain. "Luce is still just meeting everyone, and seeing Catarina again after a long time. It's a lot for her to think about. Couldn't we wait to tell her . . . everything about ourselves?"

Luce smiled gratefully.

"I'm Imani. I'm one of the ones who broke the timahk the same way you say you did. But I don't think it has to mean we're dishonored. It can mean . . . we wanted different rules, or we wanted to be honorable in a different way." Imani's voice was barely audible.

Yuan laughed nastily. "Try telling that to any queen in the world, Imani. Any tribe! No mermaids would ever accept us! They'd only think of us as . . . soiled. Ruined. And they'd be right!"

For an instant Luce just stared around, uncomprehending. What could it mean to say that no mermaids would accept them when they were living in what looked like the biggest tribe she'd ever seen? But Yuan had said it wasn't a tribe, and no one seemed to be in charge. Unless, somehow . . .

"All of you?" Luce asked. She could barely hear her own voice.

"Oh, now you get it! All of us except the refugees. And even if we disgust them they don't have a lot of choice about putting up with us." Yuan's strange grin came back. "Yeah, everyone here broke the timahk, one way or another! We all got thrown out of our tribes. Not for the same reasons, though. Tania over there got into a fight, for instance, and Jo was caught trying to call her mom with a cellphone she found on the beach."

Yuan nodded toward a girl with her hair dyed an artificial ruby red. Jo was wearing a huge necklace made from dozens of algae-slicked plastic toys and tangled string, and she kept squirming and biting the back of her own hand.

"Well, I don't believe that Jo is dishonored either," Imani objected. Even when she seemed angry her voice was low and soft, almost cooing. "She's not *soiled*."

Luce looked around. Jo wasn't the only mermaid there who had strange tics or eyes as restless as swarming gnats. "And that's why you don't have a queen?"

"No queen!" Yuan agreed fiercely. "Even if we're filth, at least we're free! It doesn't matter what we do. We can't be any more worthless than we are already."

Luce began to wonder why Catarina had been silent for so long. She was still clutching Luce tight in her arms, and her face was hidden against the side of Luce's neck, but her breathing sounded different now, raspy and somehow thoughtful.

"It *always* matters what we do!"

Luce looked up, surprised, and suddenly realized that the words had come from her own mouth.

"Not us," Yuan insisted. "We're *twice* lost. The humans lost us the first time, then we were lost to other mermaids, too. Now there's nothing left to lose us, except *life*, and the way things are going, that shouldn't take long either!"

"And the world, which is *really* in trouble now," Luce said sharply. She still felt amazed at herself. "And each other, and all those mermaids out there who are getting murdered with no way to even defend themselves. We need to figure out a way to stop that."

Everyone was staring at her, harder than ever. Luce felt embarrassed, but even more than that she felt possessed by an unexpected urgency.

"We don't need the timahk anymore!" Luce added. "The timahk doesn't even make *sense* now that the humans know about us. Maybe we're dishonored, but that's not the kind of honor that matters now! And we don't need purity either. We just need to change what's happening."

For several seconds no one said anything. Catarina finally released Luce from her embrace and dipped quickly under the water before coming up again with streaming hair. Now that Luce was floating alone in the water dizziness rippled through her head.

Why didn't anyone answer? They must all think she was insane, Luce decided. Even in this band of desperate outcasts she was simply too weird to fit in. There was no place for her anywhere in the world . . .

"We have a queen *now*," Catarina announced. Her chin was raised proudly, and there was a calm glow in her eyes even though they were still swollen from crying.

Luce felt confused and suddenly unbearably tired. What was Catarina *talking* about? What were any of these crazy, damaged mermaids trying to say to her, really? They didn't understand her, and in fact they made no sense to her, either.

"No *queens*," Yuan snarled frantically, and Imani curled a gentle hand on her shoulder. "We don't need one, and we don't even deserve—"

"Yuan, Yuan, wait! We're still *mermaids*. No matter how many times lost we are, we can't lose that! You *know* what that means." Imani smiled with sudden brilliance. She was so lovely, Luce thought, with her heart-shaped face and up-tilting eyes. But Luce still wasn't sure what they were arguing about. The whole world was out of joint, so slippery and unbalanced that words couldn't even hold on to their meanings anymore.

Yuan was gnawing her lip, but she didn't answer. No one did.

Imani looked around, waiting for someone to contradict her. No sound disturbed the quiet except, very distantly, a chorus of car horns. Then she turned her eyes straight on Luce. "It means we'll know the one who's meant to be queen by her song."

10

No One's Queen

"Show them, Luce!" Catarina's eyes flared with pride as Luce looked around, suddenly understanding what they expected from her. She'd fled from the divers and somehow wound up at an audition for a role she didn't even want.

Luce felt a secret thrill at the thought of how amazed Catarina would be by what she could do with her voice now, and just as quickly stifled it.

"Not here, though," Jo put in worriedly. She bit her hand again, jogging a plastic duckling at her throat. "We'll have to swim far out, out where everything is completely empty."

No one bothered to ask Luce if she wanted to be queen, of course, or if she had other plans. As the mermaids dipped below the surface of the bay, skimming in a long procession back toward the Golden Gate and the open sea beyond, Luce wondered what she should do. All around her mermaids streaked and rippled, dimly shining, until the dark water seemed banded by living light. Streetlamps like flocks of glowing birds crowded the hills on every side; whenever Luce surfaced the droplets on her lashes dazzled her with refracted stars. If they did want her to become their queen, then how could she look for Nausicaa?

She didn't need to worry, Luce decided. Even if they were impressed by what she could do, they'd definitely change their minds once they found out what her rules would be. Like J'aime, they'd be furious that she didn't want to use her voice as a weapon. But what if they *did* agree to follow her, even when her ideas went against everything mermaids had always believed?

They wouldn't, of course. But if they did?

Remembered voices brushed through Luce's head. *That's going to be a lot of dead mermaids who you did* nothing *for!* J'aime snarled, and the words interwove with Nausicaa's murmurs: *Maybe someday someone will change our story. Maybe you will, Luce. Then the story will be new, even for me* . . . Would Nausicaa want her to do this? Her father called her name just as Dana laughed in sudden delight, her laughter dancing with the midnight water.

Luce swished her head to clear it and swam on, coils of Catarina's hair flickering in the corner of her vision. If they agreed, well — Luce glanced around again, and Imani smiled over at her then with so many of them working together, maybe she could think of something? Maybe she didn't have to fail these unknown mermaids in the way that she'd failed her old tribe.

They slipped below the bridge. Container ships piled high with stained metal boxes were still passing out to sea, even this late at night. The mermaids kept far below the surface, their bodies twisting against the sharply roughening water as they left the bay's shelter. Then they kept on in silence, and Luce felt a brooding sense of ceremony as well as a growing tightness in her stomach. What if those black boats were prowling nearby; what if Luce had inadvertently led all these girls to their deaths?

Imani caught her wrist and tugged gently upward.

They came up in a surging sea, bright faces scattered like floating lanterns on the waves. On this side of the bridge the rising hills looked dark and wild, scrawled over by the pale writhing trunks of cypresses. Luce got the impression that there were even more mermaids now than there had been down under that warehouse. Two hundred? More?

No matter what she did it was probably just a matter of time before the divers discovered them and their refuge in the bay became a trap. After all, the Golden Gate was the bay's only exit, and it was quite narrow: could the humans close it off somehow and take their time tracking down all the mermaids stuck behind it?

"Cat thinks you're a big deal, but you have to understand—this isn't how we do things here. It's going to take a lot to convince us —" Yuan broke off. Luce was already humming very quietly. She closed her eyes to concentrate, to feel the smooth flow of her voice as it began dividing into multiple notes like a stream parting into a dozen bright rivulets. Her body rose and dipped with the waves, and Luce poured herself into the music. Each note became a half-forgotten dream from years before, or the memory of a beloved hand stroking back her hair. She was all alone inside a hundred weaving strands of song, each one free and sweet and liquid, each one calling to the water. Then she let the notes rise, twisting skyward. They mounted toward the clouds, leaped, wrapped themselves around spiral curves like the innards of a seashell . . .

Luce's reverie was faintly disturbed by the cries of the mermaids around her. She half opened her eyes, still holding her song in the same complex, swirling suspense. She'd had a fair idea of the form the water would take in response to her song, but the reality was beyond anything she'd expected. Seeing it almost made her break off in astonishment.

The ocean around them had become a fountain. The crowd of mermaids was surrounded by rising streams, but the streams didn't shoot straight up like the jets of a fountain in a park. Instead the water wrapped the midnight air in gleaming ribbons at least twenty feet tall, winding and writhing. Mermaids rotated to see, bright arms stretched like wings. Some laughed giddily or cried out; some were silent with wonder. Water rose in helixes that curled around one another high over their heads and then turned into looping archways or into sinuous, lethargically falling leaves.

It was too much for Luce to sustain for long. Her song collapsed, and the water jets abruptly crashed down. The sea rocked faster with the impact. Splashes radiated in all directions, and the assembled faces were licked by flying blots of foam. Luce felt herself flushing under the heat of hundreds of stares. She'd hurt Catarina so terribly once before by showing off like this, and now she'd made an even bigger display of herself. She wouldn't have blamed anyone there for thinking she was nothing but an embarrassing egomaniac.

Now the clatter of falling water was fading. The silence seemed so dense and pressing that Luce half imagined it would be impossible to move until someone spoke.

"Luce?" The voice was Catarina's, very soft. "How did you . . . I know your gift, but that was . . . ."

"It's not a *gift*, Cat," Luce murmured defensively. "It's just something I taught myself how to do, and—and other mermaids can learn it, too."

"That's why the divers want to kill you even more than the rest of us?" Imani whispered. Her eyes were wide and starry, staring around at the drifting whorls of foam.

"They want to kill me because I smashed their boat," Luce

said. She barely registered her own voice. "After they murdered everyone in my old tribe, I called a wave that threw their boat into a cliff."

There was another lull. Luce shifted uncomfortably, wishing she could leave.

"Well . . ." Catarina was pulling herself together now. "I don't see how anyone *could*, but . . . is there anyone here who doesn't agree? Luce has to be our queen from now on. Even if she did break the timahk."

Something in Luce hardened; her chest knotted with the urge to resist. She couldn't quite put her finger on it, but she was sure that what Cat was saying was wrong somehow.

"A twice lost queen for the twice lost mermaids," Yuan mused morosely. "And at least she can fight. I guess I agree . . ."

That *is no one's queen*, Dana had once said of Luce. Dana'd been in a rage at the time, but hadn't she been right anyway?

"Cat?" Luce said suddenly. "I don't agree."

"LUCE!" Cat's voice whiplashed through the cool night.

"No—I mean—I never wanted to be queen, Cat! I always told you that. We've had queens for thousands of years, and—and *every-thing* has to be different now! But if everyone really wants me to, I'll be something else."

Luce was quiet for a moment. She was thinking of her father, remembering something he'd said to her years before. *Then* she'd really been the person Catarina imagined: clean and innocent and honorable—all those things she couldn't possibly be any longer. But still . . .

Catarina moaned impatiently. "Then what *are* you, Luce?"

He'd said, *You're my secret weapon, honey. You've got the mind of a great —*

"General," Luce announced, looking up. Her mouth suddenly

curved into an irrepressible smile, and she didn't feel nearly as embarrassed anymore. "I am the mermaids' general."

Murmuring spread like a wave through the assembled mermaids. Imani looked dismayed, but Yuan's tail flicked with excitement. "Because this is *war*!"

"Yes," Luce said softly. "This is war. They're trying to kill all of us."

She inhaled hard, doing her best to gather her strength. In a minute she'd have to start explaining how she wanted to do things. Even if they were impressed by her now, very soon they would regard her as a traitor. The sky above was suffocated by clouds and darkness dragged at the waves.

"And maybe they will, but we'll take millions of them with us!" Yuan trilled. Her eyes were shining, her movements quickening like fire.

"Luce, is this really . . ." Imani started, and broke off.

"If I'm going to be general, though," Luce went on, trying not to think about what would happen next, "we need new rules. We need a new timahk, and we're *not* going to do things the same way we used to. I'm only staying if everyone will follow my—" Luce couldn't quite make herself say the next word, but Yuan did it for her.

"War is war! We have to be strict about it! Of *course* we'll follow orders!"

"Okay, then." Luce braced herself. "No killing humans."

A wild clamor of voices broke out, just as Luce had known it would. Catarina's eyebrows shot up, Yuan's mouth gaped as if she was choking, and someone Luce didn't know was shouting, "She's crazy! She's totally crazy!" But Imani was smiling to herself in a way that let Luce know this was exactly what she'd wished for.

Not *everyone* was rushing to condemn her. Some of the faces around Luce were enraged, but others looked confused, or curious, or even hopeful.

"No killing? Just when we're starting a *war*?" Yuan shrieked indignantly. "But how?"

"How many *thousands* of humans have mermaids drowned?" Luce demanded. To her surprise the pandemonium quieted a little. Was everyone actually prepared to listen to her? "We've been sinking their ships for centuries now, doing the same thing over and over again, and it hasn't helped anything, or *changed* anything, or even made us *feel* any better! It's not like we've protected other girls from being hurt the way we were, because there are new mermaids all the time! All we've done is convince the humans that they *have* to wipe us out."

"*War*, Luce . . ." It was Catarina. "I know you've said before that you think we shouldn't . . . *humans* . . . I really couldn't take you seriously . . . But even if you do believe humans deserve to live, well, war is no time to be insisting on this . . . this wild idealism!"

Luce wondered if Catarina was right, but she didn't care. If leading the twice lost mermaids meant committing more reckless murders, she knew she wouldn't be able to stand it. "A new kind of war, Cat! We need a way to protect ourselves, and—and I can teach everyone to control the water the same way I do." Luce desperately hoped she was telling the truth about this, but after all, Dana and Violet had learned. It must be possible. "But if I do that, I have to know no one will use their power to kill unless they *absolutely* have to, in self-defense, or if it's the *only* way to save another mermaid. There can't be any more killing for fun, or for revenge."

"This is ridiculous," Yuan snarled.

"You said you'd follow orders," Luce snapped back, then had to fight to keep from grinning in surprise at herself. Where had this sudden confidence come from? "You *saw* what I can do. I've proved I have the right to be in charge, and if you can't accept that"—Luce looked around— "then I'm going. I won't lead this war in any other way."

The silence stiffened as Luce waited for Yuan to turn away in contempt, for a clamor of voices to tell her that they didn't need a pathetic freak like her as their leader and she should just get lost and never come back.

It didn't happen.

She kept waiting, half-eager for the blasting anger that would free her from responsibility for these strangers. But it just didn't come.

The crowd of mermaids stayed quiet. Dozens of faces glowed softly, lofting up and down on the foam-streaked waves, and while some of them were biting their lips or grimacing, no one said a word. Luce could hardly believe it.

"Well, *generalissima*," Catarina purred sarcastically, "then doing things your way is the only choice we really have, isn't it?"

Luce's first impulse was to feel wounded by the edge in Cat's voice until she saw how proudly her former queen was looking at her. But there was something else in Cat's gaze as well: a tension, a coiling darkness.

"Cat . . ." Luce suddenly felt horribly shy again. "But . . . I mean, I need to know . . . Does everyone here agree? No more killing people?" She didn't sound anything like a general, Luce thought. She sounded like a nervous child. Luce made an effort to sharpen her tone. "Is there anyone here who *isn't* willing to follow me on my terms? Um, raise your hands."

A few mermaids fidgeted, their elbows shifting up slightly. Then they glanced around and lowered them.

"We *need* her," a pale stranger said. "She's right: until she teaches us how to do what she can, it'll be a total disaster if they find us! Right now we're all basically waiting to die."

Of course; that was the only reason most of them were prepared to go along with her bizarre ideas. Luce wondered if she was effectively blackmailing everyone into giving up killing. But she didn't see what else she could do.

"Okay," Luce breathed out. "Okay." She couldn't leave now. *Nausicaa? Am I finally doing the right thing? Will you find me, since I can't search for you?* "Then we're starting training tonight."

11

Tadpole

"Good morning, tadpole." Sudden light blazed through the tank and its anteroom, until the air appeared brass yellow and solid. As Secretary Moreland had expected, there was no answering flick of her blue tail, not yet at least. "Good *morning*." He was bellowing into the speaker until feedback throbbed against the glass; she wouldn't sleep through *that*.

Anais's voice was among the voices on that recording he'd listened to on an afternoon he chose not to remember—except that he remembered it all the time. They'd piped the same music into her tank a few days ago, for the occasion switching off the mechanism set to shock her in response to those particular frequencies, and she'd casually identified all the singers later. Most of them were among those Anais had seen die, but the other possible survivors—Catarina and Dana were the names he recalled—would also be of tremendous personal interest to him if they could ever be captured alive.

This creature in the tank was a source of the musical infestation that persisted in his mind. The limpid trill of mermaid song reverberated through his thoughts as insistently as his own identity, as ineradicably as the word "I." And even though Anais wasn't about to risk singing, he could still feel the presence of her voice, her compressed song, whenever he visited her. Blocked and bottled in her throat, it still whined and jarred, fighting to get free. Moreland could practically see it, a kind of mouthy pulse chewing away at nothing just above her clavicle.

He could never allow himself to hear her song again. But he could watch the song juddering away inside that pearly neck, and better yet he could command its owner. "Now, tadpole. If too much TV is what's bringing on this lethargy of yours, we can take it away. We can take away whatever is necessary to put some spring back into your *step*." He leered to himself at his choice of words. "Get over here."

As he expected, the sky blue tail reared up from behind her barricade of cushions and flung off a few sullen drops.

The blue of her scales, the blue of the water, interacted strangely with his eyes, scraping them with a distinct electric pain. "*Yesterday*, Anais." Blue and gold swished lazily through the water, and he grinned. The tank wasn't so big; in an instant she was almost at the glass.

"Why can't you just let me *sleep*?" Anais spoke these words in a faintly musical whine; almost musical enough to trigger a shock, Moreland suspected. Certainly musical enough to be tantalizing. "If you need to bug me, why can't you do it *later*?"

Even sulking and not outstandingly bright, Anais was still enchanting. For an instant he lost track of what he was planning to say. "One salient feature of owning you," Moreland observed, "is that you talk at my convenience, my *dear*." The mermaids' voices continually prodding at his mind had been keeping him from sleeping. Even when he did drop off, the endless song seemed to scrape all the peace out of his body, leaving him hollow and exhausted. It was better to come here and stare through the glass at the root of the problem: his distasteful, transfixing little pet, his vile beauty.

Her fins were switching. He'd been around her enough to recognize that as a sign of acute irritation. He smiled. "Tell me something. Do you consider yourself—a *person*, Anais?"

She looked confused, and Moreland enjoyed that as well. "Sure."

"'Sure, Mr. Secretary' or 'Sure, sir'," Moreland corrected. "Do you have any idea who you're talking to? The barest inkling?"

She didn't answer that, but her tail was flipping faster. They stared at each other. There was something searing and unnatural about the azure of her eyes, something that was more than just blue.

"So you're not *more* than a person, or *less* than a person?" Moreland pursued after a moment. "Just an ordinary girl after all? Despite your many unseemly attributes?"

"I'm not ordinary!" Anais reared back in offense. "Duh."

"More than a person, then?"

"I guess more." Anais considered the question with uncharacteristic seriousness. "More. I mean, if I weren't locked up in this stupid place and people could see me, I'd be a huge star! You said that even *Luce* . . ."

"Has become an Internet sensation? She has. Before that video of her got out, only idiots and fanatics could have bought into the idea of mermaids existing. And even now any self-respecting adult should be convinced that the video is a hoax, but"—Moreland gritted his teeth— "there aren't enough adults out there who deserve that label."

"But—isn't it real? It looks just like her!"

Moreland ignored that. "The problem is the *more*. That little something *extra* you tails take on with your transformation. The *more* is what's making people believe that the video is authentic. Even passive magic is worse, is more disgracefully *violent*, than a bomb. All the mental signals that make up a decent, regular, hardworking life are disrupted. You're left with nothing but *noise*, buzzing and whining . . ."

Anais stared, too perplexed for the moment to attempt an answer.

He'd never talked to anyone this way before. He was glad no human being could hear him coming off so half-cocked, like some kind of *poet* . . . He couldn't stop himself, though.

"The same *more* is what makes your kind subhuman, though. The same *more* that turns grown men into whimpering fools. Do you know what that video proves, Anais?"

For the first time, she looked genuinely frightened. Moreland found it delightful. He glared at her expectantly, his eyes demanding a reply.

"What?" Anais whispered at last. "I mean, what does it prove?"

"*What, sir?*" Moreland prompted.

"'What, sir?'" Anais muttered. Her tail was thrashing and she'd backed away from the glass. But she didn't quite have the nerve to swim back behind her cushions, much as he knew she wanted to.

"Ah." Moreland grinned. "The video proves that even if, by some untoward *miracle*, your kind learned to resist their murderous urges tomorrow—even if the mermaids never sang to a human again—*well*."

Anais's eyes were wide. Another first. She was truly anxious to hear what he had to say. Her golden hair spread out in an enormous, shining web behind her shoulders.

Moreland waited another few seconds. "It's not the *singing* that proves mermaids have to die, Anais," he finally crooned. "It's not the evil in all of you, or even the threat you pose to commerce. It's the *more*. It's what we see in that video, the quality that makes human minds collapse into imbecility. You little abominations don't have to *do* anything to commit violence. You just have to be your charming selves. You *do* see my point, don't you, tadpole?"

"Just because *Luce* was *stupid* enough to let some humans tape her, doesn't—"

He cut her off. "It's not just Luce, tadpole. It's all of you. I'd rather," Moreland lied, "have both my legs blown off than watch that video again. Do you understand me? It's only my duty to my country that makes me endure, for one instant, the fact that you tails persist on the same *planet*."

Every word he spoke, it seemed to him, followed the contours of the mermaids' song in his thoughts. Even railing against the mermaids only served to provide their melodies with unexpected lyrics.

He wanted his mind back. That was all. His mind intact and determined, unfurrowed by their awful music. But maybe that was impossible.

Maybe one day he'd open his mouth, in the middle of a speech or an interview on TV, and that hateful *song* would scroll out in place of language.

"Are you going to kill *me*?" Anais asked. From her shell-shocked gaze it was clear that this possibility hadn't occurred to her before. "You—Secretary Moreland, I'm trying so hard to help you! It's not my fault!"

Moreland amused himself by scowling brutally at her. She cowered. Even if Anais and the others *could* be restored to human form, wouldn't they still be tainted to the core? The possibility might be worth pursuing, though, if only for strategic reasons.

After a moment he relented, reversing his scowl into a broad, affectionate smile. "Of course we won't kill *you*, tadpole. You've become—very special—to everyone in the know. We practically consider you a mascot."

Anais turned her smile back on, but her eyes still looked worried.

"You haven't killed her yet?" Anais's question, reverberating from the speakers, came as an unwelcome disturbance. "Luce?"

"We'll get her soon enough," Moreland snapped. "It's a *long* coast, tadpole. Doing electromagnetic surveys of the whole damn thing, identifying likely caves—it's not quick, and it's not cheap. It's work."

"You mean you don't even know *where* she is?" Her voice was almost pitiful. Captivity, it struck Moreland, was starting to wear on her.

"We'll find your little friend soon," Moreland sighed. In fact, there'd been no sign of Lucette Korchak since she'd interrupted that raid fifteen days before, killing another operative in the process and taking that tribe's last surviving mermaid away with her. It rankled him to think that she might slip past the Mexican border and escape from him for good.

He was starting to get tired. Anais drifted in place with the water breaking against her lower lip. Sorrow only made her imperious beauty more potent, her azure eyes more haunting. Moreland regarded it as an improvement. Even more intriguing was his impression that grief came as a surprise to her, as if she had never considered the possibility of such an emotion before. Experiencing this much emotion had come as a surprise to him too, in fact. A very disconcerting one.

Maybe he could sleep. Maybe his sleep would even be restful for once, and the endless song would stop scraping at him like a bow against a violin. He straightened himself to go. "Good night, tadpole."

"You told me it was morning!"

"Why, Anais," Moreland scolded. "It's whatever time I say it is."

* * *

In a cave not far from Montcrey a man in a sleek black diving suit knelt in crimson water. His arms were wrapped around the body of what appeared to be a girl about nine years old—only the faintly light-slicked, greenish cast of her skin showed that she had ever been anything else. Her head tipped back onto the diver's shoulder, her bloodless lips hung open, and her wet, caramel brown hair clung to his suit.

Against orders, the diver unfastened his helmet and knocked it off. Bloody water splattered as the helmet thudded down not far from the man's spear gun. It exposed the face of a wiry young man with sharp cheekbones, a bony nose, and drooping eyes.

"Replace your hood *immediately*, sergeant! We're not through here!"

The sergeant didn't so much as look up. Instead he began fumbling with his gloves. His hurry made his movements awkward and the girl's limp body got in his way, but eventually he managed to free his right hand and slide his fingers onto the side of her neck just under the jaw. He kept moving his fingers, pressing in different spots, long after it should have been obvious that he wasn't going to find a pulse. His hand felt numb against the girl's chilled throat.

"Sergeant Waller!" His major's voice came out of his helmet in an electrical whine. "You know the procedure!"

"She looks just like *Sophie* . . ." Sergeant Waller moaned. "Just like . . . before she . . ." Of course none of his comrades could hear him now that his helmet was clanking against the rocks, but he didn't think about that. It was only the microphones built into each helmet that allowed the team members to communicate with one another.

Without considering what he was doing he pulled the girl closer and kissed her lightly on the forehead.

"You'd kiss a dead rattlesnake, too?" the major complained; a trace of sympathy buzzed behind the static. "These bitches just *look* like girls. Just picture all the innocent people that damned tail has killed and I guarantee you won't feel sorry for her."

"Looks like Waller's another waste case," someone drawled. "Probably time to put him down as nonviable, major."

Waller heard the words, but they seemed abstract and senseless compared to the girl's cold cheeks and glossy eyelids. He kept kneading her throat. Maybe it was just the lack of sensation in his fingers that kept him from finding a heartbeat.

The major sighed. His helmet changed the sound into a kind of gusty whistle. "Even *dead* these tails keep doing a number on us."

Waller only knew that he wasn't going to leave her. The Operation Odysseus teams made a practice of abandoning almost all of the bodies in the caves, only occasionally bringing back one for dissection—after all, leaving them was a lot easier than trying to explain them. Maybe, just maybe, she'd eventually revive. (Waller didn't let himself look at the wound in the girl's chest. Vaguely he told himself that it would only distract him from more important things.) He'd be there when she woke up; if he could just get her somewhere warmer . . .

The major nodded to his men. In a few seconds Waller's arms were jerked back and the cuffs snapped shut around his wrists. The dead girl slumped into the water as he thrashed, her face shifting down behind thickening veils of red. "Get his helmet on him," the major ordered. "Gonna have to drag him out of here."

The drawling man kicked at a submerged form. "This one ain't turned back yet," he observed, trying to puncture the darkening mood. "Sushi, anyone?"

No one laughed.

12

Slight Miracles

Everyone had gone back to their home under the warehouse to sleep—all except for Luce and the fifteen mermaids who'd once been queens of their own tribes. Luce wasn't surprised to find that included Yuan and Imani, since they'd both acted so confident, but there were other mermaids gathered in front of her who didn't seem like the type: Bex, who had a scattered, disturbing energy around her, and Graciela, who seemed too withdrawn and other-worldly. They gazed at Luce expectantly, and she cringed a little. She'd promised them that they would be able to master the water, but for all she knew that might be a lie. "Once all of you get the hang of it," Luce announced, trying to make herself believe it, "then we'll divide everyone else up and the queens will each be in charge of training a group."

That made sense, didn't it? Wasn't that exactly how a real leader would do things? Luce closed her eyes for a second, remembering how well Dana had learned to control the water without Luce helping her at all: well enough to turn her power against Luce in her fury.

"Luce? Are you okay?" Imani was looking at her with worried dark eyes.

Luce tried to look calm and composed, but she could tell that she wasn't doing a very good job. "I'm sorry, Imani. I was just thinking about . . . something else."

Luce glanced around for Catarina, but she was suddenly keeping her distance, her eyes lowered sullenly. In her joy at finding her old queen again Luce had temporarily forgotten how difficult and unpredictable Cat could be. Even now when Luce obviously needed her support, why couldn't Cat stop making everything so complicated?

Luce deliberately turned away from Catarina before she got too upset. Letting herself feel hurt and broken really wasn't an option now, not with everyone waiting to see what she would do. "Let's get started. I'll begin by singing just one note, enough to call up a really small wave, and I'll hold it. Then when you're ready, I'd like everyone to try to match my voice. Take your time, and try to . . ." Luce thought about how to describe it. "Try to let your voice kind of spread out on the water, like you're . . . like you're touching someone you love. Once you can almost feel the water responding to you, just pull back a little bit."

Putting her secret experience into words that way made it sound half-crazy, even to her. Luce broke off in embarrassment. But Yuan's eyes were bright with fascination, Graciela was trembling like a plucked string, and Imani was beaming as if she had just caught a star on her tongue. "Um, does that make sense?" Luce asked.

How was she supposed to be a general when she couldn't even overcome her own shyness?

"It makes sense," Imani said. Her voice curled like something alive, and Luce suddenly felt certain that—how had Nausicaa put it?—that the water would *understand* Imani at least. "It makes sense the way all miracles make sense."

The hills hovered like shadows at the edge of the sky while cars flowed like a river of diamonds along the Golden Gate Bridge in the distance. Around them the Pacific rocked, its stone dark waves always beckoning them on to nowhere at all, while above the night was blinded by clouds. Like Imani said, it was miraculous. Luce realized how much she'd forgotten to notice ever since . . .

She half closed her eyes, the distant lights blurring in her lashes, and tried to take her own advice. She let out one single soft note like a palm cupping the water's cheek, like a patiently caressing hand. For several moments she didn't try to control the water at all, only to feel it, and to feel it feeling her. Until each molecule touched by her voice became a nerve, or a thought, or a moment of realization.

Luce's arms were wrapped around her chest; she caressed the ocean's skin only with her song, and soon she shared its sensations. The water woke with a tactile vibration just the way Luce's own skin had once woken under the touch of a boy whom she couldn't bear to remember. This was a kind of love, Luce thought as her song fanned softly outward. The water would do almost anything for her because they *loved* each other.

Other voices were gathering under hers. Luce knew that she should pay attention to how everyone else was doing; she just couldn't, not right now. There was a kind of sighing pressure inside her. A feeling she had no name for rose in her chest. Her voice began to lift, very slowly, and a slender wing of sea followed it. It gleamed and circled and finally broke free of the surface. Wherever she was, Luce thought, she was *home* as long as the ocean kept her in its heart this way.

She felt ready to look around now. As she'd expected, Imani

had raised a wave, thin and slight and curling like a question mark, and Bex was making flat little waves jump and fall in sudden spurts, but some of the others were having trouble.

Luce took a moment to concentrate on Catarina's voice. Cat was singing one high note very beautifully, but Luce got the sense that she wasn't really trying to beckon the water at all. But the fact that Bex and Imani were making progress at least proved that it was *possible.*

A skinny blonde in the back whose name Luce couldn't remember suddenly lifted a knife-shaped wave, then let out a little scream of surprise that sent it splashing down again. Luce smiled to herself. It reminded her of the first time she'd seen the water answer her, when she'd refused to believe what was happening.

Luce let her own note fade away. The others should keep on without her for a while. Instead she focused on listening. Yuan's timbre was a little off; her voice had a rough magic that Luce didn't think the sea would respond to. They could work on that, though. Graciela was . . . not paying attention to anything outside her own mind. But her tone was lovely, and Luce realized that the sea *was* answering her, only with a kind of fitful stirring instead of an ascent. And Catarina: Luce was suddenly sure that Catarina was deliberately singing in the wrong way. She couldn't begin to guess why, though. Maybe Cat was angry about Luce's rule against killing?

Fine, then. Cat had wanted Luce to become their leader, and if she was going to sulk about it now Luce wouldn't try to stop her.

Luce swam over to Yuan and started singing very faintly, her voice sliding under Yuan's and lightly, slowly, smoothing out the harshness in her tone. In a few minutes Yuan's voice conjured up a tiny prancing jet, and Luce moved on. She sang with each of them, her voice luring their voices after hers, until the dark sky behind the hills graded to a murky violet. The clouds were barely parting, and frills of electric blue sky showed between them.

She hadn't been crazy at all, Luce thought with relief. She wasn't a liar. Everyone there had managed to call up at least a small wave. Everyone except for Cat, anyway, who was too stubborn to make a serious attempt.

The singing faded, but no one spoke. The first hints of dawn seemed to hold the silent mermaids together in a sense of soft exhilaration. Blue glow touched them all, and with it came a shared awareness of marvelous possibility. Luce heard Imani's laughter, amazed and tremulous, and noticed in surprise that Yuan's cheeks glittered with sudden tears.

Inexplicably, Catarina swam over and hugged Luce hard, almost as if she needed to protect her from something.

The only thing that made the moment less than completely perfect, Luce thought, was that Nausicaa wasn't there with her.

* * *

"Luce?" Catarina murmured. It was just after dawn, and beams of golden light streaked across the dimness under the empty factory. The pilings looked like a forest. Rats skittered on the planks above, but apart from that everything seemed so peaceful.

Luce had just been drifting off in Catarina's hammock of shredded nylons, scraps of silk, wire and string, but she jolted awake at the sound of her name. "Can't you sleep, Cat?" She tried to keep the annoyance out of her tone. Maybe Cat had some good reason for how strangely she'd been acting.

"Teaching everyone to do what you can do . . . Luce, have you thought about what that could mean?"

Catarina's cool shoulder pressed against Luce's cheek. It was so much like the way things had been over a year before when Cat was Luce's queen, and her friend—and when Luce had still believed that Catarina had murdered her father. "It'll just mean we'll all stand a chance if the humans ever find us here," Luce said. She felt sleep brushing up inside her mind again, coaxing her to fall.

"Oh, Luce," Catarina whispered. Her voice was a low, airy moan. "You're so trusting, even after everything you've gone through. You can't imagine how much darkness and treachery there is in . . . in almost everyone. If *everyone* can control the water, if everyone can fight, they won't *need* you anymore. And if someone ever manages to surpass you . . ."

Drowsily Luce began to realize what Cat was getting at. "I don't care if somebody else takes over as general, though," Luce murmured back. "I just had to do *something,* so everyone here doesn't end up . . ." She didn't need to finish the sentence: *like the girls from our tribe. Like dozens of other mermaids we don't even know.* "I've ruined so many things, Cat. Yuan . . . I don't think she's right that the *rest* of us are soiled, but I know I am! If I'd only listened . . ."—*to Nausicaa,* Luce thought—"to you, Cat, I probably could have saved at least some of them. I can't let that happen again."

"Even though if someone else takes control, that will be the end of your little prohibition on killing humans, Lucette?" Catarina snipped. Luce was suddenly much more awake; of course Catarina must be right about that. Luce felt the hammock starting to sway and only then realized that her tail was flicking. "Though that isn't really what worries me. Even for you, Luce, it seems absurdly naïve to insist on defending those creatures *now.*"

"We . . . The humans need to see that they don't *have* to kill us, Cat!" Luce knew what she felt, but her feeling seemed too big and too awkward to fit into words. "I think maybe if we prove to them that *we* can change . . . then we can persuade them to change too?" That was part of what she wanted to say, Luce thought, but there was more to it.

It was about more than just mermaids and humans and how they just couldn't seem to stop hating each other. The whole world was in danger; the sea was stained with death.

Catarina's mouth twisted as if what Luce was saying was too ludicrous even to deserve a response. "Luce, you've announced to everyone that you won't let humans be killed, that you won't even show anyone how to protect *herself* if that means humans will be endangered! And you've said it just when the *evil* of those, those . . . Oh, I don't even want to call them animals! When their vileness is clearer than it's ever been!" Cat's voice was rising and her gleaming hair swirled against Luce's face. Luce glanced around anxiously, sure that other mermaids would overhear. "If the mermaids here don't *need* you anymore . . ."

Then I can look for Nausicaa, Luce thought, but she decided not to say that. She couldn't have explained why she felt so strange all of a sudden: thinned out into tissue, as if her muscles were airy scraps on the verge of shredding. "I . . . don't think we should worry about that, Cat."

"Luce!"

Now Luce struggled to keep her voice down. "Cat, it's so hard already! We have to get everyone trained before the humans find us, but really they could find us anytime! There's no way to know. Those boats could be here *tonight*! And there has to be some way to stop the war, but I don't know *how* to do it!"

If she started crying now, Luce thought, the tears would take over. They'd break through her skin like watery bullets and she would drown in something deeper than any sea.

"Luce, my Lucette . . . please." Catarina's fingers smoothed through Luce's hair. "Just do one thing for me."

Luce just stared at her, trying to get her feelings under control again. Cat's moon gray eyes were very close.

Cat bent until her mouth was almost touching Luce's ear. "Just don't teach them *everything* you know, Lucette. Hold enough back so that you're always the strongest one. Don't let yourself be outnumbered by mermaids with the same powers you have! That way—"

"Cat," Luce said breathlessly. "You know I can't do that."

"Luce, would you *listen* to me for once!"

"I can't! We need everyone to be as powerful as they possibly can. We need to do *something*."

Hiding from the humans was only a temporary measure at best, Luce knew. Wearily she gazed across the dawn-streaked bay. In the distance cars were already beetling steadily along the Bay Bridge, carrying early-morning commuters to their jobs.

Luce realized now why she felt so tired and so close to shattering: there was an answer to the problem, but it kept slipping away just below the surface of her mind and eluding her. She was maddened by frustration and also simply exhausted.

"Luce," Catarina whispered. "We can't stop them from destroying us. Not if they find out we're here. They'll send *thousands* of their soldiers, or they'll drop bombs in the water."

"I . . . We'll find a way. I promise we will."

"Have you ever seen humans fishing with dynamite, Luce? The men in my town did that when I was a child."

Luce groaned with weariness and threw her hands over her face. She knew Catarina was still staring at her from only inches away.

"Then I'll have to . . . think in all the ways you refuse to, I suppose," Catarina whispered. "I'll have to protect you from anyone here who might not be as loyal to you as I am. And I wonder if I'll also have to protect them from you."

* * *

Luce woke sometime in the afternoon. Catarina was still fast asleep, her gleaming copper hair fanning across Luce's shoulder, soft as the rising breeze. Luce slipped very gradually from the hammock, holding it steady as she dropped into the bay. Not far away, Imani lay asleep in a net made entirely of finely knotted scraps of white plastic decorated with dozens of milk white shells, bits of lace, and broken teacups where pink roses glowed. Her storm blue tail swayed just below the surface, winking with neon shimmer, and that white lace scarf she'd found somewhere was slipping off her short afro. Most of the hammocks seemed to be empty, though, and Luce wondered where everyone had gone.

Here and there among the trunks Luce glimpsed a silhouette. Mermaids hovered quietly, staring across the sunlit water. White mist filmed the bay and the hills were so faded they looked like clouds. At the very edge of their refuge Luce saw a sweep of glossy dark hair then a golden face turned in profile. Luce skimmed over to her. "Hey, Yuan."

"Oh." Yuan glanced over at her, tense and sad. She was leaning against a piling, one arm and her tail curled around it. "Hey, Luce."

All Yuan's cynicism and prickliness seemed to have melted in the afternoon's pearly light. Luce almost decided to swim away; it seemed like Yuan might prefer to be alone with her thoughts. Instead she lingered, watching that golden face and wondering what was behind it. "Are you okay?"

Yuan hesitated. "Same as ever." She didn't smile. "Okay and not okay. Whenever I stop moving, there's exactly one thing I can think about. Always."

Luce thought Yuan must be talking about her father again. The memory of that dreadful story still rattled painfully in Luce's mind, and she didn't really feel like hearing more of it. But somehow she waited quietly, and Yuan kept watching her.

"You must too, right?" Yuan asked at last. "When you wind up thrashing around in the water you think, well, *that's* the biggest change you're ever going to go through in your life. You think you're finished with changes, and it's all going to be cool from then on. But then when the *real* change hits, it's so much bigger than just—than getting stuck with some stupid tail. The real change . . . no one can see it, but after that you're destroyed on the *inside*. You don't deserve to be a mermaid anymore, and you can't go back to being human either. I keep wishing I could have just not *done* it." Yuan's words came like quick, despairing jabs.

Luce wasn't sure what to think. "The real change? You mean . . ."

"I mean when I saved that girl." Oddly, Yuan lifted her hand and stared into the palm as if it were a mirror. "I didn't even *try* to hide it, Luce. Can you believe that? I saved her right in front of my tribe, like 'hell with all of you'! They were too shocked to try to stop me or anything. But the whole time I was dragging that lousy human through the water I *hated* what I was doing, I *hated* that I couldn't stop myself . . ."

Luce didn't know what surprised her the most: that it was a

girl Yuan had saved or that rescuing someone had wounded her so terribly. "Do you know why you did it?" Luce asked softly. "There must have been—or, well, was there a reason why you chose her?"

"A *completely* pathetic reason." Yuan shook her head in impatience. "She looked like my best friend from when I was—from *before*. I knew it couldn't be her, like this girl wasn't even old enough, but I couldn't stop myself from acting like it was her anyway."

Luce thought she was about to say the wrong thing, but somehow she'd stopped being able to keep her feelings secret. "Yuan? It *was* her."

Yuan smiled ruefully. "I knew you were crazy."

"No—I mean, that girl you saved, she probably meant as much to someone else as your friend meant to you, right? So it was the same as if you'd saved your friend, only for—for whoever cared about that girl. You kept *somebody's* heart from getting broken." Luce stopped, surprised by the thoughts racing through her mind. *That girl was starred by love, just like your friend. The love is the same, so it doesn't matter who's feeling it.*

Maybe she could have said something that weird to Nausicaa but not to anyone else.

Yuan made a face. "You almost sound like you think humans are the same as us. Like what they feel *counts* the same way."

Luce didn't answer that. Her thoughts were still with the girl Yuan had saved; she could almost see her hair trailing through the water, her face thrown back toward the sky. "Did you see her again? The girl?"

Yuan looked shocked. "Of *course* not! Making friends with some human—what do you take me for?" Luce didn't say anything but her expression gave her away, and Yuan's cheeks flushed. "Uh, sorry. If you did—after everything I've done in my life, I guess I couldn't blame you for . . ."

Luce's face was blazing and she looked away. "Can we please not talk about it?"

Yuan hesitated. "You said it was a boy, right? The human you broke the timahk for?"

"It was a boy," Luce agreed stiffly. "Yuan, I actually—I really need to talk to you about something else, okay? I wanted to ask you a favor."

From the corner of her eye Luce couldn't help noticing how fixed and curious Yuan's gaze looked. She wasn't going to stop wondering about Luce's past. "What favor?"

"Well—you said there are a lot of other mermaids. Living around the bay? It's not just the girls here, right?" Luce made herself look back at Yuan, though hot veils of shame still seemed to press on her face.

"Tons. A few actually came out last night when you were singing, didn't you notice? And somebody was telling me that a whole new tribe just turned up this morning, like somebody came and warned them but they didn't know where else to go."

Luce felt a surge of gratitude at the thought that they'd been warned by J'aime, still struggling to save as many mermaids as she could. "I wanted to ask if you would go talk to them. To the other mermaids around the bay." Luce hesitated; it seemed so presumptuous. "Ask them if they'd like to join us for training tonight."

"You mean—if they'll promise not to kill humans in exchange for learning what you can do?" Yuan thought about it. "You even want me to ask the crazy ones?"

"If . . . if that's okay with you. I mean . . ." Luce tried to shake off her embarrassment. "I think we're going to need as many mermaids working with us as we can get. If we're really going to stop the humans."

"So you're not just talking about teaching everyone? You're talking about . . ."

"About asking them to *really* join us. Yeah." Luce considered the question then straightened herself. "Please tell them that General Luce is inviting them to join the Twice Lost Army."

13

Kathleen

"Hi," Andrew Korchak said as the door swung open. He'd arrived at a small, white, extremely pretty house, its yard a jumble of vivid flowers and its windows set with panes of stained glass. He couldn't help feeling out of place there. "Um, I'm Andrew. We talked on the phone?"

"Of course. Very glad to meet you." The woman stepping back to welcome him in was also small and pretty, with light brown hair in a ponytail and soft blue eyes. "I'm Kathleen, and this is Nick."

Andrew shook hands with her and then, a bit less comfortably, with her angular, balding husband. "I really appreciate you both agreeing to see me about this. I don't mean to impose."

"Of course not! After what you told us, we wanted this meeting just as — well, I'm sure not as *much* as you, I don't mean — but it feels very important to us also." Kathleen was leading the way down a broad hall lined in books, with small twisty tables displaying collections of seashells. Andrew couldn't help thinking how the sight of all those books would thrill Luce if she were here with him. "You can imagine, we've received some pretty peculiar messages since we posted that video, but yours— I knew right away that it was something different."

"I know I must sound like a nut," Andrew said defensively. "I've got the photos right here. I'm sure you want to see for yourselves—that this is for real." They walked into a kitchen where, to Andrew's surprise, a large wooden table was set with plates and glasses, a salad and cheese and fruit. The warm, yeasty smell of fresh bread mixed with the scent of roses gusting through the window. Heavy lilacs swooped from a vase. "Oh—I didn't mean for you to go to all this trouble! I'm . . ." He wasn't sure what to say. He'd been hitchhiking for days, not eating much, and it was all he could do not to lunge for the food. "I'm real grateful."

"Our pleasure," Nick said behind him; a little primly, maybe, but it didn't sound hostile. "But I *would* like to see those photos, Andrew, when you get a chance."

He was already pulling the pictures out of an inside pocket, spreading them out to show his hosts. What would he do if they decided it was all a lie? "This one—you maybe can't see so good that it's the same girl. She was only three there, with her mother. But this one right here . . ."

Kathleen had turned greenish white and she teetered a little. Nick moved to put his arm around her. "Oh, Nick. Oh my God, it's her!" The words came out in a long moan.

"It certainly—if that's not the same face we saw, there's an impressive resemblance at least."

"It's *her*. It's even the same expression that she had when she looked at me! You could see in her eyes that she'd been through things that, that no one should ever have to . . ." Kathleen's voice was breaking, and she bit her lower lip.

"It's my Lucette. It's the same girl who you all filmed out in the water. And—there's some terrible things happening, and—I didn't do enough to protect her before, but now . . ." He broke off when his view of the sunny room started rippling in the tears filling his eyes. He was longing to tell Kathleen everything, but he didn't feel as confident about trusting her husband.

Wordlessly Nick pulled out a chair for him, and he slumped down. Kathleen dealt with her emotion by swinging into energetic movement, bustling to fetch a bread knife and ice and a pitcher of lemonade. Andrew watched her dart around the kitchen in her jeans and pale blouse, her ponytail lashing. *This* was how he should have brought Luce up, in a house just like this one. He pictured Alyssa's dark hair tumbling as she bent to lift bread from the oven.

"So," Nick said, and Andrew jumped at the sound of his voice, "assuming you're both correct about the identity of the mermaid we saw—and I have to say I think that's a *huge* assumption for all of us to make—there's still a question I'd like answered, if you could."

Kathleen smacked the cutting board down hard enough to make the silverware rattle, and thumped the bread on top. "Would you please not condescend to me! It's not an assumption!"

Nick smiled over at him in a way Andrew found vaguely irritating, as if he'd be sure to agree that Kathleen was just one of those high-strung women who have to be humored. "All right, darling. Let's say that the mermaid's identity is an irrefutable *fact*: she is Lucette, and the earth orbits the sun. It still leaves us with one unavoidable question, doesn't it?" Kathleen was slicing bread more vigorously than seemed strictly necessary. "Why was it a *mermaid* we saw and not a teenage girl in a swimsuit? Do you think that's something you could resolve for us, Andrew?"

"When you wouldn't even *admit* that we'd seen a mermaid at all until we watched our *own* video ten times, I don't think you get to lay claim to some kind of higher rationality!" Kathleen fumed. She slathered butter on a hunk of bread and flung it on Andrew's plate in a way that made him grin uncontrollably.

"It's okay," Andrew said softly. "I can answer. But it just . . . it means getting into kind of a long story, and a lot of it . . . it might be hard for me to say. Or for you to believe, really. I'll do my best, though."

"Please," Kathleen said. "I haven't been able to stop thinking about her. Whatever you can tell me, it would mean so much! Right now all we know is what Chrissy told us."

"Chrissy?"

"The neighbor's little girl. You can see her in the video too. She said she talked to the mermaid under the dock and brought her some food, and that the mermaid was very nice and told Chrissy not to trust magic things, and that she'd been bit by a squid."

"And you believe every word Chrissy said, because seven-year-old children *never* invent stories like that?" Nick asked.

Kathleen looked like she was on the verge of an outburst, and Andrew tried to deflect it. "That rip in Lucette's ear? Must have been a pretty big squid."

"Oh." Kathleen sounded distracted. "Maybe one of the Humboldts. They've been showing up here recently. Andrew, I'm sorry. You were about to tell us about you and Lucette."

"Yeah. See, the thing is I wasn't around when she changed, but she told me about it later." Andrew barely remembered to eat as he told the story, trying to keep it as short as possible. He left out some things, like how he'd made his living during their years on the road; he didn't want his hosts to start worrying that their credit cards would disappear. But he tried to be honest about the rest of it: how Alyssa had died as a result of their rambling life, how he'd finally moved to Alaska to give Luce some stability, then how his fishing boat was destroyed in a storm not long afterward, drowning almost everyone onboard. How he wound up marooned on an island in the middle of the Bering Sea, leaving Luce alone with her alcoholic uncle . . .

He tried to stay focused on Kathleen, but he couldn't help noticing the incredulity twisting through Nick's face. He decided to limit his explanation of how he'd survived on that island to the parts that wouldn't sound too crazy, like relying on the geothermal springs for warmth in the winter and hunting seals.

Even so the story sounded dreamy, fantastical. And he hadn't even gotten to the part where his daughter showed up but transformed into a mermaid.

Andrew heard Nick's chair scrape back and turned to look as the other man stood up. "This is all very interesting, but there's a lot of yard work I still have to get done today."

"Nick," Kathleen objected, "this is important. It's important to me to understand as much as possible, and I really think—you need to hear this too."

"The only reason I agreed to go through with this was that I was hoping you'd find some closure, Kath!" Nick's knees were trembling, and his voice grew sharper with every word. "I'm waiting for you to put this—this senseless episode behind you, and stop *dreaming*. And now this man comes in here and starts spinning these fairy tales, and I have to watch you sitting there and swallowing every preposterous word without the slightest sign of critical reflection!"

Andrew couldn't resist defending himself. "A lot of what I've said you can double-check that it's true. That the *High and Mighty* vanished, and I was on it, and that I was presumed dead along with everybody else. All that's public record; you can check . . ." Andrew's voice trailed away.

"Not interested," Nick growled. "Kath, come get me when you're *done* here."

"You're not interested, because you don't *want* to know the truth!" Kathleen snapped. Then she turned pointedly away from her husband, her lips compressed. "Andrew, I'm so sorry about the interruption. You were saying?"

"I'm thinking . . . maybe I should leave?" Andrew asked.

"Only if you want to leave me seeing her in my mind all the time, and *wondering*," Kathleen said. "Something—the sense that I'm really connected to my regular life, I guess—it feels broken. Once you know that something so extraordinary is that close . . ."

Nick stalked out of the kitchen and through a back hallway. They heard a door slam. "I'm real sorry," Andrew said. "I didn't mean to start any kind of trouble for you."

"You didn't," Kathleen breathed. "The trouble was there already. Nick wants to believe that it's all because of your daughter, but really . . ."

Andrew didn't feel particularly sorry at the news that Kathleen's marriage was troubled and then noticed how not sorry he was.

"Anyway," Kathleen went on, "please tell me your story."

Andrew did: how Luce had found him and how he'd refused for months to believe that the mermaid in the water was really his daughter and not some kind of delusion. Then, once he'd accepted it, what Luce had told him about the reasons for her change. Kathleen listened intently.

"So—is she the only one? Or is this . . . this transformation through trauma something that happens to . . ." Kathleen's eyes went wide. "Oh, no."

"She's not the only one," Andrew said quietly. "We had a run-in with a pack of them later who seemed pretty pissed about Luce rescuing me. I don't know for sure, but I'm guessing it's the same for all of them. Girls who people think are runaways or whatever, lots of them are actually out there in the ocean."

They both stopped talking for a moment. There was no view of the sea from the kitchen, but it was close enough that they could hear, very faintly, the rumble of the waves.

"Kathleen?" Andrew said. "Sorry, but it gets worse. A lot worse."

She looked up, eyes starry with tears. For a second he wondered how old she was; she was lithe and youthful, but from the lines around her eyes Andrew thought she might be forty or so. About his age now.

"Tell me."

"Well, I had a visit from this FBI guy, and he told me that tribes of mermaids are out there killing people, like bringing ships down somehow. I think I got a taste of how they do it myself, actually." Andrew didn't mention that the momentary swirl of mermaid song he'd heard still went on coiling endlessly through his mind, even in his sleep. He found it both disturbing and oddly comforting.

"They kill . . ." Kathleen was staring out the window; her voice sounded as if it were journeying across strange expanses on its way to that peaceful kitchen.

"And now our government's out there killing them right back. The guy told me straight out they'd fired spear guns at Luce, back before you saw her."

"But she was so sweet to Chrissy, and I swear the way she looked at us . . . There was no malice in her face, Andrew! I'm sure she never killed anyone."

"I'm not sure," Andrew admitted. "Not a hundred percent. But she saved me, and that guy said something about her saving somebody else, too. The deal can't be so simple that just slaughtering all the mermaids is the *only* choice."

"And then anyone . . . who has a missing daughter, or a *sister* . . . they'll lose their chance of finding them again forever."

Her sister, Andrew thought. He couldn't have explained why, but he was suddenly completely certain. *Her sister's out there in that damned cold nothingness. That's why she's taking this so hard.*

"Luce said they never get any older than they were the day they changed," Andrew said as if he were answering a question. "So even if somebody went that way a long time ago, she'd still be real young. Kathleen, I know you've done a lot already by talking to me, by even *believing* me—"

"I haven't done *anything* for you; you're the one who's helping me!"

"I got a huge favor to ask."

Kathleen only looked at him. There was no questioning in her eyes, only misery. He wished he could hold her.

Andrew knew he was about to get Ben Ellison in serious trouble. The FBI agent would probably lose his job over this. *Sorry, Ben. Sorry.* Maybe he would understand there was no other choice, though; not when Luce's life was at stake.

"I was wondering if maybe you'd be willing to . . . to put out another video."

* * *

The black boat slid among the network of tiny wild islands and narrow channels north of Seattle. The sky was the morose steel blue of a thickly overcast dawn. The divers had been up all night hunting, sounding out prospective mermaid lairs that had shown up on the scans. More and more often now the caves they checked proved to be empty, though some of them had suspicious signs of habitation: piles of empty shells or trinkets dangling from the rocks. Mermaids were obviously getting away from them, but there were no hints to where they'd all gone.

It was somebody's fault, clearly. And somebody was going to have to take the blame. The government operatives had managed to decrease radically the incidence of shipwrecks along the West Coast, but if the sinkings started up again as soon as their backs were turned, it was sure going to look like they were a bunch of incompetents.

"*There's* one . . . ." The major was peering through high-powered binoculars, and he'd caught a distant but distinct glimpse of coppery fins. Not far from the mermaid there was an abrupt jag in the coast that seemed to indicate a promising cove. "About time. We'll try to come up on her nice and gradually, see if there are more of them with her."

Some of the men thought that was stupid. They'd realized by now that the damned tails could stay under for at least half an hour, sometimes much longer. They were incredibly fast swimmers, too; no human diver was a match for them. Their only real options were to take mermaids by surprise or else corner them. In this tangle of islands it would be absurdly easy to lose sight of their quarry. "With all due respect, sir," a high-pitched voice objected, "she'll dive. We should speed up and nab her before she sees us."

"She hasn't seen us," the major said confidently. "Goddamn. She's *playing*. And, wait, it looks like there're at least two of them. *Slow* approach, like I said, and stay right up against the rocks. We're about to hit pay dirt, men."

Even without binoculars they could all see the tiny figure leaping high above the waves now, her long tail breaching as she spun in midair. She was probably brown-skinned, and her copper scales gave off flashes of ruby shine even in the morning dusk. After she splashed down, a second figure leaped, smaller and paler, her tail a light smoky blue. They appeared to be taking turns seeing how high they could go, completely oblivious of the danger creeping toward them. They looked so carefree, so joyful and innocent.

The only antidote to feelings of tenderness for these creatures was, the major reminded himself, a carefully cultivated loathing.

The boat slithered closer, its darkness blending with the slick black shoreline. It almost seemed like all the stealth wasn't necessary, though. Whenever the mermaids surfaced they were always facing the other way. If it was indeed the case that some of the mermaids who'd escaped had been warning the rest of them, the news obviously hadn't reached these two.

There was the flash of a third tail, a purple one, a little way to one side. Probably there was a whole *tribe* of them lounging right around that bend in the shore. The major started calculating. If they shot a bunch of mermaids out in the water they'd have to be extremely careful not to be seen by anyone at any stage of the procedure. The operation was still dead secret. And there would be the hassle of hiding the bodies, though one of those empty caves they'd found ought to do the job.

The copper-tailed one flung herself skyward again and pirouetted in space, coming down with an enormous splash. The boat was only fifty yards away now and still the mermaids seemed utterly thoughtless, as naïve as the children they decidedly *weren't*. In a few more seconds he'd give the order to gun the silent engines, rush the mermaids, and attack. Blue-tail somersaulted then dipped below the water. It would be best to charge at a moment when all three heads were above the surface, shoot them all simultaneously before they had a chance to realize what was happening.

As if on cue, all three heads appeared close together, their shoulders gleaming in the dull blue light. They appeared to be talking, maybe laughing at something, though of course the major's helmet kept him from hearing anything outside the network of microphones and speakers that linked him to his men. He shook his head and smiled grimly.

It was almost ludicrous how reckless these mermaids were being. If he didn't know better, the major might have thought they *wanted* to get caught. Maybe they did. Maybe their guilt drove them to it. The men had their spear guns up, ready to fire. Geffen looked back at him from the cabin, waiting for the signal. He nodded brusquely at the pilot, and the boat accelerated in perfect silence, hurtling almost to the spot where the mermaids laughed.

When he looked back at the low, dim waves there was nothing. No, *that* was one of them . . . or no, it was only a seal . . .

The boat was still ebbing forward a bit from the momentum. On all sides there was only the stone-colored roll of the water, dancing trails of shadow, blackish scrolls that seemed to be hair until he focused his gaze on them and they turned back into weeds. All he could hear was the electrical hum of his helmet and the layered rhythms of his men's exhalations against their built-in microphones. He usually tuned out the noise of their breathing, but somehow it was more intrusive now, as if it might be louder and quicker than he was used to . . . as if . . .

The world started spinning, slowly at first, like a merry-go-round just getting underway.

All the major could think for a moment was that he must be

hallucinating. The dim blue world swept ragged trees across his vision as if it wanted to brush his eyes out of his head . . . then tarnished water . . . trees again, a diving cormorant, a sense of infinite distance.

"Major?"

He snapped back to the sight of his men stumbling or pressed up against the boat's sides. The helmets hid everything but their worried, disoriented eyes. They were rotating at shocking speed now, each view of trees no more than a whiplash of passing darkness. Even worse, a mysterious circular blue wall seemed to be rising around them.

It was either that or . . ."Get us out of here!"

"I can't, major! We're in a funnel; we're—"

"Gun the goddamn engines and get us *out!*"

He found himself staggering back and crashing down on top of one of his fallen men. His stomach lurched and speed hammered at his head. The centrifugal force was now so great that it was a struggle to shift his leg a few inches to one side. Through the cabin's open door he saw Geffen's body swinging in midair as he tried to keep his grip on the wheel; then the pilot lost his hold and smashed screaming into the wall. His wasn't the only voice: the screams were all amplified by the helmets, throbbing into an intolerable, collective yowl.

It had to be *Luce*. She was the only one of those damn tails who could do something like this. She'd used the others as bait and lured the boat there.

Beyond the boat there was nothing but a blue blur of void, a towering emptiness. Blots of foam flew overhead. How far were they from the surface? Their suits would provide oxygen, of course. They wouldn't drown, unless . . .

A few of the men looked like they'd lost consciousness.

The spinning slowed and the tall blue walls caved in.

* * *

"We should rip their helmets off while they're still dizzy. *Dispose* of them." The mermaids had darted some distance away then stopped to gaze back at the scene they'd created after drawing that boat to a spot where the water was especially deep. Through the rippling gray they could just make out the floundering shapes of the divers as they pulled free of their fast-descending boat, most of them dragging comrades who apparently couldn't swim on their own.

"No." The smallest of the three mermaids flicked her blue tail. "We stopped them for now, and we showed them enough that they'll be scared about what they're doing. We're not going to kill them!"

"They're murderers," the brown-skinned mermaid hissed. "They don't deserve to live."

"Dana . . . you're a murderer too. So am I. Someone has to stop first. We should just hurry up and get *away* from here."

"Dang," the purple-tailed mermaid sniped, but she was laughing in exhilaration at what she'd just witnessed. It was incredible what these two could do when they deliberately joined their voices that way, and now they were starting to teach her, too. "You really do talk like that, that crazy—"

"Are you surprised, J'aime?" Violet retorted. "I *told* you who my queen is."

14

Pharaoh's Army

It was evening again; in a few hours they'd all head out to sea for another round of training. It was going better than she'd dared to hope and Luce knew she should be happy; even Catarina had stopped objecting. But as Luce gazed across the light-streaked bay, anxiety kept twisting through her like cold wires binding her insides. More refugees were turning up every day, and while some of them were too rattled to do much but lie in the hammocks and stare at the nightmares spinning through their heads, others were all too eager to join Luce's growing army.

The bay was getting crowded. It sometimes seemed like half the surviving mermaids on the West Coast must be living there now, under warehouses and rotting piers or in half-sunk boats. There were even larvae, and of course it was hard to make them understand how important it was not to let themselves be seen. Sooner or later the humans would realize mermaids were out there, and it was just plain dumb strategically to have everyone concentrated in a relatively small area with only one exit. More than once Luce had gone to scout out the Golden Gate, just in case, trying to determine if it would be feasible for the humans to block their escape route.

She couldn't tell, though. Luce had to admit to herself that she just didn't know enough to guess; she might be worrying for nothing, or she might be setting everyone up for death by letting them stay here.

She needed to find someone who knew more than she did. And no matter how long she brooded over the problem she kept coming back to the same absurd idea.

Luce glanced back around the tangle of nets. A lot of the mermaids were out; they'd gone off on their daily foraging expedition to the south bay, where there were large wild areas on the water with a good supply of shellfish. But Imani was swinging in her hammock, eyes closed, singing very softly to herself: a *human* song, Luce realized in amazement. She'd never heard a mermaid sing a song with words before, and she paused to listen. "'If I could I surely would, stand on the rock where Moses stood. Pharaoh's army got drownded; oh, Mary, don't you weep . . .'"

Where had she heard Imani's song before? Luce swam over to her. Though Imani's hammock was made from shredded white plastic shopping bags, they were all so intricately knotted that it looked more like handmade lace. "'Oh, Mary, don't you weep, don't you mourn . . .'"

"Imani? I don't want to interrupt you, but . . ."

A tear rolled down Imani's blue-gleaming cheek as she opened her eyes. "Why shouldn't we mourn for them, Luce?"

Luce felt a rush of tenderness for her. "You mean for Pharaoh's army? In the song?"

"My grampa would always sing that song to me, back when I was really small, and I couldn't talk well enough yet to make him understand why it made me cry. But maybe those soldiers didn't even *want* to be in that army."

Luce realized what Imani was truly thinking about. "We can mourn for them, Imani. And we can change, and not drown anyone again."

Imani's looked as if she were half-enchanted by her own singing. "I've kept thinking of that song. Ever since I changed into a mermaid and found out what we do, I've kept hearing it. I hope we can make this into a war of water and music, but I'm afraid it's just going to turn into another cycle of death and more death."

Luce breathed deep, trying to calm herself. "It won't."

"If they find us we'll be able to fight them now, and I guess that's better than doing nothing, but . . . they'll die, and we'll die too. Pharaoh's army and the Twice Lost Army, we'll share the same end."

"We won't let that happen, Imani." Luce tried to sound confident. "We'll find a way to persuade them to agree to peace."

Luce expected Imani to keep arguing. Instead she closed her eyes again, spinning her tail so that her net rocked harder. "Okay."

"Okay?" Luce said. She wasn't completely sure she'd heard right.

"I'll . . . trust you on this, Luce. But I don't see how we can persuade them to do anything."

"It's going to be really"—*almost impossible*, Luce thought, but she didn't want to say that—"really hard. Imani, I think I have to go out for a while. If I'm not back in time, could you start leading training without me?"

That knocked Imani out of her waking dream. She looked down at Luce where she hovered in the water, and her gaze was sharper than Luce had ever seen it. "Really? Where are you going?"

Luce hesitated. "I have to talk to someone. If I can even find him."

Him gave it away, of course. Luce couldn't be talking about going to see another mermaid.

"Luce . . ." Imani breathed after a few moments. "About trusting you. Do you know you're asking a lot?"

They held each other's eyes, then something shifted and a slight smile seemed to flutter back and forth between them.

"Imani?" But what could Luce say, really? "Thank you."

* * *

Above the surface reflected light pleated across the water, and the distant roar of traffic echoed and warped as it flowed along the waves. Below it there was the private night where sleek-finned bodies darted and spun, the glow of mermaids crossing the wings of rays.

Luce swirled along close to the bottom, where rusty bicycles turned their wheels in the current and weeds grew in long reddish ribbons. There were rubbery amber sea cucumbers and so many tiny pink anemones that the rocks seemed to be carpeted in feathery mouths. It wasn't that long before she saw rotten pilings on her left and the line of a pier slouching down into the water. Luce surfaced to see if she could recognize the spot. There was a warehouse she thought looked familiar, its endless windows staring blankly across the bay. And sitting cross-legged on the pier there was a man, and he was looking straight at her . . .

Luce dropped under the water, down into green depths. "Mermaid?" the man called quietly. "It's me. Your friend the old ghost."

He didn't look the same, though. Luce came cautiously to the surface and stared at him. He was wearing relatively clean clothes in place of his sagging overcoats, though to guess by how badly the new clothes fit him, he'd probably found them in the street. He was cleaner, too, and he'd cut his mouse gray hair. The reek of sweat and alcohol that had clung to him the first time Luce had seen him was gone, and she could tell by the alert way he was looking at her that he wasn't drunk. She swam a little closer. "Hi."

"Hi, mermaid." He was smiling a small careful smile, obviously trying not to scare her away. "Hoped you were gonna come back."

Now that he was in front of her, Luce wasn't sure where to start. "You look better."

"I feel better. You know, I saw my own death that night. Turns out that a good shot of terror was the best medicine for me. And maybe there was something in that unreal voice of yours too."

"I'm glad . . . it helped," Luce murmured. He was gazing at her with such powerful curiosity that she was almost overwhelmed by shyness.

"But you don't actually want to talk to me, do you? I mean— you're gorgeous and magical and whatever the hell else you are. You didn't stop by to shoot the . . . the breeze with me. So what *do* you want?"

He was right, of course, but Luce felt obscurely guilty that it was so obvious. "I just wanted . . . I wondered if I could ask you some questions?"

He just stared at her, his pale blue eyes glittering in the faded lamplight. It was hard to keep going. The immense emptiness above them seemed to press on Luce's shoulders, and a rusty glow hazed across the sky.

"That night, you said you'd been a stevedore?" Luce asked.

"Eight years, after Nam. Unloaded all those ships pulling into the port of Oakland."

"I was wondering . . . Maybe you know about the Golden Gate. You could tell me . . ." Luce didn't want to give away too much; there was no way to know for sure if she could trust him. "Well, would it be possible to close it?"

The old man swayed a little from surprise. "*Close* it? The Golden Gate? Who the hell would want to do that?"

"Say, if the government, or the army . . . if they wanted to keep anything from getting through, could they do that?"

He tilted his head, thinking it over. "I guess the navy could do some kind of blockade. If there was a threat from foreign ships, not that this would ever happen, but they could line up their boats and keep 'em out."

"But . . ." Luce knew she might be saying too much, but she didn't see any other way. "What about *under* the water?"

"Because a sea serpent was gunning for Frisco, or the kraken was rising?" He laughed, a little too wildly. "Then they've got plenty of submarines. And they could plant mines."

"I was wondering more about, if maybe they could close it down with a giant metal gate? Like, if they wanted to stop things that were smaller than ships or . . . or sea serpents."

Luce watched understanding open inside his blue eyes, watched his lips purse thoughtfully. "And it's the U.S. government that you think might be doing this 'closing down,' Miss Mermaid? Can't say I'm their biggest fan." He grimaced. "I have indeed seen a dab too much to be. Anyhow, I don't think that's something you should get yourself in a big tizzy about."

"Because it's impossible?" Luce asked hopefully. She was grateful that he wasn't asking her too many questions.

"Might be *possible*, though it sure wouldn't be easy. That's not why they'll never do it, though. They'd have the shipping companies and God knows who all screaming bloody *murder* if they tried it. One of the busiest ports in the *country*? They're going to just stop that dead? Don't think so."

Luce's tail had started twitching from excitement even before she consciously understood the implications of what he'd just said to her. "You're saying they couldn't afford to let that much business stop? So if it did . . ."

"You know how they say that blood is thicker than water, mermaid? I'll tell you what's thicker than blood. Blend up a stack of dollar bills and you've got yourself the thickest substance known to man, and it's the goddamned stickiest!"

Luce was barely listening to him anymore. The Golden Gate Bridge wasn't visible from here; all the buildings of downtown San Francisco were in the way. But she was gazing in its approximate direction anyway, her tail flicking in narrow loops behind her.

"Step your foot in *that* gunk, don't care what kind of principles you think you've got; you're trapped for life. Like a poor mouse in one of those glue traps, gnawing your own legs."

No. Her idea was completely insane. It would take so many mermaids, probably thousands more than she had with her, and they'd all have to be so powerful. Luce could control an impressive volume of water, and Imani and some of the others were getting pretty good as well, but what she had in mind—it just wasn't realistic.

"Hey, Miss Mermaid?"

Luce glanced back at him, though her thoughts were still far away. No matter how much she told herself she was being ridiculous, she was still longing to dash off and find Imani and the others.

"You have any clue how famous you are now?" His pale eyes shone with an expression Luce couldn't identify, although the word "questing" occurred to her. He was looking for something, she thought. Then what he'd asked hit her, and she reeled a little.

"What are you *talking* about?" Luce demanded. Though actually, maybe she already had an idea . . .

"How about that you've gone Hollywood? How about a giga-billion views of that little movie you starred in? I wanted to see if I could learn anything about you after you saved my life. Hit the computers at this community center I go to, and hot damn if it wasn't the exact same fishtailed Girl Wonder looking back at me from the screen."

Luce's mouth opened wordlessly. Of course she'd seen those humans pointing their camera at her, and she knew the government had found out she'd been sighted. But she hadn't seriously considered the possibility that the video would wind up on the Internet or if it did that anyone would be interested. "You're saying . . . I saw them holding a camera, but I didn't really think they'd . . . or that anybody would believe . . ."

"Huge. It's gotten huge. They put it out there, you better believe it, and now it's all over the place."

"Do people think it's *real*?" Luce asked. How *could* they, though?

The old man shrugged. "If I hadn't met you personally I wouldn't have known *what* to think, Miss Mermaid who ought to be friendly enough to tell me her name, already. See, though, what you might want to think about . . ."

Luce was still disoriented by the news he'd just given her. It took her a second to focus. "Um, what?"

"Well, if you've got something you'd like to tell all the folks out here in humanland, they'll probably listen. You've already got their attention."

Luce thought about that. Of course she had a lot of things she wanted to say to the humans: so many that she had no idea where she should start. But she couldn't take the risk that the divers would find out where she was. If they came looking for her, they'd find everyone else, too.

How much harm had that video *already* done?

"You said you'd help me!" Luce began as the panic hit her. "You said I knew who to ask!"

The old man shook his head, surprised by her vehemence. "I did, sure. And you do. What did I say? How am I not trying to help?"

"No one—this is really, really important, okay?—no one can know I'm here! You can't tell *anyone!*"

Once again Luce saw understanding crash through his face like a wave. "They're looking to catch *you*, huh? Not just—to catch things like you? People from the government?"

After a brief pause Luce nodded. He'd already figured out that much.

"Why, though? They want to give you to their scientists? Send electricity through you and whiz you through their machines and find out how you tick?"

That hadn't occurred to Luce before, but now that he mentioned it that seemed like a possibility. "I guess they might."

"Good thing about ghosts." He nodded emphatically, his haphazard gray hair twitching with the movement. "They know how to keep their mouths shut. Or if they do talk it just comes out like 'whoooo.'" He cracked up laughing wildly, but when Luce didn't join in he calmed himself just as suddenly. "Nobody listens to me anyway, Miss Mermaid. But I'll keep quiet. Awright?"

It didn't seem like she had much choice about trusting him. "Okay."

"And your name is? Princess Autocrata Waveform? Mermaladia McSea?"

She hesitated again. "Luce Korchak." Why had she given him her human name, though?

"Plain old Luce Korchak? Huh. And you can call me Seb of the Ghosts."

Luce had the sense that she was humoring him, but considering how much he knew that seemed like a good idea. "You're as alive as anybody, though."

"You're not the first one to say so, Miss Luce Mermaid. A pack of morons kept on badgering me with words to that effect after I got back from Vietnam. That just goes to show what they knew, doesn't it?"

Luce couldn't tell if he was serious. It wasn't reassuring to think that her only human ally might be totally delusional. "If you're already dead, then how could you almost drown?"

"Oh, that." He grinned at her lopsidedly, and his pale eyes gleamed. "I'm not by any stretch suggesting that I won't have to die again. Now, who ever told you that once was enough? Let me tell you something, Lucy Goosey. People always think that ghosts are spirits, right? But a man's walking-around body can be a ghost a whole lot easier than his spirit can."

15

An Appeal

The man on the screen had short-cropped hair, a stubbly chin, and wry cinnamon-colored eyes. Behind him was what appeared to be a sunny, comfortable kitchen with pale yellow cabinets and a large vase full of lilacs. "Hi," he said, with an odd self-conscious smile. "My name is Andrew Korchak, and I just wanted to say something to anyone out there who's been watching that video with that green-tailed mermaid swimming out from under the dock. The thing is . . ." He held up a photo, and the camera zoomed shakily in on it until a girl with short, dark, jagged hair and frightened eyes filled the screen. "That mermaid wasn't always a mermaid. You can all see here it's the same face, right? This photo here is my daughter, Lucette—Luce—and this is her seventh-grade picture from school."

He choked up a little and looked down. From off screen a gentle voice said, "Andrew. Can you go on?"

Secretary Moreland squirmed in his heavy armchair and rapped his knuckles against the desk supporting the large monitor where this new and even more outrageous video was playing. With each rap his reddish jowls swayed and his stiff white hair vibrated slightly. Three other men in suits stood fidgeting behind him, their eyes carefully blank but their mouths twisting.

The picture zoomed back out and Andrew Korchak looked up. "Right. Well, I was away for a while. I couldn't help it, and it's too much to tell you all, but Luce was alone with my brother and he . . . he hurt her. He hurt her so much that she stopped being a human girl, and she changed into what you've all seen. Don't ask me to explain how it works. But I saw Luce after she turned into a mermaid, and that's what she told me. And there are more of them. If some young girl you used to know, could be your daughter or your sister or your friend, if she went missing, she might be one of the mermaids now too."

There was a tiny moan from the person off-screen. The focus of the cinnamon eyes shifted slightly upward.

"Kathleen? I'm sorry. I—"

"It's okay. Let's just finish. Please."

"Okay. See, our government—the U.S. government—has got some kind of Special Operations guys out there killing mermaids. Not saying they don't have their reasons. I think the mermaids might . . . they might go around drowning people. But if one of those mermaids used to be some girl you love, I bet you don't want them all dead any more than I do. You want them back and safe and human again, like I do."

The camera was pitching a little. The man looked worried, and he started talking faster.

"And even if they drown people, I know they also might save people sometimes. So I'm here to ask: if that's you, and some mermaid saved your life before, get up on this Internet and say so. Or if you think a girl you miss is out there with my Luce, get up and say so. They're pretty much kids. There's got to be something else we can do. That's all I wanted to ask you. Okay, thanks."

The camera veered faster, pointing first at the window and then at the floor. There was a sound that was probably a chair toppling over and the image went dead.

Secretary Moreland slid back his chair and stood up as slowly and imposingly as he could manage. He was a large man, tall and broad, and he tilted over his three nervous deputies as he turned to them. "Why," Moreland growled very slowly, "did I just watch this?"

A thin man flinched sharply back. "We thought it could be significant, Mr. Secretary. It seems to indicate that someone might have leaked classified information. We were concerned that it could—"

"Of course someone leaked classified information! This"— Moreland grimaced—"this *loser* didn't learn about Operation Odysseus by reading the newspaper. That's my question. *Why* was this allowed to happen?"

None of the suited men answered, though tiny jerky currents seemed to flow through their arms and feet. Moreland scowled until one of them added, "We're reasonably confident, Mr. Secretary, that the information wasn't leaked by anyone in the Department of Defense."

"I personally feel quite clear on *who* was responsible for this leak, men. If the miscreant's identity isn't obvious to you as well, then you haven't been paying attention to the subversive *drivel* that two-bit fanatic has been going around spouting." The suited men flinched. They were all too familiar, by now, with the uncontrollable rancor Secretary Moreland felt for Agent Ben Ellison of the FBI. If his superiors weren't so determined to protect him, Ellison would have been dispensed with long ago. "But that doesn't answer my question, does it? Why was that whiny mermaid sympathizer allowed to go and jabber to Lucette Korchak's *father* of all people? If the FBI can't keep their own agents in check, then the responsibility falls to you. Or didn't that *occur* to you?"

There was an awkward silence. "Sir, are you suggesting—"

"I'm suggesting that someone who thinks we can solve the mermaid problem by bringing those goddamn tails mugs of cocoa at bedtime should not be permitted to run around undermining our work!" Moreland's lips were working as if he was chewing something too big to swallow. "Where *is* he?"

"Agent Ellison, sir? He's on a flight back to Washington. Even the FBI suspects that he might have had something to do with this."

"Not *him!*" Secretary Moreland shook his head in apparent disbelief at their stupidity. "I mean that ragtag fool who's putting out these touching appeals to the public, making them think that we're trying to wipe out every cute little girl who's ever had her face on a milk carton!"

A few of the mermaids' faces really might have appeared on milk cartons, of course. But no one said that. "Andrew Korchak?" The skinny man assumed a dismissive tone. "I don't think anyone knows. He has quite a rap sheet, though. It's only because this video was released by the same woman who posted the original mermaid tape that anyone has even noticed it. Personally, I don't see how anyone could take him seriously."

"Half a million views *already*? I would think that's serious enough. If the public starts believing mermaids are real, that's—at a minimum—highly inconvenient. If they start to think of mermaids as children rather than monsters, that's worse. If we're forced at some point to disclose what the teams are doing, we need to be able to frame our activity as what it is: eliminating an unacceptable threat to anyone who has business on the water. If people start thinking that we're murdering helpless little girls instead of protecting good citizens and their nice babies and their dogs, *well* . . ."

"Sir, of course that would be an issue, but—"

"So if you're planning, at some point, to try justifying the considerable trust I've placed in you by putting you three in charge of providing whatever land-based support the teams who are risking their *lives* out there need, you might consider that one of their primary needs is an oblivious public, or barring *that*, a supportive one!"

"Yes, sir." The skinny man's eyes were still carefully blank as he nodded.

"Sir, would you prefer if Andrew Korchak was . . . no longer a possible source of concern?"

Moreland sighed and paced to a window, which rebutted his gaze with its bland beige shade. It was better than seeing the sky beyond, though, and the clouds. Ever since he'd heard that outburst of mermaid song the whole world had seemed to inspect him with a stare at once skeptical and luminous. "That would attract attention. Unavoidably. Of course, if it was the right *kind* of attention, then that might serve our purposes very well."

"You mean . . ."

"I'll handle it," Moreland announced. Now that his back was turned to them, the three men were free to shoot one another worried looks. Speculation regarding the secretary of defense's mental health was rampant in the department. "I know exactly what to do. Major Sullivan, I have a few little tasks I need you to take care of first."

No one dared to contradict him.

Moreland felt the throb of mermaid song pressing at the inside of his skull as he paced down the long subterranean corridor. Since no one was watching he allowed himself to give in to it a little, to leap and writhe in midair as he walked. He stopped controlling his face and let it squirm and grimace, and he opened his mouth and let a few misshapen notes pour out. Nauseous excitement was building in his stomach, and his hands were damp and compressed into fists.

What he was about to do was almost unbearably thrilling—terribly satisfying but in a way that galled him and made him jump. He wouldn't be able to witness the act directly, of course. Maybe that was what irked him so much. The fluorescent lights overhead glazed the marble floor in bands of sickly pallor. He was almost there. Anais would be in front of him in a minute, with her strange shimmer and her stifled voice and her beauty that only became more marvelous as she herself became more miserable.

He couldn't allow himself to *hear* her sing again, but what he had in mind was, he thought, the next best thing.

There was the steel door; he typed in the key code that so few people were privileged to know. The keys felt hot and staticky under his rapid taps. Then the door buzzed open and cool blue light came wavering across his eyes. Golden hair unraveled through the water, azure fins stirred. "Tadpole," Moreland murmured under his breath. "Tadpole, we're going to have such a delicious little adventure together."

Then something that he hadn't noticed moved. How could he have failed to see that man in the lab coat perched on a folding chair and leaning close to the tank's speaker? The pallid young face wore an expression of rapturous intimacy, but the joyful look was quickly transforming into annoyance at the interruption. For the life of him, Moreland couldn't remember that young man's name, but he recalled that he was Anais's keeper, in charge of keeping her fed and comfortable and indulging her less extortionate whims.

The young man stood up, slapping as he rose the switches that stopped sound from transmitting in or out of the tank. His receding chin and prominent forehead, combined with a large sharp nose, made his face seemed peculiarly unbalanced. His beige hair was thinning and his eyes were narrow and sad. "Good *afternoon*, Secretary Moreland."

He didn't sound at all respectful, though. And he was pouting with unconcealed jealousy. Moreland could barely control his amusement.

"That will be all for now, Mr. . . ."

"Hackett, sir. Charles Hackett."

"Oh, yes, Anais calls you *Charlie*. I'd like a private word with our little princess, if you don't mind."

Charles Hackett grimaced with open contempt. It was another sign of Anais's power, Moreland thought, that this flunky was so blatantly rude toward someone so vastly his superior. He couldn't actually disobey Moreland's orders, though. He jerked toward the exit, hunching angrily. Behind him Anais swirled, her fins twitching, and knocked silently on the glass.

"Or actually, Mr. Hackett . . ."

Hackett turned back, his eyes narrowing sharply as they reached the secretary of defense.

"I have a present for our little mermaid, Mr. Hackett. Please give it to her after I leave." Moreland pulled from his breast pocket a slim box wrapped in pink paper with a golden ribbon and handed it over while Hackett scowled. Moreland smiled in anticipation; it was a pleasure to speak all the lies he'd rehearsed that morning.

"Also, we're going to have to play that mermaid recording for her again. We have a few more questions about the singers. Tonight when you go, I'd like you to turn off the electroshock system so that she can listen to the recording as many times as she needs to. Understood?"

"Sir . . ." Hackett visibly worked up his courage. "It's not healthy for Anais to be reminded of all that. Her friends, her . . . her difficult past. She needs sensitive, caring treatment; she needs to be allowed to *heal*."

"She needs to earn her keep, Hackett. And she needs to pay us back for letting her live." Moreland aimed a smirk at Anais, who looked wonderfully alarmed at the sight of him. Aqua light roiled across her arms and throat. "She'll *heal* when it suits my convenience."

Hackett opened his mouth and closed it again and made a kind of undecided movement with his shoulders. Moreland kept glowering at him, and after a few more flutters of silent protest he shuffled out.

Moreland's hand shuddered a little with eagerness as it reached to turn the speakers back on. Anais retreated a short distance from the glass, her long tail snaking and her eyes bright and plaintive. "Why, tadpole," Moreland crooned. "I brought you a *present*. Something I think you'll enjoy very much. You could at least make small talk with me for a while."

Anais rippled a little closer. "Hi," she muttered faintly.

"Hi, *sir*," Moreland corrected, then broke into a smile so wide it made his face ache. "I've been thinking about you, tadpole. I've been wondering if there are ways we can make your time with us more pleasant. You must get so *bored* all alone in here all day."

Anais stared at him, simultaneously wary and petulant. "Of course I'm bored."

"Of *course* you are," Moreland simpered. Anais only looked more frightened in response. "That's why I'm going to give you the opportunity to do a new, exciting job for me. Broaden your horizons, help your country, and"—he leered—"have *fun* doing it."

Anais swished with ill-concealed dismay. "What do you want me to do now? I've told you *everything* I know, and you still won't let me go home!"

"Charlie is going to give you my present later. It's a cell phone."

Anais suddenly brightened. "Really? Then I can call my friends in Miami! I can—"

"For the moment, little tadpole, it's been programmed so that it can only dial a single number." He felt a restless thrill below his heart as Anais's happiness collapsed again. "You'll make a call this evening, say around nine o'clock. Your first job is to collect some information. If a man answers or if you get voice mail, you should hang up. But if a woman answers, you'll follow the instructions we're about to go over together."

Anais considered this, her head bowed so that waves of hair obscured her face. "Then will you let me go?"

"No." Moreland smiled at her. "You'll do this for the sheer pleasure of it, my dear. Because asking a few questions is only the first of your responsibilities."

"I don't want to do anything for you, then! I'd rather be bored. I don't even care if you turn my TV off! I'll just stare at the walls."

Moreland had to admit it to himself: he adored Anais like this: childish and surly and deeply depressed. It was a shame, in a way, that she would genuinely enjoy her new assignment. "Oh, tadpole," Moreland whispered, "don't be silly. This will be fun for the whole family."

"I don't *care* anymore! I—"

"Tell me something, Anais. Don't you miss your singing?"

16

Joining Voices

Seb watched from the pier as Luce waved good night to him, a little awkwardly, and headed out into the wild night. She had a long swim ahead of her before she would reach the spot where the Twice Lost gathered to practice. As their numbers grew, they all worried more about the risk that someone would spot them from a boat or a plane. Every night they traveled a bit farther from the coast, settling into remote waves and yet still feeling terribly, helplessly exposed. They put as much loneliness around them as they could, as if the night itself could be their shelter.

Even from a distance Luce could hear the music: long, thrumming, sustained tones, scatterings of brighter notes along the surface. The voices had the distinctive, oddly smooth sound that mermaid voices took on when they called to the water, coaxing and caressing. All around Luce the water shivered, and she whipped along in excitement, ducking below hunting sea lions and spinning silver balls of frightened fish.

Soon the water above her head was thick with swinging, glimmering fins, and Luce surfaced. On the dark sea the Twice Lost Army floated. Luce caught sight of Yuan, busy organizing the newer members into small groups under the command of former queens; of

Imani, working with a few of the girls who'd been having trouble. As Luce watched, one of them—a mermaid with thick light brown curls and an anxious expression on her china-doll face—lost control of her voice completely. All at once the night throbbed with savage enchantment as the mermaid's death song took over and leaped higher and brighter. The curly-haired mermaid flung herself backwards in a panic, gasping and thrashing as she struggled to regain mastery of the notes tearing from her throat. If any humans had been unlucky enough to be within earshot, Luce knew they would have had no chance at all of surviving.

Luce was about to race over to her when she saw that she wasn't needed. Imani was already hovering just behind the frightened mermaid, her dark hands lightly resting on those heaving shoulders. The vehement music calmed a little, and the doll-faced mermaid's spasmodic movements slowed. Imani was singing in her ear, a soothing, whispering resonance, luring the maddened song back down into a single note, soft and peaceful. A docile little wave curled up in front of them. And then . . .

Then Imani's voice changed again, bending into a low, bubbling harmony. Her song caught the frightened mermaid's voice in a way Luce had never heard before. It was as if Imani's song had entered into that other song and opened it like a flower opening in the core of another flower, forming a concentric swell of music that was somehow greater and sweeter than the sound of any mermaid singing alone.

And the wave in front of them doubled, trebled in size, then abruptly shot skyward and wavered in a gleaming wall with gracefully fluted sides. The moon's light refracted in each curve until a hundred long golden eyes winked out at them. Everyone stopped practicing and watched in silence. The china-doll mermaid stared in disbelief at the result of her strange duet with Imani, then let out a little shriek. The spell broke, the water tumbled . . .

And Luce's voice entered the night and caught the falling wave again. Imani glanced over at her, eyes shining with a kind of serene exaltation. Luce could feel Imani's voice singing *into* hers and feel her own song blossoming in Imani's. The sensation was entirely new to her, and also entirely wonderful. The wave-wall grew higher and smoother, its upper reaches forming dancing pinnacles, bright corkscrewing vines.

It took all of Luce's concentration to stop herself from bursting out laughing in delirious joy. *This* was what happened when the mermaids merged their power. Her voice felt lighter inside her, and the immense force of that music was much easier to sustain than it had ever been when she sang to the water on her own. Singing together in this way, they seemed to multiply their individual power into a marvelous synergy.

A few other mermaids seemed to catch on and joined in. Water rose again, sleeked up through the darkness, then again . . . The sound pulsed through Luce's head and body until even her bones seemed to sing like the strings of a guitar. She was the heart of the song, but so were all the other singers, and the curling wave-walls bent the night on all sides until they were surrounded by a bright castle made of water and sound at once.

Like Imani had said, it was a miracle: their own miracle, their personal creation.

Luce had long since given up singing humans to their doom, but she had never forgotten the addictive thrill her death song always provoked in her. But this *new* feeling, she thought, was even better. She was lost in the sound, her thoughts weaving through all the voices at once; only the gentle loft and fall of the waves gave her any sense of passing time. It was impossible to guess how long the strange new song went on, but when the music finally began to fade, the immense golden moon was rolling into the horizon, its disc misshapen by rising fronds of mist. The watery castle seemed to melt very slowly with the lowering music, its walls bowing out and then gently petaling downward.

Quiet; it was quiet. Only the dreamlike roar of the ocean and, far away, the plangent cry of a whale.

And around Luce hundreds of drifting, dimly luminous faces moved with the waves. For a few minutes it was hard to imagine that any of them would ever speak again. They had all known one another more deeply through their shared song than they ever could through words.

"War, Luce?" Imani murmured at last, and laughed a single breathless laugh. "How can this be war?"

Luce knew what Imani meant. She'd never experienced such absolute peace in her life, peace so profound that it became a new kind of shivering excitement.

"A new kind of war, Imani," Luce said. Her voice was thin, airy, but suddenly she realized that everyone was looking at her. "I promised. I promised you. We can . . . make up a new story; we can find a new way through. We can stop all the death."

She was starting to clear the magic from her mind. This was important; she couldn't stay in that watery dream-space, marvelous as it was.

"Oh, Luce, we can't make them stop hunting us with what we've done tonight! With—" The voice was Catarina's, still half-enchanted, sweet, and despairing. "We can't stop them with *beauty*."

"We can," Luce insisted. "We can. Not just with beauty,

Cat. But with what we can do. We can make them accept peace without killing anyone, not one more person." The magic was still inside her; it was hard to find her way through her own pirouetting thoughts and even harder to put the right words in the right order. "Really, Cat. Really. I think . . . I know what to do now. I have an idea."

Now everyone was *really* staring at her. The thought of telling them all what she was thinking terrified her. If her idea didn't work, the Twice Lost mermaids would be so terribly let down. But the wild expectation in those gathered faces wouldn't allow her to hold back now either. "We're going to close down the Golden Gate. A naval blockade, right under the bridge. Then they'll *have* to talk to us."

Luce knew that she'd said something crazy by the blank way the crowd of mermaids looked at her. Most of them weren't angry or indignant or excited; they just looked as if her idea was too strange to take in.

Catarina was the first to speak. "Close it down? Luce, this is—"

"With a wave. We'll raise a wave big enough that none of their ships can get through. We'll hold it there until they agree to stop."

"But then they'll know we're here!" Jo squealed. The toys wreathed around her neck rattled. "Luce, Luce, don't . . ."

"Of course they'll know," Luce said. As she envisioned it she began to feel stronger and clearer. "All the humans will know. Everyone in the world will hear about this. That's how we'll get the government to negotiate with us. I know it sounds crazy, but . . ." *It could work,* Luce thought. *It's the only thing that* might *work.*

"Then what's going to stop them from dropping bombs on us?

Luce, I want to believe in you, in all your plans. I do. But this . . ."
Catarina seemed genuinely appalled, her gray eyes gleaming with
desperate sadness. Actually, Luce wasn't completely sure how
they'd keep the human military from bombing them, but she felt
certain now they'd think of something. After that incredible com-
munal song, everything seemed possible.

"They won't drop bombs on us." It was Yuan, suddenly grinning ferociously. "Oh, you better believe they won't! If we can really raise a wave that big?"

Luce suddenly understood where Yuan was going with this
and looked at her gratefully.

"Yuan, they'll blast us right out of the water! No, our only
hope is to try to stay secret." Catarina was almost hyperventilat-
ing now.

"Cat? No offense, but you need to start trusting our dear *general*
more. Because she's totally right. If we really have enough power to
get such a huge wave standing up and keep it there—"

"We'll all be dead within an hour!"

"No, Cat, listen! If they bomb us, we stop singing. If we stop
singing, all that water comes crashing down at once. You really
think they'll send a tsunami right at downtown San Francisco?"

"That sounds fun," Bex muttered sourly. Then before anyone
could say anything in response she added, "Oh my God, guys. Kidding? I'm just kidding?"

Yuan was right. In fact, Luce thought, she was *brilliant*. "Do
you see now, Cat? I don't want to make you do anything you think
is suicidal, though." Luce looked around, and from something in
the shine of the eyes on all sides she knew that, even if they weren't
all prepared to go along with her idea, *enough* of them were. "But
this is the only plan we have, and the humans are definitely going

to know that the bay is full of mermaids as soon as we're good enough at this kind of singing to start the blockade. If any of you think that makes it too dangerous to stay here you can leave. Go back to . . . to the territories where tribes were already killed. As long as you don't sink any ships, the divers probably won't check the same caves a second time."

It was brutal advice, Luce realized. For some of them the journey would be terrible. For many it would mean returning to the site of hideous memories, even to the decaying corpses of their old friends. But it was the best she could do.

"I'm not leaving you a second time, Luce," Catarina announced through gritted teeth. Even now that Yuan had explained how the plan could work, Cat still seemed to be convinced that they were heading for their doom.

Luce didn't know what to say. "I'm really happy if you want to stay, Cat, but you don't *have* to. But I promise we'll practice a lot first. We won't try this until we're *totally* ready."

She still loved Catarina, Luce thought. Of course she did. But maybe she didn't love her in quite the same way that she used to.

Her memories of Nausicaa just took up too much room in her heart.

From the distance came the airy percussion of a helicopter. In a few moments the ocean's surface was empty of everything except waves.

It was time for them to be getting home, anyway.

17

Connections

Nick slammed the door behind him, leaving Kathleen alone and crying in the colored beams of evening light shining through the stained glass windows. *Another* fight, Kathleen thought; why couldn't they ever seem to understand each other anymore? She'd always been a firm believer that honest communication and kindness could solve almost any problem. Now, it seemed, the more honest she tried to be the more outraged and impatient Nick became. Telling him her real thoughts was beginning to feel like a mistake. When she did he'd respond with words she found hard to forgive. *Kath, one thing I can assure you of? Just one? Eileen is not a mermaid! I suppose I shouldn't blame you, but honestly, it's absolutely foolish to go around listening to some charlatan who tries to persuade you that your sister isn't dead.*

"Eileen," Kath whispered as she sat on the bottom stair with her head in her hands, "Eileen, what I wouldn't give to see you just for a second, one second before I die. Name it."

Something about that mermaid she'd seen—No, not "that mermaid," Kathleen told herself. *Lucette. Lucette Korchak, no matter what Nick says*—had reminded her of her lost sister. She'd had the same haunted expression, the same unwitting glamour that almost seemed like a kind of dark shimmer in the air around her. Especially toward the end Eileen had seemed both wounded and magical, and those qualities had only intensified as she'd deliberately taken all their mother's abuse on herself. Their mother might be on the verge of hitting Kathleen when Eileen would deliberately fire off the most offensive remark she could think of to make sure the broom swung her way instead. *Mom? You know, I've been thinking that I'd like to see if I can be the biggest slut in school.*

Then Kathleen had run off with a boyfriend, and three days later her brave, insouciant older sister had vanished for good. And now—if only Eileen hadn't died in some terrible way during all the intervening years—Kathleen was sure that she was darting through the waves somewhere, savage and free and still a freckled, impudent seventeen-year-old girl, only transfigured at the same time into something far beyond everyday experience. "Did you think I didn't need you anymore, Eenie? I do, I *still* do."

Kathleen heard her cell phone ringing where she'd left it on the kitchen table. Her first thought was that it must be Nick, calling to apologize for their fight. She hesitated on the step, not sure she was ready to talk to him yet. Or—suddenly Kathleen was on her feet—maybe, just maybe, it was Andrew calling her from some truck stop in the middle of nowhere. The thought of hearing his warm voice, of simply feeling certain for five minutes that someone *believed* her, was enough to send Kathleen sprinting precariously down the long hallway, knocking a few seashells from tiny tables as she went. Andrew didn't have a phone of his own. This might be her only chance to talk to him for weeks. Any second now the ringing would stop and the call would go to voice mail and he'd probably feel too uncomfortable to even leave her a message.

Her pale yellow kitchen wheeled in front of her. The lilacs in the vase were turning brown, but for some reason she kept putting off throwing them out. The phone emitted what was surely its final ring, and she still couldn't find it anywhere. Kathleen's shoulders jerked in frustration. No, *there* it was, half-hidden by that dropped napkin.

A strange number. It *had* to be him, probably calling from some random pay phone in back of a gas station. She could picture him clutching the grubby receiver while the sunset glared off the nearby cars, his frown deepening as she didn't answer. Kathleen was a little surprised by how hard her heart was pounding; she hadn't run all that far. "Hello?"

Silence. She'd missed him after all.

Except the silence wasn't perfect; it had a weirdly bubbly, echoing quality that reminded Kathleen of an abandoned swimming pool. "Hello? Anyone there?"

"Um, may I speak to Kathleen Lambert?" It was a girl's voice overlaid by a hint of that watery quivering. Kathleen felt an icy tightness in her stomach; she thought it must come from disappointment.

"This is Kathleen."

"Well, hi." Now the strange girl's voice took on a kind of smirking, self-conscious tone that made Kathleen wonder if this was a prank call. "Hi. I'm an old friend of Luce's. Luce the mermaid? And I need to find her dad? Do you have his number?"

Of course those videos had provoked all kinds of people to e-mail and call Kathleen, to Nick's utter irritation. Most of them seemed deranged or malicious, but there had been a few who were obviously sincere. Kathleen decided that this girl was probably lying, but she wasn't completely sure yet. "I'm afraid Andrew doesn't have a phone. If you'll give me your name and contact information I could send him an e-mail, though I don't think he checks it too often."

"I . . . That's not going to work!" The caller sounded petulant now, and the bubbling noise surged for a moment. Maybe there was something wrong with the connection? "Are you sure you don't have a way I can call him? I have something really important to tell him about Luce. Like, I know he'd want to know, okay?"

Kathleen bristled at the girl's snappish tone. "Andrew doesn't have a phone," she repeated. "You can't call him. And I honestly have no idea where he is now." The last statement wasn't entirely true; he'd sent her a brief e-mail two days before from Portland. "Your name is?"

"Catarina," the girl announced. "Luce was practically my best friend. I know all about her, like how she lived in that van while her dad was still a bum, and how her mom died when she was four. And I know *exactly* what her uncle did to her."

Much as Kathleen was starting to dislike the caller, this was enough to make her hesitate. Andrew hadn't mentioned any of that in the video they'd made together, but it did correspond quite well with what he'd told her privately. "I suppose I could give you his e-mail address if you'd rather write to him directly."

"I need a *phone number*," the girl sulked. "But—okay, you really don't have one? I guess I'll take his e-mail, sure. Maybe they can do something with that. Hold on. I have some paper . . ."

"*They?*" Kathleen thought. Then she heard something in the background that sent an unaccountable chill through her heart.

A splash.

Then another one, as if the girl was thrashing around in a bathtub. But it would be absurd to think that . . .

"Where are you calling from?" Kathleen heard herself ask shrilly. All at once her hands were trembling violently, and her body felt cold and hollow and as full of echoes as that watery space where—

"Wait. He said if you started getting suspicious, I should just . . ."

Kathleen's hands jerked strangely as she tried to disconnect the call.

Her twitching thumb missed the button. The phone dropped and skidded face-up across the kitchen table, coming to rest against the vase of lilacs. And all at once the calm afternoon air was streaked by an unimaginable sound, a terrible metallic sweetness that buzzed through her ears and tore at them. *Power*, Kathleen thought in confusion. *Power to reclaim Eileen, to punish anyone who ever hurt Eileen, anyone who tried to get in our way . . .*

Power was beauty, power was the photons pummeling her with astounding vitality, power was her body's atoms all waking up at once and pealing together like a million bells.

Kathleen didn't know when she'd picked up the phone again. She squeezed it to her ear until her skull seemed charged by that music, until a stampede of notes bit at her brain and goaded it. It was exhilaration beyond anything she could have dreamed, but it was as intolerable as it was thrilling: intolerable, Kathleen realized vaguely, because she hadn't yet reached to truly *claim* this power and this brilliance. It was all rightfully hers, every spark of it, though someone seemed to be trying to steal it from her. If she didn't reach *it* in time . . .

Kathleen couldn't have said quite what *it* was. She had an impression one instant of a castle made of stinging light, and in the next moment the castle morphed into a sort of crystalline, thundering horse with shifting facets, Eileen swinging on its back and calling to her.

It didn't matter to her that she didn't know exactly *what* it was, this electric bliss that the music kept promising her. She knew she had to hurry before she lost it forever. Most important, she knew exactly *where* it was waiting for her.

Out the kitchen door, down the sloping street, why, she was already walking—no, running, no, it was better to walk casually in case anyone else realized what she was after and got there first—the phone still crushed against her ear and the blood in her head throbbing fiercely in time with the song.

Orange sunset light exploding everywhere, astonishment flaring in the trees, wide laughing mouths raining down from the blossoms . . .

Even through the unbearable music pounding at her ear Kathleen could still hear a sound that told her the promise would soon be fulfilled. Waves, she could hear the waves. They were the charging hoofbeats of an infinite horse assembled from moving diamonds. In the horse's heart Eileen was waiting, whispering. *"Keenie, hurry up hurry up hurry up! I've been waiting for you for so long!"*

Kathleen turned a corner and saw the ocean as she'd never seen it before: countless blazing geometric planes, all transfiguring into momentary birds and stars and armies . . .

Someone who Kathleen knew had been a close friend of hers quite recently, maybe even yesterday, came up and started yammering stupidly about something and then looked hurt as Kathleen shoved past her . . .

The music and the sea were almost together now. When they finally met they would merge and expand, and Kathleen would ride with her sister in the quick of the miracle. She couldn't stand waiting anymore; she started running right down the center of the street, dodging cars, then out onto the long dock where she'd had her first glimpse of what *could* be . . .

Just for a moment that astonishing music paused, replaced by a weary sigh from the phone. "I wish you'd finish up," a girl's voice complained. "I'm getting *bored*."

Kathleen veered into a railing, gasped, and looked at water that was suddenly just water. She felt a frigid internal touch; something corrosive and evil fingered her heart. What was she *doing?*

The singing started again.

Eileen's face became as huge as a cloud; it had endless changing angles, all of them sharp with glory; her mouth opened wide in greeting.

Kathleen vaulted over the railing. She felt her sister's teeth close in.

They were very cold.

* * *

General Prudowski spread the photos in front of Secretary Moreland—satellite photos of the ocean near San Francisco taken over the previous three nights. The photos were utterly unbelievable; it was an insult to Moreland's intelligence that Prudowski was forcing these images on him at all, let alone insisting that Luce Korchak must be responsible for those watery, convoluted ramparts rearing out of the Pacific. He began wondering how he might teach the general a lesson.

The general wouldn't stop jabbering insolently about mermaids working together, and about some *plan* he had for stopping them. Maybe it would be simplest to agree, before his confusion became too obvious.

* * *

In a dorm room in Boston a chubby, sweet-faced, gold-skinned girl sat on her bed with her arms wrapped around her knees. She'd cut class that morning for the first time in her life, telling her roommate that she was nauseous and might be getting stomach flu. The nauseous part was true enough, but she knew flu wasn't the reason she felt so awful.

A camera rested on her bedspread with its pattern of cartoon cats, and Gigi looked at the cats to avoid looking at the camera. For the last seven years she'd managed mostly to ignore the memories of the afternoon her mother had drowned, the afternoon her own life had been saved so inexplicably; at least, she managed to ignore them as long as she worked all the time and blasted abrasive music to drown out the music in her head; at least, until she had to go to sleep.

But now . . . *I bet you don't want them all dead any more than I do.* Now the scruffy-looking man from that damned Internet video kept talking in her thoughts, trying to persuade her to do something thoroughly reckless.

"They killed my *mother*," Gigi argued aloud. Her mother had taken her out on a whale watching trip for her birthday, but they hadn't seen whales. "And their songs—it's like I've had some kind of brain disease ever since. Why would I make a fool of myself in public for them?"

So I'm here to ask . . . Then there'd been the unbearably beautiful music that made her want to die from the sheer force of her joy, as if she'd finally understood that the only way to love life enough was to end it. The crash, the wild deep water. *If that's you, and some mermaid saved your life before* . . .

Gigi thought of the astonishing face that had suddenly appeared next to hers in the water; it had belonged to a girl whose skin gleamed with subtle golden glow and whose body coiled away into a pinkish gold tail. The girl had looked distinctly pissed off, and she'd hesitated for several long seconds as bubbles oozed from Gigi's lips, staring at her as they descended together. Then with a sudden angry shake the mermaid had grabbed her and dragged her back to the surface, glaring furiously at the other mermaids who still trilled their incantations to the sinking crowd.

"Queen Yuan?" one of them had called out, more bewildered than indignant. "What are you *doing*?"

The mermaid called Queen Yuan hadn't answered, just taken off swimming with Gigi clutched in her arms. Gigi had gagged up salt water and wrenched her neck to take in as much as she could of the mermaid's impossibly lovely face. The music still throbbed through her, and it didn't even occur to her that her mother was dying.

Three of the mermaids followed them, calling to Yuan in coaxing voices. "Yuan, come on! You know we don't want to expel you!" And: "Yuan, she's just human! Please, *please* let us drown her. Do it for me?"

Yuan never answered them, just surged on through the waves with a bitter, stubborn expression, her black hair fanning through the pearl gray water. How long had they gone on like that before Yuan shoved her roughly onto a sandy shore, beating Gigi with her tail to make her get up? The golden fins smacked at her face, then her legs, while Yuan snarled, "Run! Stupid human, run! Inland! *Now!*"

Get up on this Internet and say so . . .

"I'll never live it down," Gigi argued back. "I'll spend the rest of my life being that dumb girl who will make up any whacked-out thing to get attention. Mike will probably break up with me. And, seriously, you think that's going to help me get into graduate school?"

What price had Queen Yuan paid for rescuing her, though?

Gigi wiped the tears from her face and picked up the camera, balancing it on her knees and staring at the empty black lens. She inhaled slowly twice then tapped a button, gritting her teeth as a small red light blinked on. "Hi. I'm Gigi Garcia-Chang and I'm here to answer Andrew Korchak's call for testimony from people whose lives were saved by mermaids . . ."

It got a little easier after that.

18

Kraken Rising

Luce woke up at sunset, when a young mermaid whose name she didn't know stopped by Catarina's hammock to give them a small heap of oysters she'd brought back from deeper in the bay. Yuan had given the job of collecting shellfish to crews of the smaller girls, who went foraging every day with scraps of net slung over their shoulders and then came back to distribute their hauls. Cat fell back asleep as soon she'd finished eating, but Luce slipped out from under the warehouse to watch the sun sinking behind the hills and jagged factories of the city. She didn't know why she felt so sad. Training was going remarkably well, and everyone seemed happier and less anxious. Behind her an encampment that now held well over two hundred mermaids drowsed and chatted and wove more hammocks to accommodate all the new arrivals, and there were many more members of the Twice Lost Army scattered around the bay. Luce couldn't help realizing how much most of them trusted her. Somehow without even knowing what she was doing, she'd found a kind of destiny.

Luce hadn't told them what Seb had said about that video she'd accidentally starred in. It seemed like too much to explain, but Luce had to admit to herself that it might be an important development. In fact, she still hadn't told anyone except Imani about Seb at all.

Millions of people had watched her swimming out from under that dock. They'd seen her hesitate as she considered trying to get a message to her father and then turn back to the sea as she rejected the idea. But maybe, just maybe, her father was one of the millions who'd seen the video. Maybe she'd managed to let him know she was alive after all.

Maybe someone whose name Luce refused even to think had seen it too. He'd know that all his scheming to get her murdered had failed, and maybe he'd remember what it had felt like to kiss her and brush his hands around her face.

Maybe he'd feel sorry for what he'd done.

The problem with entertaining these fantasies, even briefly, was that they made her miss *him*. It was disgusting to realize that she could miss someone like that, but all at once his scent and warmth and glance came back to her like sensual wraiths. He'd seemed so tender sometimes; it was still hard to believe that he could bring himself to inform on her.

He must have, Luce reminded herself sternly. How else could the government have learned so much about her?

Even as she wondered about Dorian Luce's eyes kept reflexively scanning the bay. White houses spilled down the clefts between yellow hills on the far side. Bridges crossed the horizon, rusty cranes shaped like skeletal horses loomed, and a few small boats puttered on water lacquered gold and violet by the evening sky. The noise of their engines reverberated faintly while the gulls cried above. Certainly there was nothing out there that resembled the black silent boats used by the divers, but somehow she wasn't reassured.

They'd been incredibly lucky so far, Luce thought. The only real question was how long their luck would hold.

* * *

It was after midnight when Yuan sent her messengers darting out to all the secret mermaid camps around the bay to assemble them for that night's training. Luce smiled as she watched Yuan slipping among the pilings, quick and efficient, giving everyone their instructions. Yuan seemed so much more hopeful now that she had a job to do, and she was impressively good at it. "Yuan?" Luce called.

Yuan swirled to a halt in front of her, black hair swinging in the water, and saluted with a touch of comic exaggeration. Only a touch, though. "Hey, general-girl! Whazzup?"

Suddenly they were both giggling. "Um, snap to, lieutenant-babe." Luce felt a little self-conscious; she'd never really been this silly with anyone before except for maybe her father. But she found herself enjoying it. "Yeah, girl, I got some *orders* for you. You better jump!"

Yuan whipped her tail and spiraled straight up out of the water, knocking her head against the underside of the pier. "Ow! Oh, jeez . . ."

"Are you okay?" Luce asked.

"Oh, sure." But the blow had knocked Yuan's exuberance out of her. "What do you need me to do?"

For a few seconds there Luce had felt so *young*; she already missed it. "I think we need to start posting sentinels during training. A big circle of them, pretty far out."

Yuan was rubbing her head, and she suddenly looked very serious. "I was wondering if I should suggest that, yeah. We should assign a different division to guard duty every night so everyone still gets to practice singing."

"Good idea," Luce agreed. She was vaguely impressed that Yuan had started calling the groups "divisions" too. "And Yuan? Not all the guards should stay on the surface."

Yuan looked surprised. "How do you mean? We'll see the boats coming from far enough away to get everyone out of there."

"But . . . I don't know what they could do, Yuan, but what if they sent a submarine or something? We need a ring of guards on the surface and another ring maybe, well, twenty yards down? Just in case they come at us from below." *Like orcas*, Luce thought. *Like what Seb said the navy would do if the kraken was rising.*

Yuan considered that. "It seems like if they got close enough to do that we would notice."

"Maybe we would, but just in case?" Sometimes Luce experienced a kind of tidal sense that Nausicaa was there with her. She felt that way now. It seemed to her that she was following the advice Nausicaa would give her in this situation.

Yuan shrugged. "You're the general, Luce. And, hey, should we figure out a special alarm-call?"

They talked that over for a few minutes. Neither of them was sure anyone would notice the windy call mermaids usually used as an alarm over the sound of the entire Twice Lost Army singing together, and they settled on a series of piercing trills instead. Bex joined them, along with several other girls Luce barely recognized, though Yuan clearly did. Luce still couldn't get used to the nervous, admiring way a lot of the Twice Lost looked at her.

"It's getting late," Yuan said. Her voice was uncharacteristically soft. "Shouldn't we be heading out, Luce?"

Luce glanced back into the dimness and realized that dozens of mermaids were flicking expectantly in the water. They dived, all staying near the bottom to keep out of sight, and headed into deeper waters: first under the Bay Bridge then around downtown and a tall hill topped by a single cylindrical tower. When they skimmed beneath the Golden Gate Bridge its starry lights draped like countless tangled ribbons on the fluctuating ceiling above them. It took them another twenty minutes to find the rest of the Twice Lost, already gathered and waiting to the south. They could just see the lights of the Cliff House beaming from the shore, but the waves on all sides were steep and dark.

With the new arrivals there must have been at least five hundred mermaids huddling together, their faces and shoulders forming a dimly phosphorescent raft that curved with the passing swells. Luce was startled, again, to see how much her army had grown. Yuan called the former queens together and explained the new system. Only Catarina was nowhere to be seen. "Lieutenant Cala, everyone in your division already has a pretty good handle on their water-singing, right? Okay, I'm going to assign you to lead guard duty tonight. Ten mermaids on the surface, ten mermaids twenty yards below, changing off at about half-hour intervals. Have you got that? And you'll need a signal for when it's time to switch positions that's really different from the alarm-call Luce and I worked out. It's like this." Yuan demonstrated, her voice piercing against the low roar of the sea and the dim chatter of the assembled girls. "Everybody? You've got to get this right, because you'll each be in charge of teaching it to your division."

Suddenly the night shuddered with the unearthly, metallic trilling of the alarm as everyone tried it. Luce floated, feeling almost irrelevant with Yuan working so efficiently to keep things organized. She kept staring around. The Pacific looked almost too vacant, the sky too cavernous.

"Did you guys notice anything?" Luce asked suddenly as the harsh cries died away. "I mean, before we got here?"

"There've been a few more boats than usual, I think, General Luce." It was the auburn-haired mermaid Yuan had addressed as Lieutenant Cala. Her dark turquoise tail flurried just under the surface, pale green iridescence flashing on her scales. "Just yachts, but they came close enough that we got kind of nervous. We just hung out below the surface for a while and they all went away again. I think we're cool."

"Okay," Luce said, but then she realized she didn't mean it.

"Can we start practice?" Bex asked eagerly. "You know, I thought I loved singing when we did it to drown people. But the way we sing now—it's so, so, completely great and amazing! I *never* want to stop."

"Get the guards in place first," Luce said, and then flinched a little at the grim, paranoid tone of her own voice. What was *wrong* with her tonight? "And—sorry. You should just go ahead and start without me."

"Luce?" Yuan was looking at her worriedly. "Is something, like, wrong? You've been acting kind of jumpy all evening."

"Probably everything's fine," Luce said. Her voice sounded even worse this time: strained and phony. "I just—I don't know why, but I feel like we need to start being extra careful. I'll be back soon."

"You'd *better* come back! I mean, where are you going?" There was a shadow in Yuan's gaze that contradicted her sassy tone.

"Down."

"Just down?" Yuan tried to sound like she was kidding. "Send us a postcard, okay?"

"Please—just get the guards in place. Right now." Luce

looked around at her lieutenants. Most of them seemed vaguely shocked by her strange behavior, but Cala saluted crisply and she didn't even look like she was doing it as a joke.

Luce dived.

She could see in the dark, but in this darkness there was nothing much to see except for jellyfish and a few small bored-looking sharks. To her right she noticed one of the mermaid guards dropping and then hovering head downward, held in place by the steady rotation of her fins. Luce waved to her and kept going.

Above her the first voices leaped into fluid harmonies, and for a few seconds Luce was towed sharply backwards as the water streamed upward in thrall to the music. She fought her way to the side of the strange ascending current and kept swimming straight down. Her hands spread out in front of her as if she could feel the immensity of the space still opening below.

Shadow on shadow, tangled night on charcoal deeps. She was at least fifty yards below the surface now, maybe seventy. The water's weight pressed in on her. It was easy to start imagining things, to think that there were blots in that darkness that were somehow a little denser or a little darker than the rest. Of course there might be sea lions out hunting, and there were definitely more sharks gliding by. But here and there Luce began to think that there were dark shapes that weren't moving at all, and that seemed . . .

Well, that seemed wrong. Luce thought she detected black balls of shadow spaced far apart from one another. They were almost invisible against the blackness beyond and hovered with uncanny stillness.

Then her own rapid downward movement began to make it look like the shapes were rising just as fast as she was plunging.

No. They really *were* rising. In the nothingness below her

Luce's outstretched palm was suddenly crisscrossed by inexplicable lines of pain as fine as cutting wires.

Then Luce was reeling backwards, her tail whipping and balling up around her as those razor filaments cut at her fins. A piercing, ululating cry burst from her throat. She shrieked the alarm-call without pause as she lashed her way back toward the surface, those black spheres rocketing up around her just as fast as she could propel herself. Her frantic call reverberated through the water, breaking and echoing into a dozen different voices — or, no, those were the guards she'd posted below the surface, picking up the alarm like a relay.

Again and again the lashing of her tail sent traces of sharp pain through her fins. There was something sharp and impossible to see below her: some kind of cutting mesh. And it was rising as quickly as those dark spheres on all sides, jetting up so fast that even a mermaid couldn't outrace it.

The spheres were *pulling* it up.

There were four of them, positioned at the corners of an enormous square.

The song above her collapsed into confused quiet; only a few mermaids still seemed to be singing. Luce could just make out the shimmer of tails flashing wildly away in all directions, radiating outward like blurry fireworks still far above her head. Shock waves slammed her down again as the city of towering waves above dropped abruptly back into the sea. The blade-sharp mesh raked her fins even as Luce jerked her tail up in a coil around her body, and her alarm-call turned into a sustained scream. She couldn't swim up quickly enough to escape from the mesh, not with so much water pummeling down on her. She couldn't . . .

A few mermaids were still so consumed by their song of rising water that they remained oblivious to the chaos. Luce could hear the song reverberating just to her left. Without fully understanding what she was doing she flung herself in that direction, her scales goaded by those knifing wires.

Then the current spinning upward in the song caught her, and Luce was hurtling straight up, still screaming. Her body burst past the startled singers and up into midnight air. Suddenly Luce was turning far above the surface, watching hundreds of panicked mermaids scattering in widening circles like the ripples around a dropped stone. Huge waves released by all that falling water rode outward, sweeping away even the mermaids who were still too confused to swim. Just in time, because those awful black spheres were almost at the surface now, lifting their cruel net with them.

Most of the mermaids were outside the area enclosed by the spheres. Only a few dozen were caught, their song breaking into shrieks with the first touch of the mesh as it rose below them. In those brief moments while she rotated in space, Luce understood: the mesh was meant to drive the mermaids to the surface and trap them there, while—

She heard the beat of helicopter blades above her, and now she was plummeting right into the center of the net. Mermaids flopped strangely, stretched out on the surface of the water in their struggle not to graze those wires. Every tiny movement lacerated their fins, the skin of their backs, their faces. Luce saw her followers gasping and crazed, their bodies covered in a delicate tracery of trickling blood.

Most of the ones who'd escaped from the net had disappeared below the water, but some of the bravest fought their way back through the outracing waves and hovered nearby, gaping in horror while they wondered how to help their trapped comrades. As she crashed down into the net's center, Luce noticed Imani staring at her in desperation.

"Imani! To the bridge! Lead everyone back to the bridge!"

In the split second that followed, Luce saw Imani hesitate.

She saw how much Imani wanted to ignore the order and try to help Luce instead. In that moment Luce felt nothing but a single explosive wish: that Imani would *abandon* her.

Then she saw Imani nod in assent, her eyes wide and stunned.

"Start the blockade! Now! Imani, go!"

There was a rattling noise, and Luce turned in time to see the first blast of machine gun fire cut through Bex in a line that began at her shoulder and slanted straight across her heart. A dozen jets of blood sprayed from Bex's opening chest, and her shoulders tipped away from her torso as if they were hinged. Luce saw pale eyes watching through the domed window of a round black machine.

Those sleek, compact submarines would be harder to knock out of the way with waves than a boat would, Luce realized. They were designed to travel through buffeting undersea currents, to resist the water's force. The mermaids around her were screaming in shock, and the helicopter was swooping down again.

And Luce was howling to the water, calling it to save them. She tried to calm herself and concentrate on the submersible sphere where those pale eyes gaped. At first Luce's wave lifted the nearest sphere, bringing cutting mesh right against her flesh and the flesh of the mermaids around her. More screams came, jarring through Luce's head and making it harder to focus on the water.

She had to drive the water *outward*. If she could break even one corner of the net, they would all be free to tumble out into the ocean and escape.

A fist of water, bulging and glassy, wrapped around the black sphere, and Luce's shriek-song rose higher and fiercer as she strained to force the sphere back and snap the net. The water only seethed and eddied around the sleek metal sides, unable to get a grip on it.

Streams of bullets sliced the air again, and at least two more mermaids ruptured around lines of flying blood. Luce knew she couldn't look, couldn't gasp; she could only keep *singing*.

Something like a scroll of living fire moved in the water below her, and Luce heard another voice joining her voice, entering into it and expanding it until the dome of water covering the submarine pulsed white with foam. That net had to be made of something extraordinarily strong, Luce realized, but now she heard it start to creak in shrill protest. There was a whiny snapping noise, and suddenly the sharp wires were dropping away beneath her. The sphere rolled back and downward, its motors snarling, and Luce saw its glass dome implode.

"Everyone, roll!" Luce heard herself screaming. "Roll out of the net! Dive down!"

At least twenty tangled mermaids were spilling from the net with her. The water below them was quick with gray shapes. White spreading teeth were already coming at her, and Luce barely managed to jerk out of the way.

A froth of sharks leaped against them, maddened by all the blood. Luce felt herself jostled by slippery skins. Three sharks fought over a bullet-riddled mermaid, fangs tearing into her tail even as it trembled and turned back into human legs. Luce tried to lunge for the dying girl, to somehow drag her away from the slashing teeth, but something had a grip on her shoulders. She was being dragged rapidly backwards, down and away from the frenzied sharks and the noise of machine gun fire still rattling above the waves.

"Luce, come *on*! You have to lead them away from this!"

Luce turned and red-gold hair swirled into her face.

Mermaids were squirming free of that scrum of sharks and clouding blood, whipping away into deeper water. But Luce hesitated. What if there were wounded mermaids in that mess who could still be saved? It didn't seem likely at this point, but—

"Luce, if you don't call everyone to follow you now, more of them will die!"

Luce looked at Catarina in a daze and then realized that she was right. Her own arms were laced by lines of seeping blood as thin as paper cuts, all stinging horribly from the salt water, and below them the gray forms of hundreds of sharks were lancing upward. They could outswim them, but they'd have to move fast.

"To the bridge!" Luce screamed. "Follow us! To the bridge!"

Her voice echoed through the dark sea, and mermaids who'd scattered began to race back to her. Luce threw herself into movement, her injured tail lashing out behind her. Mermaids streaked around her, their dimly shining arms reaching forward into nothingness, their fins kicking. Luce whipped her tail until it ached, listening all the time for the sound that might save them: the song of the Twice Lost Army. If they were holding a giant wave up right under the Golden Gate Bridge, Luce was almost sure the humans wouldn't dare to attack them again.

But . . . she heard only silence. Or not even silence, but the sound of air battered by what must be several helicopters now. They must have planned to catch the entire Twice Lost Army in that net and machine gun all of them together.

Maybe she'd asked Imani to do the impossible. Maybe the Twice Lost had dashed away in a hundred random directions, helicopters whirling above and picking them off whenever they came up for air . . .

Maybe nobody would be waiting for them at the bridge, and the wounded remnant that was following her now would find themselves helpless and alone. There were about twenty mermaids racing along with her, twenty-five at most: without the others they wouldn't be able to raise enough water to create a credible threat.

And without a threat it would be just like Catarina had said: they wouldn't last an hour. Should she order everyone to turn around and scatter through the ocean? They would if she told them to, Luce knew. They could give up the fight and try to find caves to hide in, at least for a while, at least until the divers tracked them down.

Was that a faint glow in the water up ahead? It might be the lights of the Golden Gate Bridge blurring and fragmenting in the water. But the glow had a green moonish cast that didn't look like electric light, and it seemed to be stirring in a long curving line, several yards below the surface, spanning most of the Golden Gate.

And then, electric lights could never make a *sound* like that: a low swell of rising music so sweet and wild that Luce's heart seemed to expand into infinite space. Even after all the horrors she'd witnessed that night, even with Bex and the others ripped to shreds behind her, Luce was suddenly suffused by an unbearable joy that was also profound grief, and she was *singing*.

Singing into the other voices even as those voices opened inside the water. Each voice blossomed inside the next, flowers inside flowers, or stars bursting inside other stars. Now Luce could see Yuan racing back and forth, pulling stragglers to fill the empty spaces in the long row of mermaids. Cala was hugging Jo, coaxing her to join the song. It didn't look like the entire Twice Lost Army, but Luce guessed that at least half of them had assembled there. And there was Imani, her head thrown back, her voice vaulting above the other voices and calling them to rise inside the gleaming wall of water . . .

Water that shuddered, flexed, bowed for a moment as if it might come crashing down again . . . Then stood up in a huge fluctuating ribbon so tall that it brushed against the underside of the Golden Gate Bridge, so long that it stretched across at least two-thirds of the channel. Luce broke through the surface to see it, suddenly utterly unafraid.

A line of stilled headlights needled the dark. All the cars had stopped where they were. People were getting out, standing in small confused clusters against the railings. Luce hoped the music wouldn't hurt them. But what they were hearing wasn't the mermaids' death songs, after all, and Seb had heard her sing to the water without it doing him any harm. He'd even said it had *helped* him.

Probably they'd be okay.

Ten or twelve helicopters vibrated above, their searchlights swinging wildly across the standing wave-wall, and Luce turned to watch them. All the beams together made her think of a giant spider with legs made of spindly light. Then one searchlight pivoted, raced along the frothing surface, and shone straight into her face. She stared back. The light blinded her and she couldn't tell where she was looking, but she did her best to aim her gaze into the pilot's eyes. Would he open fire?

The helicopter chattered on unmoving, and Luce went on singing. Around her more of the mermaids in that long chain kept surfacing, singing with her as they faced the guns above. Luce lifted her arm, still etched by hairline streaks of congealed blood, smiled at the pilot, and waved.

19

The News

Andrew looked at the drugstore's cash register and sighed. The clerk had turned away, absentmindedly leaving the cash drawer ajar. It would be so easy to take advantage: just one quick forward flick of his wrist and he'd have enough for a few days' travel. His skin was almost crawling with the desire to reach out, to casually turn and walk away with bills stuffed in his pocket.

Except, well, if he kept on stealing then how was he ever going to make a decent life for Luce, once she was finally human again? And say Kathleen e-mailed him one day and told him that she'd decided to get a divorce? If that happened how was he supposed to be good enough for her? He was almost positive that Luce and Kathleen would be crazy about each other. Luce would read every last one of Kathleen's books, she'd help out in the garden, she'd grow up and go to college and not waste her potential the way he had.

Because there had to be some way to turn Luce back. He refused even to consider the possibility that there wasn't.

He balled his hands into fists and swung his body out the door. Didn't even snag a goddamn candy bar. It was such unaccustomed behavior that he found it almost disquieting and he shuffled his feet aggressively to make the feeling go away.

On the opposite side of the drab street a small crowd had gathered in front of an appliance store. It was weird to see people bunched together like that in this drowsy little town. That store must be having a hell of a sale. Not having anything in particular to do, he wandered over to see what was going on.

The crowd seemed to be standing in shocked stillness, watching a scene playing out on a dozen televisions at once. Andrew's first thought was that it had to be some kind of big-budget Hollywood movie, the kind with incredible special effects, because, well, those screens all showed what appeared to be a huge glassy wave standing upright under the Golden Gate Bridge. That couldn't be real, simply. But if this was a movie, it was awfully slow paced. The wave fluttered and swayed near its summit, but other than that it didn't seem to move much. A crowd of people pressed against the bridge's railings, staring down, backed by rows of cars that weren't going anywhere either.

There was no sound through the window, but a news ticker scrolled relentlessly along the bottom of the screen: "San Francisco's standing tsunami, now at hour six. The wave appeared at 3:28 this morning, accompanied by unexplained music. Police have been attempting to evacuate the bridge, but they are meeting with resistance from the crowd. We are awaiting further reports."

"Is that some kind of joke?" Andrew asked. For some reason, the lingering music that always throbbed on in his head seemed to be getting a little louder. The mermaids' songs he'd heard that time had made him pass out; it was something about the unbearable way that Luce's voice had dueled with the strange mermaid's. But didn't this look a bit like something he remembered from the moment before he'd lost consciousness?

"It's real," a big gray-haired woman said sadly. She didn't turn her eyes from the screen as she spoke. "It's real, but nobody knows what's going on. There was some talk about a lot of people spotted down there in the water, but that doesn't stand to reason either."

"Sure doesn't," he told her. Unless whoever was in the water weren't *people*, or anyway not people in the strict sense of the word.

He had only a few dollars left and he wasn't about to shame himself by calling Kathleen collect. But he absolutely had to talk to her about this, right away. He had to know what she thought, and as he walked briskly away to hunt for a pay phone, an imaginary conversation was already playing in his mind: *"You're seeing this, Kath? You think that's them? It's got to be. I've got to get down there!"*

And then the words he knew he couldn't say: *"You should come with me. Please come with me. I know I ain't done right so far with my life, but now . . ."*

"Now," he murmured to himself. It had gotten pretty hard to find pay phones since everybody had a cell these days, but there was one behind the plate glass of that Laundromat down the way. He broke into a run, praying that the lousy thing wasn't busted and scrounging through all his pockets for quarters.

It wasn't Kathleen who finally answered, though. "It's you," Nick said with rough hostility. "You'll be proud to hear how meeting you has worked out for Kathleen. A thirty-nine year-old woman with everything to live for doesn't drown herself that way out of nowhere!"

Andrew couldn't understand what Nick was talking about. Who had drowned?

* * *

Ben Ellison spent the night trying to pack up his office as calmly as possible. After twenty-three years of devoted service to the FBI, it was hard to accept that he deserved to be fired so abruptly. Heaps of papers slid from the desk and cascaded onto the floor in terrible confusion. Only the images streaming live from his laptop provided any real satisfaction. The government's efforts to keep Operation Odysseus secret—to keep the very existence of the mermaids secret—had evidently come to a dramatic end. The media was going to be bombarding the White House with impossible questions now. Reporters would strike out and investigate on their own, too. There was no way Moreland would get through this debacle unscathed.

Ellison had been kept in the dark about the maneuvers of the previous night, but it seemed clear from the helicopter gunships wheeling in disorder above the bridge that there had been a major assault on the mermaids. It was also apparent that the attack had failed in spectacular fashion. Looking at that wall of water gleaming in the morning light, Ellison knew he didn't owe Dorian the promised phone call. Lucette Korchak was alive and free and wreaking havoc.

Ellison observed with relief that these mermaids obviously weren't trying to kill anyone. A vast crowd of easy victims lined the bridge, mouths agape and eyes staring. This Luce seemed to be too media-savvy—or possibly, possibly she was actually too good-hearted—to allow the mermaids with her to sing all those awed, defenseless humans to their doom. And that was precisely the kind of move on her part that Moreland would have no idea how to handle. It was utterly unpredictable, bold and daring and brilliant.

Bone-tired as he was, Ellison couldn't keep a hard, brutal grin off his face.

Whose side was he on, anyway?

* * *

Dorian woke up to Theo shaking his shoulder. "Sorry to bother you before noon, good sir, but the world is ending."

Theo's tone was ironic enough that Dorian didn't immediately feel worried. "Yeah? Somebody release a herd of stampeding dinosaurs or something?"

"Tsunami. Epic scale. If you can call it a tsunami when it just stands there. In San Francisco."

That made Dorian sit up abruptly, his heart quickening with hope. In the next moment he realized how absurd his idea was. Luce's ability to control water with her voice was impressive, but he was fairly sure she couldn't do *that*. "How big is it?"

"*That's* what you want to know?" Theo laughed. "Not something reasonable? Like, oh, 'How the fuck is that possible?' It's big enough to block off everything under the Golden Gate Bridge, is how big it is."

Dorian was halfway out of bed, hauling on the jeans he'd dropped on the floor the night before.

"It's on the news?" Dorian was groping for a T-shirt. There was one around somewhere.

"I know it's crazy, but the media does seem to be finding the event rather noteworthy, yeah. My mom can't even talk straight, she's so shocked."

Dorian was dressed and on his feet, stumbling after Theo down to the den, where Amanda Margulies sat on the green leather sofa in her yoga clothes. She was clutching a cup of coffee with a veil of cold scum on its surface, and drying tears streaked her face. Theo sat down next to his mother and hugged her warmly.

Dorian stared at the huge TV screen: on it there appeared a wall of bright water with fluted, faintly pulsating sides. The delicate rust red curves of the Golden Gate Bridge swanned above the unmoving wave, and in the background he could see the open ocean. Cordons of police boats were keeping a good distance from the bridge, shooing back the various sailboats and kayaks that jostled forward, trying to get closer to the action. And, above the clatter of gathered helicopters and the excited babble of the newscasters, there was a distinct musical thrum, sweet and immense and enthralling . . .

Dorian realized that the music was very much like something he'd heard before, except this sound was incomparably vaster and more complex: a rich, nuanced swell that could only be hundreds of magical voices thrilling together.

"What are those people doing?" Dorian suddenly asked. At the edge of the crowded bridge, a news crew was engaging in some kind of fussy activity involving ropes and pulleys. Whatever they were up to, it looked like a bad idea.

"Looks like they're lowering that camera guy over the side. Trying to get some kind of close-up? But it's just going to look like more water . . ."

The cameraperson was strapped into a harness, and his unwieldy camera was secured to his front with various cables. He clambered up onto the side of the bridge and then dropped slowly, twitching and kicking twenty feet below the line of spectators. They watched as he adjusted himself and trained his camera on the shimmering wall of water.

For a few minutes nothing else happened. There was only the

crowd standing bone-still, enraptured by that unearthly music, the swaying figure of the cameraperson, the fractured diamonds of sunlight all over the water-wall. But nothing new was happening, Dorian told himself. The situation might drag on for hours without any change. So why couldn't they look away?

Then—then something *did* happen. A small figure appeared at the wave's base, arms raised as if it were diving. But the figure was *inside* the water, bending into strange refractions. Then it twisted, leaped upward . . .

And the figure wasn't *human*. Even at this distance that was obvious.

The chattering commentators abruptly fell silent while next to Dorian Theo let out a kind of shrill, astonished moan. Of course they'd all watched the video of Luce—but this was different. No one could even pretend to believe that what they were seeing now was faked.

The leaping body on the screen rippled away into a long, lashing tail. The tailed figure vaulted smoothly up through the wave's core and came to an unsteady stop just in front of the dangling cameraperson. He reeled against his straps, legs flailing helplessly. Then he stopped kicking, seeming to lapse into mesmerized calm.

The newscasters had started babbling again, but they weren't making a whole lot of sense. "In just a minute . . . waiting for the feed to come in . . . truly an incredib—more in just a . . . bringing you a closer look at . . ."

The mermaid in the wave had something white in her right hand, and she fluttered it as a gesture of reassurance. Her tail looked more or less the right color: a light, silvery jade green.

"Trying to communicate . . . but does that mean . . . does that mean the same thing it would for us? Peaceful intentions?"

The mermaid leaned forward, parting the water in front of her face as if it were a curtain. Dorian's heart was pulsing so quickly that it felt like some small sick bird spasming in his chest.

Then the image shifted abruptly as the close-up came on. She was wearing a tattered black bikini top; Dorian had never seen her wear human clothes before, only kelp leaves. Her arms and body were crosshatched with razor-fine wounds, there was a scar on her shoulder and a notch missing from her right ear—and she was smiling so sweetly and vividly that Dorian choked.

Luce.

20

Saying Hello

Luce sang through the night, holding herself just below the surface with slight rotations of her fins and only pausing when she surfaced for quick inhalations. She was singing as the military helicopters jarring above them were joined by more and more helicopters with the logos of television networks on their sides. She was singing when the immense wave supported by the mermaids' voices turned into a furling sail of molten gold with the dawn light. Her voice webbed into the enchantment of those hundreds of gathered voices. Sometimes the music came to her like clouds of exalted laughter, sometimes as grief for the dead. But one thing was clear: for tonight at least they had won an astonishing victory. And as she had promised, they had won it without resorting to murder. Luce knew it was strange, but she felt a sense of profound triumph at the thought that the dead of that night were all her own followers, not more random humans.

Even the human soldiers, with the possible exception of that submarine pilot, hadn't died. Pharaoh's army would see that the mermaids weren't just mindless killers. And they'd see as well that the mermaids weren't about to wait around passively to get slaughtered. She'd turned her enemies into witnesses, and *that* was a victory.

It was well into the morning when Luce was shaken from her entrancement. Yuan's golden face was shining and determined, and her hand was on Luce's shoulder. "General Luce? You're off duty."

Luce didn't want to stop singing. The brilliance of her voice surging into everyone else's voices was too great, too astonishing. She kept the song going, her tone like liquefied sunlight.

Yuan looked a touch annoyed, but she was grinning at the same time. "Give it a rest, general, okay? You can come back soon. Anyway, you're already late for a strategy meeting with all your lieutenants. Except Cala—I'm leaving her in charge for a little bit."

Yuan's words reminded Luce that they weren't just playing at war. But the song was so overpowering that Luce had to struggle with her voice for a few moments before she could force it into silence. The music stopped and started in quick staccato outbursts before she finally mastered it, and Yuan laughed. "Okay," Luce managed.

"Yeah? You're all better now?"

Without the song thrilling through her, Luce was suddenly much too aware of the horror of the previous night. "Yuan? Do we know how many of us . . ."

Yuan reached out and hugged her. "We were at five eighty-three before the attack. Only about three hundred made it to the bridge at first, but a bunch more girls drifted back here during the night. We're at four twenty-two now. But the problem is—with everyone missing, we can't tell who died and who just panicked and swam off."

Luce recoiled a little. "I thought—I only saw a few of us get shot. Bex and maybe three girls I didn't know. I thought we were almost all okay! Yuan . . ."

Yuan hugged her tighter, her arms strong and comforting.

"Most of them are probably okay. I mean, they got really scared, but they'll come back once they calm down. And you have to remember, Luce, almost everybody would have died last night if you hadn't guessed—I seriously have *no* idea how you knew those submarines were coming, but I do know for *sure* that you're the reason so many of us are still alive. Okay?"

"I didn't know anything," Luce murmured. "It just *felt* like something was wrong."

"You can be sad later, okay?" Yuan said, but her voice was very gentle. "This is war. We need you to keep it together."

"Okay," Luce said breathlessly. "Okay." All at once she was struck by a realization that should have been obvious: now that the humans knew about them, that immense wave was the only protection they had.

Now that the wave was standing there, it had to *stay* standing. If there was any lull in the mermaids' singing, Luce knew they would be massacred almost instantly.

Yuan took her hand and guided her, keeping well below the water, toward a cluster of brick buildings with low docks on the shore of Sausalito.

Twenty of her lieutenants were already waiting in a circle beneath a broad, half-collapsing platform set on pilings. Catarina was there, her blazing hair fanning out across the water and her face blazing even brighter with a kind of exhilarated fury. Imani was beaming, her white lace kerchief tied over her short afro. And there was Graciela, looking almost crazed with joy, next to a freckled strawberry blonde Luce didn't recognize.

There was a brief pause while they stared at her, and Luce felt a familiar tightening in her stomach. Were they looking at her as if she was a stranger?

In the next instant there was a wild swirl of dozens of fins, and Luce found herself embraced on all sides.

"Luce! You figured it out! We *stopped* them!"

"They would have wiped us out if you hadn't . . ."

"I was so worried when you told us your plan. I can't believe it's working!"

"It's not just your singing. It's how you *think*, too. You're like a *real* general!"

"Hey, I haven't met you yet, Luce. But I'm ex–Queen Eileen, and that was just *awesome*."

Luce did her best to hug everyone back, trying not to cry. It was hard not to suspect that they were crazy to trust her this much.

Especially when she hadn't even been honest with them, really. She hadn't been lying, but she knew she'd been keeping too many secrets: about Seb, about the video . . .

And especially about what Seb had told her: that if she had anything to say, the humans might be ready to listen to her.

Even now that everything about mermaid life was changing—their whole world upended and the timahk hopelessly shattered—Luce couldn't quite shake the sense that there were some things a mermaid just shouldn't admit to doing. Talking to humans and saving them from the consequences of their own stupid behavior were both right at the top of the list. But Luce had never completely forgiven herself for lying to Dana about Dorian. She *couldn't* make that mistake a second time.

"I've got some things I need to tell you," Luce gasped out. Everyone fell silent almost instantly. Did they really think that what she had to say was so important? Luce told them the whole story: collapsing under that dock and swimming out the next day without caring that she might be seen, then her surprise at noticing a camera pointed at her. Rescuing Seb and everything he'd told her afterward.

There were a few shocked exclamations, a few sharply indrawn breaths, but at least no one told her off for behaving so dishonorably. Luce gazed around at them, wondering what they'd all say to her when the silence finally broke, and found that she could look at everyone except for Catarina. Cat was glaring at her with such obvious disappointment that Luce found it hard to meet her former queen's eyes.

"Well, everything is different now," Yuan said at last. "It actually makes sense strategically to try to get some humans on our side, right?" She sounded like she was arguing, though it wasn't clear whom she was trying to convince.

"If Luce had saved someone who *counted*, I might have to agree with you," Catarina announced. She spoke in a silky, disdainful tone that Luce hadn't heard since the days when Cat was queen. "But saving a dirty vagrant like that, only because she felt sorry for him? What possible use is that to us? No, Luce is too *impulsive*, too thoughtless—"

"He made me think about submarines," Luce pointed out, a little brusquely. "And talking with him gave me the idea about the bridge. You really think he's supposed to do *more* than that?"

"And he's why we know about the video too. If a lot of humans are already interested in Luce, then maybe they won't like it that the government is trying to kill her. Cat, I have this feeling that we're going to need all the help we can get, if any of us are going to *survive* . . ." Yuan had seemed so calm through all the craziness and violence that Luce was startled to hear the raw emotion surging in her voice.

"Look!" It was the mermaid who'd introduced herself as Eileen, pointing her freckled hand back in the direction of the bridge. "It looks like those humans are sending some guy over the side? What a weird thing to do!"

They all crowded together at the edge of the shadowed zone under the platform, watching while the cameraperson dropped in his harness. Luce realized that the camera would capture a beautiful image: the top of the standing wave leaped and fluttered, delicate wisps of foam spilling from its crest, while sheets of sunlight wavered on its flank.

"This is our chance!" Luce said, so suddenly that it took her a moment to realize what she'd meant.

"Our chance to do what, Luce?" Imani said softly just beside her, and Luce reached out and squeezed her shoulder.

"Our chance to talk to *all* of them," Luce explained. All her joy rushed back at once. Maybe there was loss and terror and trouble all around them, but she suddenly felt absolutely certain that the Twice Lost Army was doing better than anyone could have dreamed possible.

"Talking to *more* humans? Luce, can't you control yourself?" Catarina snapped.

"Talking to them is the whole *point*, Cat!" Luce's tail gave an abrupt swirl of excitement, and she grinned around at everyone, almost quaking with the force of her inspiration. Now that she knew exactly what she needed to do, she wasn't about to let Cat talk her out of it. "Hey, Imani? Do you think I could borrow your scarf for a few minutes?"

"Are you *serious*, Luce?" Imani asked. But her black eyes were gleaming with delight.

"One thing I know about Luce"—Yuan laughed—"if she says something that crazy, you better believe she means it!"

Almost everyone was giggling now, half-nervous and half-delirious. It was all just so *different* from anything mermaids had ever done before. It was strange to feel such happiness in the middle of a war, but Luce couldn't stop herself from laughing along with the others in sheer astonishment at her own daring.

"Of course I'm serious," Luce managed through her laughter. "I'm going to go up there and say hello. To every single human who's watching this!"

Extraordinary as that night and morning had been, Luce thought that what came next was the most wondrous thing of all. And yet it was so simple: just the glow on Imani's face as she reached back and untied her headscarf.

"Tell Pharaoh's army I said hello too, okay?"

"If you want to, Imani," Luce told her, "you can come up and tell them yourself."

* * *

Luce launched herself into the heart of the rising wave.

She rose above San Francisco Bay, her view of it wrinkled and disturbed by the glassy curves passing in front of her eyes. Skyscrapers warped and shimmered to her right, glass panes glittering like fish scales. The power of the mermaids' singing propelled her upward, and she had to use her tail only for balance. Tiny currents torqued and jarred around her, and she had to concentrate to keep herself from being flipped through complicated somersaults. She didn't want the humans to get the impression that she was out of control in any way. So much depended on the coming moments, and she had to be strong and graceful and persuasive.

After all, she was there to represent the Twice Lost Army.

Luce twisted to a halt ten feet in front of the cameraperson, jouncing a little with the water's irregular impulses. The man yelped and thrashed against his ropes as he caught sight of her. Luce couldn't help grinning to herself at his eyes rounded into astonished Os, his legs kicking as he tried to run through empty air. Funny as his panic seemed, she felt enough compassion to wave the white scarf. She didn't actually want him to be afraid of her.

In the widening sky behind him a dozen helicopters stuttered, but none of them appeared to be the heavy military helicopters that had attacked the night before. Luce looked again and saw that they were all pointing cameras of their own.

The cameraperson had stopped kicking and instead flopped weakly in his harness. But he wasn't looking at the white scarf; his eyes were locked on her face. The hungry adoration in his gaze almost sent Luce diving back to her friends, but then she remembered why she was there. She tipped her upper body forward until the water-wall sliced open around her face. It felt sleek and cool, like bubbling silk against her cheeks. Her fins flicked continuously to hold her in place.

"Hi," Luce called, raising her voice to be heard over the mingling rush of water and song.

At the sound of her voice his eyes bulged and he twitched again, his lips moving around the shapes of silent words. Then he seemed to find his own voice and screamed.

Luce jarred back in shock before she understood what he was shrieking: "A mike! A mike! Get me a microphone down here! Get a mike! Carol! Sam!"

This is our chance, Luce reminded herself. *This might be the best chance we'll ever have. If there's ever going to be peace . . .*

Was peace enough, though?

Now that the opportunity was in front of her, shouldn't she

try to save more than just her fellow mermaids? The mermaids weren't the only thing in danger, after all. She thought again of that field of death she'd seen on the seabed.

Above her there were confused shouts, a clatter of equipment, and then a jointed metal stalk leaned out into the air. It crooked halfway down like an insect's leg, and at its tip there was a large black microphone coming straight toward her face.

If she chose this moment to let her voice spiral into her death song, Luce realized, it could easily have an effect equal to a nuclear bomb going off. What was happening now was so extraordinary that countless humans must be watching her. If she sang that particular lethal melody, literally millions of people would probably drown themselves. The human governments would agree to whatever she asked out of sheer terror. Mermaids all over the world would expect nothing less of her. It would be terrible—but wasn't it possible that more lives would ultimately be saved if the war ended *now*?

The microphone lurched awkwardly forward, brushing right against her lips.

"Hi," Luce said again, her voice clear and definite—and completely free of any music. "We're not here to hurt anyone."

Something swished through the corner of her vision, and Luce noticed that she wasn't alone in the wave anymore. Imani was pirouetting in slow, elegant spirals on her right, and incredibly enough Catarina had swum up too and was hovering a few yards to her left.

Luce was looking to the cameraperson for a response, so she was surprised when the reply came from above her head.

"Who are you?" a woman's voice boomed, and Luce gazed up to see a carefully coifed woman in a cobalt blue suit bent over the railing clutching a megaphone. She looked both terrified and fascinated. Luce suddenly felt sorry for the woman, and a little heartsick that she'd even contemplated killing people like her.

"I'm General Luce. We're the Twice Lost Army. And these are two of our lieutenants, Catarina and Imani. We don't want to hurt anyone, and you don't need to be scared."

"Are you mermaids?" the woman bellowed back.

This was such an absurd question that Luce couldn't bring herself to answer. Instead she let her long body catch the movement of the water. She swam in suspended, curling loops for a few moments then pulled herself through the wave's flank to face the microphone again. Then she realized that the question was actually important: it was another chance to make the humans understand.

"We're mermaids now," Luce explained, "but we haven't always been. All of us used to be human."

That seemed to cause a minor uproar. Luce couldn't quite make out what the people above her head were saying; without the megaphone their voices blended with the babble of the water and the rich swell of music. But it sounded like there was some kind of debate going on.

"Why are you doing this?" the woman finally called. "You say you don't want to hurt anyone, but this wave is threatening San Francisco. How can you claim that's not an act of war?"

Luce thought about that for a moment and decided that her best choice was to be honest. "It *is* war," Luce agreed. The microphone swayed in front of her face, dark and somehow disquieting. "The human government has been killing mermaids all over the West Coast. Maybe in other places, too. They attacked us last night with submarines and helicopters, and some of us were machine gunned. We had to do something big to defend ourselves, to make them stop *shooting* at us . . ." For the first time since she'd faced the camera, Luce remembered the mesh of fine wounds covering her skin. "If we lower the wave now, they'll kill us all. We don't have any choice!"

Again there was consternation above her. The cameraperson squirmed, wide blue space crossed by bridges and hills glowing behind him.

He looked stunned by what she'd said. Maybe even appalled. Would other humans feel upset about the mermaids being gunned down too?

"So you aren't going to send this wave at San Francisco?" the woman yelled. Her hair was so stiff with gel that the wind only made it fidget a little.

"Not on purpose," Luce explained. "But if they attack us again we probably won't be able to stop it. We have to keep singing all the time to hold the water up." She spotted one of the military helicopters hanging far back against milky smears of cloud and nodded at it. "It looks like they already figured that out, right?"

More mermaids had joined Luce in the wave now. Delicate fins brushed Luce's shoulder as Yuan swept in a high arc above her head.

Now that they weren't keeping themselves secret anymore, the Twice Lost were obviously enjoying showing off for all the flabbergasted humans. Luce found herself grinning at the idea too: how the amazing beauty and power of the mermaids with her must be affecting their human viewers. Magic had ruptured the surface of their everyday world, and that magic was quick and alive and *talking back* to them.

The next moment, though, Luce was just as surprised as the humans must be.

"Do you know someone named Andrew Korchak?" the newscaster shouted.

Luce lost her balance in the wave and dropped a dozen feet. A writhing current caught her off-guard and flipped her before she was able to recover herself and swim up to the microphone again.

Her father just wasn't the kind of person most people *knew* about. Hearing his name from someone like this overly polished woman—that didn't make any sense.

"He's my dad," Luce finally managed—and then she glanced over at Catarina's outraged face, suddenly acutely aware that she'd never told Cat the story of how she'd found her father alive. "Is he okay?"

The woman ignored Luce's question. "Andrew Korchak issued a statement claiming that mermaids drown people. Is he telling the truth?"

Luce reeled in the wave's core, though this time she somehow kept herself from tumbling. Her *father* had said that? Her adored father was going out of his way to persuade everyone to hate mermaids, including his own daughter—just when the mermaids most desperately needed his help? The pain in Luce's chest and head was so wrenching, so *physical*, that her vision blurred for a moment. She wasn't sure what she was going to do next: scream out against his betrayal or crumple into heartbroken silence . . .

There's no reason not to speak of the truth, Nausicaa's remembered voice murmured in Luce's mind. And wasn't that all her father had done? Speak the truth?

But now, Nausicaa? Luce answered in her thoughts. *How could he do that to us now?*

Speak of the truth, Luce, Nausicaa told her. *If you want to save us, speak of the truth.*

"General Luce?" the woman bellowed. "Our viewers are waiting for your answer."

Luce pulled herself straight and looked into the camera. How could she make herself say this?

"It's true. Most mermaids do drown people." Luce hesitated then made a wild leap of faith. "If my dad says something, you can believe him. But *we* don't kill. The mermaids of the Twice Lost Army all promise never to kill humans except in self-defense. If we can change, that proves other mermaids can change too!"

"So you admit that mermaids are murderers. Why should we believe that you and your followers are any different?"

Luce glowered at the woman. "You can believe it because you're *alive* to believe it!" She almost pointed out how easily the Twice Lost could destroy every human within earshot then decided not to say anything about that. The impulse seemed less than diplomatic.

There were tears on her face, Luce noticed. That was all wrong. She shouldn't let the humans see her crying. Maybe, maybe, they'd think her tears were just droplets from the wave.

Voices buzzed chaotically above her. All she wanted now was to get away: away from the cameras. Away from the thought that her father might hate her. Away from Catarina's glare, and from the possibility that she'd let her army down by saying too much . . .

"General Luce?" the woman called again. "Obviously emotions are running very high at this . . . this historic moment."

"We have demands," Luce snapped. She felt half-sick from grief; the interview was getting to be more than she could bear. "We're keeping the blockade up until our demands are met. Until then everyone had better keep away from our camps. And"—she felt another stab of inspiration—"if any other mermaids out there hear about this, we could use your help! Join us."

"What are your demands? General Luce . . ."

Luce looked up at the woman with her rigid hair and shell-shocked expression. At this moment humans seemed pitiful to Luce, but they were also pretty infuriating.

"We have to think about it," Luce announced. "We'll send you a letter."

"But—"

Luce plunged. Her serpentine body flashed through what felt like a rising waterfall.

"Hey!" Imani called brightly into the mike. "I just wanted to say hi to everyone too!"

21

Voices Carry

Secretary of Defense Moreland was standing slack-jawed beside the president, a dozen generals, and half the members of the Strategic Affairs Council. He felt a shiver of icy anticipation as the microphone curved through blue air toward Lucette Korchak's face. He was sure she would sing. She would kill them all, and his heart felt both frozen and boiling at the prospect.

He told himself that it was too late to do anything about it. Sweat sleeked his palms and his mouth seemed to be crowded with brittle leaves.

His jaw fell even farther when Lucette opened her lips — and started speaking instead of singing. She sounded remarkably sweet, almost innocent, and not nearly as stupid as she should be.

Moreland was blindsided by the force of his disappointment — and for one split second of lucidity he recognized how insane his reaction was. He'd genuinely *wanted* her to kill everyone.

Then he forgot all about his own madness. There was another mermaid in the wave, a redhead, and Lucette Korchak had said the name Catarina. Another of the singers he'd heard on the recording, then: an irresistible prize, a flame-colored coin minted from fresh desire.

"When I saw that wave standing there I knew it was a game-changer," President Leopold grumbled. "But if everything this cute little *general* is saying is true, I think we're going to need a whole new board."

* * *

Andrew Korchak wasn't watching his daughter. Instead he was sitting on a park bench, sobbing so violently that the world pitched and swam in his eyes. He knew beyond all doubt that Kathleen would be alive now if she'd never glimpsed Luce. Kathleen had been trying to *help* the mermaids, and they had killed her. He was positive of that, even if he couldn't begin to guess how they had done it. It was worse than any treachery he could have imagined. And maybe it was his fault, too. Somehow those videos had brought Kathleen to the mermaids' attention.

He should have told Kathleen he loved her. While there was still time.

* * *

Seb perched on a folding chair in the community center housed in a church basement, other homeless and luckless people crowded around him. When Luce got to the part about mermaids changing their ways, Seb burst out laughing and cheering so loudly that t! volunteers ordered him to leave.

* * *

Gigi Garcia-Chang knelt with her cheek pressed to her TV screen. With one finger she followed the ever-shifting curves of Yuan's pinkish gold tail. She'd recognized her rescuer immediately, even after so many years. Until this moment, Gigi thought, she hadn't understood how terribly she'd been missing the mermaid who had saved her.

She was taking two summer classes, and then there was her part-time job in a café. Her responsibilities were a real impediment to just catching the next flight west.

But maybe she would anyway.

* * *

"Damn. How many guys do you want to bet are ordering sushi right now? Like, 'Hey, um, can you deliver this to the bottom of the Golden Gate Bridge? And, like, tell that *mermaid* I sent it'?" Theo was laughing uproariously, though from something dark in his eyes, Dorian thought his friend was trying to conceal wilder emotions behind this display of silliness.

Dorian slumped on the green leather sofa, biting his lower lip and hoping that Theo wouldn't notice his burning cheeks. His distress was partly provoked by bitter longing at the sight of Luce looking so proud and free and beautiful, and acting so brave. But that wasn't all he was feeling. He was also queasy with shame. He'd watched Andrew Korchak's appeal over and over, and he'd kept an obsessive watch on all the video testimonies that followed from it. But he hadn't quite worked up the nerve to post a video of his own.

And now—now it was way too late to do anything like that.

Within hours thousands of people—and mostly, Dorian thought hatefully, they would be young guys, and some of them would be way better-looking than he was—would be posting videos claiming they had been *personally* saved from drowning by General Luce. There would be declarations of love, offers of adoption, the works. Damaged and defiant as Luce was now, she was simply that enchanting. Adding his own video to that ruckus would just make him look like a total moron. At best it would be an exercise in pointless humiliation.

There had to be something else he could do, Dorian thought. Something to show her . . .

"But I'm the one who's going to get the date with her, because I know the secret. Mermaids can eat fish anytime they want, right? So the way to get their attention is obviously with *pizza* . . ."

Something to show her I deserve to get her back, Dorian thought grimly. *Something to prove to her . . .*

" . . . we could use your help!" Luce exclaimed passionately from the television. "Join us."

Her pale olive face gave off a subtle greenish shine. The glow shone brighter in the streaks of her tears. When they were breaking up Dorian had told Luce her problems weren't *real*; he'd told her she wanted to stay a kid forever so that she could avoid responsibility; he'd even blamed her for letting herself turn into a mermaid in the first place. And now here she was, injured and scared but still leading an army into this weirdly peaceful battle, doing what no mermaid had ever done before, while he sat on his ass.

"Or, you know? Maybe that black mermaid is even hotter. Yeah, check out that blue tail!"

"Theo?" Dorian snapped. "Could you possibly *shut up*?"

"I see no call for such an uncouth remark, good sir. I was merely expressing my sincere desire to send those exquisite mermaids a hot, cheesy pizza."

"It's a war!" Dorian growled. "Luce is wounded, okay? Her friends just got shot. She doesn't need your fucking pizza!"

What Luce needs, Dorian realized, *are allies.*

And he was ready to join her war.

* * *

A hazy pink glow filmed the water, slivered with turquoise by the ripples flowing smoothly toward the shore. Bell-shaped scarlet flowers cascaded down the cliff, lush mosses dripped, and a tiny waterfall raised a perpetual shimmering froth where it splashed into the cove. But for all the fantastical beauty around her, the emerald-tailed mermaid leaning on the shore looked somber and a little bored. Coils of black hair snaked thickly around her dark bronze shoulders, and her greenish black eyes were glazed with sadness. She'd already seen every possible permutation of beauty the world had to offer far too many times.

If the friend she was missing had been there with her, then she could have experienced this sunset as if for the first time, seeing the world with borrowed freshness and enthusiasm. But the odds that that particular friend was still alive were admittedly poor.

The waterfall's sleepy percussion changed its tone. The mermaid looked, without much interest, at a sudden fervor of bubbling, a slippery confusion of crosscurrents that beat and rose and gathered form . . .

This too was something she'd seen plenty of times before. The mermaid waited with morose patience for what she knew was coming. A new mermaid was about to appear, a metaskaza, stunned by the transformation and the devastation that had provoked it.

New fins flashed into existence under the water's disordered surface, and with them there appeared a girl with a long tail that swung erratically. Her scales were a lovely color somewhere between dove gray and lilac, gleaming with pearly iridescence. The tail went well with the metaskaza's coloring. She was a very pale blonde with deep gray eyes, and she sat up with her hands scrambling wildly into empty air. Her breath was heaving with terror and shock, and a single impossibly sweet note tore from her lips and ended in a sudden gasp.

The dark observer thought she might as well do the helpful thing: stay and talk this newly transfigured mermaid through her inevitable reaction to the change. The girl would be overwhelmed by denial, hysteria, grief . . .

She was genuinely surprised when the metaskaza displayed none of those emotions. Instead the blonde gaped wide-eyed at her own tail, hefting it uncertainly and letting it fall back again once, twice, three times. She looked amazed, yes, but not devastated or incredulous.

That was unusual, to say the least. Of course, if this girl was *sika*, someone born cold and void of true emotions, then she might not be capable of the usual responses. The dark mermaid twisted her head to check up on that possibility, peering from the corners of her eyes into the dark shimmering that winked around the blond girl's head. With a normal mermaid you could see the terrible incident that had chilled her heart to the point where she let go of her humanity; with a *sika*, cold from the beginning, there would be nothing to see.

The blonde wasn't *sika*. She'd been altered by one of those horrors that her observer regarded as simply wearisome routine.

"Oh my God!" the new mermaid exclaimed shrilly. "It's just like on TV!" Then she noticed that there was another mermaid watching her. "It is, right?" she asked. "This is just like on TV. And that video. I *knew* it was real!"

This situation wasn't just unusual, the green-tailed mermaid realized. It was utterly unprecedented. And she adored anything unprecedented no matter what it involved. "I don't know this video you speak of. But certainly, all of this is real."

"You *have* to know!" the metaskaza squealed. "And—oh, wait, can we swim that far? We have to get to San Francisco! How fast can we swim there?"

"To San Francisco? I can help you do this, yes. But why?"

"Like on TV yesterday! Didn't you *see* it?"

"I don't watch a great deal of television," the dark mermaid observed dryly.

She watched as realization, then embarrassment, flickered over the blonde's face. "Oh. Oh. Wait, so are you saying you don't know what's happening? You haven't heard about the Twice Lost Army?"

Things were only getting more interesting. "I've heard nothing of this, no. What is this army?"

"And you don't know about General Luce? We have to go *help* her!"

For the first time in several centuries, the green-tailed mermaid was briefly rendered speechless from astonishment. Her jaw dropped and her eyes widened. Within moments, though, she had recovered most of her poise. "*General* Luce?" Her look of surprise was rapidly mutating into one of absolute delight. "*General* Luce? So she still refuses to be called *queen*?"

"She's leading this mermaid army to stop the government from killing them. And there's this wave, and they're holding it up by singing, and she said on TV that they need other mermaids to come and help. *Please* . . ."

"Of course, you are right. Of course, we must rush to aid General Luce! With the next ship! I will show you how we can ride across unseen."

"Can't we just swim?"

"Not so far. We would drown. The first thing you must learn

is that you still need to breathe, and to breathe while you sleep. You must be careful of how deep or far you swim. Many new mermaids die of their ignorance. How are you called?"

"Oh. I'm Opal Curtis."

The green-tailed mermaid smiled at her warmly. "Welcome, Opal." She already liked Opal, quite a bit, for her impassioned, spontaneous loyalty to Luce. "My name is Nausicaa."

22

Reaching Out

For the next twenty-four hours the mermaids were preoccupied with figuring out the details of their new struggle. Luce was more grateful than ever for Yuan's help. Under Yuan's direction the mermaids were organized into two groups; each group would sing for two six-hour shifts every day in order to keep the wave up non-stop. It wasn't far to the clock tower at the Embarcadero, and a small mermaid was dispatched to keep track of the time. Once they divided the army in half that way it became clear that they didn't have quite enough mermaids to sustain the wave at its full force, but they didn't want to risk a disastrous collapse. Yuan was the one who got the idea of removing the singers one by one, letting the water adjust for a few moments before she beckoned the next mermaid out of the line. She posted guards, choosing those mermaids whose voices weren't as strong to keep watch.

Half of their force proved to be enough to keep the wave going, though not quite at its previous height. It wasn't ideal, but they had to hope that it would be enough. And as Yuan had predicted, many of the Twice Lost mermaids who had scattered in terror were starting to drift back, drawn by the faint resonance of the music stroking through the water. The wave swelled higher as they poured their fresh voices into the effort. Then in the early evening a new tribe of refugees showed up, and Imani immediately set to work on training them to join in.

Above them police wearing what were probably noise-canceling headphones had begun physically carrying people off the bridge. But for every one they removed it seemed like some other human would manage to sneak on and take their place. The crowd hadn't thinned at all, and now the shores were packed with listeners as well. The base of the Golden Gate Bridge began to resemble a jostling auditorium.

Luce sang through her shift from late afternoon until midnight then swam back to their hidden encampment to get a few hours' sleep. She was bleary with exhaustion, and with Yuan handling so much of the work—and so much happier than Luce had ever seen her before—Luce felt more like just another weary soldier than like a general.

At least she felt that way until she looked up and saw three younger mermaids watching her with a kind of disbelieving admiration. Luce smiled at them, but she still felt a little shy under the pressure of their eyes. She knew she might fail them horribly, and she almost wished they understood that. They should be more skeptical, Luce thought as she fell asleep, and not so innocently ready to entrust their lives to her.

Before she knew it, a gentle hand came and shook her awake for her next shift. It was lucky, Luce realized, that their new way of singing together was so thrilling or the effort of continuing it for so many hours at a time would have proved overwhelming very quickly. Even with the exaltation of that music coursing through them, how long would the Twice Lost be able to keep going with such intensity?

There were more helicopters today. And a lot of them weren't from the TV news.

Then it was noon, and she had six hours to rest and eat. But there was something else that she needed to do, Luce realized, before she let herself collapse into her hammock again.

A soft arm wrapped around her shoulders. Imani was there beside her, and in a moment Cala joined them too. "Luce? How are you holding up?"

"I'm doing okay," Luce murmured. The truth was that, the longer she floated in the bay gazing up at that sparkling translucent barricade under the bridge, the more anxious she became. She couldn't escape the feeling that she was asking too much from the Twice Lost mermaids. Something had to change and soon . . . and she'd promised the humans that there would be a letter stating the mermaids' demands. "I think I have to go see Seb. If you want to, you could come with me."

Imani shrugged. "I'll come meet him, sure. What did you want to see him about?"

"There's something I need to ask him to do for us," Luce said. "He might be a little . . . I don't know . . . unreliable? But we don't know anyone else."

* * *

Twenty minutes later they set off for the collapsing pier where Seb passed so much of his time. A day or two before, of course, Luce would have made a visit like this in the strictest secrecy, and she still had a sense that going to see a human friend was slightly disgraceful. There was a tinge of the forbidden to it, even now that she wasn't going alone.

She was going with a whole mermaid delegation. Imani and

Cala were with her, but also Graciela, Jo, and two other mermaids Luce had just met. It only seemed right that she include some of the others. After all, this was official business.

Luce had asked the other mermaids to keep out of sight, at least at first. When they reached the pier she surfaced alone, the others waiting below the water. Luce hadn't been there in broad daylight before, and the shattered holes in the factory windows formed constellations of black vacancy against the shining glass.

Seb was there, sitting bolt upright and obviously expecting her.

"Hiya, *General*." He grinned as she appeared. "Hey. Didn't know my little fishy friend was so danged *important*. You've sure thrown a whole bunch of big shots for one hell of a loop! 'Little Lucy just goosed the *president*,' was what I said!"

Luce winced a little at the thought that the other mermaids were listening to this. She hadn't considered the possibility that Seb would embarrass her—but apparently she should have. Was he drunk again?

"Seb," Luce tried. "This is serious."

"Serious is right, girl. For right now you've got them in such a knot that they don't know *what* to do, but you'd better expect that pretty soon they're going to hit you back, hard. Kablooey!"

"Seb, listen! I'm here to offer you a *job*."

That helped. Seb was startled out of his giddiness. "A job, Miss Luce?"

"I mean," Luce said, suddenly shy, "we couldn't pay you or anything. But—"

"With all the sunken treasure and rubies and pearls you all are hoarding, you say you can't *pay* me? You'll pay me, girl, and plenty!"

Luce reeled back, her face flushing hot and her stomach tight.

This was obviously a huge mistake—and it was humiliating that her friends were hearing a human speak to her with such impudence. But the fact was that they still needed help from *someone* on land. "I guess if we ever find anything like that, you could have it. We wouldn't need it."

Suddenly Seb's manner changed completely. "I was just joking with you, General Luce. Don't look at me like that!"

"But—" Luce started.

"I'd do anything you asked me, General. Tout de suite. I thought you knew that! Sure didn't mean to hurt your feelings."

"We could offer you a title, Seb."

Seb's eyes widened as he gazed at the water just behind Luce, and he jerked back a little. Luce glanced over her shoulder and saw that the rest of the mermaid delegation had broken through the surface—and, with their crossed arms and annoyed expressions, they looked more than a little intimidating. Luce was especially surprised to notice Imani's severe glare.

After a few moments Seb partly recovered. "Uh, what's my title? I mean, general, I hope you understand, I didn't intend any kind of disrespect . . ."

"Twice Lost Ambassador," Luce informed him.

A flurry of expressions passed over Seb's worn face: first shock, then wonder, and then tears came into his eyes. "Ambassador, Miss Luce? I got to say, I'm really . . . really honored." After a moment, though, his customary impish smirk twisted his mouth again. "But I do feel obliged to inform you of something. I've been lost a whole lot more than just twice!"

Luce considered that. She recalled events that hadn't occurred to her much during all the recent upheaval: watching her mother die when she was four, then her father's disappearance. The awful loss of Nausicaa, Dana's fury at her, Dorian's shocking cruelty, and the massacre of her former tribe. "So have I. That doesn't change anything. I'm still the Twice Lost General."

Seb was nodding now, but he kept glancing nervously at the other mermaids. "So what's my first assignment?"

Luce meant to smile at him, but she couldn't. Their situation was already overwhelming, even desperate, and Luce knew that what she was planning to do was going to make it even harder for the mermaids to eke out any kind of victory. "We'll come back late tonight. Can you get me a pen and paper by then?"

There was a brief pause. "Sure, Miss Luce," Seb said gravely. "I can do that for you."

* * *

When Luce flopped heavily into the hammock under the old factory, Catarina was already there. Luce flinched. She felt too drained to deal with a confrontation, but those moon gray eyes were watching her, steady and assessing. There didn't seem to be much choice.

"Cat," Luce started, "I'm sorry. I know I should have already told you—that I found my dad alive. And I know I owe you an apology for . . . for thinking you probably killed him . . ." Cat was still staring at her, and her expression didn't change at all. Luce sighed. "I am really sorry. I know I wasn't fair. I was completely sure he'd drowned, and since his boat vanished somewhere near your territory, it seemed like you must—"

"Oh, Luce," Catarina interrupted. "That doesn't matter much, does it? I certainly *would* have killed him, with great pleasure, if I'd come across his boat. He was lucky." Cat gave an odd grin. "If it weren't that I've accepted—for now—your perverse insistence on sparing human lives, I might still. Not if I knew it was your father, I *suppose* . . ."

Luce decided not to let Catarina provoke her. "Then are you mad at me about something else? I keep feeling like you are. I don't know; it's the way you look at me."

"You've certainly been full of surprises, Lucette. I'm frightened by what you're doing. I've told you that. And I'm extremely worried about you."

Luce felt an unexpected flash of pride. "Do you still think everybody is going to turn against me?" The mermaids seemed so *strong* now, and in her heart Luce knew that strength resulted from the decisions she'd made. Even Yuan seemed to have let go of her obsession with the past, caught up as she was in the elation of their new challenges.

Catarina only shrugged dismissively. "Oh, for now, of course, you're the hero. The great mermaid general, upsetting all the rules, bringing them the gift of a new way of singing, making everyone believe that they have a magnificent cause to *live* for."

Luce flared up at this. "They do! We're finally doing something better than just thinking all the time about what humans did to us, and *killing* . . ."

"They'll follow you, and they'll trust absolutely in anything you decide, Lucette. Until you fail, that is; until you disappoint them. Then, of course, they'll go back to their old ways with a vengeance. And their hero will become to them the lunatic who led them into hell."

What makes you think I'll fail? Luce wanted to ask. But she couldn't. She couldn't ask that because she knew with painful clarity how horribly unlikely it was that she would succeed. The Twice Lost were holding the human military at bay for now, and they were making what Luce believed was a truly valiant effort. But in the long run . . . she had to admit that their prospects were still grim.

"This is why you need me, Luce. Because I don't see you as a hero, and I don't even believe in your cause. If we're going to fight we should fight the way we always have, and the way *they* do: with death. You must have noticed when you were trapped in that horrible net that the humans hardly share your qualms about murder!"

"They *will*, though. They'll see . . ." Luce trailed off, unable to completely believe in her own assertion. Would they even care that the mermaids wanted peace?

"Your followers trust your judgment, Lucette. Foolishly, I think. But I don't trust you at all, and that makes me more valuable to you than any of them"

Luce tipped her head, wondering what Catarina was trying to tell her.

"I don't trust you, Luce," Catarina repeated. "I love you. As the naïve mermaid I once rescued from drowning, and as my true sister. I've tried to see you as my queen, but I can't, not when you violate every rule a queen should uphold! No: to me you are not our great leader, but only my strange little Lucette. And that means—unlike everyone else here—I can never lose faith in you."

Luce looked at Catarina's gray eyes, but they were gazing away into the blue rim of daylight beyond the pilings. Fiery hair sleeked around her pearl-colored shoulders. Luce wasn't happy with everything Catarina was saying to her, but as she looked into her former queen's face, she felt the almost infinite sadness there as if it were welling in her own heart.

And, Luce had to admit, it was a relief to think that there was somebody who *didn't* see her as a leader. Luce hesitated, then reached out and hugged Cat tight. "I . . . love you too, Cat. Even though we don't agree about a lot of stuff, and I'm going to keep doing things you think are totally crazy."

"That doesn't matter," Catarina said again. "What matters is that I stay near you and keep you as safe as I can."

"I . . . don't actually need to be safe, Cat. If I can stop the war, then I don't really care what happens to me."

Catarina ignored that. Her attention had turned toward a mermaid Luce didn't recognize: a too-skinny Asian girl, perhaps twelve or thirteen at most. Luce saw at once that this young mermaid was one of the hopelessly deranged ones. She kept writhing with a kind of exaggerated seductiveness, thrusting out her childish chest and licking one finger. Her behavior was sad and repulsive and almost impossible not to watch; it was a tic, Luce thought, like the way Jo was always gnawing on her own hands. "Like me," Catarina said. Her voice was oddly flat.

"But she . . ." Luce didn't want to say that the girl was clearly insane.

"She was *sold*. Like me."

Luce understood—and at the same time she struggled not to understand. Could a girl that young really have been sold to be used in that way? When Luce stole a quick glance at the young girl from the corners of her eyes, what she saw in the haze of dark shimmer around that sleek head was too sickening to be borne. No wonder Catarina thought that Luce's decision to protect humans was so indefensible.

"Luce?" Cat's voice had turned thin and strange. "Try to sleep. I'll wake you when . . . when it's time."

Luce obediently closed her eyes. Then through the dark fringe of her lashes she watched Catarina approach the young mermaid. Catarina whispered to the girl, her voice a steady, half-musical lull, and cradled her softly until her awful wriggling calmed.

23

The Letter

Just after midnight the little-girl mermaid who'd been appointed timekeeper came rushing up excitedly, saluting everyone she met as she told them their shift was over. One by one the mermaids under the bridge were replaced by fresh singers just returned from sleeping in odd corners of the bay. Then a few of the smaller girls returned from the south bay with their nets bulging with shellfish and promptly got into a squabble over whose turn it was to have the *honor* of giving the off-duty lieutenants their dinner. The little mermaids looked abashed and stopped bickering as soon as Luce smiled at them.

"So," Yuan said, "got plans tonight? I heard about the new *ambassador*, Luce. I know we don't have a ton of options, but the dude does sound like kind of a joke."

Luce felt an unexpected impulse to defend Seb. "I think he'll do *fine*, actually. At least you should give him a *chance* before you go around calling him —"

"Hey, general, I wasn't trying to piss you off! Okay, he sounds *outstanding*. Better?"

"We do have plans," Luce said shortly. "I need as many of the lieutenants as you think we can spare, Yuan. Because we have to write the humans a letter, and I want to make sure—that everybody basically agrees on what we should ask for."

"I thought that was the easy part," Yuan observed sardonically. "Like, oh, 'We'd be *ever* so obliged if you gracious humans might consider, perhaps, refraining from making lethal holes in us with pointy objects? Thank you quite a lot, The Mermaids.'"

"I think . . . it shouldn't be *just* about us. I mean the war." Luce looked off at the skyline. Slices of their giant wave were reflected on the glassy sides of skyscrapers, creating the illusion that there were waterfalls frothing brightly in the center of downtown.

Yuan looked befuddled. "What *else* is it about?"

"I think . . . that's why I need the lieutenants to come with us tonight. Because it's a really big decision."

Yuan flashed Luce a strange, skeptical smile. "You're about to do something totally crazy and reckless, aren't you?" She grinned, pausing for one long beat. "Well, you can count on me to help!"

Luce laughed gratefully; she was amazed to realize how much Yuan truly meant it. "Hey, Yuan? I'm sorry I snapped at you. About Seb."

"Oh, 'sokay. I know you identify with rejects like that. Even though you're so totally *not* that yourself!"

Luce opened her mouth and found she couldn't answer. She wasn't sure which part of Yuan's observation surprised her most.

"Hey," Yuan continued. "Do you want me to ask *Catarina* to come with us? It would be easy not to, like I could just make a big thing about leaving her in charge here. If you'd rather not deal with her."

Luce was startled all over again. "Of course she should come with us! I mean, why *wouldn't* I want her to?"

"I don't know, because she seems like she's always arguing

with you? Like first she was so intense about you being in charge, but now it seems like she's not a hundred percent on your team?" Yuan hesitated. "I hope I'm not making you mad again, Luce."

"It's okay." Luce thought about it. "She does argue with me, Yuan. But I trust her a lot." *Catarina's the one who doesn't trust me,* Luce thought. But she decided not to say that.

Yuan was staring at Luce with strange expectancy, her delicate mouth tensed as if it was crowded with words that she couldn't quite bring herself to say. Her tail came up behind her in a single nervous flip. "Um, Luce? I've been thinking a lot about—about that thing you said."

Luce tilted her head in perplexity. Had she offended Yuan somehow? "What thing?"

"That thing you said to me about the girl. The one I saved. Like, maybe you're right that I don't need to hate myself so much because I did that? And . . . I've been thinking about the person you saved, too." Even as she spoke Yuan was turning away from Luce. Only one golden cheek was still visible, and it was blushing. "Catch you soon, general-girl."

At first Luce felt relieved that Yuan was too embarrassed to continue the conversation—and then she felt a trace of something else, a tiny squirm of disappointment. What would happen if she *did* tell Yuan about her disastrous romance with Dorian?

And had she really helped Yuan feel better about her violation of the timahk, her fall from mermaid society? The clock at the Embarcadero glowed, and Luce passed a peculiar sculpture that appeared to be a giant's bow firing an arrow into the ground.

Above the surface there was the brilliant city: below it the wings of rays, the fins of sharks, carved sensuous swoops from the darkness. Luce reached Seb's pier with her thoughts still flowing around Yuan and the uncharacteristic vulnerability that had moved in her voice.

Soon twenty heads were floating just above the surface, the water webbed with spreading hair. Pools of milk-pale blond, caramel brown, and inky black were punctuated by Catarina's shocking fiery amber. Seb was there, wearing a reasonably presentable navy suit jacket and a much less presentable tie with a pattern of scarlet elephants on it; Luce was touched at the thought that he was making an effort to dress up for his new role. He seemed to have trouble looking at the assembled mermaids for long and kept staring down at the rotten planks.

"So, um, General Luce?" It was Lieutenant Eileen, freckled and much less assertive than she'd seemed earlier. "Yuan filled us in a little bit, but I'm confused. I thought the whole idea of the wave was to just get the humans to back off, and it's working great for that. But Yuan said—maybe you had some kind of bigger idea?"

"I do," Luce said. "But I feel like—we're all in this together. And what I want to do is going to make it a lot harder for us to win. So I think it wouldn't be fair for me to insist on doing things my way. I wanted to ask you all—I mean, maybe you'll agree . . ." Luce broke off, suddenly shy. Everyone was already struggling so hard and accepting such enormous risks because of her. How could she ask them for more than that?

"You said you thought it shouldn't be *just* about us," Yuan said. She was floating very close to Luce, and her gaze was oddly searching. "Like, of course you want the humans to stop killing us, but . . ."

"I *do* want them to stop killing mermaids," Luce said. "But I also want them to stop killing the ocean." A stunned silence followed her words, so Luce tried to explain. "I think the way humans treated us before we changed and the way they're treating the world—they're really not that different! When I was swimming down here I passed through this dead area where almost all the animals were just suffocated and *rotting* . . ." Luce heard that her voice was getting higher, sharp and fervent.

"And *that's* why you don't want to kill humans, Luce?" Catarina purred sardonically. "Because you've seen firsthand how much they destroy?"

"That *is* why!" Luce snapped. She saw the way everyone was staring at her. Of course it sounded like she was contradicting herself. "I mean," Luce struggled to clarify, "if we kill them, then they'll never get a chance to change."

"So you're saying you want them to stop global warming and stuff? Ice melting at the North Pole and the sea levels rising?" Yuan laughed. "I thought that was a problem when I was *human,* all right. Then after I hit the water I just thought, oh, *hells* yeah! More for us!"

"It's worse than that," Luce said seriously. She remembered everything she'd read and talked about with Dorian back when he'd been researching the ocean's problems. "The ocean's warming up a lot faster than the animals can adapt, and it's getting way more acidic, too, from absorbing all the carbon. That has to stop or it'll kill all the coral, and plankton, and—" Luce strained to recall the details—"I think a lot of the shellfish. And then everything that needs *those* things to live. It's completely horrible."

"And you don't think saving the mermaids is a big enough problem?" Eileen asked. "I'm not saying you're wrong, but this—it really sounds like a lot for us to try to do. You know? Like maybe we have *enough* to deal with?"

"We do," Luce agreed. "It's already incredibly hard—just trying to stop the war. I mean, I know, realistically, there's already a good chance we'll lose and then the humans will do whatever it takes to wipe us out." It was the first time she'd admitted this out loud, and she saw the shocked looks on her lieutenants' faces. They had more faith in the mermaids' ultimate victory than she did, Luce realized. "But I think—we might die anyway. And mermaids have always been—kind of stuck. Like all we've cared about is what the humans did to us, and how hurt we all are, and how much they deserve to die. But if *everything's* going to be different now, well, shouldn't we start caring about *more* than that?"

There was another strained silence. Luce looked from face to face, trying to see the thoughts shifting inside their expressions. Seb looked oddly downcast, his mouth pinched and his eyes lowered. Yuan was biting her lip, but a half-smile was very gradually lifting the corners of her mouth and there was a distinct spark in her eyes. Imani was watching Luce but as if she was observing something far behind her. Eileen looked flummoxed and possibly angry, and Cala had started *laughing* with what seemed to be wicked delight. Catarina wore a contorted smirk. Luce couldn't guess how it would all turn out.

Yuan went first. "I don't *care* if she's crazy. I'm with Luce." She saw Luce's flash of surprise and grinned at her, though there was something a little ragged in it. "What's up with that look, Luce? I *told* you that."

Luce couldn't smile back. The choice they were facing weighed on her too much for that. "Imani?"

"Honestly? I think we'll die if we push the humans that far," Imani whispered. She still had that faraway look. The glow of streetlamps turned the droplets in her dark hair into clinging pearls. "But Luce? I think we should do it anyway. We need to—go beyond ourselves. It's like we've been living in a sea that's too small for our hearts."

"Cat?"

"You know how I feel, Lucette. We've had this discussion."

Luce felt vaguely annoyed. "Does that mean yes?"

"It means I don't care. Not—" Catarina shrugged. "Not about this. Really, Luce, *plankton*? Write whatever you like."

"Cala?"

"Yes. It's seriously about time we changed everything up! I'm into it."

They went around the circle. There were some halfhearted objections, and some answers that weren't exactly agreement. But most of the mermaids there seemed ready to share in Luce's goal of protecting the ocean. And, while a handful of girls seemed uncertain, nobody actually told her no.

Nobody except . . ."Don't do it, Miss Luce!"

Seb had been so quiet that she'd almost forgotten he was standing there. Luce turned on him with a look that made him twitch back a little. "Why not?"

"Well, because . . ." Seb hesitated, his gaze flicking to Luce's face and then down again. "If you're just telling the power out there that they've gotta stop blasting your kind, it's not going to cost them much more than their pride if they back down. And their pride—whatever kind of front they put up, their pride ain't actually worth more than—" Seb brushed his fingers across the air, batting away invisible gnats. "But what you're talking about now, Miss—I mean General Luce? That'll cost them money. Money to change the way they do things. And as soon as you go messing with their finances, well, they won't rest until they've made sure that *you're* the one who pays for that. I just—"

Seb fell into a nervous silence as Catarina suddenly laughed, shrill and harsh. "I can vouch for the truth of what this *human* is saying, Lucette. Money is what drives those human *creatures* to distraction. Dearer to them than—"

Luce understood, horribly, what Catarina had stopped herself from saying. *Dearer to them than their own daughters. Dearer to them than I was* . . . Impulsively Luce caught Cat's hand and squeezed it.

Seb flicked his eyes, very briefly, toward Catarina, and then broke out nodding. "So that's all I'm trying to say, general. I want to see you live through this, and I'll do whatever I can to help make sure that happens."

"What does that matter?" Luce asked. The words burst out of her almost before she knew what she was saying. "If I can do—what I have to do—who *cares* if I live through it? I mean, you were watching us on TV. You heard what that reporter said. Even my *dad* is out there telling people mermaids are just killers, making everyone *hate* us, when we're right in the middle of a war!"

Luce's voice was suddenly veering out of her control, spiking into odd sharp notes of song as she spoke. Luce's lieutenants looked stunned, and there were a few random cries of concern. Imani swirled rapidly over and flung her arms around Luce, holding her tight and humming softly into her ear, soothing the dreadful, violent music out of Luce's voice.

For an instant Luce was angry. In the next heartbeat she was grateful. Her voice had almost ripped away from her. In another moment it might have leaped into the death song and then she could have killed Seb without even wanting to.

Luce quickly hugged Imani back. Her voice was still fighting a little inside her, and a mournful thickness gathered in her throat where she held it suppressed.

"Aw, Miss Luce," Seb said after a moment. "It's not like you've had a chance to check up on what that woman said, right? Maybe your dad didn't mean anything as bad as she made it out."

Luce tensed. "I don't want to *hear* about it, Seb." At least the song inside her had quieted; she could speak again without risking its release.

"Maybe if you heard the whole *context* of what he said, it would seem a little different than—"

"It doesn't matter." Luce felt taut, focused, and still a little angry, although she wasn't sure at what. "We've got work to do. Can I please have that paper now?"

They spread it out in a spot where the planks were relatively level. Luce was surprised to see that it was heavy, obviously expensive ivory stationery emblazoned with the logo of what must be a fancy downtown hotel. "How'd you get this, Seb?" Luce's emotions were still running high, but now she felt close to laughter.

"Oh, you know," Seb said almost demurely. "I was fast. I figured, writing to the president or whoever, you should have something nice."

Luce thought about that. There'd been an election coming up when she'd transformed, and it suddenly occurred to her that she had no idea who'd won. "Who is the president now?"

The mermaids around Luce looked blank. "Leopold," Seb said.

Luce shook the droplets off her hand. Her fingers still left wet prints on the paper. She took up one of Seb's pens and started writing in her best script, reading aloud as she went: "Dear President Leopold . . ."

"He's not *our* president," Catarina snarled.

Luce looked at her and nodded. "You're right. Okay, 'Dear President Leopold of the United States Humans, and All Humans of the World. The mermaids of the Twice Lost Army don't want to be at war. We want peace with humans as soon as possible, but there are some things we need you to do first.'"

Luce glanced around at the faces pressing in around her. No one said anything, so she kept going. "Um, all right. 'We already promise not to kill humans unless you force us to defend ourselves. If you agree to our demands, we'll lower the wave blockading the Golden Gate, and we'll do it very carefully so we don't damage anything. We'll also send messengers out to any mermaid tribes that still attack humans and do our best to persuade them to stop. In exchange, we want you to completely stop attacking mermaids. And we want you to stop killing the ocean. Global warming and the water becoming acidic and all the sea animals getting killed off are going to cause terrible problems for humans, too, so what we're asking is really for your own good.'"

Luce looked around again. Seb was grimacing, and Catarina had her head tipped back and an aloof, sarcastic look on her face. But Yuan nodded carefully. "I think that sounds pretty good. Just something to finish up. Like they taught me in school, you want to end with something that sticks in the reader's mind."

Luce thought again then continued the letter. "'We're all kids. The oldest mermaids I know were only seventeen or eighteen years old when they changed form. I was in eighth grade. Why do *we* have to be the adults here?'"

"Will they take us seriously," Eileen asked, "if we tell them that?"

Yuan grinned. "How are we giving them the option of *not* taking us seriously? Like, 'Guys? Hey, you've noticed there's this little issue with your ships getting out to sea these days, right?'"

Luce shook herself a little. "Does everybody agree? We should sign this?"

Another brief silence followed. "Go ahead," Eileen said at last. "We're in it; we might as well be *really* in."

Luce lifted the pen again, ready to sign *General Luce*. But—shouldn't she remind everyone, her father especially, who she *really* was? The pen whipped into motion, and Luce's heart surged with some strange mixture of pride and bitterness. "'Sincerely, General Lucette Gray Korchak, The Twice Lost Army.'"

That brought on a wave of agitated murmurs. "Your *human* name, Luce?" Imani whispered.

"It's *not* my human name," Luce said, a little stiffly. "It's just my name."

Catarina's tail swung up above the surface and slapped back down hard, spattering salt water across everyone and leaving tiny rounds of blurred ink on the letter. "Luce! You must remember. When you first changed, you must remember how I *told* you—"

"I remember that you told me I didn't need my whole name anymore, Cat," Luce announced. "I also remember that you never asked me how I *felt* about that."

Catarina's mouth went round with a mixture of surprise and anger; she seemed to be on the verge of some outburst. Then after a moment she closed it again.

"Luce?" Imani said gently. "Can I see that pen?"

Luce gave it to her. Imani slid over in front of the letter and stared for just an instant. Then she wrote, *Lieutenant Imani Michaela Portman*.

"Oh my God." Yuan exhaled the words. "I can't do that, Luce! I mean, my old last name—that was my *father's* name. I was so, so glad to ditch that and—"

"It's okay," Luce said. "Everybody should sign with whatever name they feel is right."

Soon the bottom of the paper was covered in a dark lace of signatures. Most of the mermaids stuck to their first names, but there were a few who followed Luce's and Imani's example. "It's so weird to even think of my old name again," a slender blonde murmured as she inscribed the name *Lieutenant Natasha Elizabeth Lindberger*. "Like one of those dogs you read about that finds their owner three thousand miles away."

Natasha was the last mermaid to sign. Seb sighed. "Should I scribble that up too?"

Luce looked at him. "Will you?"

Seb knelt on the planks. His coarse hand lifted the pen from Natasha's dimly luminous fingers. *Twice Lost Ambassador Sebastian Grassley.*

"Okay," Luce said. Even more than meeting Dorian, than becoming general, than raising a standing tsunami under the Golden Gate Bridge—this moment felt new, volatile, radiating unpredictable consequences. A thousand possible hideous endings, and as many astonishing beginnings, might unravel from this moment at this broken-down pier under the dark-eyed night. "Seb, you have a new job to do."

He nodded, then folded the letter and tucked it carefully in a pocket inside his jacket. "Get this out there, right? Copies got to go to TV networks, newspapers, the White House . . ."

"Send it out," Luce agreed. She felt breathless. "Send it everywhere you can. Soon *everyone* is going to know what we're fighting for."

Seb nodded and walked off abruptly. Luce watched him go, his hunched figure illuminated at intervals by the pooled glow of the streetlamps, sorry at the thought that she hadn't really thanked him. Cala was farther out at the end of the pier, watching something that Luce couldn't see because of the pilings in the way. "Hey," Cala called, a bit suspiciously. "I don't know you. Are you with the Twice Lost?"

"Not yet," a voice replied. Luce felt something opening deep inside her, a longing so profound that it felt like an incurable wound. "I would ask to join with you. I have heard reports of your great general, the one whose voice the water answers and who shares her skill with all unstintingly, the one who will not be called *queen*, who leads us in defiance of humans and gods alike, and who will change from the quick the very meaning of being a mermaid . . ."

Luce let out a half-sung shriek. The water followed her voice in an explosive fountain, and foam spattered down like heavy snow.

She tried to speak, and failed. Instead she screamed again, her voice carrying all the love and joy and frantic gratitude that she could not yet make herself shape into a name.

A dark bronze figure with massy coils of black hair swam into view and smiled at her.

Nausicaa.

24

Reunion

Nausicaa had never been particularly inclined to show affection through hugging or touch, but that didn't stop Luce. She leaped from the water, her tail breaching and thrashing in midair, and knocked Nausicaa several feet backwards as she crashed down and embraced her. They spoke fast but softly, their voices rushing over and through each other. "Nausicaa! Nausicaa, I didn't know if you would ever . . ."

"Dearest Luce, I *promised* I would find you again . . ."

"I wanted to keep looking for you, so much, but then . . . I needed to try to change things here, and . . ."

"You have done exactly as you ought to, Luce. Exactly as I always dreamed you would. I knew what I saw in you, and I was not mistaken . . ."

"But if it hadn't been for you, I never could have done any of it. There were so many times . . . while you were away from me, Nausicaa, you . . ."

"Yes, Luce?"

"While you were away, you *saved* me so many times!" Luce was suddenly, giddily aware that that might sound like another contradiction. How could she explain that Nausicaa's remembered voice had come for her again and again, always just when she needed it most?

Nausicaa was beaming, her green-black eyes starry with tears. "You should allow yourself more credit, Luce. But I'm thankful if I've helped you."

"No, you don't know how *much*, Nausicaa! There was this ice floe and I would have let go and drowned if . . . if I hadn't been thinking of you. And I would have killed Dorian, except I remembered what you said to me. And—"

Luce broke off, appalled by the bitter tang of Dorian's name on her lips—and just as abruptly realized that all her lieutenants were listening. Catarina's face looked greenish, her eyes narrowed and her mouth misshapen. Even Yuan was scowling. Luce realized with a jolt that not everyone there would be delighted by the arrival of this darkly powerful newcomer. "Everybody—this is Nausicaa. She came to Alaska after you left, Cat. We—got to be friends. She's a really great singer, and she'll be a big help."

Nausicaa tilted her head and smiled politely at Catarina's glowering face. "Hello, Catarina. Luce spoke of you often."

"We've already met, *Nausicaa*," Catarina snarled.

Nausicaa started. For a moment her face went completely blank and confused, then she looked up at the buildings, almost as if her lost memory might reappear in one of those broken windows. She shook her head. "I apologize. Where have we met? I can't recall."

"You can't recall?" Catarina simpered the words mockingly. "I suppose you can't *recall* Queen Marina, either?"

"Marina, yes, of course. I have not traveled through her territory for some time, however. Do you have news of her?" Nausicaa looked at Catarina again. "You were in Marina's tribe, once? Oh . . . perhaps I do remember something of you . . ."

"Marina's been dead for twenty-five years."

"I am sorry .."

"And she *never* should have trusted you!"

There was a swing and a clap of Catarina's bronze-gold fins, and she was gone.

The silence that followed lasted much too long—and Luce found herself wondering if Catarina's words had really been as spontaneous and emotional as they seemed. Maybe she'd been calculating the best way to make everyone suspicious of Nausicaa before they even got to know her.

Yuan was the one who rose to the occasion. Her jealous look was gone, and she grinned at Nausicaa with distinctly forced lightness. "Hey, sorry about that, Nausicaa. Cat's just *being* like that. She's not completely down with all the big changes around here, and she's kind of been getting moody a lot."

Nausicaa shook her head. "I should speak with her. I am not entirely sure if I deserve her anger. But thank you for your welcome. You are?"

"Yuan." A quick shiver of hesitation followed, almost too brief to be noticeable. "And if you're Luce's friend, then we're all really happy to have you."

Luce looked at Yuan, unsure if she'd heard a tiny hint of emphasis on the word "if." She decided to ignore it. "Yuan's in charge of organizing the Twice Lost Army, Nausicaa. And she's *brilliant* at it. And . . . she's one of my best friends, too." It was true, Luce realized, but that wasn't why she'd chosen this particular moment to come out and say it.

Yuan flashed Luce a look, warm but also a little sardonic. Then she flurried into action, introducing everyone to Nausicaa, reminding some mermaids that they should return to the bridge for the rest of their shift and others that they should go and get some sleep.

When almost everyone had gone, Yuan clocked her head at Nausicaa. "So, Nausicaa? Did Luce already teach you how to sing to the water? 'Cause if you're with us, that's the first order of business."

"Of course. But I have yet to learn this skill, Yuan."

Yuan was nodding. "You'll be studying with the best! Well, I'll leave you guys to it. And Luce? You're excused from your next shift. I won't expect you at the bridge until six in the evening, okay?"

Luce gazed at Yuan for a moment then splashed over to hug her. She knew Yuan was still fighting a twinge of jealousy, and it was incredibly generous of her to offer Luce extra time with Nausicaa this way. "I'd be setting a really bad example if I did that, though, Yuan. I'll be there at six in the morning."

Yuan shrugged, but she looked pleased. "See you soon, then. God, I'm only going to get like three hours of sleep."

Then Luce was alone with Nausicaa in a night filled with hovering lights, the breathing sounds of cars on distant highways, the dark scrolls of indigo clouds. A light rain was just starting to fall. They stared at each other: those were really the same blackish eyes with their look of ironic wisdom, really the same smile turned a bit grim with the weight of centuries, and the same wonderfully unpredictable intelligence sparking behind those features.

Luce realized she'd always assumed that Nausicaa had simply seen too much and grown too jaded to feel the same depth of love that Luce felt for her. She was thinking of that when Nausicaa let out a short astonished laugh and threw her arms around Luce's shoulders, squeezing her tight. "My *dearest*, bravest Queen Luce. With all the languages I know added together, I don't seem to find enough words!"

Luce buried her face against Nausicaa's cool shoulder. "I wish you wouldn't *call* me that, Nausicaa. You know I'm never going to be Queen anything."

"But Luce," Nausicaa murmured, "it has taken me these three thousand years to find the mermaid whom I *wish* to call my queen. How can you deny me that joy?"

No matter how many times she'd been lost, Luce thought, she was suddenly even more found.

As long as Nausicaa was with her, she was *found*.

*　*　*

They settled on the shore under the pier, rain seeping in slow trickles between the planks and pocking the drowsy water. Luce poured out the story of all the events that occurred after Nausicaa had left Alaska. Somehow Luce didn't mind talking about Dorian with Nausicaa, and she told her everything: how she'd been driven away from him by the encroaching ice, how she'd been swept out to sea in a storm and then found her father miraculously alive but enthralled by spirits on a remote island. She told Nausicaa how the long effort to free her father from that enchantment had made her late in returning to Dorian, and how he'd betrayed her for a human girlfriend rather than wait. How very close she'd come to killing him in her heartbreak. How she'd tried to warn her old tribe away from the area, only to find that they'd returned to their cave after Anais murdered a mermaid from Sedna's tribe.

Then how, as she was still stunned by Dorian's betrayal, she'd found her former tribe slaughtered, their cave dripping with fresh blood.

Nausicaa had asked very few questions while Luce spoke, only held her and sometimes nodded. After all, nothing about the story surprised her; she'd even predicted Dorian's treachery before it happened.

But at Luce's account of finding the torn and partly dismembered bodies of the mermaids she'd once lived with, Nausicaa was suddenly sharply alert. "That *sika*," Nausicaa growled. "Was she among the dead?"

"Anais? She must have been! Nausicaa, there were bodies all over the place. I saw *faces* split in half. I saw—"

"But did you *see* Anais? See her there, clearly dead, her body reverted to human form? If you did not notice her distinctly enough for her name to arise in your mind . . ."

Luce didn't want to search her memories of what she'd found in that cave. "What does that matter? Nausicaa, they killed *every-one*. I couldn't think about names!"

"A *sika* will always find a way to save herself, Luce. If you did not remark her face among the dead, we must believe she lives."

Luce stared. It took her a moment to process Nausicaa's words. "I guess . . . it could be possible. But even if she did escape, it's hard to see why that matters now. With the tribe dead, she can't really hurt them anymore."

"It might matter very much, Luce. It depends on the price that Anais paid for her life. It was likely bought at a cost no decent mermaid would consider."

"You mean . . ."

"Luce. What happened next?"

Luce was suddenly finding it hard to concentrate. It took a

huge effort to focus her mind and keep up the story. How the silent black boat appeared and the divers fired on her before she knew what was happening. How in the impulse of her rage and terror she'd called the wave and flung the boat furiously against the cliff, then fled in a daze to warn as many mermaids as she could. Her hallucinations and the encounter with the school of huge squids, her collapse, those humans holding a camera.

J'aime's cave. The massacre there. Then what Luce overheard about the divers' search for one mermaid in particular — *her* — and how they seemed to know far too much about her.

How she'd concluded that Dorian must have informed on her — and thereby placed other mermaids in the line of fire.

Nausicaa was already shaking her head, her fins flicking with impatience. "It was Anais who told them of you! Luce, this only proves to me that she still lives — perhaps as a captive. How has your pride kept you from seeing something so obvious as this!"

"What makes you think it *wasn't* Dorian? Nausicaa, I didn't want to believe he could do something like that either, but . . ."

"He could not. If he spoke more than he should, he did so naïvely, with no intent to harm you. Luce, I know him."

"I thought I knew him, too!"

"You know him still. Your pride and your hurt prevent you from *seeing* what you know. You make blind your own thoughts, and they wander in the darkness."

If it had been anyone but Nausicaa who had said that to her, Luce would have felt nothing but resentment. As it was, her tail was beating the water into a froth, and she twisted out of Nausicaa's embrace. "You'd rather make up some crazy story about Anais than admit you were wrong about someone — some *human*. You know why I'm glad I didn't drown Dorian, Nausicaa? Because he didn't even deserve the *honor* of being killed by me—after how shallow he turned out to be! He—"

Nausicaa burst out laughing uncontrollably, and Luce fell into an annoyed silence. Then, as Nausicaa kept on giggling, Luce found herself breaking into a responsive grin. Maybe she *was* being a little overdramatic. "Oh, such *pride* you have now, Queen Luce! I cannot begrudge you. You've earned this new arrogance, I admit that. But—"

Nausicaa couldn't keep talking. She was laughing too hard again.

And, to Luce's surprise, she felt grateful to Nausicaa for laughing at her. "Okay, *maybe* you're right about Anais, Nausicaa. Maybe. But that doesn't mean Dorian hasn't been trying to hurt me—to get some kind of revenge! They could both—"

"Ah, Luce." Nausicaa had finally mastered her laughter. "Dawn will be with us soon. You must teach me your way of singing so that the water will understand me and answer my voice. And I must learn your methods of *teaching* as well. Clearly, the next great task falls to me. Much as it will pain me to leave you again . . ."

Luce couldn't believe what she was hearing. "You *can't* leave! Nausicaa, you—are you just trying to upset me? You can't actually mean that!"

Nausicaa gazed at her strangely, almost speculatively. "We need each other, Luce. I am more aware of this than ever."

"Then how can you even *talk* about—"

"But, as truly as you need me beside you, your struggle needs me *more*. Think of what I can do for the Twice Lost! At present, you and your followers here are alone in this battle, isolated in this bay, without support. The humans have only this one group to overcome and then everything you strive for will be destroyed. But

I am accustomed to traveling great distances. I speak so many languages that their words tangle like brambles in my mind, and I am known well to hundreds of mermaid queens throughout the world."

Luce was beginning to understand Nausicaa's reasoning. She just didn't want to understand it. "So you're saying—you'll go teach what we can do to other tribes?" Of course mermaids in other countries probably needed a way to defend themselves just as desperately as the Twice Lost did, or else they would very soon.

"More than that, dearest Luce. I will carry your skill to distant tribes, yes, so that they are not entirely helpless against these helmeted soldiers. But more than that, I will spread your movement and your goals. The humans will soon have more than just the dock mermaids of San Francisco to contend with!" Nausicaa laughed again, a little harshly.

"Dock mermaids?" Luce wasn't entirely happy with Nausicaa's tone; there'd been an audible breath of disdain in it.

"Strange enough, but this is true the world over, Luce. Those mermaids outcast by their own kind gather at the margins of great human cities. They hide themselves between the two worlds, in the shadows there, under the docks or factories or in half-sunk ships. Breakers of the timahk most often become dock mermaids just like these you know."

"You know you broke the timahk too," Luce pointed out. Nausicaa had spoken with Dorian at least twice—and those were just the violations Luce knew about. In three thousand years, there might have been others.

Nausicaa hesitated. "I did."

"And so did I. I'm a dock mermaid too!"

Nausicaa smiled at Luce, her expression wry and thoughtful, and reached to stroke her hair. For several seconds neither of them spoke. "Then I will travel to the dock mermaids first, Queen Luce. The outcast mermaids of this world will be your vanguard. The Twice Lost will be the ones who create the mermaids' future."

Luce looked at her. "And after the war—if there is any 'after', Nausicaa, if we live? Then . . ."

Nausicaa smiled, but there a shadow seemed to flit behind her eyes. "Then we may still have Proteus to contend with, Queen Luce. I cannot imagine that the god who gave the mermaids their form and their destiny will take kindly to your defiance of the ti-mahk. The first mermaids, the Unnamed Twins, know me as an old friend, but even they might refuse to listen to me speak in your defense. You have not merely broken our law for yourself, after all."

Luce barely registered the words. "But I need to know what you'll do after the war, Nausicaa! I don't care what Proteus does."

"I will not part from you again."

It all made sense. Nausicaa was obviously making the right decision for everyone; Luce could almost accept that. At least, she could accept it until she pictured Nausicaa swimming away from her again. Then her emotions all roiled in rebellion, wild with unreasonable urges to somehow force Nausicaa to stay with her, no matter the cost.

Water dripped from the rotting planks, and dull gray light suffused the morning sky. Nausicaa's singing lessons would have to wait.

It was almost time to report to the bridge.

* * *

Soon she and Nausicaa swam close enough to the bridge to feel the water trembling against their skin from that overwhelming song. There were the usual animals: clouds of weaving blackish fish and scarf-winged rays—and, up above, something Luce didn't recognize. She felt a quick impulse of fear. Maybe whatever was floating on the surface was some new weapon or a trap. There were dangling lines at its base that might be the wires of some strange bomb. She surfaced at a cautious distance to take a look at it.

Roses. It was messy bouquet of pale pink roses, balloons tied among them to make them float. Those trailing things Luce had taken for wires were actually curled white ribbons. Some human, Luce decided, must have dropped them in the water by accident. Beside her, Nausicaa gazed quizzically at the flowers.

Cala appeared at her elbow and prodded the bouquet. "They've started throwing us *presents*." She sounded somewhere between exasperated and wearily amused. "The humans on shore, I mean. And they keep calling out, trying to get us to come *talk* to them, General Luce. Nobody knows what to do! And that's not even the worst thing—" Suddenly her tone veered close to hysteria.

"What is this worst thing?" Nausicaa asked.

"I'll . . ." Cala started. "I guess I should just show you. We're all staying under the surface as much as we can because every time they notice one of us they freak, and no one knows how to react."

On the San Francisco side, the bridge's base was joined by a large parking lot. As usual these days it was packed with people. Some of them had started bringing folding chairs with them or else simply sat on the pavement with their eyes closed and their heads thrown back, rapt in the shimmering music of hundreds of mermaid voices joined together. But there were others who pressed purposely forward, some with mouths wide open but soundless, their expressions eager or ravenous or crazed. Luce, Nausicaa, and Cala had surfaced some twenty yards from shore, and at the sight of them the watchers squeezed together at the water's edge began shouting desperately, waving their arms to beckon the mermaids closer.

Dozens of police wearing headphones stood stiffly among the listeners; Luce didn't understand why they were there until a tall young woman with a mohawk leaped into the water only to be promptly hauled out and dragged away in handcuffs.

And, Luce realized, some of the humans onshore were carrying signs. At first glance they might have been mistaken for the kind of signs people carry at a political demonstration. But at the second . . .

"That's what I was talking about," Cala groaned. "It's so—I never knew I could feel so *sorry* for humans, but this is just horrible!"

Faces. The signs had blown-up photographs on them, sometimes blurry or grainy from how much they'd been enlarged.

And they were all photos of girls, grayish in the overcast dawn light. In those poster-sized images tiny girls in ruffles blew out the candles on their birthday cakes, smiling teenagers draped insouciantly over leaning bicycles, and nervous-looking ten-year-olds held up just-unwrapped Christmas sweaters. And scrawled above or below or across those images were the names, printed in huge letters: MELINDA CRAWFORD, CARIDAD ROSARIO, PRECIOUS TAYLOR-HAWKINS . . .

Luce heard a low, keening cry, and then realized it had come from her own throat: noise squeezed up by the painful tightness in her stomach.

"Oh my God," Luce finally managed. "They're the parents? Of girls who vanished or . . ."

"I *know*," Cala murmured. "I know. It's the worst thing I've ever seen. Maybe *some* of those girls are mermaids now, but the others!"

Cala didn't need to finish the thought. A lot of those girls probably weren't on land anymore, but their families wouldn't find them in the water, either.

A lot of them would never be found alive.

The desperate parents screamed and pumped their signs into the air, trying to get the mermaids' attention. Luce felt the hot salt stripes of tears crossing her cheeks. She couldn't bring herself to look away from those signs. She didn't *think* she recognized any of those faces—but maybe if she just looked long enough she'd notice a familiar smile or a name she knew.

Cala noticed the intensity of Luce's gaze and nervously twirled an auburn lock around one finger. "I know. I keep staring like that too. I mean, I guess people whose daughters *actually* turned into mermaids wouldn't care enough to come and look for them. But—"

Luce thought of her father. Before what that reporter had told her, she definitely would have expected him to be standing there too. Now everything was different. "I wish we could do *something* for them," Luce sighed. "I just don't know what. Unless we recognize one of those faces."

Nausicaa was oddly silent, looking back at the row of humans watching her.

"So, um, general?" Cala asked after a moment. "We need to know the rules. I know you said the timahk has to be different now, but—well, are we allowed to *talk* to them? I know you talked to that reporter and everything, and Seb, but that was all official stuff, and I wasn't sure if everybody . . ."

Luce thought about that. It seemed a little risky. And, ready as she was to overturn the old timahk, the idea of unrestricted socializing with humans still made her uncomfortable.

On the other hand, it would be way too hypocritical to say that it was okay for *her* to talk to humans—but not okay for the rest of the Twice Lost Army. After all, her relationship with Dorian had hardly counted as official business.

"The mermaids can talk to anyone they want," Luce announced. "Let all the lieutenants know that. They can tell the girls in their divisions."

Cala's hazel eyes went wide. "Really?"

"Really. Just ask everybody to please remember that we all represent the Twice Lost Army, and we shouldn't say anything that's not true or that could make humans hate us any worse. Okay?"

"Luce," Nausicaa interrupted sharply. "This is a dangerous decision. Many of those humans are not to be trusted."

"We need to start trusting them, though," Luce told her. "Because we need them to trust us."

"You, as well as anyone, Queen Luce—you know the grief that comes of this. Allow them to draw close to humans, and soon enough a great number of your followers will be disordered by love for human males. It cannot end well!"

"I don't see why that *shouldn't* work out!" Cala interjected. "Just because we're in the water!"

Nausicaa flashed her a dark look.

"We'll . . . have to risk it," Luce decided. Cala's comment made it all too clear that Nausicaa was right, but . . ."I just don't think we can *avoid* talking to humans anymore. No matter what happens. Just—ask everybody to be really careful, Cala, okay?"

Cala leaped impulsively, her dark turquoise tail breaching and flashing in the somber gray light, provoking a flurry of shouts from the onlookers. Then she darted away to tell everyone the news. Nausicaa looked worried. Behind her, the mermaids of the morning shift were streaking below the surface to take their places in the line, while those who had been singing through the night began to break away, one by one, and head home to rest.

"Do you want to go with them, Nausicaa? You could probably use some sleep."

"I prefer to remain with you, Luce. Today I will listen and learn what I can of your singing in that way."

Luce didn't want to admit it, but she was relieved to have Nausicaa's company. The frantic cries of the people on the shore clanged through her mind, and she had to force herself to look away.

Not all the off-duty mermaids were heading back to their encampments, Luce realized. Word of the new rules had already spread, and a few mermaids were swimming directly under Luce's tail.

Heading straight for the human crowds.

25

Facing the Water

She was too far away for him to be completely sure. But as he squeezed through the mob near the water's edge Andrew Korchak caught a distant glimpse of a mermaid with short dark hair turning away and then vanishing. "Luce!"

"Yeah!" a teenage boy standing near him called, and burst into shrill, ecstatic laughter. "Go, General Luce!"

Andrew glared at him but the boy had his eyes closed, his voice humming faintly in a drowsy counterpoint to the piercingly sweet thrum of hundreds of mermaid voices. Those voices washed through Andrew's mind. They curled around each thought and shocked him with a kind of electrical tenderness. It was impossible to stay entirely clear-headed. Instead he seemed to sweep through a heart as large as the sea, and everyone else in the crowd drifted with him. It was glorious, intoxicating; no wonder all these people couldn't stay away.

He'd spent a couple of days curled up in the toolshed of an empty, rickety house with a faded For Sale sign listing in the front lawn, dreaming of Kathleen and crying. Then he'd come to the decision that, even if he hated the mermaid who had killed Kathleen and even if he wasn't so sure now that the rest of them weren't worth hating too, still, he couldn't blame Luce for that. Luce hadn't personally murdered Kathleen. That much was *almost* certain. And if he did have a few lingering doubts, well, the only way to deal with them was to talk to Luce face to face.

He'd staggered out of his toolshed—only to find Luce's picture splashed across every newspaper he saw.

General Luce. He couldn't get used to the idea that anyone actually called her that. His bookish, gentle, painfully shy little girl had become a mermaid general leading a naval blockade and giving defiant speeches on television?

Did he even know who she *was* anymore?

His confusion only lasted until he sat down with a crumpled newspaper he'd found lying in the street and read what Luce had actually said. Those words *did* sound like they belonged to his Lucette, just to the side of her that she'd usually been too shy to show to anyone but him. She was still honest and deep-hearted and strong, still doing the best she could in terrible circumstances.

And then, what that *reporter* had said to her—that woman almost made it sound like he'd started some kind of anti-mermaid campaign, when in reality he and Kathleen had been doing the only thing they could think of to help.

And Luce went and stood up for him anyway and told the world to believe whatever he said . . .

Yeah, he still knew *exactly* who Luce was. That was his girl, all right, and he never should have let himself doubt her. And he urgently needed to find her, no matter what it took, and explain how that reporter had distorted what he'd said in his video. He'd hitchhiked the rest of the way to San Francisco, and now—well, he still had a little bit farther to go.

"Hey!" The teenage boy's eyes had flown open, carried on some tremulous gust in the music. "Hey, aren't you—from that video? The guy who came out and told everyone about them? General Luce's *father*? You are!"

Great. Somehow this wasn't a possibility that had occurred to him—and attracting attention was hardly going to help him get past the line of scowling cops he could make out now between the close-pressed bodies ahead. His first irritated impulse to deny his identity, though, almost instantly shifted into the idea that he might be able to turn it to his advantage.

"Shhh," Andrew hissed. He made his tone confiding, conspiratorial. "I've got to get to her."

As he'd hoped, the boy nodded, but then he kept on nodding as if he were too entranced to stop. "That won't be easy. They're stopping everyone. Boats, anyone who tries to swim. I've seen like five people get arrested since midnight. I don't know how you can."

"How 'bout you distract the cops so I can get a head start?"

"There are police boats patrolling too, though. And then I think the mermaids have their own guards, and they might think you were trying to attack them or something."

"If I can just make it as far as the mermaid guards, they'll bring me to Luce," Andrew whispered with far more assurance than he actually felt. "They're not about to piss their general off by drowning her dad."

Well, *maybe* they wouldn't. But he'd worry about that once he got to them.

"Okay," the boy said dreamily. "Okay. But hey, will you tell her I helped you?"

So there it was. The kid would do a better job if he was feeling really motivated. "Yeah, I absolutely will. What's your name?"

"Josh Byrd. Tell her—I really believe in what she's doing? I know people are complaining that it's bad for the economy, but I think she's right to try to protect the mermaids? Tell her—"

There was a sudden clamor of jabbering voices, moaning half-musical cries, and screams from the edge of the water. Andrew tipped his head, and he and Josh elbowed their way through bodies that were now so compressed that they seemed more like some squirming inhuman substance than like actual people. Once they fought their way through to the front, they saw what was causing this fresh disturbance: five mermaids were floating only twenty feet away, looking at the crowd with what appeared to be a kind of stage fright. They were so beautiful that the sight of their faces seemed to burn Andrew's eyes.

"Um, hi?" one of the mermaids ventured, her shyness contrasting strangely with her ferocious loveliness. "General Luce says it's okay for us to talk to you."

The crowd yowled, several people who were carrying signs swung them recklessly, and the mermaid glanced around at her friends and started backing away.

"Don't scare them!" Josh yelled. "Everybody act calm! Don't *scare* them!"

One brown-skinned mermaid flicked her way just a little closer, gazing with obvious pity at someone Andrew couldn't see. Someone on the shore to his left, probably standing right at the front of the crowd. "I, uh, God, there's something I have to *tell* you. About Melinda. We were friends, and she—"

The mermaid broke off in alarm, but this time what had spooked her wasn't the crowd's uproar but an even more abrupt and disturbing silence. She visibly gathered her courage and kept speaking.

"I'm sorry I have to tell you this! Melinda's dead. I saw her get killed—by those divers with the helmets. They got her in the throat with a spear. I saw it, and I couldn't do *anything* to help her! I couldn't—I barely got away! But Melinda . . ."

Horror pitched sharply through the mermaid's voice, and Andrew suddenly noticed the long, imperfectly healed, crimson slash that began at her left shoulder and disappeared where the water covered her chest. It must have been the distracting power of her beauty that had stopped him from seeing sooner that she was hurt. He had the funny feeling that everyone watching the mermaid had noticed her wound at the same moment he did. People around him gasped, sobbed . . .

And then a woman pitched headlong into the water, bobbing limply face-down as if she'd fainted.

Beside her floated the sign she'd been carrying, emblazoned with the name *Melinda Crawford* above an enormous photo of a beaming honey-haired teenager. Water sloshed across the girl's smiling face, dragging it under . . .

Police were in the water, grappling with that unconscious body; around Andrew people screamed and tried to surge toward the spot; someone else dived and was instantly caught and flung back toward the shore. In the corner of his eye, he saw Josh leap forward shouting, crashing into three of the cops and toppling one of them.

As distractions went, it was all pretty prime—and then those mermaids were so *close*. What with how crazy everyone was acting, they'd probably never come this close again.

The only thing still separating him from the water was a low embankment of heaped rocks. Andrew stepped up onto it, seeing Melinda Crawford's face half erased by green darkness, seeing the

single police officer who turned to stare at him with a look of furious realization—and hurled himself over the edge.

Gray and salt and cold. The violent rhythmic thrashing of his
arms as he propelled himself forward, beating the low waves. Up
ahead he caught a glimpse of blue frightened eyes as a mermaid
turned to gape at him. He spat out salt water and called, "Luce!
General Luce! I need to *talk* to her!"

The rush and whorl of mermaid song was much louder inside
the water than it had been onshore. His brain seemed to tremble
and melt into strange new shapes, rippling wave forms. His vision
was divided between the gray of the sky above and the slopping
green confusion of the water. He lurched high enough to peer across
the water's surface, trying to catch sight of those brilliant blue
eyes, of the flash of fins.

They didn't seem to be there anymore. Maybe just a little
farther ahead? He kicked harder, his jeans and sneakers dragging at
the water.

Then he felt a pair of hands closing on his calf, hard, and
shoved his heel back in the direction where he guessed the face
must be. He didn't have much time left. "Hey! Mermaids! I'm General Luce's dad! I need to see her!"

A black boat zoomed in, almost colliding with Andrew's
head. He tried to dive under it, but those hands were still jerking
him backwards, and now someone else was leaning in from above
and twisting his right arm sharply up behind his back. His body
rocked crazily from side to side as he tried to pull free. But more
hands kept closing on him, and the mermaids were singing indiffer-
ently in the distance. Had they even heard him? He was already
hauled halfway out of the water, the boat's edge digging into his

stomach, when he felt a horrible staticky buzzing at his temple. He heard his own sharp scream as his limbs spasmed, and for a while the world was smeared black and senseless.

He came to face-down on the boat's curved bottom, his wrists shackled behind him and his legs somehow immobilized. Water sloshed against his cheek and his sodden clothes encased him in stiffness and cold. Someone was rummaging through his pockets.

"No ID on this guy, then?" a man asked behind him. The voice was all wrong, prickly and distorted. Like it was coming through some kind of speaker.

Someone else laughed, a little nastily. Somehow laughter sounded even worse than speech did through that veil of electrical noise. "Didn't you hear? We don't need ID. Guy already said who he is—and he wasn't talking to us, either."

"I heard him shouting something about General Luce. He isn't the first of these berserkers who's—"

"He said he's her dad. And I'd say he looks right too."

There was a stunned pause, and then the first man whooped. "We got Andrew Korchak? About time. God, we've been hearing enough about it."

"I figured he'd turn up here eventually. What do you think they'll charge him with? You think aiding and abetting the enemy will stick?"

Great job there, pal, Andrew thought. *Great job on the getting to Luce. Great job explaining everything.*

The curved shell of the boat vibrated as the motor roared. Air rushed across Andrew's back. With an effort, he just managed to crane his head far enough to catch a last glimpse of the Golden Gate Bridge, falling into a wild gray sky. The last velvety resonance of the mermaids' song faded away.

It was mid afternoon the next day when Moreland went to visit Anais, an even odder smile than usual on his face. "Hello there, tadpole."

Anais hesitated for only a second before swimming over, but she didn't look up at him. Moreland stood with his hands spread on the glass, enjoying her lowered eyes and cowed expression. "What do you want me to do *now?*"

Moreland couldn't resist pushing his luck a little. "Aren't you happy to see me, tadpole? All alone in this tank all day, nothing to do. But you know I always bring the fun. Don't I?"

"It's not the same," Anais barely muttered. She looked very pale, her golden hair matted in places. Maybe her sky blue tail was losing a bit of its iridescence as well.

"What's not the same, dear?"

"Singing to people. It's not as fun anymore, with you always *telling* me what to do, and I can't even *see* them. And I just did the last one, like, yesterday!"

"Perhaps I can address your concerns this time. I don't see any reason why you shouldn't be allowed to watch the effects of your singing . . . on our newest subject."

"What are you *talking* about?" Anais was looking up at him now, her eyes wide and her lids dark and puffy.

"Tell me something. I'm very curious to know what would happen to someone who was obliged to listen to your death song for an extended period of time. That is, if there was no water available to . . . relieve the pressure. What do you think the results would be?"

Anais gave her habitual bewildered glare while she tried to understand what he'd just said. Then she released a kind of astonished squeal. "You mean if I sang to somebody and they couldn't drown themselves? They'd go crazy!"

Moreland nodded. Mermaids' voices slopped heavily in his brain, a wave made of cold, ringing metal. "Indeed. They'd go crazy. Permanently, do you suppose?"

He'd listened to that recording of mermaid song for precisely twenty-eight seconds before he'd tried to drown himself, and each one of those seconds seemed to carry more weight than the entire rest of his life. He didn't actually doubt that someone forced to listen to Anais's death song for several minutes would sustain irreversible damage. He didn't expect Anais to give him any information that he didn't already know from personal experience.

He asked instead for the peculiar pleasure of watching Anais try to think, of hearing how she'd reply. Her face contorted as she mulled the question.

"I don't know! How am I supposed to know that? It's not like I ever *let* anybody live—when I was still with the tribe! Why do you always have to ask me these *questions?*"

For the first time, Moreland wondered if she genuinely missed her slaughtered friends; if, perhaps, she even regretted surviving. "Let's assume *permanently*, then. The victim would be left permanently utterly insane. A gibbering idiot. It would be apparent to anyone who observed him afterward that he was mad and that nothing he'd ever said should be believed. For example, his outlandish claims that mermaids are lost little girls who've been terribly hurt somehow."

Anais tipped her head. The strain of following his reasoning showed vividly on her face. "Mermaids—but girls do change because they get hurt! Except for, like, me."

"Oh, I know that. Tadpole, of course we know things—you

and I do, I mean—that we'd prefer the American public *didn't* know. And if someone goes around *telling* them those things, we'd much prefer if they didn't take him seriously."

"But—who are you *talking* about? I don't know what—"

"Ah, tadpole, quite a prize. A prize and a surprise for you. I hope you'll be pleased."

"I don't get it."

"Whom in all the wide world would you most enjoy hurting, Anais?"

"I—you mean Luce? Did you catch her? But me singing wouldn't make another *mermaid* go crazy!"

"I'd like to propose that you can wound Luce most effectively by destroying someone she loves." Moreland grinned. "*Now* are you happy to see me? I have Lucette Korchak's father in shackles just down the hall, and when you're ready I'll bring him to you."

Anais didn't look happy at the news. Moreland was genuinely surprised. She blanched and hunched her shoulders.

"You see, dear? You don't have to try to track down his phone number anymore because we've conveniently brought him straight to you. And, given what an unholy nuisance he's turned out to be, I'd have to surmise that his bitch of a daughter must take after him." Anais's expression didn't change. Moreland felt the first twinge of worry that she might actually refuse to do what he wanted. "Anais? You will collaborate with me on this little project, won't you? You wouldn't want me to think that you've . . . outlived your usefulness. Of course not."

"You wouldn't do anything to hurt me! Not after—I've helped you so much! You *wouldn't* . . ."

Moreland glowered at her sternly until her voice trailed away. She was much too precious to him to be killed, but there was no reason to let her know that. "Just follow my instructions, tadpole. That way there won't be any need for us to find out what I *would* do if I were ever forced to deal with your disobedience."

"Okay," Anais muttered.

"Okay? You'll do a nice, thorough job of destroying Andrew Korchak's mind? Not one speck of sanity left?"

"I said okay, already!"

She was hunched in the water, her sky blue tail coiled tightly and her arms wrapped around her chest. Moreland regarded her for a sustained moment, one hand lazily tracing the outline of her head and shoulders on the glass. "I'll have him brought in, then. You'll be able to . . . enjoy yourself . . . for as long as necessary. Though I think you should be able to accomplish the job fairly quickly, don't you?"

Anais didn't answer, didn't look up at him. After a moment he gave up waiting for a reaction and left the pale, soundproof room. When Moreland returned there were two guards with him leading a man in shackles and a black hood. They plopped him on a plain wooden chair and fastened him to it with a few deft adjustments. "So," Moreland said. He positioned himself directly behind the captive. "So, Anais. You were complaining that you don't get to see them properly? We can fix that for you." Moreland tugged off the hood and dropped it to the floor, letting Andrew Korchak stare straight at Anais, her azure eyes suddenly lifted to meet his. "Better? The shock system in your tank will be switched off in precisely two minutes."

Then Moreland and the guards stalked out of the room.

He could observe the proceedings through live video, for once, even if he couldn't listen. He could witness on Andrew's face the same expression that had floated on his own on the hateful day when he'd put those earphones on, when he'd *heard* her and his mind had given itself to new configurations, the dark intestinal corkscrewing of relentless song.

This was the happiest he'd been in months.

* * *

Then Anais was left alone, facing the shabby, helpless man strapped to the chair. He had short-cropped, grayish brown hair, stubble, and a look somewhere between bleak and oddly whimsical as he regarded her. One cheek was swollen by a large greenish bruise. "Heya. That guy said your name's Anais?"

Anais couldn't help noticing that he didn't seem even slightly surprised to see a mermaid in a tank.

"What if it is?" she asked sullenly.

"Did you know my Lucette? Sweet girl, short dark hair, light green tail? I was trying to swim out to see her when they busted me."

Anais hesitated for a moment. But it was a relief to have someone speak to her so simply after all Moreland's sadistic verbal contortions. "I knew her." She pouted. "So? It's not like Luce is going to get me out of here!"

She watched while the man in the chair nodded thoughtfully. "They're holding you against your will? Yeah, well. Luce doesn't even know we're in here. Doesn't look like there's much she can do for either of us. But maybe we could help each other out."

There was a shocked pause while Anais took this in. Her tightly coiled tail started to loosen and trail deeper in her tank. "Like how?"

"Well, maybe if I ever get out of here, I could let people know you're trapped. Does anybody even know about this? How they've got you stuck in here?"

Anais gave a small yelp of surprise. This guy really *was* dumb enough to be Luce's dad. "They're never going to let you out! Are you *stupid*? They won't let you out, unless . . ."

"What have they got in mind for me, Anais? They must have a pretty big reason for leaving me here with you like this."

Anais looked at him, watching his wry cinnamon eyes and scruffy intensity. He should have seemed utterly contemptible, a bum and a lowlife, but Anais found that she didn't quite see him that way. "You don't actually look much like Luce."

"Lucky for her, right?" the man asked. He grinned back at her. It was strange how relaxed he seemed in spite of his immobilized legs, his arms bound behind his back. "Yeah, Luce always looked like her mom, Alyssa. About as beautiful a girl as I ever saw. Before she went mermaid, Luce looked a little more—like, a quieter kind of pretty than her mom was. How about you?"

Anais jerked back a little. "What do you mean?"

"Who do you take after more? I mean, you had human parents and everything, right?"

He'd asked in the same casual, warm tone he'd used ever since they'd dragged him in here, but Anais couldn't escape the feeling that the question was some kind of trick. "I don't know!" Her voice came out in a thin squeal.

"You don't know?" He considered that gravely. "You don't know what your parents looked like, then?"

Anais didn't answer. It wasn't like she normally disliked thinking about her parents—they'd been rich and adoring, after all—but somehow now it bothered her to be reminded of them.

Was her own father's skeleton still clanking along the blue carpet of his office in their long-submerged yacht?

"How about Kathleen Lambert?" the man asked. His voice suddenly sounded flatter, as if he was suppressing his emotions. Anais felt an almost physical discomfort, as if the water of her tank was charged by a cold, jagged energy. "Did you come across her somehow? Like—" He stared at Anais then glanced searchingly around her tank. "Say, did you ever sing her any songs, maybe?"

Anais decided not to look at him anymore, and her mouth twitched up into an awkward smirk. Those two minutes were definitely up by now.

Even with her eyes averted, she could *feel* the man regarding her somberly. "That's how it went down, then?" he asked. "They made you kill Kathleen, and now you're supposed to do me, too? Not that I can get to an ocean too easy, tied up like this . . ."

"He doesn't *want* you to drown." Anais was surprised to hear herself mutter the words. "He wants you to go crazy."

"Crazy, you say? So just don't do it, Anais. You don't really want to, do you? Look, I promise you I can fake crazy just fine. Then once I'm out I'll tell everyone you're in here. I'll get you help. How 'bout that?"

"I have to do what he says," Anais whispered. "If I don't do it he'll kill me, like he'll drain my tank, or they'll electrocute me, or . . ."

"You *don't* have to. We can trick him."

"I—" Anais was astounded by the words that had formed in her head. She didn't want to say them, but they kept repeating in her thoughts, aching and clamorous. "I—but you won't be able to tell Luce anything! You'll just be a vegetable, like, too retarded to even talk!"

"I loved Kathleen. I want you to remember that forever, all right? I *loved* her."

Anais couldn't keep those insistent words *quiet* anymore—and they wouldn't make any difference anyway. No one would ever know she'd said them. "Uh, tell Luce I'm sorry about this."

Anais sang.

26

Lost Humans

Luce was secretly dismayed to see how quickly Nausicaa mastered singing to the water. Nausicaa was an amazing singer, but Luce had hoped that she might have trouble picking up this particular skill. Within three days Nausicaa was lifting waves big enough to curl over her head, and she'd already started training Opal, the blond metaskaza who'd traveled with her from Hawaii. Luce tried to focus on her work, on helping to train new arrivals and keeping up morale, but she couldn't completely fight off a sneaking depression as she realized how soon Nausicaa would be leaving her.

On the fourth day after Nausicaa's arrival, Luce woke in the late afternoon to find Imani next to her, looking concerned. "Hey, Luce? I'm afraid you're going to be upset about this."

Luce jerked upright and gazed helplessly through the azure-streaked shadows, searching for Nausicaa's dark silhouette. "Is she gone?"

"She said to tell you goodbye. She said it would be easier for both of you if she left while you were asleep, but she'll come back as soon as she can."

"Why didn't you *wake* me? What if something happens to her out there, and I never . . . Imani!"

Imani was stroking Luce's arm, trying to calm her down, but it wasn't working. "I . . . thought she might be right. And I thought it might be better for everybody else here too. I understand that Nausicaa's incredibly important to you, more than any of us, but that hurts . . . some of the girls. And if they saw you get too upset about her leaving—I don't know—it might be pretty bad."

Luce groaned, thinking of Catarina. Cat had taken to sleeping in one of the other encampments ever since Nausicaa had showed up, singing on the shifts opposite Luce's and conspicuously avoiding her. A few of the other lieutenants had been acting a bit edgy too. It was as if they thought Luce was committing a crime by loving Nausicaa as much as she did.

"I know it's not fair," Imani went on gently, almost as if she could hear Luce's thoughts. "But it can't just be about what you want, Luce. It has to be about what's best for the Twice Lost Army, about keeping everyone together, okay? You have to at least act like you're fine."

Luce stared off, unable to reply. She knew Imani was right, but she still couldn't help resenting what she was saying. Now that she was general she wasn't allowed to cry or break down just because of how *other* mermaids might feel about that? Since when did she not have a right to her own emotions?

"It's going to be time pretty soon for our shift," Imani pursued, still stroking Luce's arm. "You look tired. You need to eat, and you need to be strong for us. When the war is over you can scream at me for this or cry or do whatever you need to, and I promise I won't complain."

Luce turned to look at Imani, with her midnight face and searching eyes. Blue light curled like feathers on her dark cheeks. "I'm sorry, Imani."

"Why?"

"If I'm acting so wrong that you think I'd *ever* want to scream at you, I must be . . ." *Really selfish,* Luce thought, but instead of saying the words aloud she shook herself. "We need to get to the bridge early, anyway. We should see if there's any news . . . about the letter." Ever since Seb had wandered off with her missive, Luce had been waiting for a report, for any sign of how the humans might be reacting to her proposal. Some of the Twice Lost had started to make friends with certain humans on the shore, and there were already a handful of budding romances. If Luce's letter was discussed on the news, the mermaids would be sure to hear *something.*

Imani leaned in and hugged her silently. All Luce's grief and weariness and worry surged in that embrace, only to be met by the strong, sweet containment of Imani's arms.

* * *

As they were rounding the Embarcadero, a young mermaid came dashing toward them through the deep green water. "General Luce! Lieutenants Yuan and Cala sent me to find you! They're talking about us on the news!"

"The humans got the letter?" Luce asked breathlessly. "How did you find out?"

The little mermaid saluted, in a messy, embarrassed way. "They got it! They keep talking about it! And we can go watch the whole thing! On TV!"

Luce was perplexed. "TV? How do you mean?"

"They—two of those humans, the really nice ones? The woman with the brown hat? Who came looking for their daughter, except they say they know she's gone? They brought a way for us to watch. Come see! General . . ."

Imani was smiling indulgently, but Luce was struck by the deep sadness of her expression. "I guess we'll have to look for ourselves, Luce." She touched the little mermaid on the cheek. "Would you go ahead and tell everyone we'll be right there, please?" Then Imani's face tightened in a way Luce had never seen before. She looked sharply away as the younger mermaid raced off.

"Imani? What's wrong?"

Imani just shook her head, still turned away from Luce even as they swam. Wings of light brushed across the surface ten feet above Imani's head, and a school of tiny silvery fish parted around her slim dark body like a strange cloud-shaped ball gown. Her storm blue tail cleft the water, flicking strokes of neon brilliance through the dimness.

"Imani?" Luce reached out and touched her softly. "Is there anything—"

"No one's ever going to come looking for me, is all. Seeing all those humans who actually *care*, Luce, when—it's hard for me. I wish they wouldn't come here! No one ever loved me but my grampa, and he died."

Luce wasn't sure what to say; it seemed clear from the images she could see in the shimmering indication around Imani's head that she'd already lost her immediate family by the time of her transformation, just as Luce had. And then the fact that Luce's own father *still* hadn't come to join the human crowds seemed to prove that he must not care about her at all anymore.

But Imani definitely didn't need to be reminded of how many mermaids were in the same situation she was. "Your grandfather's not the only one who ever loved you, Imani." Luce hesitated but only for a moment. "I mean, you know *I* love you, right?"

Imani glanced over at her and managed half a smile. When

they came up for a breath the water-wall gleamed ahead of them, foam sliding from its crest in a cascade of pearls. Pale mist wrapped the red bridge in bands of suspended glow.

* * *

A tangle of mermaids with arms around one another's shoulders clustered near the shore not far from the bridge's base, facing a tightly compressed crowd of humans some fifteen feet away. Police officers stood among them, tense and bristling in the headphones that protected them from the silky wash of enchantment endlessly throbbing from the singers under the bridge An older human couple sat cross-legged at the front, pressing affectionately together. The woman wore a floppy brown hat and tweed coat and had a large laptop propped open on her knees, its screen turned toward the water. As Luce surfaced with Imani beside her several humans cried out softly, and the mermaids parted to make room. "Isn't that her?" someone onshore murmured.

"Shh. Yes. Don't scare them again!"

Luce's tail fidgeted as she approached that mass of staring faces. Could it really be safe to come this close to a human mob? But there was the screen in front of her, with a newscaster introducing a man Luce had never seen before, his stiff white hair like frosting above a heavily jowled reddish face. The woman supporting the laptop looked kind and thoughtful, and she considered Luce with a mixture of warmth and open curiosity. "General Luce? I'm honored you could join us. I'm Helene Vogel."

A bit nervously, Luce swam close enough to shake the woman's outstretched hand. A few people gasped, and Luce abruptly swirled back to the waiting mermaids. "Hello, Ms. Vogel. Thank you for letting us watch the news with you."

"My pleasure. I'm sorry the volume doesn't go up any louder than this."

Luce didn't see any reason to explain that mermaids had much better hearing than most humans. Her attention was caught by the faces chattering on the screen in front of her; there was something unpleasantly fascinating about the man being interviewed, with his emotionless ice gray eyes and twitching half-smirk. A banner at the bottom of the screen read "Secretary of Defense Ferdous Moreland."

"It's plainly impossible," Moreland was saying indignantly, "that these vicious entities were ever *human beings*. Those claims are pure propaganda."

"But the facial resemblance?" the newscaster objected in a weak voice. "There are records of a Lucette Gray Korchak. A troubled eighth grader who was presumed to have committed suicide in Pittley, Alaska, in April of last year. So are you suggesting that *General* Lucette Gray Korchak is actually someone else?"

The image was suddenly replaced by two very close-up faces juxtaposed side by side. On the right was Luce, wounded and exhilarated and fierce, as she'd leaned from the wave's flank during her conversation with the reporters. On the left was what Luce recognized with a jolt as her seventh-grade portrait from school, her gaze scared and full of longing. Together those two faces created an unsettling stirring, a sense of something irreconcilable and rasping and wrong, because they were so much the same but also not the same at all. Objectively there was no real alteration in Luce's features between the two portraits, apart from the notch missing from her right ear, her fine crisscrossing wounds, and the strange internal luminance that gave the mermaid version of her face the feeling of a beacon floating in infinite darkness. It was precisely the sameness of the two faces that created such a disturbing sense of impossibility: how could the commonplace childish prettiness of her human face translate into the volatile, raking beauty of the face on the right? Luce heard murmurs around her and realized that both Yuan and Imani were squeezed against her sides as if they needed to protect her from something.

The screen switched back to the interview. "Our research suggests that these creatures can assume a resemblance to their victims," Moreland intoned heavily, then paused for effect. "The *real* Lucette Korchak—an innocent although seriously disturbed child—was almost certainly murdered by this monster who has hijacked her identity."

Around Luce mermaids cried out in indignation and disbelief. But didn't some of the humans facing them look troubled, uncertain? Luce couldn't completely blame them: it had been hard even for her to stand the dissonance between those two faces. Even as she remembered the cold metal stool where she'd sat for that school portrait, the bleak room and glaring flash, she could still feel a kind of shudder of persuasion in Moreland's words.

Moreland kept going. "We also need to remember what happened to Kathleen Lambert of Grayshore, Washington, when she made the mistake of getting involved with these unnatural beings. It's certainly a striking coincidence that Ms. Lambert turned up drowned so soon after videotaping this self-styled General Luce. Anyone out there who's considering aiding mermaids, or trying to *contact* them—" Moreland's voice became a bleak growl—"would be well advised to keep Ms. Lambert's fate in mind."

Yuan stared. "What is he talking about? You said somebody filmed you, Luce, but—"

Luce felt nauseous. "I don't know. I only saw those people

with the camera for a few seconds!" Had the strange woman Luce had glimpsed that day somehow died *because* of her? But that made no sense at all.

"The woman who put out the first tape of you was found drowned," Helene Vogel confirmed softly, her hat sliding over her eyes. "People have been talking about it. I'm not accusing you, General Luce . . ."

Luce stared up at the humans lining the shore, bewildered and heartsick. Their skin was damp with fog, hazy with the faded afternoon light. No matter how she struggled to put a stop to the killing it seemed that there was always death, and more death, and maybe in some obscure way it was her fault . . .

"General Luce," Helene Vogel asked, gently but steadily, "*did* you kill that woman? Or order her killed?"

Luce shook her head miserably. "I didn't. I wouldn't. I'm so *sorry* if . . . if she died because of . . ."

Helene nodded. "Then don't allow anyone to manipulate you into *feeling* responsible, general."

Yuan's arm was tight around Luce's shoulders, silently urging her to be strong, and meanwhile the voices from the interview kept beating into her mind. She needed to focus on what they were saying, no matter how she felt.

"So—I know you've stated before that there's no possibility of agreeing to the Twice Lost Army's demands—is it correct that General Luce's letter doesn't change the White House's position on that?" The newscaster's voice pounded on like a drum.

"I've said it before and if necessary I'll say it again," Moreland droned. "We do *not* negotiate with mermaids!"

That made Luce jerk back in shock. "But—why shouldn't they *negotiate* with us! It just means *talking* to us. Like we count."

"And as for resolving the blockade of San Francisco Bay?" the newscaster pursued. "You've appealed for patience, and of course there's been a real outpouring of support from the business community so far. But—"

"All options are still on the table," Moreland snapped. "Naval traffic will be redirected to alternative ports until such time as we're ready to move on this."

Luce bit her lip and leaned toward Imani's shoulder. Her eyes squeezed shut with the effort to hold back tears. Beyond the darkness of her closed eyes the newscaster nattered on, thanking Moreland for taking the time to talk to their viewers. Why were mermaids the only ones who were considered unworthy of meeting in conversation? If the humans wouldn't even *talk* to them, it was hard to imagine what else the mermaids could do.

There were a few commercials for cars and alarming-sounding medicines. How much longer could she ask the Twice Lost to go on this way if there was no hope of negotiations at all? A blurt of shrill music announced a return to the news program.

"Well, we've all been wondering about the crowds who can't seem to tear themselves away from the Golden Gate Bridge," the newscaster's voice suddenly thudded on. "It's certainly hard to understand why some people in the Bay Area are expressing support for the mermaids."

"That's San Francisco for you!" a man's voice smirked.

The female newscaster gave a dull laugh. "That's certainly one explanation, Tim. But now we're getting reports that even in Chicago—far away from the *crazy* Bay Area—there's a demonstration happening right now. A crowd estimated at around five thousand people is marching in support of the Twice Lost Army. To you, Constance."

Luce looked up again—and what she saw was even more intolerable than Moreland's bland, cold face had been. The screen showed a large procession of people carrying signs. And right there, unmistakably, at the very *front* of it—

"Oh my God!" Cala squealed. "That is just so *sweet* of them!"

Two teenage boys were leading the march. A large banner stretched between them was emblazoned with the words *All Life Came from the Sea*. A wild wind stirred the tarnished bronze-blond hair of the boy on the left, and his expression was grim and determined even as his dark-haired friend grinned absurdly.

But even *worse* than that—

"Oh, I *love* that boy!" Cala called giddily. "Do you see what his *shirt* says? That is just the sweetest, most adorable thing—"

Yuan wasn't looking at the screen anymore. She'd suddenly craned forward to stare into Luce's face. Luce wouldn't meet her eyes.

"He's got no *right* to call himself that!" Luce snarled. "Cala, it's not sweet at all! It's like he's *stealing* our name!"

The bronze-haired boy wore a black T-shirt, and printed on it in huge white block letters were the words—

"Twice Lost Human? Luce, he's totally being nice! He's just saying he's, like, on our side. And he's *cute*."

TWICE LOST HUMAN. How could he dare—after everything he'd done—how could he possibly have the gall to *call* himself that?

"Cala," Yuan said coolly, strongly. "Cut it out."

"I just don't think he means it like *stealing* our name! He—"

"Don't you get it?" Yuan's tone was oddly matter-of-fact. "That's Luce's boyfriend. She doesn't need to hear you going on about how sweet he is!" Luce reeled in the squeezing crowd of mermaids, spinning toward Yuan in outrage. Yuan only raised her eyebrows. *"Isn't he, Luce? That's Dorian."*

All Luce wanted was to dive away and disappear. Eyes, both mermaid and human, came at her from all sides, curious and demanding, as if they wouldn't be satisfied until all of Luce's private suffering was dissected in front of them. She felt stripped and prodded; coarse fingers seemed to go fumbling through the chambers of her heart. Luce choked wordlessly, her tail lashing against the tails around her, wild with the urge to escape.

But Imani's arms were around her and so were Yuan's, and she was still their general — and their friend. She *couldn't* just run away from them. Not anymore. She inhaled hard, forcing her tail to slow.

"Luce?" Yuan said. "I didn't mean to hurt you. It's just — "

"He *was* my boyfriend," Luce announced flatly. "He betrayed me. For a human girl." She couldn't believe that she'd actually spoken those words aloud.

"And you let him *live?*" Cala asked, wide-eyed — then looked self-consciously at the humans watching them.

"No," Luce snapped. After all the horrible things Moreland had said and then the shocking appearance of Dorian, her emotions still seethed inside her, threatening to sweep her away. "I *made* him live. He *wanted* to die."

"Either way," Yuan said sardonically, nodding at the screen, "it sure looks like he wants you back! Why do you think he's doing this?"

The news show cut away from the protestors. Now the two newscasters were talking about a movie star who had just been arrested for drunk driving.

The sudden disappearance of the marchers hurt Luce more than she would have believed possible. Could Yuan be right? Luce gaped at the screen, where Dorian's absence seemed to form a cataract of emptiness. And far too many people were still watching her.

"Let's get to work," Luce said. Her voice sounded dead. "It has to be almost six by now."

For once, her followers ignored her. "But if they won't even *negotiate* with us—I mean, what's the point of trying so hard?" someone muttered behind her.

Most of the humans waiting by the bridge were friendly, but Luce knew there had to be spies mixed in with them. "We'll talk about—about our *options* later. But we're not giving up that easily!" Luce braced herself to say something she didn't entirely believe. "That Moreland guy was bluffing, anyway. Couldn't you tell?"

Still no one moved. "Luce?" Cala whispered nearby. "Do you still love him? Dorian?"

Before Luce could get upset by the question she was distracted by a commotion some distance to their left. A young, strikingly handsome man in a beige trench coat was fighting his way toward the water on that side, where there were fewer police—and where a lovely chestnut-haired mermaid Luce didn't know had actually come close enough to rest her crossed arms on the embankment. With a touch of bitterness Luce thought that the two of them were probably falling in love; they seemed to be gazing at each other with ravenous fascination. "You're amazing," Luce heard the young man say. "It's hard to believe that anything could be so beautiful. How can you be real?"

The mermaid's reddish fins fluttered up behind her, haloing her in falling droplets. "Well, thank you. I'm really not about to vanish or anything, though."

"Noooo," the man drawled, and Luce looked at him more

sharply. "No, I know you're just as real as me. And you have such a sweet face, such gentle eyes." His voice was purring, seductive. "It's hard to believe you could kill people. Have you really done that?"

Luce wondered if she should try to interrupt the conversation, but her friends pressed in around her; it wouldn't be easy to get over there. And anyway, she *had* said her followers could talk to anyone they wanted. But this was starting to feel a bit uncomfortable.

"Oh, I used to," the mermaid acknowledged casually. She tucked her long hair behind one pale, exquisite ear. "But I really do think General Luce is right, like, there wasn't much of a future in hunting ships and everything. I'm pretty much over that stuff now."

"Pretty much?" the man crooned. Both his hands sank deep in the pockets of his long coat. "Do you think one of the people you killed might have been this woman?"

The mermaid's eyes went reflexively to the photo the young man suddenly held in front of her—so that she didn't watch his other hand as it came up pointing a gun. Luce was already screaming at the chestnut-haired mermaid to dive. The girl had just time to pivot her head quizzically in Luce's direction before the air cracked wide and a blood-bursting hollow opened where her perfect ear had been.

27

Ringing

"We made the news!" Theo was already busy with his phone, scanning through the Internet results about their march barely over an hour after it was over. They were sitting in a dark café, all thrift-store chairs and tables plastered in collaged pictures cut from magazines. "Look, you can totally see us! I think you look better than I do, though. Why did I have to make that stupid face? You're doing this killer noble-and-determined thing. Wait, I'll go back in a minute, you can see . . . And—ooh, shit—it looks like some freak-azoid shot some random mermaid's head off right afterward. You don't think the Twice Lost will decide to wipe out San Francisco, do you? To retaliate?"

Dorian's heart slammed up in his chest, and he reached to snatch Theo's phone, but his friend was too fast, jerking the phone far out of reach at the end of one ropy arm. "I made a point of saying that she was *random*, good sir. 'Some random mermaid,' I said quite clearly. So you'd know I wasn't referring to that very not-random mermaid whom you're going to such lengths to impress."

Dorian relaxed but only slightly. "Luce is okay? But, Jesus, one of them *shot* . . . Was Luce there?"

"Kind of hard to tell." Theo was back to watching tiny images scrolling on the phone's screen, images made even tinier by the fact that he was still holding his phone as far from Dorian as he could. A taxidermy pheasant loomed from a bookcase behind him, its beak gaping as if it couldn't believe what it was seeing. "Oh—wait, it looks like she was. You can see her in the background of this one. She's screaming." He pulled farther away, anticipating Dorian's leap from his chair.

"Let me fucking *see* that already!"

"It looks like General Luce, screaming loudly. Surely you can take my word for that?" Theo groused even as he surrendered the phone.

A still photo on the screen showed a man in a trench coat aiming a gun at a mermaid who was looking away from him, her waves of vibrant chestnut hair startling against the pale gray water. She was looking in the direction of two crowds separated from each other by an expanse of sea: one gathering of humans and one of floating mermaids, both a short distance away. And there in the center of the mermaid crowd was Luce, her mouth wide and her face frantic and contorted as she shrieked in warning.

And he couldn't hold her, couldn't comfort her, couldn't do anything to *help* . . .

"Hey," Theo said. There was a sudden note of seriousness in his voice, maybe even of concern. "General Luce will probably hear about the march, since it was on TV? And then she'll know there are people who want to help, and we're not all rabid mer-bashing jerks, right? And that might make her feel a little better?"

"Maybe," Dorian muttered. But the march he'd helped organize suddenly seemed pathetic, overshadowed by this outburst of violence. How could the support of a few distant humans make up for seeing one of her followers murdered that way?

"Hey, you want to text those girls we met? The hot one—wearing all the gothy shit?—said something about a party tonight. Want to go?" Theo nudged Dorian's arm, trying to make him look up again.

"I can't deal with a party." For Dorian that image of Luce's screaming face veiled the shadows. He needed to get home to his own computer, find out everything he could about the day's events in San Francisco. "You go, okay?"

"I got the distinct impression they really wanted you to come, though. They were just talking to me because you seemed all like brooding and romantically unapproachable. You seriously need to give me lessons in that, dude. And they were all really into your T-shirt." Theo eyed Dorian's black shirt covetously. "Would you make another one for me?"

Privately Dorian thought that Theo was about as un-lost as they came. But whatever. "Oh—sure. Just get me the shirt you want and I'll do the screen print." He considered the idea for a second. "Maybe that's what we should call the whole movement? Twice Lost Humans?"

"Oh!" Theo stared. "Yeah! That's way better than whatever those other names were, like 'Human-Mermaid Solidarity Front.' Too freaking long."

"Right." Dorian shook himself and stood. "You go on to that party. I'm going back to the house. I want to do some work on the blog."

"If I drive you it's going to be way out of the way. She said they live way over in—"

"I'll take the bus." He wanted to be alone with his thoughts anyway.

"But we could just go to the party for, like, a couple hours? And you could work afterward?" Theo pleaded.

Dorian just shook his head and lifted one hand in a perfunc-tory goodbye before he stalked out of the café. The city was glazed in the moist heat of a midsummer evening. Slabs of deep blue air rested between the elegant brick row houses and vintage bou-tiques. Dorian caught himself staring into one window at the man-nequins in their cowboy boots and quirky veiled hats, wondering how Luce would look—as a human, of course—wearing that mid-night blue dress with the pearl embroidery around the neckline.

* * *

The tall narrow house where Dorian now lived with Theo and his mother was dark when he reached it. He was relieved by the op-portunity for solitude. Maybe he could find out more about what Luce and all those other mermaids had been doing, hanging around so close to the humans onshore; maybe he could find videos that would reveal more of her reactions, more of her feelings. In that squeezing, jostling crowd there must have been several cameras pointed Luce's way. Dorian sat on the bed and curled around his laptop, clicking eagerly.

At first he found mostly dross: a sappy tribute song for the Twice Lost that had gotten inexplicably popular, another song that made fun of the first song, some clips of various senators de-nouncing the mermaids at press conferences. But then he noticed "Twice Lost Mermaids Watch the News" in the sidebar. His hand shook a little as he started it.

It was a strange video. Whoever had shot it seemed fixated on Luce and the mermaids who were pressed around her. The camera never swerved from their faces or showed what it was they were looking at with such intensity. There was one corner of a laptop screen visible but it was facing away, toward the water. By turning up the volume as far as it would go Dorian could barely distinguish their voices, interspersed with the louder voices of the humans onshore and the babble of a news program. Someone was being interviewed, and after listening for just a few moments Dorian made out enough of what was being said to understand why the mermaids all looked so upset.

But — whoever that man was who kept droning on — what he was saying was plainly ridiculous. Luce had never been human, even though plenty of people remembered her as a regular schoolgirl? She'd murdered *herself*, stolen her own face? Nobody would believe that, would they? Then the stuff about Kathleen Lambert: old news as far as Dorian was concerned, though clearly it wasn't old to Luce. He watched her raw dismay and craned to hear the faint notes of her voice. He could catch only a few blurry words.

Dorian couldn't sit still any longer. He started pacing, his stomach tight, watching the screen from the corner of his vision. He was doing everything he could think of, but it wasn't *enough*. Luce could still die any day. He stopped to stare out the window at the dark street, the trees like masses of congealed night, the lonely glowing rounds under the streetlamps.

Then — wait, what were they showing now? Dorian wheeled around. The mermaids sounded excited, and then Luce was speaking again, her voice raised in anger so that Dorian could suddenly hear every word: "He's got no *right* to call himself that! Cala, it's not sweet at all! It's like he's *stealing* our name!"

It took him an instant to understand what they were talking about. It became clearer with every sentence that followed, even with the mermaids' voices coming through fragmented and murky.

Luce had *seen* him. She'd watched him marching on her behalf, *fighting* for her . . .

Furious or not, she had seen *him*.

Dorian's nails were digging into his palms. His knees trembled, and he felt sick and wild and exhilarated. Even thousands of miles away he'd found a way to make her understand how much he missed her—whether she wanted to know that or not. It was as if he'd sent her the strangest love letter imaginable, a message cast out wildly into space, and against the most phenomenal odds she'd *received* it. With a sudden flash of vanity, Dorian remembered everything Theo said about how noble and determined he'd looked in that march. Good.

"You *see* now, Luce?" Dorian hissed out loud. "You see? You can be a general or whatever, but I'm *with* you, and I'm not going anywhere!"

He had no right to call himself Twice Lost? Dorian imagined arguing with Luce, pointing out that he'd been lost the first time when the mermaids killed his family—and the second time when he'd broken up with her. But he could only communicate with her in such awkward, indirect ways.

Well, then, he'd organize more protests, blog like crazy, put up a Twice Lost Humans page on every site he could—

His cell phone started ringing. Dorian's first reaction was annoyance at the interruption—but what if it was something important? What if it was news about *her*?

"Hello?" His heart was pounding, and his tone came out strained and breathless.

"Is this, um, Dorian Hurst?" A shrill-sounding girl. Dorian was fairly sure the voice was new to him. Maybe it was one of those girls Theo said wanted to meet him so much? He half expected to catch the clamor of a party in the background: Theo calling out and music blaring and people giggling.

But no, everything was silent. Maybe, dimly, there was a kind of electrical buzz. "Yes?" Dorian asked curtly.

"Are you at home?" the girl's voice inquired pointedly.

"Yeah. Who is—"

"Alone? Because I really need to talk to you without anybody *interrupting.*"

That seemed even weirder. Prickling chill brushed up Dorian's back. "No one's going to interrupt. What's this about?"

"You used to be with Luce," the girl pursued curiously. "Right? You were actually her boyfriend? In *love* with her, like you thought she was just so special?"

Nobody knew about that except for Zoe and Ben Ellison, and Dorian felt reasonably confident that neither of them would blab. Or, well, maybe some people in the government knew it too, but this girl sure wasn't from the FBI. "How do you know about that?" Dorian demanded. There was a sudden fogginess in his head and he fought to clear it. "Who *is* this?"

The girl didn't bother to answer his questions. "What did you *see* in her, anyway? She's such a little freak, and she's not even that pretty. *Seriously?* And she has hair like a boy. I can't believe any guy would want to—"

"I don't know who you are, and I don't know *what* your goddamn problem is, but Luce is incredible. Just look at what she's *doing* now!" Dorian growled—and suddenly he knew that he was making a mistake by letting the strange girl bait him into this conversation. He wasn't thinking straight. Something was wrong here.

"I'm not really supposed to be getting into a big discussion with you," the girl confided. "I'm just curious. I never understood why anybody thought Luce was *anything*. But actually I'm only supposed to—" He could hear her suck in a breath and there was a very slight sloshing noise.

Zoe and Ben were the only *humans* who knew about his relationship with Luce. But—

It was in his head before he knew what was happening. For a fraction of a second Dorian felt it even more than he heard it: an icy, crawling vapor that licked through his ear and then stroked slowly upward. Music, Dorian realized. The sensation was transmitted through a sharp soprano voice so cold and so powerful that it burned, wrapping up his thoughts and crippling them.

And, at the same time, carrying the *promise*. Dorian couldn't have said exactly what was being promised, but he knew it was bright and thrilling and brutal. His skull was an immense black space full of rotating diamonds, every facet flashing cage signals at him. If he could only decipher the diamonds' code in time, all power would be his, all *strength* . . .

Dorian was standing in the middle of the room with his phone pressed to his head, his body slowly spinning in sync with the diamonds. Any second now, he'd know *exactly* where the power was waiting for him—

And yet something inside him resisted. It was like there was a weight tugging in his chest working desperately to get his attention, right this moment, before it was too late. Telling him he *knew* what to do. Dorian squirmed irritably, wanting only to spin further into that brilliant music without any more *interference*. Then his eyes landed on the laptop screen. Right in the center a girl with short dark hair was screaming out in warning, her charcoal eyes wide and fervent.

Luce, Dorian thought in a strange burst of clarity. Her face broke through the freezing flash and darkness, broke through the singing that became a field of strobing lights. He *did* know what to do. He'd done it before, and it had saved his life.

Dorian felt his own voice in his chest as if it were a physical thing, some stubborn, heavy tool that he was grappling with both hands. His voice seemed to be caught somehow, and he strained to pull it up. And then, with a burst, he was *singing*.

Singing back to the mermaid on the telephone, her painfully lovely soprano battling with his rough sung shouts. Dorian echoed the pulsating, starry notes of her song as well as he could, fractured them, and then changed them into a song of his own. And with every note he sang, he could feel his voice seizing hers and tearing it out of his mind. He didn't understand how the hell a mermaid could get hold of a phone, but he still recognized with absolutely lucidity what was happening.

An unknown mermaid had called him up, and she was working as hard as she could to murder him.

She didn't know who she was messing with, did she? For a few moments she sang more loudly, trying to overwhelm him, and Dorian countered her, his voice battering its way up the scale into a horrible off-key yowl. This was actually starting to be *fun*.

The girl gave an abrupt gasping cry of frustration, and stopped singing. Dorian paused too. She wouldn't catch him off-guard a second time.

"Stop *doing* that!" the mermaid barked.

Dorian laughed harshly at her, his mind still wild with the dregs of enchantment. His head felt like it was splitting open, but the pain wasn't enough to erase his brutal delirium. He'd beaten death *again*, just the way he had when he'd first encountered Luce.

"You don't understand!" the mermaid shrieked. Suddenly Dorian realized that she was genuinely panicked. "You don't understand! I have to do it! I can't just let you—" She started to sob.

And all at once Dorian knew who she was. He'd never met her, never heard her voice before this evening. But Luce had talked about her, and the sickening power-crazed exultation he'd felt from this particular mermaid's enchantment revealed her essence, the very quick of her personality. Her song gave her away like a fingerprint. He *knew* her. Through and through.

"Hey, Anais," Dorian said.

She immediately stopped crying with a shocked inhalation. For several seconds they were both completely silent apart from Dorian's breathing.

"I *know* it's you," Dorian told her at last. But it still made no sense that she had a phone. And how did she get his number? "I *recognize* you. Where are you?"

"Did *Luce* teach you how to sing back at us like that?" Anais finally burst out furiously. "I bet she did. And now—God, if you don't die, how am I going to *explain*—"

"Explain to who?" Dorian asked roughly. This wasn't the first time a mermaid had wanted him dead. "Anais, who told you to do this? Tell me where you are!"

The sloshing noise came again—and it seemed to have a faint echoing quality, as if she was calling from an enclosed space. "I can't talk about it," Anais finally whimpered. "If you tell people he'll *kill* me."

He. A human, then? A *human* had made Anais do this? It was the craziest thing he'd ever heard. "Can you get out?" Dorian asked. "Anais? Who's going to kill you? Are you locked up somewhere?"

She hesitated. "I don't even know where this is. And I can't talk about it! I told you that!" There was another pause. "Can you at least *pretend* to be dead? Like, hide so he doesn't find out that I couldn't do it? I tried!"

"No," Dorian said shortly.

"But I told you! He'll probably kill me for real! You have to die, or—"

"Tell him I'm doing just fine, whoever *he* is. And tell him I'm going to keep fighting back."

Anais burst out singing her death song again, but this time the melody came out stumbling and distraught and sloppy. Dorian sang back, opposing her. It was easy now. He was almost bored, but he knew he had to keep her on the phone for as long as he could. He had to find out who was *behind* this.

Anais moaned, raspy and despairing. Then the line went dead.

Dorian immediately hit Redial. He heard the phone ringing three times, followed by a weird buzzing sound. "Anais?"

No response. He called a second time, but now her phone didn't ring at all. There was no busy signal, no recording telling him to try his call again. There was simply nothing.

Kathleen Lambert, Dorian thought suddenly. She'd died far away from here. Dorian had never met her, never even heard her name until after she was dead. And yet he was sure that he'd touched Kathleen's death from the inside: a slick, starry, horribly frozen chamber. He'd almost *shared* that death with her.

And maybe he wasn't the only one. His legs wobbled and he sat down hard in the middle of the shiny wood floor. Maybe Anais had a list of names that she was crossing off, one by one. Nobody besides him knew how to fight off the enchantment of mermaid song. They wouldn't stand a chance.

But maybe—and Dorian was already dialing, his heart jarring and his hands trembling with urgency—maybe she was making her next call right now, and—

"Dorian. I was planning to call you as soon as I was calm enough to talk. *All* I asked, *all* you had to do, was to keep a low profile, keep your head down and enjoy your very privileged life! That's your *job*. And instead I see you on the television news? Marching to *support the mermaids*? What kind of willful, quixotic, suicidal provocation *was* that? I've worked so hard to protect you, and you spit on that with this . . . this infantile defiance!" Ben Ellison paused, out of breath.

Dorian had never felt so happy to be yelled at in his life. "She didn't already get you! Listen, Mr. Ellison, if a strange girl calls you, she's not actually a girl. You need to hang up right away, okay? Or if you don't somehow you need to start singing *back* at her, or sing before she can even start, and maybe she'll give up."

"I can see that you might prefer to change the subject, Dorian. But really, you—"

"She just tried to murder me!" Dorian yelled. "Look, I'm calling to warn you, okay? A mermaid just called me up and started *singing* to me. I almost—let her get to me, but I'm okay now." For an instant Dorian wondered if that was true. He still felt lightheaded, his thoughts slicked by a residue of song.

There was a shocked pause at the other end. "A mermaid *called* you, Dorian? Do I understand you correctly? You're trying to convince me that a mermaid called you on the *telephone*?"

"It was Anais," Dorian snapped. "Anais, the really evil one from Luce's old tribe? I'm positive. I think she's trapped somewhere, and somebody's making her kill people. Like, as some kind of slave assassin."

The silence this time went on for even longer. It had an airless quality, staggered by revelation. "Mr. Ellison?" Dorian asked.

"I haven't been able to reach—" Ellison began, and stopped. He was wheezing audibly.

"We have to warn *everyone*. I can't keep a low profile, okay? I mean, Anais might kill—I don't know—anybody who's put out a video or whatever, Luce's dad or . . ."

"That's who I can't locate," Ellison said grimly. Dorian rocked a little as he caught the implication of the words. "Andrew Korchak."

28

Acts of Grace

The air was still surging with Luce's scream as a gray-haired man in a dark business suit lunged at the killer from behind, flinging one arm around his throat and slamming the gun from his hand. It jumped into the air, a blurry blackish shape, and then clattered down the rocky embankment and into the bay.

Luce, Imani, and Yuan were pressing forward to reach the dying mermaid, but their tails were tangled and some of the girls in their way were too stunned to move and only screamed or gaped, their breath coming out like torn rags. By the time they managed to break free of the crowd the humans were already there, and for once the police didn't stop people from clambering down into the water. The dead mermaid's head slumped sideways, her wound a deep crimson crater surrounded by a drifting corolla of red-brown hair. Dark spatters of brain soiled her ivory cheek, and her green eyes were wide and empty.

To Luce's amazement half a dozen humans were on top of the killer, pinning him face-down on the pavement. Many of them had been friendly enough, but it still astonished her that they would turn against one of their own kind for a mermaid's sake.

Yuan cried out as the humans began to lift the mermaid from the water. "Luce, stop them!" But there such obvious tenderness in the way that old woman cradled the devastated head, such care in how those two tough-looking teenagers gathered the still-twitching tail in their arms.

"It's okay, Yuan," Luce said impulsively. "It's too late to save her, and . . . they're doing the right thing."

"She belongs in the water! Even dead! Don't let them take her!" Five people were now holding the mermaid at different points along her slim body, carefully climbing back ashore with her. Her scales already had that papery, faded look Luce had seen once before, and reddish flecks began to dance in the somnolent breeze. Someone spread a black coat on the asphalt. They laid the mermaid on top.

"They *have* to. It's about . . . about their kind of justice, too." Would the humans really punish that young man in the trench coat for what he'd done, or would they decide a mermaid's life didn't matter? After all, she'd admitted to killing in the past herself.

Then Luce heard humans crying out in dismay and amazement. The mermaid's dull ruby-silver scales were curling up, fluttering, peeling away. Even as they peeled they were somehow disintegrating into a kind of speckled reddish smoke that shone slightly against the gray air. Then, like something emerging from a mist, Luce caught the shape of a foot with tightly curled toes . . .

And the body resting on that black coat wasn't a dead mermaid any longer, but a dead human girl. The skin on her legs looked damp and smeary and long-unused, and her empty green eyes were suddenly less vivid. All around them humans had started gagging and sobbing and sinking to their knees.

Of course, Luce realized. *She* knew perfectly well what happened when a mermaid died—but the humans crowding the shore hadn't known. Luce heard a yowl of despair so loud that it cut through the rest of the clamor and then saw that it had come from the killer, his head craned to see the dead girl as he struggled in the handcuffs one of the police must have clapped on him. His handsome face had turned crimson and blotchy. "Well. That'll make it easier to convict him of murder," a police officer announced morosely.

"Murder? It wasn't murder! Murder means killing a fellow human being, not a thing!" the young man in the trench coat yelled back at him.

"A human corpse proves a human was killed, I'd say."

The same gray-haired man who'd tackled the killer was tugging off his suit jacket. He kept his eyes carefully averted from the dead girl—out of respect for her nakedness, Luce realized—as he spread his jacket over her body. Hiding it from the crowd. From the absolute silence of the mermaids around her, Luce knew that they were touched by the same thing she was: the kind, dignified generosity of that gesture.

This was why humans were worth saving. No matter what evils they committed, they were also capable of such unexpected sympathy, such grace.

They *were* worth saving. Even if they had to be saved from themselves.

Luce noticed that Yuan was crying. "I thought they'd all just ogle her, *paw* at her," Yuan whispered. "I thought they might do things to her body."

Imani hadn't spoken once throughout the whole awful event, but now she turned and leaned her head softly against Yuan's tear-streaked face. There was a glint of something metal in the human crowd and Luce spun toward it, afraid that it was another gun. But no, it was just a camera. There seemed to be quite a few of them, actually.

"Doesn't this show that Secretary Moreland was lying just now?" a woman asked. "On television?" No one answered her. The breeze dragged steadily across their faces, drying the tears of humans and mermaids alike.

"We have to get back to work. No matter how we all feel. It's way after six; the singers from the last shift have been going for way too long," Imani murmured the words even as tears were still welling in her midnight eyes.

"We'll sing for her tonight, though," Luce said gently. "All night. We'll sing to the water as her . . . her . . ." she couldn't remember the word at first. "Her elegy."

Imani nodded. Wearily the mermaids slipped away from shore, heading out to take their places in the ranks under the bridge, while the mermaids who were finally off-duty streaked below them, their dimly phosphorescent skin glancing through green waves.

* * *

The singing of the mermaids under the bridge sounded sad and strange that night, without its usual undercurrent of sweet shared delight. As Luce dropped under the surface the line opened to welcome her: two mermaids she didn't know took her hands, one on each side, and squeezed them. Actually, Luce realized, she did recognize the blond girl: wasn't that Opal, who had traveled here with Nausicaa? Opal's voice had a slow, ghostly vibrato. The mermaid on her other side looked Hispanic, and she sang in such a sweet, lambent voice that Luce was surprised she wasn't a lieutenant.

The evening felt endless, and yet all its many moments seemed somehow to be the same moment infinitely repeating. The lights from the bridge slit the water above them with a thousand blade-like lines of light, and once a dolphin swam close enough to nose curiously at their fins.

As the song soared endlessly onward, surging from her core and up to merge with the rising water, Luce couldn't help thinking of the last time she'd sung in mourning over a mermaid's death. It had been that horrible dawn when Miriam had committed suicide by crawling onshore—when, in the frenzy of their grief, her tribe had sunk the cruise ship that was carrying Dorian's family as well as Dorian himself, and Luce had seen him for the first time, staring down from the ship's railing and singing back at her in cool defiance. At least this time the mermaids weren't expressing their sadness through more murder!

Luce felt selfish for even thinking of Dorian at a time like this, but as she sang on and on into the light-slivered night she found herself wondering again if it was possible that Yuan was right. Could it really be that he'd marched on behalf of the Twice Lost, even worn that T-shirt, as a way of trying to tell her he was sorry for breaking her heart? Had he broken up with Zoe? And after all the callous, uncaring things he'd said to her, was it really possible that he wanted her back? The fused voices of hundreds of mermaids eddied through Luce's mind and sent her thoughts spinning on dizzy trajectories.

She caught herself thinking that Dorian really *had* looked beautiful at the head of that march, with his hair dashed by the wind, his expression so strong-willed and serious.

Was it possible that he still *loved* her?

When her shift finally ended Luce kept on singing. New mermaids arrived and took the places beside her; Luce barely noticed Opal and the other singers leaving to go back to their encampments. She sang well past midnight, then on into the new dawn, even when her tail began to tremble from exhaustion.

She had too much emotion to contain in her small body; she had to let it out somehow, turn it into music, and she could *never* stop. Luce's voice was roughening, crackling, but she drove it up to meet the vibration of the water above her.

Then Yuan was there, her hands on Luce's shoulders, actually tugging her out of the line as Graciela arrived to take her place. Luce strained back, but now that she saw the expression on Yuan's face—a mixture of strict and concerned and mocking—stopping began to feel a bit more manageable than it had moments before. "Come *on*, general-girl. You're going to go home and sleep whether you like it or not. And eat, a *lot*. And maybe talk to me about all that stuff we saw on the news last night. Okay?" Yuan shook her a little.

Luce's voice ebbed away. Without the song sustaining her she was suddenly unbearably hungry and so tired that she was tempted to simply collapse on the nearest beach. "Okay. Okay." Yuan towed her to the surface, and Luce breathed deep and stared around at the dawn-smeared bay in a daze. Far away Alcatraz sat in a slick of lemon-colored light so brilliant that the whole island appeared to be levitating. "Thanks, Yuan."

"Oh, my *pleasure*. Somebody's gotta make sure you don't go off the deep end, right?" But Yuan suddenly sounded a little distracted. She was looking toward the shore. At this distance the humans and their posters looked quite small, and Yuan was squinting at them. "Uh, Luce, what does that look like to you? I mean, it *couldn't* be . . ."

Luce saw what Yuan was talking about. "That poster on the right? That does look like you! But Yuan . . ."

"It *couldn't* be someone from my family! It's been—God, almost fifteen years or something? And then—" Yuan looked down. "I mean, I used to get grounded if a boy called me up or *anything*. You'd think killing both my parents would be enough to get me disowned!" She gave a heart-rending laugh.

Luce focused on the image. "I think it might be a picture of you as a mermaid, actually. And it says—it says *Queen* Yuan. No last name."

Yuan visibly relaxed. "Probably just another guy with a mermaid fetish, then. What a relief! Want to go tease the groupies for a minute? Could be fun."

"It looks like a girl."

Tired as she was, Luce was too curious not to swim a little closer with Yuan in the lead. People started waving to them, but Yuan's eyes remained focused only on the human who had come for her. Then she stopped and grabbed Luce's arm. "Oh, God. Oh, Luce, I wish that *was* my aunt or something! Anything would be better than—"

Luce could see the girl more clearly now. She was chubby and pretty and had golden skin that beamed orange in the dawn glow. "Do you *recognize* her?" Luce asked. Then the girl spotted them. She dropped her poster and started waving both arms wildly in midair.

"Yuan! Queen Yuan! It's me!" the girl shouted. And all at once Luce understood.

"That's *her*?" It was the girl Yuan had saved, the girl Yuan had despised herself for saving, the one whose survival had cost Yuan her tribe and her role as queen.

The girl who was both Yuan's secret heart and the crack in her heart.

"Oh, God. She's gotten so much *older*. But I have to talk to her. Do I have to talk to her? Luce!" Yuan's nails sank deeper in Luce's flesh.

"Queen Yuan! You saved my life! I came all the way from Boston to *thank* you!" the girl called out. She was looking around at the police, as if she might be considering making a leap for the water.

Yuan's face looked greenish, her stare confused.

"You don't have to talk to her if you don't feel like it, Yuan. If you want I'll go over there and tell her that . . . that you don't think it's a good idea," Luce whispered.

Yuan shook her head. "I *have* to. It's my fault she's alive at all! I feel"—she gave that strange laugh again—"responsible."

Luce considered that. "I felt that way too." She hesitated. "With Dorian. Like I was tied to him somehow."

Yuan's grip on her arm eased, leaving deep red crescents where her nails had been. She groaned. "You get home safe now, general-girl."

29

Disappointment

"Anais, my dear. It appears that you've hardly been putting forth your best *efforts* of late. Just when I was hoping that I might have some good news for you soon. But I can't help you if you won't help yourself," Moreland explained to the speaker set into the glass wall. Anais was in the tank, of course, but she was refusing to emerge from behind her pillows. He could barely see her azure fins flicking irritably in the crystalline water.

He took a breath and continued. "We're close to a breakthrough, tadpole. Any day now we'll have the means to restore your kind to their lost humanity without damaging them. Isn't that wonderful? Of course, if you changed back, you'd be promptly convicted of so many murders that you'd never see daylight again. I was just starting to think that I might be willing to ask the president to pardon you, and to see about getting you your inheritance as well. And then"—Moreland's voice turned to a growl—"I found myself *gravely* disappointed in you. You failed me, tadpole. After the extraordinary trust I've reposed in you, you didn't merely permit that boy to live. You actually went to the extreme of *introducing* yourself?"

Anais mumbled something. From the sound of it, her face was probably buried in a cushion.

"I can't hear you, Anais. If you have something to say for yourself, you might do better to speak *up* and *enunciate*."

Anais lifted herself on her elbows, just high enough that her tousled head appeared from behind a pink satin mound. Her lids were swollen and raw, and she seemed to have some kind of rash on her cheek. "I said I didn't *introduce* myself! And I really *tried* to kill him! He just—he lived anyway."

"You should know better than to lie to me, Anais," Moreland snarled. His anger rose in him with an icy, buzzing sensation. "This isn't amusing. Do you know what this boy is *saying* now?" He hadn't shown Anais any of Dorian's inflammatory videos or postings about the attempt on his life, though. She might guess at some of the contents, but she couldn't actually know what Dorian had said. "Luckily his claims are so extravagant that no one in the media—no one *serious*, at least—is paying any attention. But the mermaid lovers and other fringe types are only too eager to believe his story of a mermaid assassin named Anais *controlled by someone in the government*. Now, where do you suppose he got that remarkable little morsel of information?"

It was actually worse than that. Dorian had repeatedly named Secretary Moreland himself as the most likely culprit. He'd said that since Anais's old tribe had been slaughtered, it was logical that she might have survived by surrendering. He'd learned far too much, and he was shouting all of it to the four winds. "I have a press conference later," Moreland fumed. "Anais, if I'm obliged to deal with *questions* about this—" He let the unspoken remainder curl into a threat.

Anais muttered something again. She was back in her pillows.

"Yes? What was that, Anais?"

"I said, then maybe you shouldn't have made me try to kill him! You knew he used to be with Luce! It's not my fault she—she probably taught him—so he can—" Anais broke off with a keening cry and slammed a pillow into the floor.

For a long slow moment he considered her. "So that's it, is it, tadpole?" Moreland rasped at last. "You didn't *want* to kill him?" He simpered out the words, crudely mimicking Anais's chirpy voice. "Now, why would that be? You thought you might like to take your old enemy's boyfriend away from her and get *cozy* with him yourself? If you simply explained that you're a poor little captive and that you never wanted to commit those nasty murders at all, maybe he would ask you to the prom?"

Anais turned pointedly away from him, grabbed some random gadget on the artificial shore, and threw it as hard as she could at the blue cement wall. There was a percussive crack and black plastic shards flew everywhere. He had forgotten how strong she was. Anais paused and deliberated over her remaining possessions, then selected some sort of hand-held video game. *Crack.* Moreland watched her with a hard empty smirk on his face. The best way to punish her was to deny her the pleasure of a reaction.

She pulled out one of her ornate dresser drawers and hefted it experimentally by one corner, shiny tops and bracelets tumbling into the water. She swung the drawer onto the hard blue pavement. It buckled and splintered, and she swung it again. Moreland was beginning to find the whole business tedious. He turned off the speaker and swung away from the glass wall as Anais worked doggedly at her tantrum.

"Sir!" someone exclaimed as he walked out into the hallway, clicking the door firmly shut behind him. Moreland turned to see the undersecretary for Intelligence, a severe man in black-framed glasses. "Secretary Moreland, there was some difficulty reaching you? There's a new development, sir. The port of Tacoma . . ."

If he could only *focus* better, without the bits of song in his head always breaking apart and jangling at him like electrified coins. "Tacoma? What about it?"

"There's . . . a second blockade there, sir. A group of mermaids there apparently spray-painted messages along the channel walls declaring their allegiance to the Twice Lost Army during the night! Obviously that implies human collusion; *someone* provided the paint. Now they've raised another of those water ramparts at the channel's mouth. The messages were signed by a mermaid using the name Lieutenant Dana, sir. If this continues to spread . . . There's an emergency meeting of the Joint Chiefs to discuss the situation."

Lieutenant *Dana.* Another of the mermaids on that recording he'd heard.

One of *his* mermaids. Irrationally Moreland found himself thinking of Dana's joining the Twice Lost as an intolerably personal betrayal. How *could* she? His eyes rolled up; fluorescent rings shone at intervals along the ceiling, tugging at his thoughts. They looked like round singing mouths.

"Sir?" The undersecretary was looking at Moreland with such an odd, concerned expression that it verged on insolence. "I was *extremely* sorry to hear the news about General Prudowski's death last week, sir. I know you worked closely with him. And then the shocking manner of his death, the way he was found drowned in his own swimming pool, must have been very disturbing."

"Of course," Moreland snapped.

Anais's caretaker—why could he never remember that pasty young man's name? Was it Freddy, or maybe Charlie?—peered out of an open door down the hallway. His face shone with pale pink hatred as he gazed at Moreland. His mouth hung open over his sharply receding chin.

"Sir? Shall we proceed?"

Moreland began walking automatically, almost brushing against that glowering face as he passed. "What about human activity?" Moreland asked. He knew that asking questions was expected of him, but in this case he also felt an ache of genuine interest. Human rebelliousness would be instigated by that Dorian Hurst boy; it would justify his steadily mounting fury at Anais.

"Human activity?"

"Those self-hating children calling themselves Twice Lost Humans. Any more trouble from them?"

"Yes, sir. There are large demonstrations going on in several cities at the moment. Most without permits. And there was an attempt to build a barricade across Route Sixty-six."

Unbelievable foolishness. Clearly there was a need for drastic action. General Luce's movement couldn't be allowed to disrupt naval traffic in any more cities, and she certainly couldn't go on attracting human followers seduced by her phony pacifism, her pretended naïve desire to protect the oceans.

The public needed to hate mermaids as much, as implacably, as he did. As for the way to make that happen, well . . .

It was unfair and outrageous that all the real effort, all the imagination and initiative, fell to him. But it looked like he'd just have to take matters into his own hands.

30

The Net

"Hey, Luce?" Imani had swum up beside her just after Luce's shift ended. They were floating together in the low waves halfway between the bridge and the crowd onshore. Luce was watching Eileen, who'd swum over to scan the faces in the crowd; she seemed to spend half her time there, swimming back and forth for hours. Obviously Eileen was searching for someone in particular, and Luce wondered who it was. And there was Yuan, leaning on the shore and talking with her new human friend Gigi again . . .

"Hey, Imani," Luce murmured. "Everything okay?" In the days since the murder, they'd fallen back into the same steady routine of singing and sleep. Nothing had really changed, except for occasional reports that mermaids in other cities had joined the Twice Lost and renounced killing and raised waves of their own. Nausicaa was doing incredible work, that was clear, and everyone was feeling optimistic. Their friends onshore told them about increasing numbers of humans protesting on the mermaids' behalf too. Almost everyone in the Twice Lost Army seemed convinced that the eagerly-awaited negotiations would start very soon, now that their movement was spreading and now that more and more humans seemed to be on their side. But as the days went by without a response from the human government, Luce only grew more anxious.

She could understand why so many of her followers were hoping for an easy victory. But this almost seemed *too* easy.

"It's about Catarina," Imani began, and Luce groaned inwardly. "She's completely stopped showing up for her shifts, Luce. And some of the other mermaids over at the Mare Island camp say she's been getting really angry for no reason and saying horrible things, like that Nausicaa persuaded you to betray everything mermaids stand for. I know she got jealous of Nausicaa, but still . . ."

Luce bit her lip. "Why does Catarina have to go and make *more* problems? Everything's already so hard, and she's just making it all worse."

Imani looked at her for a long moment, her eyes deep and searching. "But Luce . . . you're still her *friend*, right?"

Luce considered that. Delicate wands of mist stroked over the water, and by the shore it glowed mirror smooth and brilliantly silver. Gigi and Yuan were laughing hard about something, and the sight of their closeness brought tears into Luce's eyes. Even if Catarina's constant moodiness sometimes became exhausting, Luce did still love her. Maybe she *should* be the one to try harder, to reach out. "I'm still her friend. I just want her to stop making everything so complicated! Just because Nausicaa's my friend too, she doesn't need to go off and sulk and start telling *lies* like that."

"I think she's depressed, Luce. She thinks she's losing you." Imani's voice was even softer than usual. "You should go talk to her."

Luce sighed. The Twice Lost Army had swelled with the addition of refugees and drifters attracted by their fame, and a large mermaid encampment had sprung up under the wharves of the abandoned naval shipyards at Mare Island far in the north bay. The last thing Luce felt like doing was swimming that far, especially when it might mean another argument. But Imani was right: if Luce cared about Catarina's feelings, she should do something to show it. "Okay. I'll go. Imani . . ."

Imani only smiled silently, the silver water lapping around her dark shoulders.

"Thank you for . . . for reminding me to do the right thing. You always do."

* * *

Luce knew more or less where to find the Mare Island camp, but she hadn't actually been there before. When she surfaced fifty yards from its shore she was bewildered by the sweep and confusion of the island's waterfront: rusty cranes painted mustard and navy and dusty green crisscrossed the sky, a row of collapsing barracks stood deep in swaying yellow grass, and graffiti mottled the scaling white warehouses with names densely layered in ruby and silver scrawl. Bridges arched everywhere behind the island, their iron beams a complicated geometric lace against the mist covering the hills. Swallows dipped overhead. It was as lonely in its way as the distant coast of Alaska had been. In that whole decrepit expanse she didn't see a single human being.

But somewhere under the water, Mare Island wasn't deserted at all. Luce dived again, skimming along the jagged piers that rambled out into the bay. She could hear voices licking through the water but so bent and trembling that it was hard to tell quite where they were coming from. She was swimming away from the tangle of cranes and desolate buildings, out to where a broad dark pier glowered just above the water's surface. A charred, half-fallen shed leaned at its end, and as Luce approached it girls' voices seemed to drift closer to her.

"General Luce! You came to see us!" It was the tan-skinned mermaid who'd sung beside Luce through the night after that shocking murder. "Um, do you remember me?"

"Of course I remember you. I was so sad that night, and hearing you sing—it helped keep me going." Luce hesitated. "But I don't know your name?"

"Thanks. I'm Elva." She suddenly sounded shy. "Did you swim up here for a reason?"

"I have to find Catarina," Luce said softly.

Elva's expression darkened as she pointed into the deep shadows under the pier. "She's back there, all the way at the shore. Look, if she gives you a hard time . . ."

Luce tried to smile, but her insides were tense with dread. "It'll be okay." She dived, dipping and weaving her way through a forest of swaying fins. There were even more mermaids here than in the encampment near Hunter's Point. The low dark space was densely webbed with nets and hammocks. Mermaids curled half-submerged, dreaming or whispering.

Luce found her former queen slumped on her side on the gritty pebble shore. The pier formed a ceiling less than a foot above their heads, its rotting beams glittering with condensation and grubby with soot. Catarina's arm stretched up the beach, her pale hand emerging from her pooling red-gold hair; she turned her head just enough to glance sullenly at Luce, then buried her face in the fiery tangles again. Luce reached out and lightly touched her shoulder. "Hey, Cat?"

Catarina pivoted her head again. "Hello, *generalissima*. You seem to have gone out of your way for once."

Luce suppressed an impulse to snap back at her. "Cat, things shouldn't be like this with us! I don't really understand why you're so angry with me, but —"

"Angry?" Catarina raised herself slightly. Her stunning face was oddly blotchy and streaked with black dust. "Is that what I am, Lucette? Angry that you're still so childish that you can't see through Nausicaa and her ridiculous flattery? Is *that* what you think?"

It took an effort, but Luce kept her voice level. "I really didn't come here to fight with you, Cat." She paused, wondering if she should ask the next question, not sure she wanted to know the answer. "What do you have against Nausicaa, anyway? You said something about her and Queen Marina . . ." Queen Marina, whom Catarina had adored and followed and lost when the queen left the sea out of love for a human and died on the shore. Luce couldn't quite believe that Nausicaa would have done anything truly wrong to Marina, though.

"Indeed." Catarina exhaled sharply. "Indeed, just as Nausicaa is doing now with you, Lucette. She appeared out of nowhere, telling her preposterous stories of living with the first mermaids, of spending thousands of years in the sea and escaping death again and again. And Marina believed all of it, blindly enchanted with her. For three months Marina completely forgot the rest of us. She behaved like the tide chasing after the moon."

Catarina was just jealous, then. "If that's all that happened, you shouldn't have made everybody think that Nausicaa did something untrustworthy! Cat, those things you said when Nausicaa came, I mean, all of that *really* wasn't fair."

Catarina glowered. "Nausicaa *is* untrustworthy. She abandoned Marina in the night, with no explanation, no goodbye. For so great a queen as Marina, to have her devotion discarded so callously . . . She never fully recovered her former strength of mind, Lucette. She was half-broken, remote. And it was not long afterward that Marina sought consolation by throwing herself into the arms of that *human*. If it hadn't been for Nausicaa's heartlessness . . ."

Luce flinched, thinking of how recently she'd woken up to find that Nausicaa had vanished. And then, Catarina . . . "But *you* left *me* without saying goodbye, Cat. Don't you remember? Up in Alaska I came back to the cave and you were just gone. I don't see why it's so different when Nausicaa does the same thing."

"I had no choice!" Catarina snarled. She moved to sit up, but the filthy planks above stopped her. "For Nausicaa *everything* is a choice. Anyone who cares for her is simply a temporary amusement, Lucette. As you will certainly discover! But I had *real* responsibilities. I had to do whatever I could to save our tribe from that *sika* Anais. The only possibility open to me was to leave you, and to trust that you would behave with honor and become their queen!" Catarina laughed bitterly. "I gave you too much credit, it seems. Queen is too trivial a title to tempt you. You require much more than that!"

For a moment Luce was distracted by anger at Catarina's insinuations. Her tail thrashed the murky water into froth and she looked away into the dimness, fighting to compose herself. Then it hit her: "that *sika*"? Luce was certain she'd never heard Catarina use that word before: the word for a mermaid who'd lost her humanity not through suffering like the rest of them, but simply through her own essential coldness, her utter inability to feel or to love.

Luce had learned that Anais was a *sika* from Nausicaa, in fact, along with everything a *sika*'s nature implied. But Catarina had never even mentioned it as a possibility.

"You knew Anais was a *sika*?" Luce asked. Her voice came out thin and high and oddly detached from her, a rag of sound brushing through the shadows. "Did you know that all along?"

The dim glow of Catarina's face showed the flickering shifts of her expression all too clearly: surprise, an instantaneous blink of something like alarm, then a slight self-conscious smirk. Streams of copper-shining hair obscured one of her moon gray eyes. "Well . . . I knew there was nothing to see, of course, in the indication that surrounded her. Nothing like a story to be captured with a sideways glance, as I can still observe the story of what your uncle did to you. But as for what that meant . . . I suppose I knew that Anais *might* be one of such mermaids as I had heard described some years before, a *sika*."

"But if you knew," Luce began, her voice still that thin strange scrap drifting on the air between them. "Cat, if you knew you should have *warned* everyone as soon as Anais joined us! Why didn't you . . . we could have thrown her out of the tribe before . . ." *Before so many people died, before the tribe went crazy sinking all those ships, before she killed those larval mermaids. Before she tried to murder Dana and Violet and me,* Luce thought.

Catarina looked away, and all at once Luce knew *exactly* why she hadn't taken action to prevent Anais from worming her way into the tribe and destroying it.

"Had you learned what a *sika* was from Nausicaa, Cat? And because you just didn't want to believe Nausicaa was right about *anything* . . . you pretended everything was fine with Anais until most of the girls in our tribe were on her side, and it was too late?" Luce stopped talking. She felt as if all the air had been ripped from her lungs, as if her heart was seized in a vice that squeezed all the blood from it and kept it from beating.

Cat still wouldn't meet her eyes, and Luce knew it was true.

Catarina had actually *allowed* Anais to take over the tribe out of the spite and envy she felt toward Nausicaa. She'd willfully ignored the warnings she'd heard years before Anais was even born.

"Cat?" Luce's voice came out jagged, accusatory. "Cat, is that what happened? You should have driven Anais away the second she showed up, and you just didn't do it? And then you left me alone to deal with *your* mess?"

Catarina glanced at her for just a fraction of a second. The gray shine of her eyes stabbed through the shadows, flashed away again. "I suppose the question seems so easy to you, Lucette. You would never doubt anything Nausicaa told you, not even the most outrageous lies. After all, if you did, you would also have to doubt the sincerity of her *friendship* for you. But Nausicaa never told *me* lies too charming to question. So why would I believe a single word she said?"

Anais's out-of-control attacks on ships had provoked the humans to the point of slaughtering their old tribe. Luce closed her eyes and saw girls' faces veiled by water stained ruby; she saw throats gashed wide and bubbling with blood.

"You should have believed Nausicaa because she was *right*! She was always telling the truth! You just didn't want to listen . . ." Luce moaned.

Anais's actions had helped bring on the *war*.

"Of course you take Nausicaa's side! I knew you would, Lucette."

"I am *not* taking Nausicaa's side, Cat!" Luce's voice was high and sharp enough that other mermaids under the pier turned to look at them. "You're the one who wants to make everything be about *Nausicaa* and how much you hate her. I'm taking the *mermaids'* side."

The silence went on so long that it seemed to flex and coil like a snake. Catarina drew herself up, her beautiful face stiff and haughty, and gazed at Luce with regal disdain. "Luce, do you dare to suggest that I am *not* on the mermaids' side?" she hissed at last. "You accuse me of this, when you love *humans* so much that you degrade not only yourself for their sake, but you even lead your followers into the same degradation? When you would accept any humiliation from that human *boy* of yours if only he would pretend to care for you!"

A cold, airless rage choked Luce's heart, clotted in her throat and eyes. There was nothing she could say in the face of such despicable cruelty, especially coming from Catarina. Between the low planks and the beach darkness waited, like some heavy, compressed substance. Something about that darkness felt to Luce like contempt made visible.

She wouldn't answer Catarina. She would never answer her again.

"I have no place here, in this absurd army of yours. I should leave," Catarina murmured at last.

Do you think I'll beg you not *to go?* Luce thought bitterly. *After what you just said?*

"Does it mean nothing to you, Luce? If I leave here? We may never see each other again." Catarina's voice was veering up the scale, wild and plaintive.

Luce finally turned to look at her. Catarina's gray eyes met hers with a shocked, scattered brilliance. Cat's cheeks were bone white, and as she saw the look on Luce's face she visibly recoiled. Her recoil transformed into a sudden, violent rippling like a flame in the wind, and she vanished under the water. Luce could just see the golden shimmer of her tail streaking away.

For half a second, Luce felt nothing but a kind of savage relief that Cat was gone. Then something in Luce's stifled heart burst free, and she gave a trembling cry and dived after her.

* * *

Luce had forgotten what an exceptional swimmer Catarina was, how extraordinarily quick and fluid she was even for a mermaid. The water of the north bay was murkier than she was used to, beige and unpleasantly brackish; Catarina's golden fins showed only as a kind of bright disturbance far ahead. "Cat!" Luce called into the opaque water. "Cat, I'm sorry!" She knew how well sound traveled through water; surely Catarina must hear her?

Then Luce couldn't catch even a glimmer of distant fins any-more, even as she drove herself faster. When she surfaced for a breath there was nothing around but the lonely shore with its scat-tered palm trees and rusty metal huts leaning in auburn grass. Bridges like the skeletons of snakes were slung across the pale sky.

But if Catarina was determined to leave she could be going in only one direction: back toward the Golden Gate and the wild deep sea beyond. Luce gathered her strength and dived again, her tail lashing behind her. Once Cat reached the open ocean, Luce would lose all hope of finding her. A black slash of wings broke the water just in front of her, startling her into reeling abruptly side-ways, before she saw the cormorant sweep toward the surface again with a silver fish in its beak.

Still, Catarina was nowhere, not even when the city loomed ahead again, not even when Luce came up to see the dull red curves of the Golden Gate Bridge not too far away. Mermaid song vi-brated through the water, stroking Luce's fins with tremulous mu-sic, and the wave beneath the bridge still shone like a wall formed from millions of shivering crystals. The sun burned through a fine haze, and light like grainy brush strokes danced around her. "Catarina?" Luce called, but the air suddenly pulsed with a loud, disturbing noise that drowned out her voice.

Luce looked up to see the helicopter whizzing overhead. Of course there were always helicopters around the bay now, sent by different news channels as well as by the military, but they never came this *close*. The military ones usually just circled high above the bridge, watching the mermaids below.

This one was darkly drab, heavy but sleekly formed, menacing: definitely the same as the ones that had attacked them before. And it was swinging rapidly lower. Something Luce couldn't quite make out swagged from the helicopter's base until it was almost skimming the water. Then with an agitated rippling the surface broke and whatever that dangling thing was dipped into the bay, slicing deeper as it neared the bridge with disquieting speed. Luce raced ahead. The glassy sides of the towering wave juddered with the pounding air from the propeller. She heard screams unraveling from the human crowd lining the bridge, saw people shift and jostle and slam one another in a panic as the helicopter rushed toward them, its blades ripping so close to their gathered faces that Luce feared they would be slashed to bits.

At the last possible moment the helicopter changed course, pulling steeply straight upward. Luce had a brief moment to feel relieved.

Then she recognized what the helicopter was dragging with it, out of the bay and up into the gusting wind.

A net. That thing hanging from its bottom was a *net*.

And now it wasn't empty.

The helicopter rose, its blades hacking at the air. Below it a tangle of mermaids — ten? a dozen? — jerked and thrashed against the net's strands. Luce flung herself across the water even as she stared in desperation. Netted arms bent randomly around rippling, translucent fins in subtle shades of bronze and celadon and smoky peach; ribbons of long hair tumbled through the mesh; dark and pale hands wrenched at the strands, trying frantically to tear their way free. Then the helicopter stopped its ascent and simply hovered high in space: higher than the bridge, higher than any wave the mermaids could hope to command.

Didn't the humans understand that —

"They'll die!" Luce heard herself screaming into the sky. "You have to put them back in the water! They'll die!"

If the helicopter's crew heard her, they gave no sign of it. But other mermaids did. In a moment Luce was surrounded by clamoring girls: "Luce, what are they *doing*? Aren't they afraid we'll let the wave go?" "What are we supposed to do?" "You have to make them stop, Luce! You *have* to!"

The standing wave still shone in the misty, smoldering sunlight, but Luce saw that it was starting to dip and wobble a little. Too many singers were abandoning their places, racing out to see what was happening.

"We have to keep singing!" Luce yelled. "No matter what! Everyone, *get back* in the line!"

Luce saw reluctance, even anger, in the faces around her. "They're killing our friends!" Eileen snarled back at her. "We'll go back to singing once they let everyone out of that net. How's *that* for a compromise?"

"And what about all those humans onshore? What about the ones who are just there to help us? Are you going to let *them* drown?" Luce's voice was savage as she wheeled on Eileen. "Get *back* to your place, Eileen. What if one of those humans is that person you keep waiting for?"

Eileen's face blanched and she swirled back a few feet under the impact of Luce's glare. "Fine. I guess you have a point." She crooked her strawberry-blond head at the other undecided mermaids. "Come on, everyone. You heard the *general*."

Eileen was just turning to go when two appalling sounds called her back.

The first was a thin, strangely pale-sounding scream from the net above. It prickled on the air like a million motes of galvanized dust.

The second was a loudspeaker. A rough, staticky voice boomed down through the treble of that scream. *"You have three minutes to lower the wave completely and end the blockade. Repeat, you have three minutes only. If you do not comply, the captive mermaids will be allowed to die. Release the wave now, and the captives will be released."*

It was so insane that for an instant Luce could only stare up at the helicopter, flabbergasted. They must realize the impossibility of safely lowering so much water in such a short time. If she obeyed them, she'd unleash a tsunami. A speeding field of water would crush the city, and thousands of people would certainly die.

The humans in that helicopter were *ordering* her to destroy San Francisco.

The air shook with another high, sustained scream, and then another. The mermaids in the net were starting to go into convulsions as their tails began to dry out. The net rocked and heaved in the air high above until it looked like a single shapeless, tortured animal.

For a few seconds there was nothing Luce could say. Around her other mermaids gaped with the same staggered hopelessness she felt herself; beside them the standing water-wall buckled a little more, and odd blobs and sashes of water began to tumble down its brilliant flank.

"Luce," Jo begged beside her, "just tell everyone to stop singing! Just let the wave go! Even *you* said we could kill to save other mermaids! You *said* so! And we don't have any choice, not when they're . . . when we're . . ."

The mermaids were being *tested*, Luce realized.

Whoever was ordering them to release the wave understood perfectly well what the consequences would be. For some strange reason, the humans in that helicopter *wanted* the Twice Lost Army to kill—to kill as many people as possible.

"Hold the line!" Luce screamed. "It's a trick! They *want* us to kill everyone!"

Yuan was there, but closer to the bridge—thank God Yuan was suddenly there, gazing at her with a look of appalled understanding—and Luce saw her nod sharply once before she dived, pulling two other mermaids with her. Luce could hear Yuan shouting down the line, "It's a trick! *Defy* them! Get back in your places and *sing*! No brave mermaid would ever take orders from a human! Show them that! *Defy* them!"

Oh, Yuan. No one is like you. No one else could be so strong.

"But Luce . . ."

It was Jo, pointing up now with one wild white arm, biting at her other hand until droplets of ruby blood burst through the skin.

"Hold the line! Keep singing!" Luce shrieked again. At least *some* of the mermaids nearby seemed to be singing to the water again, dipping under the bridge as they sang, though the wave was tilting now and fissured at its top into uneven, jutting swags.

Luce's head throbbed with the shivering screams of the mermaids above her. Her face was slick with tears as she turned to join the mermaids singing under the bridge. No matter what, they *couldn't* let the wave collapse. Not even if those mermaids in the net had to die—to save thousands of human lives.

Jo grabbed her arm, jerking Luce back so sharply that she gasped.

"You now have exactly two minutes. Lower the wave completely within that time or the captives will all die."

There wasn't even a way Luce could offer herself in their place. She could scream until her throat ruptured; the helicopter's crew would never hear her.

"Luce!" Jo shouted in her ear. "They've got Catarina!"

The net jarred again, and suddenly Luce saw red-gold hair like a rivulet of liquid fire pouring through its holes. One of the frenzied, shrieking voices far above suddenly brightened and clarified, catching Luce's heart in a shining net of its own. Jo was right. That could *only* be Catarina, tangled and quaking with the other captives.

If Luce didn't order the Twice Lost to unleash the tsunami, Catarina would die in agonizing pain within minutes.

And she would die believing that Luce hated her.

* * *

Luce couldn't move. The bay might as well have locked up completely, become an endless sheet of ice gripping her. All she could do was gaze from that fiery trace of Catarina's hair dangling against the white sky, to the soaring water-wall under the bridge, to the ragged skyline of San Francisco. On the shore some people were fighting to crush their way onto the already dangerously over-crowded bridge or to run up the hill—though if the wave was re-leased, they would certainly never manage to run far or fast enough to save themselves. A few humans were taking advantage of the confusion to dive into the bay. Luce could see their arms splashing up through the salt water as they swam doggedly toward the mer-maids, though they were still quite far away. They would drown, too. The air around Luce's head pulsated with screams and the vio-lent percussion of helicopter blades—and there seemed to be more helicopters now, including some that were whirling rapidly to-ward the one carrying the net.

The mermaids in the net shrieked and spasmed. Luce knew exactly what they were feeling: a white pain like needles made of pure sun drilling in on all sides, pain so piercing and terrible that thought and hope and breath were all extinguished. But it was still in Luce's power to save them. They were still *alive*.

"This is your final warning. Release the wave now."

Yuan's human friend, Gigi, was alive too, though, probably on the shore nearby. So was the man who'd spread his jacket over the murdered mermaid. So were countless humans whose hearts Luce couldn't guess at: hearts that would vanish forever under an on-slaught of water strong enough to lift trucks and level buildings—*if* Luce gave in and obeyed the helicopter's insane command.

Already some of the singers were surfacing again, their voices fading away in a kind of dazed mutiny. Without them, the water-wall sloped precariously. Then one watery swag broke free and plummeted into the bay. The surface rose in an abrupt, fifteen-foot swell that lifted Luce and Jo and the others skyward and dropped them again. It raced toward the shore, broke into countless flying shards of foam, grabbed people and threw them like twigs. And *that* was only a small piece of the water the mermaids were supporting, a single loose scrap of sea. Any more than that . . .

Luce heard herself singing. The song broke through her awful entrancement, and she saw other mermaids turn to stare at her. She felt her new strength touch them as their voices rose again, and then their strength flowed back into her. A circuit of shared power woke the deep green waters. Her throat felt thick and knotted, but the voice that tore through it was vibrant, sweet, and powerful. Tears streamed from her eyes, joining the sea. Luce sank below the surface, her song a hovering cry for everything that was lost, for those who were dead and those who were dying now. She saw the Twice Lost holding hands in that endless chain below the bridge, their heads thrown back and fins shimmering. Yuan was there, fiercely corralling uncertain mermaids into the line, passionately driving her voice into fusion with those hundreds of other voices. There were Opal, and Jo, and Graciela, all singing, all reaching out their hands to other mermaids, urging them to keep going—no matter what happened.

Even if the song came out like sobs, even if it wavered, it still *held*. And with the song their towering wave oscillated and jumped . . .

But it didn't fall. It didn't *fall*.

The screams of the netted mermaids were gradually ebbing away, thinner and lighter. Luce gagged for a second with the knowledge of what that meant—then forced her voice into the song again. The others were singing more loudly too, and now along with the infinite grief in that song there was a new tone of defiance, sad and calm and still somehow ferocious all at once.

Luce closed her eyes, feeling herself suspended in an expanse of water and music made one. Almost all the screams had slipped into silence now. The glassy darkness surrounding her filled with the knowledge that Catarina was almost surely dead—and that Luce herself had made the choice to kill her queen and her friend.

Her song twisted on like a living thing, vital with determination. But while her voice still lived, Luce was sure her heart hadn't survived.

* * *

A rattle of gunfire burst through the immense upwelling song. Lost in numbness beyond grief, Luce could only feel a dull chill in place of fear. That helicopter's crew was enraged by the mermaids' disobedience—of course; of *course*, those lunatics had started shooting in frustration. Soon the bombs would fall, and the water would burst with crushing waves of energy. For some reason those people up there wanted San Francisco destroyed, and they weren't about to take the mermaids' no for an answer.

It was all over, then. Everything she'd tried to do was about to be obliterated. In a dark, mournful way Luce wondered how many of the Twice Lost would die and how many would flee before there weren't enough of them left to sustain the wave. Maybe, just maybe, they could buy some of the humans onshore enough time to escape from the inevitable cataclysm.

She'd killed humans before, Luce thought dreamily. It seemed fair enough that now she would die trying to save at least a few of them. And then Catarina was dead because of her, and soon

Luce would die too; that seemed right as well. She almost smiled as she reached out her hands, touching the water around her as if it were an enclosure of glossy diamond. As the guns cracked again Luce's voice rose to meet their outbursts, wild and sweet. There were no words to her song, but it was still shaped by an emotion so strong that the music seemed to take on language: *I accept it, I accept it, I accept* . . .

"Luce!" It was Yuan. Luce wouldn't stop the song until a spear or a bomb stopped it for her, but she opened her eyes to gaze at Yuan, trying to reassure her without words. *You can leave, you can live, but I'm staying. I accept this.* "Luce, something crazy is happening! Those helicopters—they're shooting at each other! Not at us!" That made no sense, Luce thought hazily. Yuan obviously didn't know what she was talking about.

Yuan pulled at Luce's elbow, and Luce resisted her, suddenly stabbed by fear again after that long cold lull. It wasn't death that horrified her, but the thought of seeing Catarina's lifeless body swinging in the sky. "Luce, this is important!" Yuan gasped. "We *have* to understand what's happening—we can't just ignore it! *You* can't."

Yuan leaped, grabbing Luce around her ribs, then spiraled her tail so forcefully that they both rocketed to the surface. Yuan actually caught Luce's short hair in one hand, jerking her head back to make her *see* . . .

Two helicopters waltzed around each other, rising, dropping and swooping with balletic grace. Strangely, Yuan was right; they didn't seem to be shooting at the mermaids under the bridge or even paying any attention to them. Behind the two aircraft the clouds had parted, showing long sinuous sweeps of bright blue sky, and the spinning propellers cast ribbons of reflected sunlight into the air. The spectacle would have seemed mesmerizing, even gorgeous, if it weren't for the net full of dead girls dangling horribly from one helicopter.

Serene if it weren't for the staccato gunfire that spat abruptly, slicing straight across the helicopter's tail.

The helicopter carrying the net sputtered as the bullets cut through it, as its tail sheered away and plunged into the water in a ring of spray. It seemed to stagger in the sky, crippled and shocked, then began descending in a long wobbling fall like a bird caught in a turbulent downdraft. The victor hovered just above, watchful and threatening, as its prey dropped toward shallow water. The net touched down first, then the wounded copter sank in defeat just ahead of it. Small dark boats converged on the spot.

Beside them the wave still held, tall and unyielding.

There was a disturbance in the water behind them. Luce glanced around, confused, and saw one of those human swimmers nearby, her arms flailing with exhaustion. A golden, chubby girl, her drenched clothes flopping around her. She pulled her head up, gasping, trying to say something—and Yuan gave a piercing cry and caught the girl in her arms. "Gigi! Gigi, are you crazy? You should have been running uphill as fast as you could! What would have happened if . . . if we hadn't managed to—you would have *drowned*, and—"

"I *couldn't* let you go through that alone, Yuan! How could you think for one second that I would? Oh, God!"

Alone? Luce thought wearily. Had Yuan really felt alone until Gigi arrived?

Where was Nausicaa now?

And even if he was angry or disappointed in her, why had her father *still* not come to look for her? Luce knew she'd done horrible things as a mermaid — but hadn't she earned his forgiveness yet?

And Dorian? Could he be thinking of her now?

Luce stared back toward the circle of boats surrounding the downed helicopter. People were loading blanket-wrapped corpses onto the boats. And one of those veiled bodies was Catarina's.

Who was she, *what* was she, now that she had allowed her friend to die?

31

Always a Price

The larvae tank wasn't nearly as luxurious as the tank where Anais lived: it was an uncovered glass enclosure half-filled with bubbling salt water, set in the center of a bland white room. There was no need for the soundproof barrier that sealed Anais from the world. Larvae's attempts at singing weren't much more than eerie, dissonant squeaks that didn't threaten anyone. The tank contained a small artificial shore, crudely formed from coated plaster, so that the larval mermaids would have somewhere to sleep, but apart from that there wasn't much for the mushy little creatures to do. Charlie Hackett, who was extremely proud of his growing reputation for handling the captive mermaids well, had brought them a few random toys: pink plastic dinosaurs with glittery eyelids and docile smiles, a teething ring with a row of bright beads sliding in an endless circle, a battered Barbie doll in a golden swimsuit. As he entered their room, rolling the small gurney in front of him, he saw half a dozen larvae tussling in the tank, their stubby pastel tails flopping as they wrestled. They were squeaking fitfully, and after a moment Charlie Hackett recognized the source of the trouble: one especially temperamental larva had the Barbie and wouldn't let the others play with it.

That made his decision easier. Because what he had to do now was definitely the worst part of his job. Coming back from yet another shopping expedition—they'd sent him out that afternoon to replace some of Anais's broken belongings—he'd been disheartened to find the order to select one of his small charges for an experimental treatment. And they hadn't even left him any time to check in on Anais, to refresh his mind with an infusion of her bright beauty. "Now, Snowy," Charlie murmured. He'd named the troublemaker larva Snow White for her pale bluish skin, midnight hair, and beautiful sapphire eyes. "Now, Snowy, you know we've talked about this. You have to learn to share with your friends, and if you can't . . ."

Something in his tone warned her. She looked up at him, burbling apprehensively, and dropped the doll. Her deep blue eyes rounded in wordless appeal. The others trilled out airy, piercing cries and shrank away from her into the corners. They'd seen more than one of their small companions carried off before, though he'd been careful to keep them from knowing what happened next.

Charlie Hackett grimaced. He needed to hurry up and get this over with, before those yearning eyes got to him. He sank his arms into the water, up to the elbows, and gripped Snowy by the waist as she tried to wriggle away. She pawed his hand softly and crooned. Trying to talk him out of it in the only way she could. He looked away from her plaintive little face and hefted her, swinging her dangling silver fins clear of the glass, and plunked her down on the gurney. She was already emitting a series of harsh, quick, bursting shrieks. He pinned her expertly with one hand while he used the other to bundle her tail in a pile of dripping, salt water–soaked towels that would protect it from drying out too soon, then turned to the task of strapping her to the gurney.

He couldn't stand those eyes, their frantic blue gaze lapping at his face like hungry waves, and he draped another towel across the top half of her face to stop her from gawking at him. That helped a bit, though she was still shrieking. Her muffled fins thudded rapidly against the steel like a dog's wagging tail beating at a chair. As fast as he could, Charlie Hackett spun the gurney around and thrust it ahead of him.

An older, drab-faced man and an older grayish woman stood up a bit awkwardly as he charged through their door. Both of them wore lab coats, and a rolling table of equipment waited beside them. The woman already had the syringe in her hand, holding it not far from her own cheek. Her face was tight and perturbed, and—unusually—she didn't greet him as he entered. The skin around her eyes was purplish, crumpled and heavy. The man was making notes in a black logbook. A video camera, pointing downward, was positioned over the taped markings that showed where the gurney was supposed to park. With only a tremor of hesitation, Charlie Hackett rolled the larva to the correct spot. Then, without thinking about what he was doing, he caught Snowy's tiny, spongy hand and squeezed it protectively.

He'd already watched four larvae die in this room, and he had no faith in the potion in that syringe. Snowy had at most twenty minutes left to live. Her tail thumped on and on, a nervous stifled drumroll, but at least her shrieks had died down to a whimper.

That wouldn't last, of course.

"Her name is Snowy," Charlie Hackett said. "Snowy." Naming her—forcing these doctors to *know* her name—was the best approximation of courage he could manage.

The man glared at him imperiously, but the woman gave a weary nod as she approached, her needle glinting in the pallid light. This business was taking a toll on her, too, Charlie Hackett noted with some satisfaction. It was only fair that she should suffer for what she was about to do. For an instant he was tempted to tell her so, loud and clear. Then he looked down and obediently turned Snowy's arm outward for the injection.

"Snowy," the woman breathed out. Tentatively she touched the larva's damp shoulder then twitched her hand back with evident repulsion. "Snowy, it's going to be okay. I have some medicine here for you that will help you feel better. All right, hush now. You're going to feel . . . just a little poke." The needle slipped into the larva's arm, the plunger depressed, and the silver tail kicked so violently that a drenched towel slumped off the gurney and landed on Hackett's ankle with a squelch. Snowy started yowling. It didn't sound quite like a normal baby's cry; it was shriller, stranger, touched by a hint of unnatural music: a noise that made human flesh quiver and shrink.

When her screams started, they wouldn't sound much like a human baby screaming, either.

"Remove the rest of the towels, please, Charles," the woman said quietly.

He did it, tugging them free of the jerking fins and dropping them in a sodden heap to one side. Then, for the first time, he wondered *why* he had done it. But wasn't it better for Snowy to have someone she loved and trusted at her side now rather than to find herself abandoned to uncaring strangers? It was only by doing exactly what they told him that he could have the opportunity to be here for her and the other larvae—just as he had to obey Secretary Moreland if he wanted to spend time with Anais. If he didn't follow their instructions exactly he would be fired, and then what would become of Anais without him?

"Take the towel off her face, too. We need a complete record of the effects."

Hackett removed the towel silently. He was doing it for Anais, his darling, golden Anais, so that he could stay here, so that he could continue to serve as her protector and her knight.

Snowy's blue eyes swung wildly around the room as if she was looking for someone who might save her. Her brilliant silver tail dashed violently against the cold steel table. She screamed again and again, her racked body slamming against the restraints so hard that her stomach began to weep beads of blood around the straps. For two full minutes the humans stared mesmerized at the dying larva, their minds like sails filled by her screams.

Then Charlie Hackett felt himself breaking through entrancement as if it were some slick membrane. He groaned sharply. "It's not working! It's not working! Just do *something* for her!"

The lab-coated man looked up from his notes. "It's hardly appropriate for you to second-guess our work. It's a new formula, it should —"

"I'm upping her dosage," the woman interrupted. Her voice was barely audible over that throbbing scream. Another needle drew a bright clear line across the air, straight into Snowy's neck. The little larva was in convulsions now, and the luster dimmed on her silver scales. They had turned the color of old tin, as dry as scabs, loose-looking and ashy.

Snowy couldn't even scream anymore now, only sigh. Charlie Hackett knew from experience what that meant: she was near the end. Her scales were flaking away, winding into a kind of silvery smoke. Her spasms ceased, her blue eyes closed, and she shuddered. She seemed surprisingly quiet all of a sudden, actually, her small body suddenly gone soft and limp. Her hands made tiny fists then opened again. She gave a long exhalation.

And then two babyish legs sagged on the gurney. Snowy lay silent, unmoving. The gray woman moved forward and rested a hand on that small pale chest, feeling for a heartbeat.

He might as well get back to the rest of the larvae, Hackett thought. It would take at least an hour of coaxing and petting before they would be calm enough to eat their dinner. And then there was Anais, who probably hadn't heard any of the bizarre, incomprehensible news coming out of San Francisco. He wasn't supposed to tell her anything about the outside world, of course. Talking too much was the kind of small defiance he felt ready to risk. And as his reward she would murmur to him, turn her azure eyes on his face, laugh and play and tell him her secrets.

Snowy's corpse had a faint blue tinge and a subtle luminous quality that marked her, even in death, as having once been something more than human. Hackett ran a hand over his face and turned to leave.

A whispery moan came from the air behind him. The woman gave a sudden cry.

Charlie Hackett spun around. The moaning stopped for an instant and then came back more loudly.

There was the thump of a small foot kicking steel. Two sapphire eyes opened, and then Snowy let out the full-throated cry of a hurt human toddler. The change in her voice startled Hackett even more than the change in her body, even more than the fact that she was miraculously still alive. She suddenly sounded like any other frightened child.

The gray woman was unbuckling Snowy's restraints with trembling hands. She scooped the howling little creature up and cradled her close against the coarse white lab coat. "Oh, you *poor* little thing, you *poor* little thing. Oh, you're going to be *fine* . . ."

The drab man nodded sharply. "Mr. Hackett? Fetch us another one."

The words jarred through Charlie Hackett; his shoulders heaved up and his voice came out as a yelp. "*Excuse* me?"

"We have to ascertain that this larva lived through the transition because of the new drugs. Until we can replicate our results with a second larva, there's nothing to indicate your *Snowy*'s survival wasn't just a fluke like that mermaid in San Francisco we've been hearing about. It might be rare, but apparently in exceptional cases mermaids do survive the transition without the benefit of medical intervention. There's no room for doubt here. Another one, please."

Hackett stared, outraged and breathless. Snowy bawled in the woman's arms. "I do have *other* responsibilities," he managed at last. "It's after six, and I haven't had a chance yet to feed the larvae their dinner, and I haven't seen Anais in *hours*."

The lab-coated man's bland affect was punctured by sincere surprise. "Anais?"

"I'm responsible for making sure her needs are met, not just for being your errand boy! She's been kept in solitary confinement for months now, and the potential damage to her mental health is—"

"Anais isn't here anymore, Mr. Hackett. I assumed you'd been informed."

"Anais isn't . . . Of *course* she's still right where I . . . She couldn't just get up and *walk*." Had his golden beauty escaped through the plumbing somehow or used some unfathomable magic to melt a tunnel to the sea? But then . . . wouldn't she have asked him to come with her?

"Secretary Moreland ordered her prepared for transport two hours ago. I personally saw her being loaded into the special tank truck that was used to bring her here. She was on a gurney, much like—" here the drab doctor allowed his face to show just a flutter of malice—"much like this one you used to bring us Snowy. Larger, of course."

"But didn't she—" He couldn't ask if she'd cried, if she'd begged to at least be allowed to say goodbye to him. "Didn't she say anything?"

"She appeared to be heavily sedated. Presumably as a precaution against singing, although the men moving her were also wearing protective helmets."

Sedated. His Anais drugged, unable to cry out for her one true friend, her champion. If he had only been here, he would have torn her from that gurney with his hands suddenly gleaming like gilt steel and run with her in his arms all the way to the sea. And with her by his side the cold, compounding waves would be no obstacle. But instead he'd been sent out of the way on purpose, to guarantee that no one would defend her. His rare beauty, his strange jewel . . .

"You do realize we're at war," the gray man said. His voice came as a terrible violation of Hackett's thoughts. "I am not a sadist, Mr. Hackett. I don't enjoy torturing . . . creatures of ambiguous status . . . especially when they happen to resemble human children. But changing mermaids back successfully will mean the end of the war. They'll abandon the Twice Lost Army in droves once we can offer them a different, better life. You'd agree that that's a noble objective, wouldn't you?"

How stupid Moreland had been. So distracted, so unhinged by Anais's mere presence that he hadn't even considered what

Hackett might do for love of her. But he was Anais's one true friend, and he'd taken what precautions he could on her behalf. If anyone ever brought any accusations against her—accusations concerning the deaths of Kathleen Lambert or General Prudowski, for example—he could prove that Anais had been cruelly exploited, forced to act against her will.

"Another one, please, Mr. Hackett. Then we can all go home. Believe me, I'm every bit as tired and hungry as you are."

Anais hadn't wanted to do those things any more than he wanted to go pluck another sacrificial larva from the tank.

The thought consoled him as he gripped the gurney's cold metal handle and—obediently, miserably, with all the rebellion sapped from his body—turned and rolled it out the door.

Somehow it was the squeak of the wheels that changed everything for him.

Somehow, in that moment, his own obedience became unendurable.

*　*　*

A man lay on the pavement of an alley in Washington, DC. He was humming a melody that seemed to trace drowsy circles in the dusky air around his head. He hadn't understood before, he hadn't *understood*, but now he knew that the only true language was music. Even his thoughts no longer took the form of words but instead were transcribed as elaborately coded blurts of sound. He knew what words were, of course, when he heard them: they were the unmusic, squawks not bright or rare or beautiful enough to *mean* anything.

He only wanted to join with the songs and the world they revealed. That world had contours of impossible purity. Its empty spaces fell from resonant claps of the moon. Sometimes he was in the music. Sometimes he *was* what it sang, his being summed by the sequence of its tones. But more often his body got in the way. He could understand that. Flesh and bone were bulky; they annoyed the music with their intractable mass.

He was lying on the pavement now, very still, in the hope that the music might forget that he still had his body with him. He stared up, face to face with the extreme blue that showed between two brick walls. In a dim way he knew that the car had left him here some days before—an octave or more of days, each one full of light like the slap of a bird's wing against his eyes. Perhaps he'd been expected to go somewhere else, but he heard the world so *clearly* here that movement seemed wasteful, even absurd.

One of the back doors along the alley vented food smells. A woman opened it and leaned out, searching, then spotted him. She set a paper plate full of eggs and toast down on the cement and let out three sharp cymballine hisses—*tss, tss, tss*—as if she was calling a cat. The door clicked shut.

He didn't go in pursuit of the food. Perhaps later. At the moment he'd almost coaxed the music into rendering him in its true voice again, making him the substance of its melody. It sat on his chest, considering him. Two round lights parted the alley like shining throats. The music rumbled thoughtfully and then ground to a stop.

"They left him here," a voice said. "I wasn't supposed to know. I wasn't supposed to know anything. It's funny that I know *everything*, then, isn't it? Except the only thing that really matters, where *she* is . . ."

"I'm truly sorry," someone answered gently—and those words, strangely, *did* seem meaningful. They carried a certain familiar warmth that was in itself a form of unexpected music. "I do hope you'll make the decision to take your information public. To expose the way Anais has been used. Of course I've been aware for months now that they were holding her and that she'd been providing information, but it never occurred to me that even someone like Moreland might use her as a weapon!" The voice tipped across space with each word: there was the face, swinging like a lantern in a car's open window. "Andrew's probably long gone, of course. But I'll get out and search, just in case."

Andrew. That was surprising. That was a sound that formed a skin, and inside the skin there was a person . . .

"I want Moreland *dead*," the first voice moaned. "Whatever is the worst nightmare he could have, the worst torture, for *taking* her from me . . . She's been through so much, and she's *fragile*, and he has no idea how to care for her."

The man on the pavement had stopped listening. The sky's blue blast was louder than words.

Then he felt a sudden grinding pain and heard himself shout. His body curled involuntarily, bringing his head and chest up into shadow-damp air. He didn't know it, but someone had accidentally stepped on his hand. The pressure pulled back, and his hand hurt much less.

Another cry came, not his own. And the man on the pavement discovered that the cry came with a face: tan, with large, sympathetic brown eyes and silver hair. It came attached to a name.

He didn't seem able to speak. Instead he sang the name, slowly, groping his way through the syllables with raspy music. "Ben . . . Ell . . . iss . . . son?"

"Andrew! Good God, you've been here in this alley all this time?"

He couldn't answer that. But it didn't matter.

The wonderful thing about music was that whatever was true was also obvious: as obvious as those large hands grasping him and hauling him to his feet.

* * *

"Anais." Moreland breathed her name out, hard, as he climbed into the back of the truck and then pulled the heavy doors shut behind him. Was she finally awake? He was hot-faced and palpitating; his jowls trembled, pale lilac in the blue skeins of light from the narrow upright tank where she floated. He was standing somewhat below her in a channel the same width as the tank, high walkways on either side of him and, far up on the left, a lever that would swing the glass open and send the water, and the other contents, flooding out.

He'd been driving up and down random streets or sometimes just sitting in the parked truck for hours, in DC and later in Baltimore, through the previous evening, then on through half the night. They'd given her too strong a dose of sedatives; she just couldn't seem to come to. But surely by *now* . . .

Someone had fitted inflatable water wings of the kind used by swimming children on both her pearly arms to prevent her from drowning while she was unconscious. A single bulb shone just above her. Her golden head flopped and her long hair spread through the water like radiant yellow veins. He caught a gleam of sleepy azure as she gazed at him from the corner of her eyes and then closed them again. "Anais, my precious one, you *want* to talk to me. *Now*, even if you're still feeling poorly. You do. I've brought you here," he gasped out, "to offer you your freedom."

She raised her head and stared at him, her skin blanched and ashy in contrast to his damp flush. "I don't trust you," Anais slurred. "I don't. There's some kind of trick."

At least she was talking again. "No trick, beauty, I assure you. But a price, of course. There's always a price, isn't there?" Unbelievably, in the far-off city of San Francisco , the wave still shimmered in an upright mirror below the Golden Gate Bridge. He'd expected mobs in the streets screaming for mermaid blood. Instead the crowds filling blue suburban parks, dark highways, and city bridges across the country were calm and quiet, their faces gilded in the cupped light of candle flames. They sang in mourning for the mermaids who had died that day: died so that thousands of humans would live.

Worse, they were acclaiming General Luce as a *hero*.

And as soon as the missing secretary of defense was located, President Leopold would surely demand his resignation. But his own destruction hardly mattered as long as he could leave a solid record of accomplishment behind him "Not *so* high a price, Anais, I promise. Nothing you can't do in a few hours."

"What kind of *price*? You've already made me work so hard, and I'm *tired*, and I don't even care about getting my house back anymore! I just want . . ." She leaned her face on the tank's wall, her mouth a compressed pink blob on the glass, her cheek a slick pale dab.

"To be the way you were, free and blissful in the ocean. Of course I understand that, dear one. Of course. To be the way you were before you sold yourself to us. I suppose, relatively speaking, you were innocent then."

Anais didn't answer.

There wasn't enough time left for him to indulge her self-pity. "You bought your *life* from me, Anais. Now buy one more thing.

You only have to complete one final task, and you'll have your freedom again forever. Even your humanity and your inheritance from your parents, if you decide you want those things. I can arrange it all for you," Moreland lied. "But there's always a price, isn't there, for anything worth having?"

The Twice Lost Army was still spreading to other cities around the United States; it seemed there was a new blockade every day. Half an hour after General Luce's astonishing act of resistance he'd heard the first reports of a wave rising outside of Liverpool in England. Tomorrow the Twice Lost might appear in Holland, then in France, then possibly on the north coast of Africa.

This wild expansion of their movement was the Twice Lost Army's greatest strength, but it also might be their downfall. If General Luce had proved stubborn, well, she was only in San Francisco Bay. And it wasn't as if mermaids on the opposite side of the country could telephone her for instructions.

"You want me to drown someone else for you?" Anais asked. "And then you'll let me go?" She tilted her head, gazing blearily at the truck's dark metal walls.

"Anais," Moreland scolded. He waved a finger at her. "Do you think you're worth so little to me? Do you really imagine I would give you up in exchange for a simple murder? And whenever I begin to forget how deeply your last effort disappointed me, that humanity-hating boy radical always seems to pop up on TV again at the head of *another* march, declaiming this, that, and the other. After *that*, Anais, do you think I would rely on your competence as a killer?"

Anais didn't seem to be listening. She reeled slightly under the impact of his voice, but her eyes stayed dim and insensate. The neon orange water wings held her arms sloppily akimbo so that they dangled from the elbow. "Where?" Anais started vaguely. "Wait, where are we? Why am I, why did you . . ."

"You're here to do something that could make a real difference in the world." Could she pull it off? Suddenly he wasn't entirely sure, but she was the only hope he had left. His voice thrummed; his heart heaved and stammered in his chest. "We're two miles from Baltimore's Harborplace. As I said, this a chance for you to earn your freedom. You've been so sad locked up, haven't you? Promise me you'll do this one thing for me, and I'll—" He hesitated, nauseous at the prospect of losing control of her. But if everything went well tonight they would only be separated for a few hours, just a very few, and then . . ."I'll release you into the harbor. You'll do your job, and then you can choose the life you want next. Human or mermaid. It's simple."

Once everyone discovered he'd personally orchestrated the attack on the Twice Lost Army earlier that day, he'd assuredly lose much more than just his job. But Anais knew nothing about that, and in any case his plan would render such considerations quite irrelevant.

Her head rocked a little. "Baltimore? Can't we go to Miami?"

"No, tadpole, we can't. The mermaids of Baltimore only declared themselves members of the Twice Lost Army two days ago, and they've raised a feeble little excuse for a standing tsunami, at least compared to the one in San Francisco. They seem weak and disorganized, which suggests they might very well listen to a charming girl like you. And our intelligence network believes they haven't contacted the local human population yet. It's the best opportunity we could have. With any luck you'll find them entirely ignorant of what happened today."

"What happened today?" Anais repeated. She was distracted, her thoughts churning behind her eyes as she tried to make sense of everything he was saying. "What do you mean?"

"What you'll *tell* the mermaids here is that you've just changed form. This very hour. You'll explain that you saw an attack on the Twice Lost Army on TV immediately before you changed. Tell them that General Luce was captured and tortured to death in front of the cameras. I'd suggest you describe it, my dear, in sickening detail; describe precisely what you'd like to do to Luce yourself. *Then* tell them that just before she died she cried out the order for the mermaids of the world to release their waves and drown the cruel and treacherous humans." Moreland tried to smile, but the ache in his chest and the musical throb in his mind sent his lips torquing into a strange sloping curl instead. He knew he looked hideous. "You'll have to be very persuasive."

"But . . . did that happen? Did Luce really say—"

"Suppose it happened. As far as *you're* concerned, Anais, as far as winning your freedom goes, it absolutely happened. What do you care what the truth is?"

This had to end. Everything had to end; the music had to be stripped from the sea, from his mind, the murmuring enchantment purged, so that he could simply *rest*. Even prison would be a relief if it could lock out those voices.

But prison wouldn't be enough. He already knew that.

Anais was still bleary from the drugs. It had the odd effect of making her calculations all the more apparent. Her sly smile advertised her thoughts so distinctly that, had their situation been less desperate, Moreland would have found it comical.

"Okay," Anais chirped, her smile so oddly heavy that her

mouth seemed carved from some impossibly dense stone. "I'll do it. Exactly what you said."

"How touching, Anais. I'm moved by your enthusiasm for your work. Whatever our differences, we've always come together to serve a greater cause, haven't we?"

Anais nodded, too carefully, her smile unaltered. "I like being helpful."

"Oh, I know, tadpole. I have hours of recordings that prove exactly how helpful you've been. And if I need to, I can play those recordings through loudspeakers at a very high volume, not just above the harbor in Baltimore but up and down both coasts. You know, in some of our conversations you expressed views that might be perceived as . . . perhaps a touch disloyal . . . to the great General Luce."

It wasn't true. He'd given explicit orders that none of his conversations with Anais be recorded—for reasons so obvious that Moreland worried even *she* might realize he had to be lying. No sane man would tape himself instructing a captive mermaid to commit a series of murders.

Maybe Anais was still under the influence of the sedatives. Or maybe she just didn't think of him as sane. Either way, her face greened with dismay as the threat sank in. "They'll tear me apart! If they hear *anything*—those things I told you—they'll . . ."

"Ah, but they won't have the slightest inkling of how you've *helped* me, tadpole. Because you'll do exactly what I've told you to do. I'll be waiting to see the results of your work. And then"—*and then and then and then, darling Anais, you'll be the one to cure me, to save me*—"you'll report back to me here, as soon as the water recedes enough to make the shore passable. Once you do that I'll honor our agreement, and you'll be entirely free of me for the rest of your life. Do you understand?"

She nodded.

Thank heavens, she nodded. And she didn't even ask him *why* he wanted to see the Baltimore waterfront destroyed.

To her the urge for destruction must seem self-explanatory, Moreland thought. As natural as waves.

The truck was already parked so that its back end protruded over the harbor. Moreland swung the back door wide open, giving Anais her first view in months of lacquered violet water and star-shattered sky. A hot, humid sigh of late-August air brushed in while in the distance Baltimore's new standing wave wobbled, starlight pitching on its unstable crest. He was short of breath, and there was an awkward lull as he struggled to heave himself onto the walkway. The steel edge dug into his belly as his legs kicked in midair.

Not that long ago he'd been so strong, so agile, his body swift and unpredictable and deadly. Just as Anais was still. As he righted himself on the platform he saw her glorious form hanging in the blue water like a twist of golden, blue-fringed flame. "Anais," he said. His hand was on the lever now, poised to set her free.

She watched him with intense interest. "I used to think I hated Luce, *sir*," Anais said suddenly. She delivered the word *sir* with a vehement sneer. Her azure fins switched. "But now maybe I actually like her."

Anais waited for him to ask *why* her feelings had changed. He stared at her, breathing heavily, and didn't oblige her with the question.

"I like her because she's made you so miserable. And pathetic. And because she's showed everybody what a *loser* you are. You're so messed up and weak now, it's even better than if Luce had drowned you. Because this way you've suffered for longer. And," Anais added with a smirk, "I've gotten to *watch* it happening. Almost every day I've seen you getting more and more wrecked."

Moreland smiled at her. His face felt slippery and distorted, wet and rotten. "A man can't be more than a ship, Anais," he said, without quite knowing what he meant by it. "A ship, a song, and a shore." The words felt true even if he didn't understand them. "Remember to take your jewelry and your shirt off. Before you swim out there. Otherwise those other mermaids won't believe you've just changed."

He grasped the lever tighter, dragging down with all his strength. The glass wall swung outward, disgorging a wild and sudden flood that sparked with the pink and azure of Anais's racing tail, the gold of her streaking hair.

The violet water leaped as it received her. Moreland gazed down into dim lapping depths and saw nothing. To his left the masts of moored sailboats gouged black lines from the starry sky; he'd parked in a lonely spot near a boat club. Behind him a highway hissed and whispered.

Faintly, faintly, he could hear the mermaids singing. They were singing as they always did in the rough sealed pit of his mind.

But now they also sang in the sweet dilating sky that knew nothing of him.

32

Catarina Ivanovna Smekhov

The room had bars covering its single window, but apart from that it could have been a room in a hospital. The sky beyond the bars was the blue of late evening. She was lying in a plain, clean, very white bed, wearing some sort of equally white nightgown. The dry powdery feeling of the sheet covering her was horrible, but she didn't move to throw it off. What would be revealed would surely be even worse than the revolting sensation of cloth on skin. Apart from the bed there was a night table and a chrome armchair with olive cushions. A half-opened door showed a small bathroom. And of course there was another door near the foot of the bed. That one was closed, naturally. It would be locked.

Just in case, though, she should check. The question was whether she could reach it without glimpsing the horror concealed by the sheet, without sensing more of its configuration than she absolutely had to. Catarina inhaled deeply, reaching for courage.

Only a moment later, she found herself obliged to breathe again. Her lungs intruded on her consciousness and *demanded* it.

She became furiously aware of the continuous, repetitive wheezing of breath into her chest, instead of single breaths spaced far apart as they ought to be. With a simple act of will, couldn't she make her breathing stop? Catarina closed her eyes and pictured the deep green of the Bering Sea crossed by fans of sunlight. She pictured her fingers spreading out, parting the sun into rays; submerged cliffs whipping past beside her; water like streamers in her hair. She could stay here in this glassy airlessness for a long, long time. She simply wouldn't allow herself to surface, no matter how that aching pressure swelled inside her, no matter—

Catarina gasped, and her eyes flashed wide as breath tore through her again. Her vision of the sea abandoned her, and instead she saw the pale, oppressive walls. She completely forgot the door. If the air kept on invading her in this insulting way, she would never be able to return to the sea. She'd never be able to forget what had happened to her body: this sudden *deformity*.

Breath was the first thing she had to conquer. Everything else could wait. She squeezed her eyes tight again, pulled a pillow halfway over her face, and dived into her dream of water . . . She'd swim deep, far down where the light turned thick and somber, where a whale might pass within reach of her trailing hand.

There was no need to head for the surface. Not for at least half an hour, at *least* . . .

"I'm sorry if we've been neglecting you," someone said.

Catarina exhaled with such force that bile rose into her mouth for a moment. Her face was hot and damp, and she was ready to scream from frustration. She didn't move the pillow to see who had spoken, but she did notice the sound of the door closing again.

"It's incredible. We have an actual lieutenant from the Twice Lost Army staying with us, and everyone's so caught up in the drama of the moment that they can't even come check up on you," the someone continued. It was a man, probably fairly young. Catarina found his nervous, placating tone distinctly annoying. "I guess the first thing is, can I get you anything to eat? What would you like? I can order delivery from twenty different places, so please don't hesitate . . ."

Catarina threw the pillow away from her face and sat up slightly. The man stopped talking.

Young but not that young. Perhaps thirty. Moderately good-looking, with light brown skin and neat black hair and a strong, narrow face with prominent bones: not quite what she would consider handsome. Still, he was attractive enough that Catarina couldn't help thinking that, if circumstances were different, she might enjoy drowning him. "Murderer," Catarina murmured. "I need nothing from you."

The man recoiled, wide-eyed. "Of course. You could only think that. But what happened to your . . . companions, the attack with the net, that was *completely* unauthorized. That's why everything here is in such chaos. No one understands what happened or where that order to attack came from. There seemed to be two conflicting executive orders given at the same time, but one of them was faked. I have to say, your general showed remarkable strength of character in her response. We were all watching the whole thing on television, expecting the wave to come smashing down at any moment, and we were all stunned when General Luce refused to give in. It made a tremendous impression. She was faced with such a tragic, such an *impossible* choice . . ."

Catarina leaned her head heavily against the wall. Somehow in the brief time since she'd regained consciousness she hadn't remembered the other mermaids in the net with her at all: their suffering the same as hers but still impossibly remote; their writhing and dying the same as hers, shared and yet incomprehensible. Their *dying*: that was what this man was talking about. All of the others must have died. And she, somehow . . . She'd heard that in very rare cases mermaids could survive leaving the water, but she hadn't quite believed it. And why would *she* be the exception?

When she'd called this man a murderer she hadn't been thinking of the other mermaids at all but only of herself. Of those two grotesque, suggestive bulges she could see running down the lower half of the bed . . . Hot shame rose in her face, confused and horrible. Her mouth was full of a strange sensation, something like burning pins.

"The president has already conveyed his apologies to your general for the loss of life. But—you could say that's only a formality—any talk of tragedy is a formality—but the mermaids aren't alone in grieving for what happened today. Much of the country is united in mourning for your friends. Catarina, I *promise* you that . . ."

She couldn't let herself cry in front of this stranger. A hot, buffeting force was rising inside her, and its unwelcome winds were salty with tears.

"*Lieutenant* Catarina, I mean. I certainly don't want you to think I don't respect your rank."

"Please leave me." She could barely manage the words. Her throat felt raw; she'd screamed so long, so wildly.

"I'm . . . not sure you should be left alone, lieutenant."

"I am not a lieutenant," Catarina muttered.

"But . . . General Luce introduced you that way. On the news, immediately after the wave first went up. I'm sure I recognize you."

"Luce was wrong. She is often wrong. Mermaids *died* today because Luce was wrong."

The man pursed his lips as if he wanted to start an argument, but then he shook his head. "Just Catarina is good, then?"

"*Queen* Catarina."

He'd been standing at the foot of her bed the whole time, but somehow her reply moved him to walk closer—it was almost unbearable to see those stalklike legs scissoring along, to think of her *own* body—then pulled the olive chair to her bedside and sat down, watching her with focused speculation. "I'm Rafe Naimier. Honestly I'd probably be more comfortable just calling you Catarina. Calling anyone queen doesn't come too naturally to me. Can you live with that?"

Catarina kept her face turned away from him. The bed was made of white metal bars. Through the bars she could see plaster, also white and covered with small round blobs like bubbles rising in water.

"Can I ask you something? If you don't think of yourself as a lieutenant, then do you consider Luce a general? I noticed that you called her simply Luce just now, without her title."

"No. Luce is not my general." Catarina thought of the net, the astonishing pain in her tail, and the scrape of scales against her back and lips as the mermaids around her shuddered and died. She must have lost consciousness at some point; her memory gave away to dark bewilderment. Now the cold metal of this bed frame was digging into her cheek. "So many of us are dead. To call Luce a general—it doesn't help the ones who died in that net. The word has no meaning."

From the corner of her eye Catarina could see him nodding. "So what *would* you call Luce?"

"What would *I* call her? A heedless, destructive child! *Wild* with power, thoughtless of the honor that all mermaids must live by!" The words rolled out as if they didn't belong to her, drowsy and incantatory.

"You don't like Luce, then?" Rafe's voice was soft and curious.

"No, I don't. I *love* her." Catarina rolled her head from side to side, feeling the metal ribs striping her face with their chill. "Luce was a little sister to me. Ungrateful, impossible, but still much beloved. And I was her queen." Rafe didn't answer, but somehow his silence had a warm, receptive quality that made Catarina want to tell the story. "I saved her *life* when she first changed, when she knew nothing of our ways or of what her transformed body could withstand. I followed her into the depths to pull her back, at great risk to my own life! And that was not the only time I rescued her. And after all that, to hear the things she said to Nausicaa!" Catarina reared back and slammed her forehead into the bars. The ache was almost comforting. She reared again.

And then Rafe's hand was there—his *human* hand, as warm as earth in sunlight—cradling her forehead with just enough pressure to keep it from hitting the bed frame again.

The heat of his touch entered through her skin, suffusing her face and then brushing deeper. Catarina jerked sharply away from him, glaring into his dark eyes. "I won't allow you to hurt yourself, Catarina," Rafe said apologetically. He pulled his hand back and held it out for a moment as if he weren't sure what to do with it anymore. "I won't touch you again, unless . . . What did Luce say to . . . Nausicaa—was that the name? Luce said something to Nausicaa that was very hard for you to hear."

Catarina scowled at him. His touch had woken her to the discomfiting awareness that she'd already said far too much to a strange human; worse, to someone who was holding her as a prisoner. "Why do you *ask* me such things?"

Rafe held his eyes on hers. "Why? Because I care about the answers."

"It was wrong of me to speak to you at all. Please leave me

now. It is a violation of the timahk for a mermaid to speak with a human. It dishonors me."

She meant to look away from him again, but somehow her gaze seemed linked into his. His face was very serious as he waited, letting the air hold her words, letting them linger like unwinding smoke. Then he spoke again very quietly. "*Are* you a mermaid, Catarina?" He let his eyes travel, just for a moment, to the two elongated shapes under the sheet, then turned to look at her face again.

Catarina let out a sharp hiss.

She wanted to sing—to sing him to death—but the fear of what her voice might sound like now gagged her. A sickening silence filled her chest.

Rafe nodded gently, taking her silence as some kind of answer. "You have an accent. It's subtle, but I keep noticing it. Are you Russian?"

It was a strange change of subject, Catarina thought. But she still felt relieved that he had dropped his earlier, intolerable question. "I *was* Russian, once. Now I do not belong to any nation in the way a human would."

"Where were you born?" Rafe's voice was careful, neutral; Catarina was vaguely aware of how much effort he was putting into controlling his tone. Still, she felt again that inexplicable impulse to answer him.

"A town called Anadyr. On the Bering Sea. Not that this is of any importance to me now, of course."

"You don't consider your own life history *important*, Catarina Ivanovna?"

A bullet made of silence seemed to explode in Catarina's chest. Airy shards scattered, shocking her with a kind of white pain.

Then the silence dissipated, and Catarina's voice came back to her as a scream. "WHAT did you call me?"

"I believe I'm speaking to Catarina Ivanovna Smekhov, born in Anadyr, Russia, on February fifth, 1961. Reported missing by her parents in January of 1977. Catarina, you have a name that means much more than *queen*. You have a history—"

Catarina screamed wordlessly. Any words now seemed hideous, an insult to feeling. Without quite thinking she lunged up on the bed—up onto her *knees*.

Realizing that made her scream again, both hands flailing out into empty air. Those lumpy, bony things holding her up were much too weak. Her legs felt muddy, saggy, teetering; she was already pitching forward, her head swinging helplessly toward the floor.

Rafe caught her by her shoulders, tipping her back onto the bed.

With all her strength Catarina slapped him across the cheek. But even her arms were so much weaker than they used to be. The blow felt sloppy, flimsy. Rafe was standing over her now, holding both her wrists in an oddly light grip, looking at her as if he were staring through a window and into a deepening sky. She waited for him to strike her back, to pulp her face with furious blows. She would welcome a beating; this body she had now deserved no better.

Instead he let go of her wrists and sat back down. "Would you have preferred if I'd let you fall?"

"Can you do anything besides ask *questions*?" Catarina snarled. She was sitting on her heels in a tangle of sheets, and her new legs were trembling under her. "Only a weak man does that. That way he never has to give an answer!"

"So take a turn doing the asking, Catarina." Rafe shrugged. "I'll tell you the truth."

"You said they reported me *missing*. So tell me, if you sold a thing—if you sold your watch to the pawnbroker or to some filthy man on the street—would you run and tell the police that it was *missing?*"

For a moment Rafe just looked blank. Then his eyes altered; all their darkness seemed to be falling to some terrible depth. His lips parted and pinched closed again. "No. I absolutely wouldn't do that."

"So you say," Catarina hissed.

"I also wouldn't sell something that didn't belong to me." Rafe's breathing came fast and strained.

"What do you mean by that?"

"I mean you didn't belong to your parents. You weren't theirs to sell! You only belonged—you *still* only belong—to yourself."

"Then let me leave here."

Rafe stared. "I don't think you can even *walk*. Not yet. You need time to build up your strength. And the idea of you wandering through the streets, Catarina, in the shape you're in now—"

"I can swim! Only take me to the bay. I can beg Luce, she can try . . . perhaps she can sing me into my proper form again." Catarina swallowed. "Please, Rafe."

"I was wondering when you'd finally use my name," Rafe observed quietly. "Do you think I'm your jailer, Catarina? That it's up to me if you stay or leave? If I tried to take you out of here we'd both get caught before we reached the elevators. That's the reality now. I'm not your jailer, so it's not in my power to free you."

He was lying, Catarina thought bleakly. For a while there she'd half believed he might be better, different, than the men she'd known in her human life all those years before. She turned away from him, tugging the sheet up around her head.

"I was expecting you to ask me a question," Rafe said to her back. "I thought you would say, 'If you're not my jailer, Rafe, then what *are* you?' But now it looks like that might be a misplaced hope. Your only interest in me is what I might be able to do for you. Isn't that true?"

Was it true? Catarina suddenly wasn't sure, but she wasn't about to give him the satisfaction of telling him so. She stayed curled away from him, shrugging the sheet a bit higher.

"I'm a research psychologist, actually, Catarina. I've done studies on the effects of severe trauma: people in war zones, victims of . . . of human trafficking. The Department of Defense brought me in to prepare a report on mermaid psychology. That's why I have the opportunity to be here with you now. And a colleague of mine here has been working on a database of missing girls who we suspect might have become mermaids; there were only two Catarinas on the list. That's how I was able to guess your real identity."

Catarina couldn't let that go. "You mean that *name* you said? *Smekhov*? It has nothing to do with me! Luce might demean herself by using a human name, but even for her that is not her *real* identity. That identity fell away from her when she changed. And even if I've . . . lost my proper body, lost it for now . . . I don't accept those *noises* you say are my name! Dogs barking, goats bleating as their throats are slit, are more my name than those! Ivanovna! That you could *dare* to call me Ivanovna!"

"Your patronymic. 'Daughter of Ivan.'" Rafe said softly. Then he seemed to realize something. "Oh, Catarina, I'm *sorry*. I should have thought . . ."

"Surely when that man sold me for cigarettes, he sold my name as well! What *right* does he have to be called my father?" Catarina rolled over to glare at him.

A tear glittered on Rafe's cheek. He wasn't looking at her. "No right at all, Catarina."

"And you dare to speak of our *psychology*, as if you knew anything."

Rafe started laughing bitterly, brushing the tear away with the back of his hand. "I don't think the Department of Defense is going to be too pleased by my report, honestly. They might be glad to hear your opinion that I don't know what I'm talking about."

Against her own will, Catarina was curious. For several seconds she struggled to suppress her desire to ask him the question and then failed. "What will you tell them, then?"

"That you're no different from humans. Psychologically a mermaid is indistinguishable from a human who's been through a similar degree of trauma. The only real difference is the physical manifestation. Suffering transformed into beauty, into magic. It's fascinating."

"I am hardly a human," Catarina muttered. She felt an impulse to flick her tail—and instead felt bare feet kicking at the white sheet.

"You're . . . both, I'd say. Human and mermaid. That's what's so intriguing about you, Catarina. You have an exceptional richness of experience and identity. I mean, are you a beautiful young girl? Or are you a woman in her early fifties, with a lifetime of struggle and exploration behind her? On paper, of course, you're the much older version of yourself, born in 1961, and not a teenager at all."

"I'm sixteen years old!"

"*And* fifty-two years old. Simultaneously." For the first time

Rafe grinned at her, almost rakishly. "Now, I'll be the first to admit that you look simply *fantastic* for your age."

Hearing him say that made her feel so old, so weary. In a way he was right: she could sense all the long years dragging at her back, years that split the ocean waves with grief and death and pleasure. But Catarina also suspected that Rafe had reasons of his own for wanting to think of her as an adult and as at least somewhat human. She meant to stare at him contemptuously but instead looked down at her hands. She was annoyed to feel herself flushing.

"I'm sorry," Rafe said after a long moment. "It's inappropriate for me to tease you."

Catarina shrugged.

"Can I return to an earlier question? I'll understand if it's too private, but I do care . . . about how you see things. About what matters to you."

Catarina twisted away from him, but her body was tense and her head cocked as she waited for him to speak.

"What was it that Luce said to Nausicaa? That hurt you so much?"

Catarina leaned on one hand, thinking. If he was telling the truth, if he actually cared about the answer, well, nobody else did. Her breath rushed on, much too quickly, filling her lungs and then abandoning her again.

"Luce said—" Catarina paused, feeling her chest rise and fall, curling her unaccustomed toes and then spreading them. "She said to Nausicaa, 'While you were away, you *saved* me so many times!' As if even absent Nausicaa meant more to her than I could while staying faithfully by her side! As if the times I saved her were *worthless* in comparison!"

Rafe was silent, but his silence had a slow, serious tone to it that Catarina understood as if it were speech. "That sounds extremely painful," he said after some time. "You're saying you saved Luce's life repeatedly, but for some reason she couldn't acknowledge that, only what Nausicaa did for her. Is that right?"

She wouldn't look at him, but after a moment she nodded.

"Excuse me for asking you this, Catarina, but . . . am I correct in thinking that you've been involved in sinking ships? With the deliberate intention of drowning people?" Rafe was using the same extremely careful tone she'd noticed earlier, his words seemingly placed one by one on velvet.

"I've drowned many hundreds," Catarina answered dully. She was surprised to find that the statement felt strange to her. "Of course I have. The humans are owed our vengeance! It was only this madness of Luce's that made me cease to kill."

"And yet what you want most is to be recognized for *saving* someone, for saving Luce. Catarina, what does that tell you about yourself?"

Catarina looked at him.

"To me it says that you'll get much more of what you truly want from life if you try approaching it from a different angle." He grinned again, and his dark eyes sparked with sudden amusement. "It sounds like bringing vengeance isn't actually all that fulfilling for you."

"You mean that I should be like Luce is, with her *plankton?*" Catarina snarled. Rafe just smiled at her, his look calm and warm.

Before she could stop herself Catarina realized that she was smiling sadly back at him, smiling even as her first uncontrollable tears began to flow.

33

Regret

The blue-black water seemed boundless, pierced by myriad points of starlight. After months of living in a tank only five feet deep, with no room to leap or spin or plunge, this wild, welcoming space intoxicated Anais. She yanked the idiotic inflatable swimmies from her arms immediately. For half an hour she dived as deep as she could and then spiraled her tail and went rocketing back to the surface, over and over again. She swooped until dizziness reeled through her and green lights scattered themselves across her eyes. It occurred to Anais that she'd never really noticed before how incredibly fun it was to be a mermaid. If it weren't for that flabby-faced old lunatic and his *assignment*, wheeling through Baltimore's night-covered harbor wouldn't be so bad at all. Mermaid song licked through the water on all sides, until she seemed to part countless ribbons of music with every stroke of her fins. It did sound a lot like the odd, smooth tone Luce had always used when she called to the water, only much *more* so now: the same tone multiplied, curling and rebounding and blossoming as it passed through dozens of different voices. But that kind of singing wasn't so great, Anais thought sullenly; it wasn't *real* singing at all. It wouldn't kill so much as a five-year-old kid!

Moreland been right about one thing. However reluctantly, Anais had to concede that much. If she approached these strange mermaids and claimed to be a metaskaza, her ruffled ivory silk top and the diamond studs in her ears would instantly mark her as a liar. After a few moments of hesitation, she pulled the studs from her ears and dropped them, then wriggled out of her shirt and let the current loft it away. It flowed like a moon-colored kite through the darkness. Now Anais was as naked as the water around her, and she bared her teeth as she watched the silk fluxing away into a small pale blot. *Moreland* had given it to her, she thought. Of course she didn't want it; of course she felt better without it clinging to her skin.

But nakedness alone wouldn't be enough to convince these unknown mermaids that her story was true. Anais had never encountered a newly transformed mermaid herself, but she'd heard enough stories to recognize that her own reaction to the change hadn't been typical. She should seem stunned, bewildered, stricken. She stopped swimming and simply hovered in water that now graded from jet black to violet-gray along its eastern fringe. Dawn was coming. Anais held herself in place with tiny ripples of her fins, carefully assuming the emotions she knew would be expected of her. To her, it felt like getting dressed for a party. She furrowed her brow, widened her eyes, and bent a scared, sagging mouth just as someone else might adjust a scarf.

Anais was aware of her peculiarity: the veils of dark shimmering that any other mermaid would see clinging around her didn't *reveal* anything. With her there was no horrifying story displayed in a language of winking darkness. That made her different from other mermaids; all the others were marked forever by flickering images of whatever heartbreaking event had stolen their humanity from them. Anais had always been glad to be set apart from the pathetic, broken girls she lived with in the sea. But in a situation like the one she was going into now, a distinguishing feature like that might be dangerous. She needed a story of her own personal horror, and she needed to describe it with enough shaken, vulnerable intensity that the mermaids might start to *think* they could see it happening when they gazed into her shimmer—or at least feel bad about not seeing it.

Anais thought for a moment and chose the story she would tell.

On her face the emotions she'd selected shifted and flowed: grief, consternation, denial. She was ready. She came up and sighted the high, palpating wave heaved up as an imperfect barricade across the harbor's narrow mouth and made for it. Pale lilac dawn glazed a tangle of freeways with dripping blue; on the other side of the harbor some kind of old fort loomed in a mass of sullen gray. It would be better if she didn't swim straight up to the Twice Lost mermaids who were singing under that wave; instinct told Anais that it would be more convincing if they found her instead. She swished closer, stopping some fifty yards away from the wave's base. Then she let her body go limp in the water, and let out a few wild, stabbing, fragmented notes. Just as if she hadn't yet developed any control over her voice. Just as if the power of her own singing terrified her.

As she'd known it would, that outburst of music brought two mermaid guards dashing over so quickly that she hardly saw them arrive: a sweet-faced younger girl with hair streaked in shades of deep gold and soft caramel and a thin, nervous brunette, maybe seventeen or so, who looked at Anais guardedly. Anais gaped back at them with assumed terror and then shook her head violently and threw her hands over her eyes. "Oh, God," she moaned. "Oh, God, this just can't be real!"

"Hey," the younger girl soothed. "Hey, it's okay. You're going to be okay! We're here to help you. My name is Sadie, okay? We'll be friends. You don't need to be scared."

Anais peeked between her fingers, then howled and covered her eyes again. "Oh, no! I don't know what this is, and I don't know what you *are*." A stolen glimpse told her that she'd miscalculated; Sadie's tender look had altered into a flash of skeptical surprise. Of course: everybody in the world knew that mermaids were real now. "I mean, I guess you're mermaids like everyone is talking about, but I just can't believe this is happening to me! After what my *uncle* did—I couldn't take it anymore! But I never thought—"

Sadie and the brunette mermaid both responded to Anais's statement on cue, turning their heads to gaze sideways into the dark, cloudy sparking hovering around the newcomer. "That's so weird," the brunette murmured after a moment. "I can't see *anything*. Sadie, can you?"

Anais lowered her hands enough that she could watch the two strangers. Sadie's lips were compressed and her brows were drawn; a shadow danced in her eyes. "I can't. I've never seen anything like this! Paige, I'm not sure . . ."

There was only one way to deal with this. Anais burst into frantic tears. "He kept hitting me whenever he got drunk, but *this* time . . . this time he . . . oh, I can't say it! And I was so, so scared, because I knew . . . if I stayed, he'd try it again! Oh, God," Anais sobbed, then carefully dropped her voice into a whimper. "Please help me."

"Of course we'll help you!" Paige cried. Her arm was already wrapped protectively around Anais's shoulder. "Mermaids *always* help each other, okay? And your uncle won't find you, and we won't let anyone hurt you *ever* again!"

Sadie bit her lip and didn't say anything. That was okay, Anais thought; she could work with one sympathizer to start with. She leaned against Paige and cried harder.

"But . . ." Anais sputtered. "But you can't *promise* that! They'll come for us, and they'll catch me and hurt me. I *know* it! Just like they did today, when they caught General Luce . . ."

For several seconds Paige and Sadie didn't react to that at all apart from the glazed look that came over them. Then Sadie's hand shot out and gripped Anais's shoulder dangerously. "You'd better explain what you're talking about right now!"

"Sadie," Paige whispered urgently. "Sadie, calm down. We'd better take her to Lieutenant Tricia. That way she can explain to everyone at once."

Sadie was glowering, her mouth opening to speak, when Anais yowled abruptly and cut her off. "Oh, God, you mean you don't know? But I *can't* be the one to tell you; I just can't say it. It was so, so terrible! She died so *slowly*, and they kept on . . . kept on . . ."

Sadie's sunset-colored tail was lashing in vexation. It reminded Anais that her fins should be flicking, too. "She's lying," Sadie hissed. "Paige, I can tell!"

Anais did her best to look wounded. She began rippling her tail so vigorously that her whole body gyrated.

"Why would she lie about something like that!" Paige yelled. "Sadie, nobody would just make that up. Why—if those filthy humans *killed* General Luce, we're going to make them pay for that! Come *on*. You have to explain everything to Lieutenant Tricia. I don't care how hard it is for you to talk about it!"

Anais went slack in the water, passively letting the two strangers grab her by both arms and drag her toward the glimmering, upright wave. Serene golden light rose like a mist on the horizon, and the wave concentrated the dawn's glow into brilliant pleats and falling streamers of unbearable purity. Below the wave was the line of mermaids, their hands linked except now and then when one of them broke free and rose to the surface for air. And in the center of the line was a harsh-looking girl with vivid green eyes and ash brown hair who had to be Lieutenant Tricia. There was something in Tricia's look—something stubborn, furious, and full of raw, unexamined emotion—that made Anais think she might be in luck. She shot Anais a hard, slightly contemptuous look. But for all Tricia's apparent toughness Anais detected a quiver deep inside it: Tricia was already fighting a continuous undercurrent of panic.

The way to deal with Tricia would be to channel her fear and feed it back to her until it amplified into hysteria.

"So who's this?" Tricia barked. "The last thing I want now is to get stuck training some sad little newbie!"

"We didn't ask her name," Paige groaned. "Tricia, she says—"

Tricia nodded brusquely. "We'll get to that. What's your name, new girl?"

Again a tremor of instinct warned Anais in time. "I'm Regina. I— Oh, no, you'll be so *angry* when you hear what they did to General Luce, and maybe you'll blame me for *telling* you . . ." Anais deliberately sent her voice wavering higher.

"I bet Regina's not even her real name," Sadie muttered. "Tricia, *listen* . . ."

"To *General Luce*?" Tricia burst out, and Sadie fell silent. Anais could feel the agitation she'd put into her tone moving through

Tricia like a transfusion of tainted blood. "Regina, you start talking right now! Who—did they *dare*—our general—we'll—"

Some of the mermaids began deserting their places in the row to find out what was happening. As the crowd thickened the wave began to totter. Eager, reckless girls pressed in, clamoring with questions, and Tricia's obvious anxiety danced and dabbled over them like a living, serpentine thing.

Anais allowed herself to shoot Sadie a look of such dark triumph that, if any of the others had seen it, it would have given her away completely. Sadie's indignant cry was instantly lost in the uproar.

"Everybody shut up!" Tricia yelled. "Just shut up and listen! Our *general*, our great general, she's—"

"Dead," Anais moaned dramatically. "General Luce is dead! Whenever she was just about to finally die they would pour some water on her scales and then she would start slowly drying out all over again! They did it live on TV, to send us a *message* they said, and it went on for hours! I've never seen anything so, so terrible! And right when she was dying she said that trying to make peace with humans had been a big mistake!"

"A message?" Tricia shrieked. "We'll send them a *message* right back! We'll—"

"No we *won't*," Sadie snapped. She swirled forward and stopped with her face immediately in front of Tricia's. "We'll send someone to find out if *Regina's* telling the truth. And if she isn't, and I already know she's *not*—"

"Find out how?" Paige sneered. "By asking the *humans*? The same humans who just *tortured* General Luce to *death*?"

"We don't even know Regina! I'd trust a human more than I trust her!"

"Since when do *you* make the decisions here, Sadie?" Tricia was rippling savagely, her dark green fins kicking rhythmically. "What is this? A mutiny?"

Sadie reacted to this by lifting her head and unfurling her gorgeous amber tail to its full length. "It's only a mutiny," Sadie announced, "if I disobey my *general*, Tricia. And you know what? That's not you. Everybody who follows General Luce? We are keeping this wave standing!" Sadie swam backwards, pouring her voice into the song. Anais couldn't help but notice at once that Sadie was an exceptional singer. Her back was arched and dawn glow lit the swanlike curve of her throat. She fought the immense weight of the water above her, flooding it with her clear ascending voice. The wave above was bent, crumpling, as a few mermaids parted ways with the crowd and rushed to join their voices with Sadie's song.

Anais's distress was perfectly genuine now. She watched in anxiety as the Twice Lost mermaids of Baltimore chose sides, each of them using her voice to declare her allegiance to Sadie or to Tricia.

One by one they joined either the ranks of the singers, or the ranks of the silenced.

* * *

The giant wave above them teetered, bent halfway up its height like some doddering ancient man. Anais watched it from a spot a yard below the surface, gazing at the wave as if through a rippling glass pane. The singers strained to keep the wave up, their voices turning hoarse and wild as they tried desperately to support a volume of water that suddenly seemed to be staggering from its own weary immensity. On the freeway the cars' windshields flashed bright palms of dawn, and people shrunken by distance walked along a promenade that followed the harbor's curves. They didn't seem to realize that anything was wrong.

For several minutes Anais couldn't guess which side would win. At least two-thirds of the mermaids here had joined her and Tricia in embittered silence, their hearts poisoned by what she'd told them. They waited around her at various levels so that the water flicked with fins and swirled with bright hair. And as she watched the wave slumping farther forward, its crest writhing from the thrust of the mutineers' frenzied song, Anais began to feel just a trace of the same emotion that had unaccountably possessed her on the day she'd sung to Luce's father. It was a sensation of hollowness in her chest, as if a delicate creature that lived there had suddenly escaped from her and all she could feel was the brush of its departing wings. Anais didn't have a name for what she was experiencing. Luce or Yuan or Nausicaa could have told her that it was regret.

But if she told the truth *now*, the timahk would hardly be enough to protect her.

"Sadie's right," Anais whispered. Her golden hair spun across her mouth as if it wanted to stifle her, then danced up and blinded her eyes. "I was lying."

No one reacted to that. They were all transfixed by the sight of that crooked wave, somehow both lurching forward and yet suspended midway through its fall. Maybe they hadn't heard her at all.

"I was lying!" Anais yelled. "Sadie, I was lying!"

Sadie heard her, and for a moment—for a pause briefer than a heartbeat—astonishment crushed the song in her throat.

34

Healing

Luce sang through her shift automatically. Catarina was dead, a dozen other mermaids were dead, but the war was still a living, lashing thing that had to be fed and tended. She was feeding it her own body and her song, just as earlier that day she had fed it her heart. Inexplicable things had happened over the last several hours. The president had denied responsibility for the attack, even sent her an apology, and the crowds onshore kept screaming her name . . . but none of that changed anything. The war was still famished, endlessly demanding, and she was still its unwilling keeper.

For once her song meant nothing to her, though magic still flowed from it. And at midnight when Cala arrived to replace her Luce slipped silently away. No doubt at the encampment there were friends waiting to comfort her. Yuan and Imani would hug her and assure her she'd done the right thing, the only thing, that she'd had no choice . . . and Luce knew she couldn't bear to hear any of that.

Instead she swam deep, hugging the shore. For at least an hour she wove randomly between black pilings and lightly brushed the pink kiss of the anemones, stared into bone white sea stars draped across rotten beams. She couldn't face her fellow mermaids, but something was pulling her along, and when at last she came up near a collapsing pier she knew what it was. That hunched figure sitting at the pier's end was just as heartbroken as she was. Every line of his back showed it.

Seb, Luce thought with surprise, might understand what had happened that day. At least he might understand it *enough*. She dipped low again and came up in front of him.

He didn't seem surprised to see her and raised a hand in greeting. His worn face looked severe and mournful under his uneven hair. His hideous tie flapped in the wind, and he'd pulled his blazer as tight as it could go. For a human, Luce realized, it was a chilly night—in San Francisco even August offered no guarantee of warmth—and there was nothing she could do for him.

"I'm sorry I didn't come sooner," Luce said. "To thank you. You did everything right."

Seb just looked at her then shook his head. "Well, it's a real luxury, isn't it, Miss Luce? When you *can* do the right thing, because there's one truly right thing to do?"

Luce was suddenly aware of the water cradling her, gently and faithfully. She looked at Seb with gratitude. "Yes. That is . . . a luxury."

"So maybe I'm the one who should thank you, for giving me such a nice clear-cut *right* thing to do. Helping the mermaid who saved me when that's not enough for her and she's gone and set her heart on saving *more* than that? That was an easy one, Miss Luce. I haven't had so many opportunities in my life to do anything as right as that. I've mostly been doing something at least halfway wrong, just fighting to get at one little *speck* of right that was mixed in with it somewhere." Seb kept on looking at her. For all his tattered absurdity his gaze was as transparent as glass, and grave comprehension shone through it. "And I know you know about that."

Luce felt something blocky and horrible in her throat. She looked away, unable to answer him, and wrapped her arms around a piling for support. Hoops of apricot light cast by the streetlamps pranced on the water. Luce looked at those beaming rings and thought she might fall through them and plummet into another world. "I killed them, Seb. Mermaids who trusted me."

"I know you did, Miss Luce. I watched the whole thing on TV, along with practically everybody else on this planet of ours. It was as horrible as anything I ever saw, even in Vietnam, and I'm no slacker where horror's concerned."

"I had a choice. I let Catarina die. I *decided* that."

"You *made* a choice. That's why everybody here in humanland thinks you're the big hero tonight. They're taping your picture in their windows. You're looking out all over, on all the streets, with those sad eyes of yours. It's gonna change things for sure, what you did."

"I'm not a hero," Luce murmured dully. "I never was. Catarina was right about me."

"I know you're no hero," Seb said seriously. "They set you up so you'd be a monster no matter what you did. And now a monster's what you are."

Luce nodded. Far from feeling offended, she was grateful and wildly relieved that Seb understood her so well. She looked at him. He was shivering from cold because he'd thrown away those filthy coats he used to wear—thrown them away so he could look better for his role as her ambassador. "I wish I could help you, Seb. I wish we did have treasure and pearls for you. I'm *sorry* . . ."

"Thanks, Lucy Goose. And I wish you knew that a monster like you is worth twenty heroes."

Luce leaned her head on the piling and closed her eyes. "Please don't say that."

"I've known heroes, Miss Luce. Plenty of them. You know I even knew that Secretary of Defense Moreland back when we were both young? Big hero, that one. So I'm kind of an authority on this stuff, and I'm going to tell you whatever truth I've got in me to tell."

She swayed in the darkness. Around her hovered empty spaces shaped like her father, Dorian, Nausicaa, Catarina. No wonder everyone always abandoned her. She was a monster made of nothingness; she was ruin and desolation wearing a beautiful mask. Everyone knew that, but no one would admit it—apparently not even Seb, although she'd thought he understood.

"Hey," Seb said. "I'm glad you're here."

It took Luce a long moment to realize that he wasn't talking to her.

"Oh, God," Yuan said. "Poor Luce. She just doesn't get a break."

Luce cringed—at Yuan's presence, at her sympathy, at the concerned looks she knew both Yuan and Seb were firing her way.

"She's got the shadow sitting on her heart tonight," Seb said as if that were the most rational explanation in the world. "She's feeling what it is when you have to know exactly what kind of a monster you are, and you can't look away from that."

"She's going to have to," Yuan said firmly. "Look away, I mean. I didn't come searching for Luce so I could try to cheer her up. There's . . . something she has to deal with."

"Oh, Lord," Seb said. "Don't make her do *more* tonight! Just look at her."

"I see her," Yuan agreed. Suddenly Luce felt Yuan's strong, smooth hands on her arms, gently unwrapping them from the piling. "I'd let her stay here if I could, Seb. Really. But this is important. Luce?"

Important, Luce thought with grim sarcasm. "What's so important *now*?" She barely muttered the question.

"They could be lying," Yuan conceded. "But if they're not—and I *really* don't believe they are, actually—"

"Yuan," Luce snapped. "What do I have to do *now*?"

Yuan's gentleness was gone in a flash. She gripped Luce by both shoulders, spun her savagely around, and gave her such a quick, jarring shake that Luce opened her eyes in exhausted surprise. Yuan's golden face appeared, fierce and radiant and loving. "You have to come see your father, Luce. He's by the bridge. And he is *not* okay."

* * *

With those words everything changed. The night seemed to inhale, to stretch itself wider and darker in all directions.

Luce gave an apologetic wave while Seb sadly watched them from the pier. Yuan was already towing her away and talking as they swam. "Luce, listen, about your dad: it's bad. He's not *physically* hurt, but . . . it might be something a mermaid did to him? And I don't know, but there's this nice old guy who brought your dad to the bay, and he keeps saying . . . that maybe you can help somehow? Come *on*."

They were already swimming under the water. The darkness ran like quicksilver around Luce and also straight through her veins. She was the pulse in the night, the racing surge, and Yuan's words seemed to signal her from far ahead, bright and strange in the distance. She drove herself on, faster and faster, until Yuan was trailing just behind her. Past the Embarcadero and its shining clock, below the looming hill with its pale tower. As the bridge neared, Luce lunged for the surface, staring frantically at the crowd onshore. Humans were gathered there in greater numbers than ever; they all seemed to be holding candles and their faces floated on the dark like glowing balloons. Instead of jostling they stood quietly with arms around one another's waists, staring wide-eyed at the brilliant streaks of reflected light playing on the soaring flank of the water-wall. Many of them were weeping quietly. The rush of mermaid song suffused Luce's mind so completely that it took her a moment to understand that the humans were all singing too, in a long incantatory drone of rising and falling harmonies. It was their best effort to sing along with the mermaids under the bridge, Luce realized. They couldn't contribute magic to the mermaids' struggle, but they could offer compassion and the strength of their hearts. Tears swarmed into her eyes. But she didn't see her father.

"He's farther along, Luce. Around the next bend, on the ocean side. We tried to pick a spot where you could have a little more privacy, but it's still pretty crowded."

Luce dipped again. On the bridge's far side was a hill with strange bunkerlike buildings and terraces set into its slope. The singing human crowd had grown big enough now to submerge the bunkers in a tide of bodies: people sat and stood on the decks and rooftops, their candles sending pitching waves of light across their faces. The shore here was paved in cement, defined by a row of large rocks mortared together.

And at the base of one building, very near the water's edge, was an empty doorway. And poised in that doorway . . .

Her father, but also—not her father. Her father with everything that made him who he was somehow missing. His face and body looked slack and empty, and another man—a thickset, strong-looking man with tan skin and neat silver hair—was holding him firmly upright. Luce swam closer, a strange paralysis gripping her heart, her eyes helplessly drawn by the awful vacancy of her father's face. To think that she'd blamed him for not trying to see her . . . Even when he'd been snarled in the spirits' enchantment on that lost island, he hadn't seemed as profoundly injured as he did now. His body was like a shell for the void.

Even worse, she could *hear* the strange shapeless emptiness that was waiting for her behind his cinnamon eyes.

Even worse, the void was *singing*.

Luce was gripping the shore before she even knew what she was doing. Some of the people on the roof had started calling to her, crying out her name. The silver-haired man stepped out of his doorway, Andrew Korchak's vacant body still sagging against him, and half turned to silence the crowd with a single imperious hand. "General Luce isn't here for you," he announced, sharply. "She's here to see her father, and he's not well. Please respect that." He kept on staring into the faces above until they quieted, then he nodded with a certain curt efficiency and carefully lowered Andrew until he was sitting loosely cross-legged just behind the row of rocks that separated him from his daughter. By stretching her arm through a gap between two rocks Luce was able to catch his hand and hold it tight, and all the time she was listening to the void's slow, musical purr, attuning herself to its thrum and its cadence. To fight it she had to become its intimate, as familiar to it as its own echo.

Who had *done* this to him?

The silver-haired man sat down too, watching her intensely.

Luce didn't look at him or at Yuan, who'd swum up beside her. Imani was there too, Luce realized dimly, and Graciela, waiting in silence to see what Luce would do. Nothing mattered, though, but the yawning devastation in her father's eyes. He was so close to her, but his gaze never alighted on her. That gaze went everywhere and nowhere as if it saw everything undifferentiated, as facets of a single complex sound.

"General Luce?" the silver-haired man tried. "I'm sorry that you have to see this, especially after everything that happened earlier. But I thought you should see your father as soon as possible, in case time is a factor in . . . in your ability to effect a cure. Assuming a cure is *feasible*. The effects of a malicious, deliberate assault by mermaid song . . . well. Dorian insists that you have the ability to heal this kind of damage, although I have to say that seems like a great deal to hope for."

Dorian's name was enough to make Luce glance up sharply at the silver-haired man, but only for an instant. Almost immediately her eyes went back to her father's face, to his head fallen over at a steep angle and his wandering gaze. But looking up, even so briefly, reminded Luce of the crowd watching raptly from above as if they were in some kind of bizarre theater built from night and sea. "I can try," Luce breathed out. "I can *try* to heal him. But I'm going to have to sing to do it. I mean sing in ways that might not be safe for the people here. Hearing me—I don't know what that will do to everyone. They should leave."

In the corner of her eye, the strange man nodded thoughtfully. But for some reason he didn't get up and go.

Yuan began swimming back and forth under the pallid bunkers, calling up, "General Luce needs to sing. It could be dangerous. You should leave for your own safety, okay? Everybody please leave!"

Some people started climbing down from the roofs and vanishing behind the buildings. But far too many lingered where they were, and Yuan's voice began rising in frustration. "We're trying to be responsible here! We're asking all of you to GET—AWAY—NOW! Why don't you all get moving? This is serious business!"

"We just want to listen," a young woman in a red parka answered from a curving cement roof. "We won't bother you."

"It's dangerous!" Yuan yelled back. "Don't be stupid! This isn't a rock concert!"

"I'll take my chances!"

Yuan wheeled around to look at Luce and raised her hands helplessly. Luce groaned. Her father was as hollow as an open wound, and these stubborn, reckless humans wouldn't get out of her way and let her help him. Luce gave her father's unresponsive hand a quick squeeze and swirled back a few feet to look up at the crowd. Her tail coiled around her. "Please, *please* leave! Now! I don't want to hurt anyone, but I can't just keep waiting!"

"General Luce?" It was the man who'd brought her father. "The way you need to sing to your father—it must be a way of singing that's meant to help, not harm. Isn't that correct? You won't actually be singing in a way that would persuade the people here to drown themselves."

"I don't think anybody will *drown*," Luce agreed. "But I can't *tell*; it might hurt them in other ways. I just don't know, and there's already been—so many horrible things have happened already—and if anyone *else* gets hurt because of me—" She closed her eyes in despair. Maybe she should just seize hold of her father and drag him away from here, across the bay. Maybe she could take him to Alcatraz.

"It's *really* going to be fine, Luce," someone said. The voice ached inside her, as warm and reassuring as her own blood, but somehow she couldn't place it at first. "You can sing without hurting anyone. I know that for a fact. Mr. Ellison? Can we get him closer to her, like on the other side of the rocks?"

Now she knew who was there. Luce looked up again, her vision scattered and silvery with tears. Dorian appeared at the center of a web of light. He was helping the strange man to maneuver her father's limp body over the line of rocks and into the shallow lapping water where Luce waited.

It was all too much, too painful. Luce closed her eyes again, trying to squeeze the darkness so close that it would never leave her. She caught her father's lolling head between her hands and held on gently, keeping him from sliding down into the water. And then she heard him trying to speak. The word came out as a lowing, broken note. "Lu . . ." her father half groaned, half sang. "Lu . . . ssss."

And very softly, very delicately, Luce began singing back to him.

Her voice spread through her father's mind. He was full of a trilling emptiness, yes—but that void didn't possess *all* of him. Instead he was fragmented, torn apart by that darkness. Aspects of him shone far apart in that vacancy like suns separated by the immensity of space. Luce's voice reached through his strange internal night and gathered pieces of his consciousness, until those suns weren't scattered but instead hung like apples from a single blazing tree.

Luce heard herself singing slow, high notes that traveled along sweeping curves, touching everything in her father's mind that had gotten lost. She sang the webs, the reconnections, but her own voice sounded to her like the deepest possible silence. There was still the endless thrum of mermaid voices under the bridge. There was the subtle breathing of the wind. But even in concert with those sounds the silence was perfect, just as actively present as any music. It rose in *harmony* with the music.

In that silence her father would hear his own thoughts again.

In it he would recognize himself again. And the world, which had been washed away by some uncanny, destructive flood of sound, would come back to him with its sky and its ground and its trees. Those things would seem real to him again, without any music.

By the time Luce let her voice softly die away, she knew that he wasn't completely cured—but also that he was much, much better.

And so was she. At least she was well enough now to open her eyes and face the world outside her own private darkness.

The people on the hillside were crying silently, each one consumed by a lifetime's worth of emotions all streaming into wild release at once. None of them spoke.

Dorian was sitting cross-legged only five feet away from her. His cheeks were tear-streaked and his ochre gaze seemed to cradle her face. She looked away from him, suddenly embarrassed.

And her father—he still swayed uncertainly. He looked weak and sleepy. But he also looked like a person and not like a shell filled with yawning night, and his eyes met hers with dreamy recognition. "Hi there, Luce," he whispered. "I was trying to get to you. I wanted to explain . . ."

Luce hugged him, trying not to break down and sob. "Explain later. You need to go somewhere warm now. You need to get in dry clothes and then sleep for a long time. Okay?"

"That sounds about right," Andrew Korchak agreed vaguely. He lifted his hand from the water and watched with perplexity the drops falling from his fingers. "How did I get here, Luce? I was just trying . . . I saw you in the water, and I tried to swim out to you. And after that . . . there was that room made out of glass, and I was talking to your friend."

He was still half-crazy, Luce thought: still shaken and disoriented. "Tell me everything later. And if you need me to I'll sing to you again, and soon, soon you'll be *okay*." Andrew Korchak nodded hazily, then stood up and clambered over the rocks. He curled in a ball on the pavement and sighed. Maybe he was already asleep.

Luce looked toward the silver-haired man. Like everyone else, he was gleaming with tears that seemed to illuminate something deep inside him. It was only now that Luce realized how much this unknown man had done for her. "I haven't thanked you yet. For bringing my dad here. And I don't know your name."

"I'm Ben Ellison." He smiled at her sadly. "I'm glad to finally meet you, general. Dorian always speaks of you . . . very lovingly. And now I truly understand why."

Luce's eyes went wide as the realization hit her. How could she have forgotten? Ellison, Ben Ellison: this was the same FBI agent who'd tried to make Dorian betray her. Even without meeting Ben Ellison she'd always hated him, always regarded him as an implacable enemy.

But he'd helped save her father, and she couldn't hate him anymore.

"Hi, Mr. Ellison," Luce said a bit awkwardly. "It's nice . . . to meet you, too. I really, *really* appreciate your helping my dad this way. Can you please take him somewhere safe now? I think I shouldn't try any more tonight."

"I have a hotel room waiting for him," Ben Ellison assured her. "General, I'd very much like . . . to speak with you again soon. Your old acquaintance Anais did this to your father"—Luce jolted, stunned to realize that Nausicaa had been right *again*, and that Anais had in fact survived the massacre of their old tribe—"and her current whereabouts are unknown. Obviously she could be extremely dangerous."

Luce nodded, but she was so overwhelmed that she could barely take it in. Anais was still causing extraordinary harm; Anais was still out there somewhere . . .

"Luce?" Dorian whispered. But she couldn't bring herself to look at him.

"Dorian, are you coming with us?" Ben Ellison asked. "We're leaving now." He tried to lift Andrew from the ground, and a few people from the crowd came down to help. In a moment a group of half a dozen was carrying her father, probably to a waiting car. He'd be safe, Luce thought, and eventually he'd recover completely.

"I'll come later," Dorian called. Even without glancing at him, Luce knew his stare hadn't once shifted away from her face. "Luce, I know you must be really mad at me, and you've gone through hell, and I don't blame you if you hate me. But—"

"Not *now*, Dorian." The voice was Yuan's, coming from just behind Luce's left shoulder. "We all know you love her, okay? And I've been really impressed by your whole Twice Lost Humans thing. But this is not the time. It's not fair to ask Luce *anything* tonight."

It was strange, Luce thought. But somehow now that she heard Yuan say it she knew it was true: Dorian *did* still love her. What she didn't know was how she felt about that.

Dorian tilted his head toward Yuan. "Who are you?"

"I'm Yuan." There was a brief pause. "And I'm pretty sure I want the same things you do for Luce. I think we're on the same side. But everything's changed since you knew her."

Dorian gave a kind of abrupt, wheezing laugh. "Yeah. Changed. Yeah, it has. You have no idea, Yuan. While we were on the plane coming here Ben Ellison told me something that's going to change *everything*."

Even Luce looked toward Dorian now. He sat like some wounded prince at the edge of a battlefield, his skin golden and his bronze-blond hair overgrown and knotted.

Yuan stared at him. "Dorian? What are you talking about? Are they ready . . . are they going to end the war?"

"I don't know about that," Dorian said wearily. "I hope so. It's something else—about you guys. About mermaids. You can change back into humans if you want. They've found a way. You can all change back, and it won't kill you."

Yuan let out a shriek of pure amazement, and an answering outcry poured down from the hill.

At first Luce thought it was a cry of surprise, maybe even of joy, provoked by what Dorian had said. The storm of voices kept getting louder, growing and booming. The sky seemed to thunder with human shouts, and Luce realized that the uproar had spread to the mass of people lining the Golden Gate Bridge, to the hills above them, maybe even to the far shore of Sausalito.

And it no longer sounded like a cry of amazement. The tone had darkened to a howl of fury and dismay. Imani, Graciela, and Yuan rushed close to hold her, tugging her away from the shore in alarm. All of them were buffeted by a torrent of outraged sound. They spun in place, bewildered. A woman was yelling at Dorian.

In that vast clamor Luce couldn't make out what she was saying, but she saw the desperate look that came over Dorian's face, the way his body wrung with sudden despair as he scanned the water for her.

"Luce! Yuan!" Dorian screamed. The mermaids were floating together thirty feet out, scared to approach any nearer. He caught sight of them and waved his arms wildly; Luce thought he was beckoning them over and shook her head in anxiety. "Get out of here now! Swim away and hide!" *Hide?* Luce shuddered with the first gasp of understanding. "The mermaids just destroyed Baltimore!"

35

The Sea Inside

If it had not been for the vast tumultuous crash that turned the inside of the harbor into slashing crosscurrents as strong as waterfalls, for the shock waves slamming forward with irresistible violence, for all the froth and the mermaid bodies hurled in disorder, Anais wouldn't have had the slightest chance of escaping. She was sent tumbling with the rest of them through a labyrinth of foam that rose in veils and hid them from one another. A surge like an angled geyser caught Anais and shot her up and over. Strange green fins smacked at her face; a hand wriggling like an anemone burst out of a wall of crystalline foam and grasped her wrist. Anais craned forward and bit the hand savagely, and it let go. Then she was speeding away, although at first she was too disoriented to guess at her direction. When she surfaced she saw cars drifting like bubbles where the freeway had been minutes before, an off-ramp snapped in two halfway up its arch, buildings slumped over into heaps of angled walls and rubble while high wild waves leaped through the city streets.

Moreland had promised her that she could be human again if she wanted to. And she couldn't keep being a mermaid, obviously; as soon as the Twice Lost recovered from the shock and realized

what she'd done they'd be after her. And once they caught her . . .
Her only option was to leave the water as soon as possible before
dozens of enraged mermaids shredded her fins, twitched her scales
off one by one, then opened her veins with raking nails. But when
she looked around she couldn't recognize the spot where Moreland
had left her anymore. The streets channeled eddying waters spangled peach and bronze by the rising sun. She had a vague sense that
she'd slid into the harbor somewhere on the left, near those slips
where dozens of shattered and upended yachts now slanted across
the jetties, their white hulls grinding together with each new impulse of the maddened sea. Anais dashed in that direction. Soon
she was weaving between the submerged cars on the freeway,
sometimes ducking below rolling human bodies dressed in bright
summer outfits. A German shepherd with blood pouring into its
eyes from a head wound snarled furiously at her as it swam nearby,
but with a quick lash of her tail Anais darted out of reach of its
jaws.

Lush green trees cast endless shadows over the dawn-
shimmered water as she turned up a street of partly collapsed red
brick townhouses and small, uninteresting shops that had sold
plumbing supplies and carpeting. The water was high enough that
she skimmed alongside second-story windows, sometimes peeking
in at beds whose sheets suddenly hovered above them like huge
waterlogged wings. Anais passed a teenage girl who was standing
on her dresser in a room whose front wall had torn away so that
rags of its flowered wallpaper bellied in the currents. The girl was
gasping so hard that her breath sounded like tearing flesh. In the
green water below a drowned white cat thudded against crushed
bits of furniture, shoes, and uprooted saplings, followed by an unmoving boy no older than four. A silver fish peered out of his open

mouth. Anais felt her heart beating so quickly that it merged with the sound of her blood into a single skittish clamor. She'd only done it because Moreland had *made* her, she told herself. But somehow that didn't calm her down or ease the yawning, rattling sensation in her chest.

The water was smoother now, gradually lapping into the calm that comes after utter devastation. Birds trilled in the protruding crests of uprooted trees lining the street; sirens howled in the distance. Wherever she looked, Moreland was nowhere. A torn daisy grazed Anais's shoulder, heading out toward the sea. She didn't think about it, only about the black van that *had* to be around here somewhere. No matter how much she hated Moreland she needed him now to rescue her from all this awful chaos.

Then a garbage can lid came spinning straight at her, clapping her on the head. She glowered at it in irritation as it cycled on toward the harbor. It was traveling faster than the daisy had been.

A chair swung itself through roiling water, smacking her arms and bruising her tail. The drag of the current was against her now, and she had to fight to keep swimming inland. Her fins flicked against the cold metal dome of a car. Lace curtains billowed from a second-story window, and now they were well above her head.

With a sudden jolt, Anais became aware that the level of the water was dropping. Fast. The flood was receding from the ruined blocks along the waterfront.

And she couldn't find Moreland *anywhere*, and soon she might be left beached and helpless on a field of silt-filmed debris, her tail slowly drying in the brightening sun. She toyed with the idea of turning back to the harbor and trying to escape into the open sea. But the harbor's neck was quite narrow, and it seemed much too likely that the mermaids she'd deceived would catch her if she tried it. Anais could already picture the water streaked by their rapidly converging bodies, their hands contorting with desire to sink into her throat. She hovered where she was for a few moments, the water bubbling past her as if drawn by some immense drain. Then she began slipping along with the flux.

Where had Moreland gone? How could he have abandoned her now? It was, Anais thought, so terribly unfair. Doorways flashed by. She was drifting backwards now. Something razor-sharp gouged into her scales. She screamed and rolled sideways to escape it and only succeeded in slashing herself more deeply. Anais curled in place, turned awkwardly on her side, and saw that her tail had snaked deep into the broken windshield of a car strangely canted on a pile of fallen tree trunks. The hole where her tail was lodged gleamed back at her like a mouth lined with gleaming diamond teeth. The water kept pulling out from below her as she struggled to free herself until she was draped across a row of serrated glass jags, her upper body tipped across the car's steeply angled hood. A long curve of her tail was exposed to the summer air now and her fins flapped helplessly against the driver's seat. Blood streamed down the car's scraped silver paint and blossomed in the greenish tide. With every twist and spasm Anais felt the glass stabbing her anew. Hot sun settled gently on her scales. Droplets of water flared like sparks, and soon Anais felt the pain of a deep internal fire. Her tail smoldered unbearably; it was all far beyond any suffering she'd ever imagined.

With a desperate effort she managed to tilt her body off the hood until her torso dipped into the outflowing sea. The sloping trunks below appeared through the reddish clouds of her spreading blood as she braced herself with both hands, then heaved her tail up and free of the slashing glass and jerked herself violently forward at the same time. Pain raked through her and gouts of blood spurted from wide ragged cuts. Her azure fins shredded as they flopped across the jags again, and she landed screaming in the water: water that was now no more than three feet deep. Bleeding and frantic, Anais swung her lacerated tail. She had to get back across the highway and into the harbor again before the falling water left her stranded.

She hurled herself through the retreating tide as best she could, asphalt and broken bricks and spilled garbage only inches from her face. Behind her blood trailed in crimson plumes. But there, just ahead, the highway shone in a long plane of glittering water interrupted by cars and trucks knocked askew like hundreds of small lacquered islands. And beyond the highway there was a large gymnasium caved in on one side, rows of treadmills heaped in muddy confusion—beyond that, the broken, swaggering masts and boats turned belly-up that promised deep water. If she could get there, at least she wouldn't have to face that horrible burning in her tail again, that immolation buried in her own flesh . . .

The deep gouges in her tail slowed her movements, sending blades of cold agony through her with every beat of her fins. She was no more than a foot above the pavement now, and as she skimmed across the double yellow lines at the freeway's midpoint she began to understand that the water below her might run out and leave her floundering before she reached the gleaming green depths on its far side. Terror charged through her muscles, and her tail began to lash in wild defiance of the pain. With every stroke her shredded fins slapped horribly against the coarse pavement and pebbles grated against her raw wounds. But she was close now, so horribly close; already she was crossing the yacht club's parking lot on a plane of water so shallow that she had to constantly crane her neck to avoid dragging her face across the stones and torn metal thrown everywhere by that enormous wave. The masts now were just ahead, and suddenly instead of skimming above asphalt Anais saw the dark stained beams of the boardwalk that ran out between the ruined boats. In only moments she would plunge into deep water and sink her tail far from the harsh, pursuing sun, the naked air.

Wood slammed into Anais's belly, and the last cascade of water dashed back to sea without her. Salt water pooled under her flailing tail and then gradually drained away through the cracks between each plank. The harbor glinted. How far away? Was it six feet? Eight? It struck her as impossibly distant. Sunlight fluttered onto her scales like butterflies. Then, as Anais smacked and thudded at the planks, those butterflies burst into penetrating flames.

Something dark squealed as it loomed above her, cutting off the sun. Sharp, repetitive screams burst in her throat like tiny exploding stars. She was filled by fire, and her wounded tail thrashed uncontrollably. Her torn fins caught against rusty nails and ripped again. Everything seemed blinding bright, set alight by pain. A car door slammed close by.

"Aaaah," a voice groaned. "Aaah, no, no. My Anais . . ." Rough hands shoved and then rolled her like a sloppy, blood-spattered carcass over splintering wood. She couldn't stop screaming.

Then . . . then the wood came to an end, and Anais dropped through empty air. She landed with a splash in the green harbor. Flotillas of debris bobbed thickly around her. Her tail soaked up the cool, quenching water while she gulped harsh, staccato breaths. Someone was close by. Someone was dropping into the water next to her and binding her shoulders in huge greedy arms . . .

At first the delicious relief of simply being in somewhat less pain was enough to keep her from caring who was gripping her. The fire in her scales was doused, drowned, and even if blood kept on unraveling from her salt-stung wounds she was *alive*. If she could just make it past Sadie and the others she would still have a chance. Though, come to think of it, she was feeling awfully weak and sleepy. Maybe she should rest before she tried anything like that.

A heavy hand pawed at her cheek and hot, humid breath gusted into her ear.

The sodden wool of a large expensive suit pressed against her side. Two thick legs kicked and then found purchase on a sub-merged pier. That *someone* was standing slightly above her now, the water's surface just reaching the knot of his tie, so that she sagged a little in his grip.

Anais's relief was replaced by the intensely disagreeable aware-ness that Secretary Moreland had saved her life. Couldn't it have been a younger, hotter guy? Someone more like Dorian? Her tail flicked with irritation, but that only made her torn fins burn. Vaguely it occurred to her that she'd lost a lot of blood. She didn't feel well at all. Clouds of tiny black fish seemed to swim through her head.

"Anais," Moreland moaned into her ear, "Anais, it's all over. Everyone knows, everything's been exposed. But thank God, it's all over! Oh, Anais . . ."

"I want to be human again," Anais snapped. It was disgusting to feel him squeezing her this way. It made her feel so cheap. "Like you promised! I want to be human, and I want my house back, and all my parents' money. And I want to *never* see you again!" She gave a quick, revolted squirm. "Get *off* of me!"

It took her a few moments to understand that the high, whin-ing sound in her ear was coming from Moreland's throat. "Ah, tad-pole," Moreland wheezed out at last. "I'm afraid I can't accommodate you. It's much too late for that. The jig, as they say, is up. In the last fifteen minutes or so there's been simply astounding news blaring over the radio. And it's all about me and you. It appears that your Charlie Hackett secretly recorded tapes of the two of us talking, and now he's gone and given everything to the news channels. Everyone knows the little tricks we've been getting up to, and they're not pleased with us at all."

Anais didn't understand what he was talking about—and even more, she didn't *want* to understand. *Too late?*

"Anais," Moreland crooned. "Anais, darling. Sing me to sleep."

Anais thrashed hard enough that he loosened his grip slightly. She turned to look into his jowly, contorted face. His gray eyes slopped in their sockets like dirty water as he gave her a kind of simpering smile. He reached to stroke her hair. She felt too weak now even to try to shake him off. The water below her looked dark as wine, wrapped by unwinding blood.

"Sing me to sleep, Anais. That's the only thing I still want. Sing me to sleep, once and for all, and then . . . you'll be free, free, free to go."

Her head pitched a little. He should take her to a hospital, Anais thought blearily, not keep jabbering on about singing. And anyway, she didn't *feel* like it. "No."

Now it was Moreland's turn not to understand. "No?" He stared at her. The front of his white shirt was tinted pink with bloody water. "No? Anais, I'm sure you don't mean that!" His awful, whimpering laugh disgusted her. "What could possibly make you happier than killing me?"

"I said NO!" Anais whined. She *really* wasn't feeling well now. She needed a nice soft bed where she could sleep. "I don't *care* about killing you. And I'm sick of doing what you tell me!"

Moreland gaped at her for another long moment. His face seemed oddly blurry and the sunlight was much too bright. Pink-tinged water jostled around their shoulders as his caressing hands slid with a slow, contemplative movement toward her neck. His thumbs brushed her windpipe. "Sing to me, Anais!"

"I already told you no."

There was just a hint of pressure on her throat now. She thought she might fall asleep right there in his hands.

"You *will* do what I tell you! Anais, we don't have much time!" He was trying to stay calm, but his voice lurched into high, trembling notes. He shook her, quick and sharp. "Sing to me now!"

Anais closed her eyes. The sea inside her seemed as red as jam; it was full of layered crimson lights that throbbed like jellyfish. "I don't *care* about you," Anais slurred. His hands were tightening on her throat. It felt awful and constricting, and she made a drowsy effort to pull the hands away, but somehow when she grabbed for his wrists she kept missing. "I don't care what you do. Whatever."

She barely heard Moreland's strained cry as he threw himself from the submerged pier, still choking her, and tried to drive his way deep below the surface. He thrashed down a few feet, keening desperately the whole time, his suit-clad legs kicking wildly at her gashed scales. Anais flopped limply, her closed eyes consumed by that deep red sea. Her mind was dissolving, becoming part of the ruby water. In a remote way she was aware that they weren't far from the surface. No matter how Moreland thrashed, the two of them formed a buoyant tangle that refused to sink, and Anais's fins curled like a sail and resisted the water.

Her body floated like a raft, belly up in the harsh summer sun. Moreland flailed and wept and splashed, driving his knees into her stomach to make her sink. They went down and wavered back up into the air again and again. Anais's golden hair spread into a second sun on the ruby water.

He'd been right, she thought. It was all over. And then even that final drop of awareness poured out to join the sea.

36

Cresting the Wave

Imani's voice was so soft that Luce didn't understand at first how effectively her friend was taking charge. "Graciela, you need to swim as fast as you can to the Mare Island camp. Wake up everyone there and tell them it's time to evacuate. Get everybody here right away, okay? But you need to keep calm so they don't panic; we don't know for *sure* yet that the humans will attack us. And Yuan, I think you're the best one to go to all the little hidden camps; you know better than anybody where all of them are. We need to get every mermaid in the bay inside the wave or under it, now. That way we'll all be close to open sea, and the humans won't be able to trap us in here. Okay?"

Graciela looked at Luce for confirmation of these unexpected orders, and Luce nodded heavily. "I think Imani's right. That's the best thing we can do." It *was* a good plan—and after everything that had happened in the past twenty-four hours it was an immense relief to have someone else assume the work of leadership. Graciela and Yuan saluted and darted off, their quick forms gliding under the water-wall and back into the far recesses of the bay.

"Luce?" Imani murmured. She was gently leading Luce forward. The smooth, ascending wave rippled gracefully, whorls of wandering light caught inside it in glimmering suspension. "I hope you don't think I was out of line, I mean by giving orders that way? I didn't mean to act like *I* was the general. I just did it because, after everything you've been through, I thought you probably needed a break."

All Luce wanted was to lean her head on Imani's shoulder and forget the world. "Thank you, Imani. You were right." Luce hesitated, watching the golden curls cast by far-off streetlamps climbing high through the towering water-wall. The sweet vibrato of mermaid song mingled with the disturbing clamor of humans weeping and shouting on the bridge above. Luce had briefly lived in Baltimore years before, and she pictured the city reduced to sea-battered ruins. With the time difference it was probably well after dawn there, and the morning light would sharply expose the full extent of the destruction. "Imani, I don't think I *should* be general anymore. I think I'm . . . really broken now. After . . ."

Luce couldn't finish the sentence, but Imani's dark eyes flashed with understanding. "If you were broken you wouldn't be able to heal anyone else, Luce. And you just did."

Strangely, Imani's words provoked a kind of rebellious weariness in Luce. Those kind words struck Luce as almost disrespectful, as if they showed that Imani didn't take Catarina's death entirely to heart. Imani was still guiding her forward and now the vertical sheets of water gleamed only a few yards ahead.

"Hey, Luce?" Imani asked softly.

Luce turned. The expression of Imani's mouth was uncharacteristically mischievous, but her usual deep tenderness still glowed in her midnight eyes. "Yes?" Luce asked.

"Are you serious? You want *me* to give the orders tonight? Because if you mean it, I've got an order for *you* right now."

Luce tipped her head, feeling weak and incredulous and—in spite of herself—quickened by curiosity. "What is it?"

Imani's grin widened impishly. She looked lovelier than ever, Luce thought, even if her delight seemed incomprehensible. "That's what I like to hear! Okay, I don't want you to sing to the water tonight, Luce. I have a *way* more important job for you. It's something only you can do too."

Luce waited. The vibrancy of Imani's smile was starting to affect her just a bit, as if flecks of joy dappled the surface of her despondency.

Imani raised one arm and pointed high above. It took Luce a moment to realize that Imani was indicating the raging human mob lined up along the bridge. "Don't sing to hold up the wave. The rest of us can do that. Sing to *them* instead."

Luce swayed from disbelief. "Imani! There's no way—you *can't* mean—" When their situation was so sad and desperate, when the humans might attack at any moment, how could she be so irrepressibly gleeful?

Imani laughed. "For real, Luce? You really thought I wanted you to *kill* them? Of course not. I want you to sing to them the way you just did to your father. They're all suffering tonight; can't you hear it?" Imani paused. She had the exhilarated look of someone who had just made a tremendous discovery. "I want you to *heal* them."

Luce stared. "It's too dangerous, Imani! It's too *much* for them, too beautiful for them . . . to absorb." She was thinking of Dorian, his crazy otherworldly rapture when she used to sing for him—and he had much greater resistance to mermaid song than any human Luce had ever met.

"It didn't seem like it hurt those people who were listening to you on the bunkers just now," Imani argued. She was still beaming.

"And anyway I *need* to learn how you do that, and now seems like a fantastic time to get started, right? I'll come up to the very top of the wave with you and I'll just listen, and listen, until I can feel exactly what you're doing." And then Imani burst into a peal of blissful laughter.

It was too much for Luce. "I don't understand how you can act so *happy*, Imani. Even if they won't attack us as long as we're in the wave, we still have to sleep *sometime*. Soon they'll start searching for our camps. And you're acting like this isn't serious at all!" Her voice wavered.

In reply Imani caught Luce's wrist and spiraled her tail, launching both of them upward through the wave's glassy core.

They vaulted through a high upward dive, the dancing pane of water across their eyes making the skyscrapers flutter like wings and furl like rising smoke. Even in her grief and fear, Luce was consumed by the beauty in front of her. It didn't matter if she died, since this splendor would live on without her. And still Imani's tail was flurrying and still they were shooting higher and higher inside the wave, looking down on houses scattered like confetti across the distant hills and the bay's variegated shades of smoke and dust and moon all joined into a single rippling symphony.

When they broke through the wave's crest the girders crossing the bottom of the Golden Gate Bridge loomed only few feet above their heads, and the air popped and reverberated with stamping feet and raspy human cries.

"We loved the mermaids! We trusted them; we *marched* for them! And we believed them when they told us they'd given up killing, and now — now there are at least ten *thousand* people missing in Baltimore," someone howled immediately overhead. "General Luce needs to answer for this!"

She *did* need to answer for it, Luce realized. But she couldn't answer with words. They'd never believe her.

Luce and Imani looked at each other. Imani's dark heart-shaped face had lost its giddiness; instead she was intent, rapt with concentration as she stared into Luce's eyes. The droplets in her dark hair held the first hints of dawn in a crown of radiating rose-colored sparks. "Luce?" Imani whispered. "You asked me how I can be so happy now? After so many mermaids died yesterday and now that Baltimore's flooded and all these people hate us?" Luce nodded slowly, unable to look away. Imani was illuminated by a kind of transcendence that Luce had never seen before. "I'm happy because we've *won*. The Twice Lost have won, and the war is over."

The madness of Imani's words left Luce paralyzed, silenced. The water frothed and gurgled around their chests, and they bobbed and fell with each tiny variation of the music swelling below them. "Imani . . ." Luce finally managed. "That's not *true*. There's no way we can win, not now that mermaids have destroyed a human city! They'll *never* stop thinking of us as monsters now."

Imani was unperturbed. She reached out with both hands and squeezed Luce's shoulders. "No, Luce. I knew we'd won as soon as I heard you singing to your father back there. I knew we can do exactly what it will take. There's only one way you can answer for what happened and that's by *singing* it."

"Imani . . ."

"Trust me, Luce. You know I've always trusted you. I *promise* you they'll understand."

"It seems *crazy*," Luce objected. But somehow she'd started smiling. Imani might be out of her mind, but in this strange transported mood she was also magnificent.

"You get started, general. I'll be back in a few minutes. I have to go give some orders."

Luce shook herself as Imani streaked back downward. Luce watched Imani's dusky blue fins flicking away. Above her people stomped and wept and moaned, their voices beating the air into agitated rags.

Luce thought of Dorian: of how he'd fought for her, of how he'd worked to help save her father, and how he'd come here to find her. She thought of how she used to sing to him beneath the undulating green of the aurora while the harsh Alaskan nights lingered on, and the taste of love turned to music on her tongue.

And then the memory became a living sound in her throat: a single low note that brushed the shrieking faces above her like a rain of light kisses, like a wind that could carry away all their tears.

A thousand distraught voices fell silent together as Luce's voice rose. They couldn't see her, positioned as she was directly under the beams supporting their feet, but they still recognized at once that the music streaming from her was entirely different from the kind of mermaid song they'd grown used to hearing. It was new, with a magic that wasn't meant to enchant the water at all. It wasn't even meant to enchant the humans who heard it.

Instead it was a song that wanted only to join with them, to share in their grief and terror and then, by sharing those unbearable feelings, to let them spin away in notes as fine as strands of drifting silk.

As she sang to them, Luce began to understand. With absolute tenderness she accepted the hatred and rage of the people above her. She turned those tortured emotions into music, let them expand and float in vibrating sonic clouds. And as she sang that darkness, the crowd on the bridge discovered that darkness was no longer *necessary*. They could let it go.

A shadow seemed to press down on her. Luce glanced up in momentary alarm and saw the bridge's planks were only a foot above her head. The wave was rising higher. In a flash she understood that more mermaids were singing to the water now. The first of the mermaids gathered by Yuan and Graciela had arrived, and they were merging their voices with the bewitching chorus below. That was why Imani had gone: to gather as many voices as possible, to swell the wave in a show of strength.

Luce leaned back, letting herself drift toward the frothing edge. The wave was wide enough to support her beyond the dark roof formed by the bridge. As she approached the drop, the currents became choppier, more effervescent, and it took increasing concentration to maintain her balance with subtle loopings and flicks of her fins. She was still singing.

It occurred to her that, if any of the humans on the bridge had a gun, they might well open fire to avenge the dead of Baltimore. For a fraction of a second she hesitated, imagining the way her heart would feel as a bullet winged through it like some bright metallic bird with sharply bladed wings.

Then she gave a last slight kick of her fins, and propelled herself out where the crowd on the bridge could see her.

Some of the faces were still crumpled with anger or slack with confusion but others were crying or simply staring into her face with wide, accepting eyes. Luce felt a kind of jolting in the wave around her. Its crest cleft into two long parallel waves, still rising, and fanned out to enwrap the bridge's roadway without engulfing it or spilling more than a few droplets onto the people squeezed against the railings. Luce was lifted high enough that she could feel the air around her cheeks warmed by the crowd's mingled exhalations. Some of them reached out to touch her, and Luce reached back, her fingertips grazing theirs as she swam slowly along a wave that echoed the bridge's form.

To all of those she passed Luce sang her grief for the thousands of humans slaughtered in Baltimore. Hearing her they gazed with recognition, understanding that her sorrow for them was as deep as her sorrow for the mermaids she'd allowed to die as the price of sparing the city at her back. And then Luce felt a cool, swirling presence at her side and looked to see Imani, her eyes wide and wondering in the amber dawn as she listened thirstily to Luce's new song: a song that had left death far behind.

37

Aftermath

Luce had been battered by too many overwhelming emotions not to collapse into numbness at the first opportunity. As the news began to come in, as it became clear that the humans *weren't* going to attack, Luce couldn't even feel surprised. And when the reporters gathered jabbering onshore and asked for her reaction to the torrent of astonishing information coming from Washington she could only offer them drowsy, irrelevant replies. Soon Yuan and Imani were doing most of the talking. Half of the Twice Lost Army was still singing below the bridge, but everyone who was off-duty seemed to be too excited to sleep. The bay was full of darting, leaping figures, and their fins flashed colored reflections across the water's glossy skin.

Luce slumped in the shallows near the bridge's base with her head leaning on a rock while her friends spoke and gestured vivaciously beside her, only occasionally nudging her when the reporters bought up issues they weren't sure about. Behind the reporters a crowd of humans pressed and shuffled, but all those people didn't seem to be frightened and enraged anymore. Instead the mood was peculiarly light, even buoyant. People cried for the dead of Baltimore, but they also cried from relief: like Imani, most of them seemed to believe that peace was finally at hand.

"Yes. That's Anais," Luce confirmed sadly when they showed her the photo of the dead golden-haired girl with a badly bruised throat who'd been found naked and hopelessly drained of blood in the secretary of defense's clinging arms. "We were in the same tribe once, up in Alaska. She was . . . really dangerous . . . but still . . ." Luce went back to staring at the late-morning sunlight speckled across the bay's low waves.

"Secretary Moreland confessed to sending her out as an agent provocateur with instructions to trick the Baltimore Twice Lost into attacking. Can you tell us something about Anais that might help explain why she would agree to do that?"

Since Luce was looking away the reporter had addressed Yuan instead. "Well, Luce is the one who *knew* her; I never actually met—"

"She was a *sika*," Luce murmured vaguely. She didn't look around.

·   "A seekah?"

"Oh—yeah." Yuan took up the question in authoritative tones. "See, a lot of mermaids are angry. But a mermaid who's a *sika* isn't angry, just empty. They'll do anything because they can't really feel, so it's like they have to do evil, crazy things to feel anything at all, and nothing *means* anything to them."

"Similar to what humans would call a psychopath?"

"Pretty much, I guess."

The conversations went on and on. Luce couldn't understand why this Secretary Moreland guy—wasn't he the same one who'd said on TV that she was impersonating the real Luce Korchak?—hated mermaids so much that he was ready to sacrifice thousands of human lives simply to persuade the world to share in his hatred. But, unfathomable as it was, that appeared to be precisely the case. The tapes of his conversations with Anais certainly proved he was a madman, capable of extravagant evil. On the news they said Moreland was delirious now, gibbering, but telling everything over and over again as if he couldn't believe it himself. He'd admitted that he was the one who'd sent out the helicopter with the net too. Catarina and the other mermaids caught that day had died because of him. And he'd also arranged for the murder of certain humans, ones he considered his enemies. That part was on the tapes: they revealed that he'd been using Anais as an assassin.

He didn't care if everyone knew the truth, not now that he'd lost Anais, now that he'd been pulled off her floating corpse by the first rescuers to arrive at the scene. He only wanted to die, and to die by a mermaid's enchantment. He was begging the mermaids to show him that mercy in gratitude for his confession.

Luce didn't think any of them would.

Poor Anais, Luce thought. A gray glaze seemed to cover the water, or maybe it only covered her eyes. She felt sick and achy. Her head seemed to be drifting by itself down to Imani's shoulder.

"When Dorian Hurst of the Twice Lost Humans started claiming he'd been subjected to an attack by a mermaid assassin via *telephone* and that he'd fended her off by singing back to her, his story struck most people as pure fantasy. But now it appears that Hurst was in fact targeted by Secretary Moreland," someone said loudly onshore.

Luce jolted out of her hazy half-sleep and sat up, her mouth suddenly opening in wordless indignation. Anais had tried to kill *Dorian?* How *dare* she?

"*That* got a reaction from you," Yuan observed, smiling slyly at her. "You know that while you were singing on top of the wave earlier, Dorian was here the whole time? He wanted to go up on the bridge and jump off into the wave so he could see you. God knows how he thought he was going to squeeze through that crowd up there, but anyway. I told him no, to just let you do your thing, and he could come visit you at our camp tomorrow."

Luce was now so wide awake that her eyes ached. Everything felt cold and sharp even though it was a beautiful warm day, and she found herself sitting bolt upright. "You told him *what?*"

"He's *earned* it, Luce." Yuan was firm. "I know he hurt you, but he's earned a chance to make his case. Maybe he's earned more than that."

"But I—" *I can't see him,* Luce thought. *I can't face it.*

"And maybe you've earned some happiness too. I mean, the war might be over for real soon. There are just too many humans on our side now for them to keep on fighting us, right? And you know Dorian had a lot to do with that." Yuan was watching her with an expression Luce couldn't decipher. "What did you think about what he told us, anyway? That mermaids can turn *back* if they want to now?"

Luce shook her head. It felt like her skull was filled with loose silver sparks. She was beyond exhausted. "Yuan! We don't even know if that's *true.* And even if it is . . ."

"I'll be the first in line!" Yuan grinned in such a strange haphazard way that Luce couldn't tell if she was joking or not.

Either way, her thoughts were still on Dorian. "There's no way he'll be able to find our camp," Luce murmured. It sounded like she was trying to convince herself.

"Oh, I think I gave him pretty good directions." Yuan was still smiling. "Don't sweat that part, general-girl." An outcry started up in the parking lot behind them, and Yuan jerked around, raising herself as far as she could in her effort to see through the clustered humans. "Whoa, Luce. Look! What the heck?"

All the mermaids along the water's edge turned to look. As usual the parking lot next to the bridge's base was packed with people, sitting or standing, some with signs or cameras, singing or debating the latest electrifying fragments of news. That was normal. What wasn't normal was that for once many of the people there were climbing back up onto the road above, shuffling and scrambling onto the hillsides as they tried to clear a path . . .

A path for a chain of black-windowed limousines. The cars advanced patiently, solemnly, but they were obviously determined not to stop before they reached the land's limit.

Imani caught Luce's hand and squeezed it.

Soon the limousines stopped. Doors opened, and a dozen men and women in dark, crisp suits stepped out. For all their poise, they seemed a bit uncomfortable as they looked around at the water-wall still glimmering like an immense ghost under the Golden Gate Bridge, at the jostling crowds and the wide expanse of the bay. They didn't seem to notice the watching mermaids, low down and half-concealed by the line of rocks. "We're here to speak with General Luce," a man called out.

"I *bet* you are!" Yuan called back. "She's right here!"

The man started apprehensively, caught sight of them, and assumed a professional smile. He was very handsome, slim and straight and black-haired, with vivid blue eyes. Luce sat up as far as she could without exposing her tail to the warm air. The black-haired man walked forward to meet her; Luce was suddenly aware of her ragged bikini top, her scars, and the missing notch in her ear. "Hi. I'm General Luce."

"General." He nodded, looking her over in exactly the way Luce had feared he might. "I'm Ambassador Prescott, authorized by President Leopold of the United States of America to formally request negotiations with representatives of the Twice Lost Army." His mouth tweaked a little as he tried to repress a smile of amusement. Yuan's forehead looked tense. Luce thought that he was having trouble taking her entirely seriously; after all, to him she must look like a child.

For a moment she was almost cowed. For a moment she almost saw herself through his eyes, as an absurd, pretty little schoolgirl with a tail like shiny mint candy—but with enough power that she had to be humored.

And then she remembered who she *really* was, along with everything she'd gone through to become who she was now. This ambassador was in no position to condescend to her, and she knew it.

"I speak for the Twice Lost Army," Luce said. She kept her tone as calm and straightforward as she could manage. "Does President Leopold want peace?"

Ambassador Prescott looked a bit graver now. "He does. He'd like to meet with you in person to negotiate a treaty."

Imani squeezed Luce's arm, hard. It was only then that the enormity of what was happening sank in. Her mouth seemed clotted with ashes and her heart drummed.

"We're ready to negotiate anytime," Luce told him carefully. At first all she'd seen in Ambassador Prescott's eyes was crystalline blue vanity, but now she began to see the possibility of something better than that. "We want peace, too."

Prescott nodded so soberly that even Yuan stopped glaring at him. "We believe that you do, general."

38

Dorian

The kayak steadily wove its way among the pilings under the factory next to Islais Creek. On all sides the mermaids chatting in swaying hammocks fell silent as they saw the human boy, his expression somewhere between nervous and determined, being escorted into their secret redoubt by Lieutenant Yuan. He looked around at them in turn, the dim shine of their bodies like sleepy comets in the shadows. "Where's Luce?"

"Our *general* is still asleep," a small mermaid, no older than eight, called defensively from the water. "Yuan, don't you think we should let her rest?"

"She's been asleep for like twenty hours straight already," Yuan said. "And this is important, too. Would you please go wake her? Tell her she has a visitor."

For the next few minutes Dorian's foot could be heard tapping gently but rapidly on the kayak's hull. "Yuan," he whispered, "what if she *really* doesn't want to talk to me? I completely blew it with her, and she's probably going to think that I'm not worth her time."

"If she refuses, she refuses, and then you get to deal with that," Yuan agreed. She smiled. "But I don't think she will."

A soft rippling disturbance approached beneath the dusky surface and then stopped ten feet away. Even through the dark water Dorian could see that the submerged tail flashed a light silvery green, and he groaned and leaned sideways, one hand floating tentatively toward her. If Yuan hadn't caught hold of the kayak he would have capsized. "Luce?"

Dorian and Yuan could both see the luminous form slip closer to the surface, hesitate, and then retreat again.

"At least give me a chance to tell you how sorry I am. Please."

Luce's head parted the waters. She started to say something, then stopped and twisted a bit. "Hi . . . Dorian."

For a moment Dorian just stared at her: she had the same spiky dark hair as ever, the same long charcoal eyes and broad forehead and slightly sharp features. The same unbearable beauty still radiated from her, undiminished by her scars. So much about her was exactly the way he remembered that it only made the aching strangeness of her expression harder for him to accept. "Hey, Luce. I'm really . . . happy to see you."

She gazed at him searchingly. He wondered what she saw. "Does Zoe know you're here?" Luce asked quietly.

The question startled him. "Oh—yeah. We were just texting about it last night. She wished me luck." He caught Luce's look of perplexity and hurried to explain. "Zoe and I broke up a long time ago."

Luce was still watching his face as if she were trying to see into an undersea crevasse many fathoms deep. It was both painful and thrilling. "Why?" she asked.

"Why? Because Zoe's not *stupid*. She knew I still loved you."

Luce looked away from him and down. Her tail was curled behind her and he could see her fins stirring just below the surface.

"Um . . ." Yuan began. "There are a few wharves on the other side of the factory? You'll have more privacy back there."

Luce nodded. Without glancing at Dorian again she began to lead the way, and he paddled after her. The war had changed her so much, he realized. Maybe too much?

She led him out into the blazing daylight and then below a small dark slip with a half-sunk motorboat still tied to it. A monstrous metal construction scabbed with rust, maybe some kind of ancient machinery, loomed from the waves nearby, and the water ran in chevrons of taupe and lemon yellow and milky turquoise. Luce sat close to the water's edge, her tail coiled tight around her, and caught the kayak's side in both hands. Its hull lightly scraped against the pebbled seafloor. She was very close to him now but she still wouldn't look up, and suddenly Dorian realized why. The fringe of her lashes gleamed with tears. She was trying not to cry in front of him.

He reached out and curled his fingers around her damaged ear, then—so lightly that his fingers barely grazed her—he stroked the side of her face. "Luce, I'm *sorry*. I know I screwed up. I was completely in love with you the whole time, even when I was breaking up with you. I mean, I loved you so much that it just made me angry, like, that my feelings were out of my control. And I took that out on you." Luce glanced up at him so quickly that he felt himself lanced by phosphorescent beams. Then her eyes lowered again. But to his surprise she didn't pull away from his caress. If anything she might have drawn slightly nearer to him.

"You broke my heart." Close as she was, Dorian had to strain to hear the words. "You said my problems weren't *real*. And then I found my old tribe massacred." Again there was that quick flash of her eyes. "What's not *real* about that?"

Dorian sighed. He deserved this. "I was being an asshole because I was trying to make you mad enough to kill me! God, Luce, you've been leading a *war*. I'm not so dumb that I think that's not real!" He was caressing her cool, wet face with both hands now. "Look, I know I don't *deserve* for you to forgive me. I'm asking you to anyway."

"*Forgive* you," Luce murmured. She sounded doubtful.

The chill under Dorian's fingers was suddenly interrupted by a tiny splash of warmth: a tear against his thumb. "Please," Dorian said. He heard his voice crack.

She leaned her cheek against his palm and took a long deep breath. What was she thinking?

"Do you forgive *me*?" Luce asked at last. Dorian didn't know if he was more amazed by the question or by the fierce sweetness of the gaze that she suddenly fixed on him. "Even for helping to kill your family? Because I don't think you ever really did before. No matter what you said. And I understand if you can't, but if you can't there's no *point* in—" She broke off with a moan.

"That wasn't the only thing I couldn't forgive you for." Somehow saying that sent a shock through him. Truth rose in his mind like bubbles and then popped horribly.

"How do you mean?" Luce's voice was still very soft.

"I couldn't forgive you for always getting to be the hero when I *wasn't* one."

They were looking at each other so intensely that the air seemed to ring. "So go *work* on being a hero," Luce said. "If that's what you want."

"I did." For the first time since he'd found her again he felt himself grinning at her. "I mean, not like you, Luce. But I really tried my best. That's all I've been doing for weeks now. And I know everything we did at least *helped*."

"The Twice Lost Humans, you mean?"

Dorian felt the thrill of seeing her responding smile. Possibly, just possibly, there was still hope for the two of them. "Yeah."

"I was so *mad* about that. You using our name."

"I know," Dorian whispered. And before he was entirely conscious of what he was doing he'd leaned forward and kissed her.

The kiss was a bright banner unfurled and beating in the wind. It was an expanse of water suddenly waking with a surge of blinding ripples. It was his heart made manifest, and it felt like a triumph that comes unexpectedly when all hope has long been lost. He heard her gasp and pulled her closer still.

Then Dorian kicked his legs out of the kayak and landed on his side in the shallow water, his arms binding her fervently. For a time they tangled sweetly, Luce's fins flicking and curling around his ankles. General or not, Dorian thought, Luce was still *his*. They still belonged together, and he told her that with a slow whirl of deepening kisses.

Then she pulled away—not far enough to leave his embrace but enough to break the kiss and rest her forehead on his chest. He gazed down at her, his hands still glossing gently around her faintly shining shoulders, her back, the nape of her neck. "Luce . . ."

"Everything's changed," Luce murmured. "Everything is different now! Dorian, I can't even *explain*—"

Dorian felt his heart plummeting. The world became nothing but ice, falling stones, blackness. She couldn't *explain* why she could never love him again? Was that what she meant? "What can't you explain?" His voice rasped out of him.

"I mean . . . if everything is different now . . . why hasn't *this* changed, too?" Luce looked up at him, her eyes shining and vulnerable, spangled with hints of desperation. "Why do I still love who I've *always* loved?"

"You mean me," Dorian said proudly. He brushed his cheek against hers.

"You and my dad. Dorian, do you know—have you heard anything about him since—"

"Oh." He was ashamed now that he'd been so consumed by his own longing that he'd forgotten to tell her the news immediately. "I saw your dad this morning. He had breakfast with me and Ben Ellison. Luce, he's way, way better. He still seemed—kind of out of it, like, spacy?—but he's not all insane and catatonic anymore. You did an *amazing* job. Ben's so impressed that he can't really talk about anything else. I don't know why. I mean, I *told* him you could do that, but I guess he didn't believe—"

"What did my dad say?"

Dorian hesitated. He wanted to have this conversation with her, but later, once her responsibilities to the Twice Lost were completely out of the way. But Luce's look was so worried and tender that he couldn't hold anything back from her. "We talked about you." He paused again. "About what you're going to do after the war is really over, like once there's a treaty and everything. Your dad's already thinking about—you know, where he should live, and what would be best for you."

Dorian was still hedging, but Luce was quick enough to guess what he was really getting at. "You mean, you talked about turning me human again?"

Now he was afraid of bringing up all the fights they'd had back in Alaska: fights about exactly this question. "Well, maybe. It is—an *option* now. If you want. But maybe you'd rather keep being a mermaid general than go to high school or whatever."

Luce leaned her forehead on his chest again. She held him tight, and, in the way of mermaids, there was a long, long silence between each of her breaths. He could feel the intensity of her thought as if it were a physical thing turning against his skin. "I *can't* be a general anymore," Luce whispered at last. "As soon as there's a treaty, I'm going to . . . let go of all that."

He didn't want her to see how happy that made him. It might seem like he was gloating. "You *can't* be general? Luce, why —"

"I let my friends *die*, Dorian. I'm — broken inside. The Twice Lost General should be — somebody whole."

Why did those words send a spasm of cold panic through his heart? "You mean when those mermaids got netted? Luce, you didn't have any choice!"

Luce's gaze turned skeptical and even harsh. "Of course I had a choice."

"You mean to try and save them by wiping out San Francisco?" Dorian's laugh sounded rough, almost hysterical, even to him. "That isn't much of a —"

"I didn't say I had a *good* choice. And I'd do the same thing again. But Dorian, you . . ."

That distant look was back in her eyes. He could almost see ghosts slipping through her irises like trails of mist. "Whoever was in that helicopter wouldn't have let the mermaids go, Luce. No matter *what* you did. Right? They were obviously lying to you. So you shouldn't keep blaming yourself!"

She was looking away, watching the streamers of light that raveled and split on the bay. Then she smiled. It would have been better, Dorian thought, if she hadn't smiled. "And do you think that's what Catarina was telling herself? While she was dying?"

There was nothing he could say to that, really. He was almost relieved when Yuan came toward them, splashing much more than she needed to, to tell Luce that they'd received a message. President Leopold would be arriving the next day.

Dorian clambered back into the kayak he'd rented. Water streamed from his sopped clothes and puddled at his ankles. He tried not to show how upset he was that Luce was suddenly too distracted to even kiss him goodbye.

She had work to do.

* * *

Luce rushed off. She had one last job for Seb. She found him in his usual spot and talked with him for a few minutes before heading on to the bridge. She'd slept through two of her shifts since no one wanted to wake her, and even after her long sleep she still felt peculiarly weary. The memory of Dorian's kisses and of everything he'd said to her lingered in her thoughts, softly smoldering.

The Golden Gate Bridge swanned through the fading grandeur of a deeply golden afternoon. Below it the water-wall was noticeably lower than it had been before. Of course now that the mermaids weren't afraid of being slaughtered anymore they were singing more softly and in some cases not bothering to show up for their shifts. The pervasive sense of peace had washed away the urgency of the war. It wasn't really time to lower the wave yet, not until they had a treaty signed. But Luce couldn't completely blame her followers for relaxing their guard.

There was Yuan, leaning against the shore and talking to Gigi again. Luce was surprised and a bit embarrassed to notice that they were holding hands. Giddy mermaids pirouetted in the water, no longer shy at all in front of the human crowds. And there was the usual press of people with their signs, their blown-up photographs of lost daughters. Luce skimmed the images out of habit, not expecting to recognize anyone — and did a double take at the image of a girl with wavy ruby-dyed hair.

JOHANNE ARIANNA SPIELDOCH.

Luce swam a little closer. She knew the pale, anxious face that glowed between those red curls. The woman holding the sign was chubby and worn-looking, wearing an eccentric flowing robelike dress in an odd shade of murky purple and several huge necklaces that reminded Luce of the strands of clattering toys that Jo always wore. In fact, that woman's aged and worried face *was* a lot like Jo's if all Jo's brilliant beauty and youth had been stripped from her.

Beside Luce, a few mermaids had stopped to see what she was staring at. Luce glanced around and saw that one of them was Cala, now just as wide-eyed as Luce was herself. "Cala! Do you know where Jo is?"

"She's on shift," Cala whispered. "I guess she didn't notice? Or maybe — she might not want to see that woman. Maybe she's trying to avoid her."

Luce remembered Yuan's explanation of why Jo had been kicked out of her former tribe: *Jo was caught trying to call her mom with a cell phone she found on the beach.*

"I think that's Jo's mom," Luce said breathlessly. It occurred to her how poignant it would be for all the other humans onshore to see someone find a missing daughter when their own children were still lost, but she couldn't help that. "Please go tell her."

A few moments later Luce heard Jo squealing and watched her streak like an arrow toward the shore. The police had stopped keeping people out of the water. The woman in the purple robes was squealing too as she stooped and tripped her way over the rocks. "Mom!" Jo was shouting. "Mom!"

Luce couldn't help crying as she watched them clutch at each other. Jo didn't seem like a mermaid at all anymore, not with her mother's arms around her. She could hear them laughing and sobbing, and now and then she caught a broken fragment of conversation. "But I thought you'd be fine with Aunt Janet!"

"Mom, Aunt Janet is a total psycho! You wouldn't *believe* all the things she did! I thought you didn't love me anymore. I thought—"

"No, baby, no. Never. I was confused, and—I couldn't function very well for a long time. I had to stay—in the hospital. But I always loved you! Losing you was the worst thing that ever . . ."

Luce turned away, and found herself face to face with Imani. "I should be happy for her," Imani whispered, watching the reunion onshore. "I *want* to be happy for her. But I can't."

Maybe seeing Luce with her father had been just as painful for Imani. Luce flinched and looked down, obscurely ashamed.

Assuming Dorian's information was correct, then very soon mermaids all over the world would start leaving the water. It was strange to think of the mermaids who'd sung beside her standing up on human legs again, tugging on borrowed clothes, and walking off into unpredictable new lives—lives in which they'd grow old and maybe even have children of their own. Jo would go; even Yuan had said she'd go. But there were others who would choose to remain in the sea forever. Luce didn't have to ask to know that Imani would stay a mermaid for as long as she lived.

Imani smiled wistfully, but a hint of bitterness still showed in her eyes. She nodded toward Jo. "Have you made a decision yet, Luce?"

Luce was startled. Imani seemed to have read her thoughts. "You mean—"

"I mean about leaving the sea. If it's true that we can. You have—a lot more waiting for you on land—than some of us do. Your dad and your boyfriend. No one could blame you for choosing that."

Luce searched her heart for an answer to Imani's question. All she found was painful uncertainty, a bewilderment of fierce currents that pulled her this way and that. "I don't know."

For a long moment Imani looked at her with an expression of soft disbelief. "I think I know what you'll decide. And I'll really miss you." Luce opened her mouth to object, but something dark and knowing in Imani's gaze stopped her. "You don't have to worry about me, Luce," Imani added in a half-whisper. "I've found my calling."

39

Negotiations

Luce waited by the shore, surrounded by a ring of all the Twice Lost lieutenants. The parking lot had been entirely cleared except for several dozen men and a few women in stiff black suits: the president's security detail. Even the mermaids were wearing a kind of uniform, since one of their human friends who owned a clothing store had donated twenty-five identical burgundy velour tank tops for the occasion. "But you're sure they know to let Seb and Dr. Perle through?" Luce asked anxiously. "Seb *said* she'd agreed to come."

"Stop stressing, general-girl," Yuan said sardonically. "Working out a treaty with the humans? That's so insane it ought to come naturally to you."

They could see the advance of black-lacquered cars on the road above. "We don't know enough to know what we're *doing*, though," Luce murmured. "That's why we need Dr. Perle. She seriously knows *everything* about the oceans, like about what will help . . ."

Yuan was grinning rakishly. "It's funny to hear you going so fangirl."

Luce bristled a little. "Her book was *amazing*. Dorian got it from the library, and I read it back in Alaska. She's been doing deep-sea exploration for years, like going way deeper than *we* can! And—"

The limousines were turning into the parking lot, lining up one by one. Their windows sleeked across the pale day like wet black brushes; Luce half expected them to leave strokes of darkness on the air. She realized that she had no idea what the current U.S. president looked like. So many people were stepping formally from those cars; he could be almost anyone.

No: she knew him by the way people stood around him, their posture slightly curved and deferential. She knew him by the assertive way he met her eyes, just visible above the line of rocks. For all his coifed hair and severe tailoring he still looked rough and craggy to her, his face composed of complicated peaks and deep folds under his salt and pepper hair. His expression took on an aggressive archness as he watched Luce. Even from a distance, she realized, she made him uncomfortable.

Then, to Luce's astonishment, a chauffeur opened yet another gleaming door, and Seb of the Ghosts stepped out looking extremely sheepish but also remarkably well-dressed and groomed. He offered his arm to an older woman who was emerging after him. She had neat, fluffy gray hair to her shoulders and wore a trim gray pantsuit with a bright silk scarf, and her expression was so wise and gracious that Luce immediately wanted to be like her someday.

She just *had* to be Audrey Perle. Luce was watching her so intently that she didn't notice the president and his delegation approaching until they were ten feet away. "General Lucette Gray Korchak?"

Luce looked up. "Yes, Mr. President?"

"Just President of the Humans. Isn't that what you call me?

Even though you girls are living in U.S. territory. International waters don't kick in until you're a good few miles out that way." He gestured toward the horizon. He sounded like he was kidding, or at least trying to make her think he was kidding. The snide, offended undercurrent in his voice was obvious enough.

A Secret Service man rushed over with a chair. President Leopold waved it away and sat down on the rock, leaning toward Luce in a way she didn't entirely like. There was a slightly misted look to his eyes, as if they were windows hit by a hot breath of enchantment.

Luce considered what he'd said anyway, tilting her head as she thought it over. "Did you even believe mermaids existed? Until a few months ago?"

"Of course not. I'm not about to believe in fairies or unicorns either."

"Well, if you didn't believe we existed, then how could you represent us?"

President Leopold nodded at that. "Touché, general. Touché. But if you all get your legs back and start trotting off to school you'll be citizens again, won't you, with the same rights and — pay attention now — *responsibilities* as everybody else?"

That made her start a little in spite of herself. "Is it true that we *can* change back now?"

"The Pentagon used to have a tank full of those baby mermaids you all call 'larvae,' general. And now they're telling me we've got a bunch of babbling human infants to tend to instead. They still look a little greener and shinier than your average babies, so I hear, but apart from that they're doing fine. So, yes, indeed you can. We'll send down some doctors to help you all out with that soon."

Luce wondered nauseously what the Pentagon had been doing

with a collection of larval mermaids, but she couldn't wonder for long. Leopold was still speaking.

"Now, I'm told you have a couple of—what should we call them?—interspecies advisors who aren't exactly batting for their own kind today." He gestured with his head toward Seb and Audrey Perle, who were now standing much closer with two of the suited men flanking them.

"They aren't *batting* for anyone," Luce said a little curtly. "Because this isn't a game, Mr. President. Anyway, if this is about peace, then nobody has to choose sides anymore!"

From the way he stared at her, Luce knew she was halfway enchanting him without even wanting to. A different mermaid might have known how to use that to the Twice Lost Army's advantage, but his fascination just made her feel fidgety. "Well. You're just full of the zingers today, aren't you, general?" he purred.

"May I introduce you to them, Mr. President?" Luce said. Exaggerated politeness seemed like the best way to handle his disconcerting reaction to her. She waved Dr. Perle and Seb over and couldn't repress a smile at Seb's bashful, half-stumbling advance. "President Leopold, this is the Twice Lost Ambassador, Seb Grassley. And you must be Audrey Perle?" Luce was suddenly just as shy as Seb. "The great oceanographer?"

"That's a kind way to put it," Audrey Perle said, smiling, and held out her hand to shake.

President Leopold turned a slow, shifting look on Seb. "And how did *you* meet our lovely general, *Ambassador* Grassley?"

"She saved me from drowning, Mr. President," Seb muttered. He couldn't make himself look up.

"I see."

Luckily for Luce Audrey Perle wasn't self-conscious at all.

With a few deft words she brought everyone's attention around to the question of the treaty, and soon negotiations were starting in earnest.

As Luce had expected, the parts about how humans and mermaids would treat one another were easy: nonaggression and full amnesty for the mermaids in exchange for an end to all the Twice Lost Army's blockades and a promise: not only that the Twice Lost wouldn't attack human ships, but also that they would send envoys to any mermaid tribes that still *did* hunt ships and persuade them to stop. Basically it amounted to assurances that humans and mermaids would let one another live in peace.

The parts about how humans would treat the oceans, though, were much harder to settle; that was why they needed Audrey Perle. The mermaid lieutenants had trouble hiding their boredom as the discussions dragged on. Various human assistants sat nearby busily drafting different versions of the treaty while Audrey Perle waved her hands with brusque animation, debating what percentage of U.S. waters should be designated Protected Zones safe from fishing boats and discussing carbon-reduction timetables and energy policy and on and on. Luce did her best to be attentive—this was what they'd fought for, after all—but there were times when she had to admit to herself that she had no idea what they were talking about. Now and then President Leopold would snap at Audrey Perle, saying, "Nonstarter. Try getting *that* through this Senate!" or "Our lovely general might have to take that particular matter up with Japan."

It was some kind of victory for the Twice Lost, Luce supposed, but it wasn't nearly as clear-cut and glorious as she'd imagined. And were they really going to have to go raise waves around *Japan* next?

Pale dusk was just starting to silver the bay when Luce realized that the humans had finished. Someone was running a printer. "This is a ridiculously informal way to be putting a peace treaty together," President Leopold observed waspishly. "But this is one of those times when the smart thing to do is to roll with what life deals you."

Luce's lieutenants were snapping out of various states of idleness and lethargy now that the treaty was finally in front of them: three sheets of white paper on a clipboard. The pages kicked in the breeze, dense with fine black print. President Leopold was already scratching his signature across the bottom.

Luce looked up at Audrey Perle. "Do you think it's good?" Even now that she'd led an army, her voice sometimes came out sounding uncomfortably fragile and childlike.

Dr. Perle's answering gaze was patient and sympathetic. "Truthfully, General Luce? It's far from perfect. But it's also better than anything I'd hoped to see in my lifetime."

Luce wanted to end the war so desperately that she didn't trust herself. She might be giving in too soon. She might betray everything they'd struggled to achieve out of sheer emotional depletion. "Do you *really* think I should sign it? I mean—" Luce broke off, dismayed not so much by the thought of continuing the struggle herself as by the prospect of asking all the other mermaids to keep going, too.

Dr. Perle watched her, the wisdom in her olive eyes like a steady glow. "This treaty will make a tremendous impact for the better, general. So, yes, I really do think you should sign."

The papers fluttered in front of Luce. She read them through, still feeling weary and doubtful. Her lieutenants began whispering. Of course, Luce thought, they were impatient to get this all over with. The black letters winked like fish in a moon-colored sea. There was President Leopold's jagged signature, and there was the line for hers. Seb smiled wryly—or was that a grimace?—as he handed her a pen.

She signed.

Around Luce mermaids started cheering and clapping. Even most of the Secret Service men applauded. "Time to lower the wave, Luce?" Yuan asked giddily. "I've got it all figured out. I'll pull one singer out every few minutes so the water level has plenty of time to adjust without causing any problems. We'll do this nice and slow and safe. It will probably take all night, but then *damn* will it be time for a party! Sound good?"

Luce couldn't even answer. She just nodded.

The cries of celebration were spreading from hill to hill. Mermaids spun high in the air, shrieking and laughing. People had started dancing on the bridge, and Luce saw a few mermaids who had swum to the top of the wave trying to leap far enough into the air to exchange high-fives with the humans leaning against the railings. Cars honked, and soon the uproar spread from the bridge and across the city until the entire bay seemed to reverberate like an immense liquid drum. Everyone was delirious with joy.

Everyone except her. Luce made herself go through the motions, first shaking hands with dozens of excited humans and wishing them all a good evening, then trying to look happy when her friends launched themselves at her in wild hugs that sometimes turned into playful wrestling or sent her tumbling through lilac-gray water.

The Twice Lost had won, more or less. They'd won against incredible odds, and for the first time in history mermaids and humans were reconciled. They were right to be ecstatic.

The problem for Luce was that she couldn't forget the price they'd paid for their victory. As soon as she thought no one was looking, she slipped away, skimming recklessly out toward the open sea. She hadn't swum out into the savage waters far beyond the shelter of the bay since the night when the submarines had attacked the Twice Lost—not since she'd seen Bex cut in half by a spurt of machine gun fire. Even now Luce didn't really know how many mermaids had died that night: dozens of girls were still missing, but there was no way to determine who was dead and who was simply hiding.

At first the song of the Twice Lost still purled around her. It curled and ebbed like a second ocean made of music, a timbre that infused the waves and answered their secret songs. Then she went on, and the music slowly faded out behind her.

And as she swam she kept noticing something that looked like a golden lantern trailing ribbons of light. It kept pace with her the way the moon does, only it followed her through deep sea rather than clear sky. It would vanish for long stretches as if disappearing behind rooftops or trees, then Luce would catch sight of it sailing along beneath her again.

The fifth time she saw it, she understood what it was: the face of a sleeping girl, her long golden hair rippling in her wake like tentacles. The face wasn't attached to a body, but its expression offered a sense of enveloping peace.

Anais, Luce realized. She didn't know if the fact that she was seeing Anais meant her mind was going. And it was astounding to see Anais looking so utterly serene, so sweetly transfigured . . .

The face blinked away again. There was only a hint of golden rivulets, a subtle fluctuation as if the darkness was straining to remember the glow it had held moments before. Maybe the face was behind something, a stingray or a tangle of kelp? Luce didn't know how far she'd gone beyond the bridge, but her body was rocked by deep swells again, disorienting after the calm enclosed waters of the bay. The pressure thickened as she swam deeper, layers of sea heaping above her back.

The golden girl reappeared, lambent and drowsy and still somehow precisely the same distance away from Luce, although she *had* to be much farther from the surface now. Anais's face guttered, its deep internal light disturbed by a play of darkness. For an instant Luce thought that Anais's lips were moving, as if she was murmuring something in her sleep.

Rationally, of course, Luce knew that Anais was dead. Her lifeless body was thousands of miles away from the surging Pacific. Even now scientists might be stroking her flesh with shining blades, opening her cold chest to search for any sign that she'd been anything but human. Whatever she was seeing, Luce reminded herself, it wasn't *actually* Anais.

She could tell herself that, but she couldn't persuade her heart that it was true. She couldn't stifle her longing to know what Anais was saying and to talk with her one last time. Maybe, now that they'd both lost so much, they would finally make sense to each other.

"Anais?" Luce called. Even the dusk light was gone now, crushed by the enormity of the water above. Night saturated the deepening brine, and an immense weight began to squeeze Luce's ribs from all sides at once. "Anais? Can you wake up? There's something I need to tell you."

But what? Luce thought. Anais had saved her own life, though only for a time, by betraying her fellow mermaids. She'd murdered larvae, she'd tried to kill Dorian, and she'd deliberately shattered

Luce's father's mind. But somehow, unfathomably, Luce couldn't make herself feel any anger toward her old enemy. All she wanted was to heal the hatred between them, soothe the malice Anais had felt toward Luce ever since —

Ever since Luce had helped transform Anais into a mermaid. It had been the only way to stop Catarina from drowning her, but still . . . All at once Luce understood what was troubling her, what made her blood fight inside her as she stared at those always-retreating, gold-lashed eyelids: whatever Anais had done, Luce's own choice was at the root of it.

"Is that why you hated me?" Luce asked softly. "Because I *changed* you, and maybe you would have rather died the way you were?"

Anais's lids fluttered at bit as if she were gliding through the fringed edge of a dream. Her long hair waved as if it was trying to communicate with an unknown but graceful sign language. Luce had completely forgotten how far she was from the surface now, or at least she didn't care. Anais had something to say to her, something *important*, and this was their final chance to forgive each other.

"Anais?" Luce called again. The sullen weight of the water gripped her body. It kneaded the air from her lungs and mashed own her scales against her flesh until they felt like biting coins. "If that's the reason . . . everything went so wrong, then I'm really sorry. I'm sorry for everything that happened to you because of me. Please . . ."

Anais blinked dark and gold, dark and gold. Her eyes finally opened, but they were the whitish blue of nimbus clouds and seemed perfectly blind. The last time Luce saw her she was smiling.

Smiling like an evil dream. Luce's lungs were burning.

Well, she told herself, *you said you didn't care what happened to you, Lucette. Not as long as you could end the war.*

40

The Forever World

"So she went off to get some sleep, Cala," Yuan said a little brusquely. "I don't know if you've noticed, but Luce has been seriously burned out ever since those mermaids got pulled out of the water. Whatever. I wish she'd stayed up to celebrate with us tonight too, but it's more important for her to rest." Yuan and Cala were hovering ten feet below the surface. Through the thick rippling ceiling above them the wave-wall appeared like a long rag of glowing lace. It was already significantly lower. Yuan had been gradually removing singers from the line for hours, and Cala thought Yuan's nerves must be fraying from overwork and exhaustion.

"She isn't in her hammock," Cala said. "I checked there first. Yuan, I know you're busy! I wouldn't bother you if this wasn't serious."

"Then she's with Dorian. Good, I like him. I think he'll really help her recover from all this craziness." Yuan's lips pinched as she surveyed the line of mermaids. "Awright, that's been long enough since the last one. Hey, Eileen? Lower your voice nice and slowly, okay? You're done here."

Eileen nodded, her strawberry blond hair tossing with the

movement. Filaments of light from the bridge curved around her face as her song began to drop through a long series of fading, silky tones.

"She isn't with Dorian, either," Cala insisted gently. All at once she was afraid that Yuan wouldn't be able to cope once she understood that Luce was truly missing.

"How do you know?" Yuan's snappishness only made Cala more concerned. "Of course they wouldn't be making out right where everyone could see them!"

"Because he's been looking for her too. Paddling around in that kayak. We've both been searching every place we can think of, and she just isn't anywhere. Yuan, I don't want to freak you out, but we have to send out search parties or *something*."

For the first time Cala saw Yuan's eyes light with genuine concern. Eileen was just leaving the line, swishing below them. "Hey, Eileen?" Yuan called down.

"Yeah?" Eileen reared back to look at them, her tail sweeping above her head in an immense C.

Everyone was just so *tired*, Cala thought. The exhilaration of victory seemed thin and wispy now compared to the weariness of their long struggle.

"You're not off duty after all. I've got a brand-new assignment for you. General Luce is missing, and we need to get as many lieutenants as we can to organize search parties. Get a few of the girls who are just playing or whatever and go. I'm giving you the coast around Sausalito."

Eileen groaned. "The war's done, Yuan. If Luce wants to disappear she can go right ahead. I've got somebody *else* to look for."

"Like who?" Cala snapped.

"My sister, Kathleen Fain. She hasn't showed up here yet, but

I know she's *going* to." Eileen looked so miserable that Cala melted. "The only thing that would stop her would be if she's dead."

Eileen swirled onward, and Yuan grimaced with exasperation. "I'd come help you search if I could, Cala. But I've got to keep on directing everyone lowering the wave until it's completely finished." Yuan sighed and tipped in the water as if she wanted to lean her head on something, but there was nothing there except a twinkling constellation of tiny silver fish. "Luce—she wouldn't give up on herself *now*, would she? I mean, we won the war, and nobody really believed we'd be able to do that! Luce seriously better not have done anything stupid. I'll kick her *ass* if she—"

"That's exactly what I'm worried about," Cala admitted. "Luce giving up. Like, she might think nobody needs her anymore? Now that we've won?"

"Of *course* we need her!" Yuan's beautiful face was crumpling even as her voice rose furiously. "And what about her dad? And Dorian?"

Strong as Yuan was, Cala thought, the strain was obviously getting to be too much for her to handle. "I'll organize the search parties. I just need to be able to tell everyone you agreed we should do that. Okay? Yuan, you don't have to worry. We'll find her."

"Report back here *right* away if you find anything! I swear, Luce is getting bitch slapped if she even *thinks* about doing anything besides being totally happy from now on! You *tell* her that!"

Cala wanted to say something playful and comforting in response, but she couldn't think of anything that would make Yuan feel better. "I'll report back as soon as I can."

There were mermaids chatting with the humans onshore, and Cala headed over there to look for volunteers. In some cases mermaids were kissing new human boyfriends. Late as it was Helene and Ray Vogel were reading aloud from a huge illustrated volume of fairy tales to a circle of the youngest mermaids. From the longing on their small faces, Cala knew that many of them had never had anyone read them stories before.

"Hey," Cala called, too softly. No one turned around. "Hey, I need help! Luce is missing and she might be in trouble!"

That got their attention. Ten minutes later Cala had managed to get three small groups together and sent them out to search in different directions: along the north and south sides of the bay, with the third group heading out into the open sea.

Cala thought of how Luce had looked just after she'd signed the treaty—her blank, faded gaze, her forced smiles, her air of weary abstraction—and wondered if the search would prove futile.

* * *

"What a scrap she is," a gruff voice said nearby. "A rag of skin and scales. Easily destroyed, easily thrown away."

Even though someone was speaking, Luce supposed that she was still in the ocean. The medium that contained her was cold and terribly heavy; it ebbed and pitched. And yet somehow it felt not like the Pacific on a chill night in early September but like everywhere and always. It felt like the place where days and years burst their membrane-fine skins and poured into a single fluid sphere. *The forever world*, Luce thought vaguely. She thought of continents and seas ripped into confetti and gusting out of the map. She could see nothing, not even darkness.

"To what purpose?" This time the voice was a girl's. "What we have before us is the rag, but is that rag truly Queen Luce? Or is Queen Luce the changes now wrought on the world?"

Luce felt an icy current wrapping her body. It was strong enough to bind her arms to her sides. Then with a kind of contemptuous flick it sent her rolling, and seized her again.

"She should end here. Her every act has been defiance." A pause. "She has led *all* your kindred into defiance. And so I choose to lead her to these depths, here to abandon her. Her mermaid's form is forfeit, and she will die very soon once I take it from her."

"Children do defy their parents," a different girl observed cynically.

"They may, when those parents are human," the low voice rumbled in annoyance. It sounded half sea.

"No. When the children grow *up*. When their ideas are no longer only the ideas their parents have offered them. When they think beyond what they've been taught." She paused. Luce had the sense that this unknown girl was about to give voice to something she found difficult, even frightening. "For these thousands of years the mermaids have been your obedient children. Perhaps it was time for one of us to change that."

Luce felt her muscles squeezed and buffeted. Whatever held her pressed in with bruising force. Her eyes merged with the endless nowhere.

"I *saved* her!" The sea voice was now a roar. "I saved her and I offered her great gifts, and she repaid me with this rebellion, this contempt."

"She repaid you by leading the mermaids into a future you never imagined for them," the first girl said coolly. "Everything between mermaids and humans is different now. Queen Luce has repaid you with *transformation*. Surely that is your own coin?"

The deep voice growled. "You listen to Nausicaa too much."

Luce tried and failed to cry out at that. *Nausicaa? Where are you?*

"I listen to what my own long experience tells me. So does my sister. Even the sea is too confining when your destiny is settled for you, and when that destiny describes so small a circuit." The girl paused again. "Queen Luce should be with us. She's earned that choice."

"She's earned nothing but death!"

"We *claim* her. Luce is ours. As we were first, so is she the first of the mermaids as they will now become. And we refuse to see her harmed."

The sea rumbled in Luce's head. Her whole skull roared like the inside of a seashell. There was a sound like vast currents quarreling. Sheets of water seemed to grind against one another until they squealed like iron; Luce's empty eyes suddenly poured down tracks of blue phosphorescent flame.

Then, very quietly, she was no longer everywhere. Though it was impossible to guess precisely what had changed, Luce could sense that she was now somewhere quite specific. Her body was a point in space, it was enclosed in latitude and longitude, and the world was again banded by magnetic pull.

The time was no longer always, but *now*. She was weak and nauseous and—though she knew beyond all doubt that she'd been hopelessly far from the surface when her consciousness had merged with that strange forever—a cool breeze was brushing across her face. It took her a moment to understand that, and to remember to breathe.

Everything was dark, but that was because her eyes were closed. The process of opening them seemed confusing at first, but with an effort she managed it. Dark sea, towering night, and in the distance a star of piercing radiance high on a cliff. Behind it rolling tree-fringed hills. To the star's right a long expanse of beach shone like a pale fissure in the darkness. "Is that light the Cliff House?" Luce asked aloud.

She felt a quick swish of displaced water as someone nearby spun around in surprise. Ten feet away from her a dark head swung to see who'd spoken.

Luce had never imagined that it would even be possible for Nausicaa to look so utterly discomposed, so flabbergasted. She grinned at her friend's dropped mouth and rounded eyes; Luce couldn't have explained why, but she wasn't surprised to see Nausicaa at all. She'd just emerged from the *always*, after all, and Nausicaa was Luce's private always, the ocean continually cresting in her heart. "But . . . Luce?" Nausicaa stammered at last.

Luce laughed and swam over to her, then realized again how weak she was. "Let's swim to the beach. I think I might faint soon." She leaned her head on Nausicaa's shoulder.

"Luce!" Nausicaa hugged her tight and looked around. "But where . . . are we?"

"That looks like the Cliff House. I thought I went farther south than that, but . . ."

"Near San Francisco, then?" Nausicaa was regaining a hint of her usual poise, though she still seemed uncharacteristically shaky.

"I guess so. Where do *you* think we are?"

Nausicaa gave a crazed laugh. "When last I *knew* where I was, I was watching from a distance as the lights came on for the evening across the vast city of Alexandria. In Egypt, Luce. It might be ten thousand miles away from this place. I had just left the Twice Lost mermaids there." She shook her head, her dark curls ruffling. "I thought that was only moments ago. But perhaps . . ."

Now it was Luce's turn to be unsettled. "Egypt?" She thought for a moment. "Then . . . did you go through a place that didn't seem like it was anywhere exactly?"

Nausicaa bit her lip. "I heard myself speaking. How did I hear that, Luce, unless it was a dream? I heard myself in conversation with the first mermaids, the Unnamed Twins. But I often dream of them, of course; they were my dear friends when I was newly in the sea." Nausicaa stared, searching through billows of memory. "But now I think this was no dream. There was a discussion . . . about you. And I believe that they . . . extended an invitation, Luce. To the two of us."

That made sense, Luce thought. She nodded, and then her head seemed to keep nodding by itself. Her eyelids swagged, and her face felt warm and watery. "I . . . really need to sleep. I can't talk now."

Nausicaa gazed at her in sudden concern and began towing her toward the shore. Luce saw the light of the Cliff House prancing and swinging through the dark. It was lucky that Nausicaa was holding her, Luce realized hazily, because she couldn't possibly hang on to consciousness any longer.

* * *

When Cala's search party found them it was well after dawn. They couldn't wake Luce and so they carried her home, Cala and Elva in the lead with Luce's tail slung across their arms, Nausicaa swimming behind and supporting her friend's head at the surface. Nausicaa studied Luce's jagged dark hair and long crescent eyelids, wondering at how transfigured she was. Her features were the same as ever, but even in her sleep Luce now had the aspect of a mermaid who'd been in the sea for centuries.

They passed beneath the Golden Gate Bridge. The huge standing wave was completely gone now. The bay gleamed mirror-smooth, without even a line of foam to show where the blockade had been.

Luce didn't wake up to see it. But on the shore not far to their right, mixed with the usual crowd, there were doctors in white coats, gurneys, and ambulances.

The mermaids had started turning back.

A girl in a borrowed bathrobe tried to stand on legs as wobbly as a newborn calf's then toppled slowly sideways. Her skin had a faint greenish shine.

"Hey," a slightly tattered man with cropped hair and cinnamon eyes shouted across the water. He waved his arms high overhead, looking straight at the group carrying Luce. "Hey! You've got my girl! Is she okay?"

"That's the general's dad," Cala sighed. "How are we supposed to explain what happened?" Then she raised her voice. "She'll be fine, Mr. Korchak! We promise! She'll come see you later!"

Nausicaa gazed at him with interest. For the first time she wondered if she might have to let Luce go forever. She pictured Luce stumbling toward her father on human legs and looked away.

41

Promises

"Heya, general-girl," Yuan said as Luce at last opened bleary eyes. She barely knew where she was, but Yuan's determined face was clear enough. "Damn, it's about time you woke up! I'm here to say goodbye."

"Goodbye?" Luce asked in confusion. "Yuan, where—"

"To Boston. With Gigi. She's got to get back to college." Yuan made a face. "And I'm going to go finish *high school*, of all insane things. There are these human groups organizing to, uh, *rehabilitate* ex-mermaids, so it looks like I'll have some help."

It took Luce several more moments to understand what Yuan was talking about. Then she groaned and sat up abruptly. One reaching hand found Yuan's shoulder and squeezed it. "Yuan, are you serious?" All at once Luce felt like crying. "You're really leaving the water?"

Suddenly grave, Yuan said, "Yeah, I am. Because you were right, Luce."

"How do you mean?"

"When you told me that Gigi was actually my best friend. That I saved her *because* she's—the person I love most in the world. I didn't know that when I was pulling her to safety, but I know it now." Yuan waited a few moments for that to sink in. "But we're really hoping you'll come and visit us, Luce. You and your dad." She paused for a moment. "Or you and Dorian. We'll have a blast together! And you and Dorian could maybe look at colleges in Boston too, right? 'Twice Lost General' is one hell of an extracurricular, so I bet you can go anywhere you want."

Luce shook her head. She still felt obscurely sick, and she was bewildered to realize that Yuan took it for granted that she'd be turning human again. Imani had made the same assumption. Why did her path seem so obvious to them? "I can't think about *college*. I don't know what I'm going to do."

"Sure you do!" Yuan was sincerely shocked. "I mean, what about your dad?"

"If he needs me to take care of him . . ." Luce swayed a little as she considered the question. "If he's not all the way cured, then . . . I guess that would be the right thing to do."

"Of course it is! Family has to come first, Luce." Yuan saw Luce's stunned look and grimaced. "Okay, I know that probably sounds hypocritical, coming from me. But your dad is a good guy and mine was a monster. You do appreciate the distinction, right?"

Luce didn't answer that. Instead she dropped from the hammock and hugged Yuan hard.

"You gonna come see me off, general-girl?" Yuan was straining to keep her tone light.

"Of course I'm coming. But I'm not actually anybody's general," Luce murmured. "Not anymore."

"Yeah? Who is?" Yuan didn't wait for an answer before diving abruptly. She whipped away at top speed and then vaulted over a sea lion with her pink-gold fins gleaming in midair. *It's for the last time,* Luce thought. *Yuan's never going to leap that way again.*

A long procession of mermaids followed her. Some of them had larvae cradled in their arms.

* * *

Yuan held her arm out for the injection. Then a group of human volunteers carried her inside a small white room made of folding screens while Gigi looked on with worried eyes. Luce caught a final glimpse of Yuan's fins twitching as the air hit them.

She'd hoped—even assumed—that the drugs would make the transition painless, but that clearly wasn't the case. Soon they all heard Yuan's thin, keening screams. Luce had to throttle her own impulse to scream in sympathy, to send a wave that would lift Yuan and pull her back to them. Luce clenched her teeth instead, her heart charging and her nails digging into her palms until they were flecked with blood. This was Yuan's choice to make, and no one had a right to interfere. By the time Yuan came stumbling out in a borrowed lilac sundress and bedroom slippers Luce's face was slick with tears.

"I'm cool," Yuan slurred. "Seriously, it's not that bad." Then she fainted into Gigi's arms.

She's alive, Luce told herself. *She'll be fine. That's all that matters.*

Silently some of the mermaids around her started handing larvae to the doctors. It was terrible to think of the infantile little mermaids suffering that way, but everyone knew it was better than the fate that waited for them in the ocean. As human children they could be adopted; they would grow up and possibly even find happiness. In the sea they'd be unlikely to survive for long.

The afternoon took on the feeling of an endless ceremony. Now and then a mermaid's face would start to waver, crossed by alternating doubt and longing, and then she would nod to herself and call the doctors over, looking back at her friends who were still in the water with puzzled sorrow. It was hard to watch, but Luce knew that it would feel worse to swim away.

It was at least an hour before Luce realized that her father was there, well back in the crowd; she couldn't tell if he'd just arrived or if he'd been standing there quietly all along. He looked older and sadder than he should, but he definitely didn't seem crazy anymore.

He was watching Luce somberly, so lost in thought that he didn't react when she smiled at him.

"Oh my God!" Elva screamed next to her. "Luce, look!"

Luce turned away from her father just for a moment. She couldn't tell why Elva was splashing so excitedly and waving at a handsome human couple who were picking their way gingerly through the crowd.

Her father was gone when she looked for him again. Where *was* he?

Elva grabbed Luce's arm and shook it ferociously. "Luce, don't you see?"

Luce's head swung in bewilderment. Elva was still pointing to the human couple: a tall slim man with a narrow, light brown, sharp-boned face. A remarkably beautiful redhead was leaning heavily on his arm. She was long-legged, wearing teal cowboy boots and skinny black jeans with a fuzzy sea green sweater — and when she met Luce's eyes her foot halted in midair. If her boyfriend hadn't held her by her narrow waist she might have fallen.

Luce heard herself gasp. That lovely girl looked horribly similar to Catarina; she even looked at her with Catarina's gray, wounded eyes.

"Catarina!"

Suddenly Elva wasn't the only mermaid screaming. Voices were shouting on all sides, "Catarina! Cat! Cat! Cat!" It was becoming a chant now, but Luce still couldn't quite believe it. Her insides were watery, roiling; her heart seemed to be caught in a whirlpool.

The redhead slowly approached as if she couldn't hear the clamoring voices, and her eyes never left Luce's for a moment. Her steps were unsteady, and Luce briefly wondered if she'd hurt her legs somehow.

"Cat?" Luce couldn't believe she'd said that name.

The redhead didn't smile, but now that she was closer there did seem to be a subtle green-golden cast to her skin. She was at the line of rocks separating the parking lot from the bay when she staggered and dropped to her knees.

Luce didn't know she was reaching wildly forward until her hand found the redhead's hand in midair and squeezed it. "Oh God, Cat . . ."

"I'm sorry, Luce. I know the things I said to you were unfair and unkind. I hope we can be reconciled." Catarina delivered the words as if she'd rehearsed them, her voice clipped and formal. Beside her the dark young man knelt too, gazing at Catarina with ardent tenderness.

Luce started sobbing. She didn't care that humans and mermaids were staring at her or that she might seem weak. Sobs wrenched from her so fiercely that she thought they might tear out her heart. She clutched Catarina's hand above the row of stones and wept from gratitude.

Catarina laughed. Not harshly but with relieved delight. "I didn't know if I should dare to come here! I was afraid you would be disgusted at the sight of me, my Lucette. Rafe told me that wasn't true. He said you would be overjoyed to know I lived. He said it was important that we meet again, you and I. I had to wait until your treaty was signed to gain my freedom, but then I was terrified to show my face here. For hours Rafe persuaded me."

Luce looked at Rafe through her tears and reached out her free hand to him. "Thank you," was all she could say.

Rafe grinned. "You're very welcome, general. It wasn't hard at all for me to believe you still loved Catarina."

He went for a walk while Luce and Catarina talked and sometimes cried, their words coming fast and overlapping, oblivious to the world around them. It didn't take Luce long to notice how often Catarina said Rafe's name and how her eyes seemed to deepen whenever she mentioned him. It was strange after all of Catarina's vehement hatred for humans, but this was unmistakable. "Are you in love with him, Cat?" Luce asked.

"I never knew there *were* such people. I did not imagine a man like Rafe could be possible, Lucette! If you knew the humans I grew up with, if you had met my parents or those men who bought me, you would understand why I believed all humans were bestial. Vile. To learn so late . . ." Catarina shook her head and let out a plaintive laugh. "But Rafe says that all of us base our conclusions on our experience and that I could not be expected to do otherwise. Still, when I think I would have gladly *drowned* him, removed such a great heart from the world without a thought, I feel . . . as I suppose you sometimes felt, Lucette. I can only focus on the future so that shame won't consume me."

"What are you going to do?"

"Attend university. First I must complete intensive studies, though. I can only read the Cyrillic alphabet that is used for Russian, for one thing; I never learned yours." Catarina's gaze was momentarily far away. "When I finish my education, I want to work . . . on behalf of girls like me."

For a fraction of a second Luce thought she meant ex-mermaids. Then she realized it wasn't that at all.

Catarina completed the thought. "I mean, girls who were sold."

Luce nodded. "That sounds like a completely amazing thing to do, Cat."

Dusk was falling. Catarina was starting to glance around, and Luce knew her former queen was waiting for the man she loved to reappear. It was both heartbreaking and wonderful to realize how soon Catarina would stand up and walk away with him. And, Luce knew, there was something she had to ask first. "Um, Cat? Do you miss being in the ocean?" Luce hesitated, afraid that she might make Catarina angry. "I mean, are you sorry you changed back?"

Catarina glanced at her sharply, as if she guessed why Luce was asking this particular question. "Miss the ocean? Of course I do, Luce. I didn't choose to be made human again. Humanity was forced on me. And yet I choose it *now*, now that I know what it can mean." She smiled ruefully. "All I'm sorry for is that I have to use a name that comes from my father."

Suddenly Rafe was there, listening and smiling to himself. Luce hadn't noticed him approaching, but now he reached to lift Catarina to her feet. "In a few years," Rafe said softly, "we might change that."

Catarina paused to say hello to a few of the other mermaids, Rafe close beside her. Then she looked around: mermaids and humans were talking and laughing together under the hazy rust-colored glow of scattered streetlamps. Yuan slept in a lawn chair with her head on Gigi's shoulder, her slippered feet sticking out from under a blanket, while well-wishers stopped by with gifts of clothes and books to help Yuan make the transition to her new life. Catarina glanced back at Luce. "It's all your song, Luce. It's your song come to life!"

"How do you mean?" Luce asked. Catarina looked magnificent and brave standing there, and also somehow much more grown-up than she'd ever seemed before. Her hair no longer shone with its own internal luminance, but it still flowed like fire in the lamplight.

"Your song always promised *forgiveness*, Luce, don't you remember? It promised forgiveness and reconciliation so sweet that people would joyfully die for it." Catarina smiled wryly at her. "Who would have thought that any mermaid's promise would be so truly fulfilled?"

* * *

The scene at the shore had turned into a party. Mermaids were singing to the water, not to raise a blockade but to create spiraling fountains, wobbling parapets, and floating liquid stars while the humans onshore laughed and applauded. The mermaids had turned into such *showoffs*, Luce thought, but the idea made her smile.

She hadn't seen Nausicaa or Dorian all day. It wouldn't be surprising if Nausicaa had simply gone exploring, but, especially now that she'd seen Catarina so deeply in love, Dorian's absence triggered a low, painful vibration in her chest. Maybe he'd realized he didn't want her back after all.

Luce skimmed out into the bay, floating on her back and watching the full yellow moon. Voices bubbled over the water. She swept slowly around the curve of the coast, under the bridge's red complex spine, and then rolled over and over, stretching and feeling water curling like plumes around her scales. It still felt strange to see the surface here so flat and placid now that the water-wall was gone. Only a handful of people were perching on the bunkers. It still wasn't exactly private, but Luce's head felt clearer.

"I'm so *worried* about her," a voice said quietly, and Luce's heart stilled. "You know how Luce can sing to heal people? I feel like we need to find someone who can do that for *her* now. She's just—she seems pretty messed up."

"Luce is sorely hurt," Nausicaa agreed, "but perhaps these are not the kind of wounds that *should* be healed, Dorian. Perhaps what wounds her now is wisdom."

Much as Luce loved them both she wished they wouldn't talk about her. She wished everyone would just stop talking about her once and for all. From the corner of her eye she spotted them now, huddled close together. Dorian was perched on a boulder, the soles of his high-tops just grazing the bay while Nausicaa's feral black hair gusted across his knee.

"I don't think that's *wisdom*. I think it's like posttraumatic shit from the war. She's going to need serious therapy or *something*. I mean, it's going to be hard enough for her to deal with going back to school, especially since everybody's going to recognize her!" Dorian's voice was sharp and plangent. It was strange to discover that he'd given so much thought to what her human life would be like. Luce hadn't considered how she'd feel in a human school at all. "She's always going to be—kind of greenish, right, even once she's human? And there's that triangle torn out of her ear. I guess she could grow out her hair and hide it that way, but . . ."

There was an awkward pause. "Truthfully I hope that Luce will make a different choice than this you envision, Dorian. She doesn't belong to the land now."

"Yes, she *does*. She can't just stay in the sea forever! That's not like a real life at all."

The currents furled and licked at Luce's fins and the moonlight sank into her eyes. *What's not* real *about this, again?*

"I promise you that I will not try to influence Luce to remain in the sea with me, however. And I hope that you will show the same forbearance, Dorian. Luce must decide for herself."

"I'm not showing any *forbearance*. Me and her dad both need her! She'll be way happier with us, and she'll be safer, and — there has to be some way to get her help. Somebody will help her dad pay for a great therapist. Luce has all these fans now. Some of them *must* be rich."

Luce had heard enough. It was probably too late to find her father tonight, and somehow he was the only one whose opinion Luce cared about. She swam back to the mermaids near the shore: there were Cala, Opal, Graciela, all engaged in a kind of mad ballet where they leaped in synchrony with jets of rising water. It was a shame to interrupt them, Luce thought, but it was the last time she would. "Hey! Can I ask you guys a favor?"

"A favor? You mean it's not an order?" Opal laughed. Her ivory hair fanned like an explosion as she deliberately crashed down right in front of Luce, dousing her with an immense pale cascade.

"It's not an order," Luce said seriously as water sheeted off her cheeks. "That's all finished. But I do want to get everyone together for one last meeting back at the camp." She hesitated. "I'm going to be leaving soon."

"You mean you're going human?" Opal demanded, wide-eyed. She looked dismayed but she didn't wait for an answer. "Okay. We'll go find everybody."

Luce tried to smile reassuringly. "Can you please make sure Imani's there? I haven't seen her in a while."

"That's because she's busy practicing singing to heal people the way you can. She's like completely obsessed, and she's already working with some of the really crazy mermaids? I know where to find her, though." Opal paused. "Just because the war's over doesn't mean we don't still need a general, Luce. What if something goes wrong? Or you could just be queen instead. You don't have to *leave* us."

Luce found that she was too choked to answer. After a moment Opal nodded and swam away.

* * *

Half an hour later Luce made her way past the creek and under the huge glowering factory. The planks at its base were tar-slick and dripping. It was dirty and decrepit, and Luce's heart wrenched at the thought of leaving it behind.

The dimness among the pilings was packed with mermaids, more than she'd ever seen there. Faces like veiled moons bobbed in the water. The hammocks sagged under the weight of coiled tails, all flicking their soft colors through the dark. The chatter fell silent when Luce appeared. "Opal says you're leaving," someone called. "Just like Jo and Yuan."

"I am leaving," Luce confirmed. Now that she wasn't general anymore her shyness came rushing back, and she struggled to suppress it. So many faces were turned toward her. "I can't be a general anymore. And . . . I'll miss you all so much. You've been amazing. You've all been so *brave*, and that's why we won. But the main thing is that you need a new general now. That's what I wanted to say."

Luce glanced around to make sure. There was the new Twice Lost General, gazing down at the water. But what if she refused to take on the role? She was always so gentle, but Luce had caught glimpses of passion and ambition in her as well.

"Who?" Eileen asked, a bit curtly. "How are we supposed to decide that?"

"We're mermaids," Luce pointed out. Suddenly she found herself smiling. "That means we'll know the one who's meant to be *general* by her song. And . . . anyone who's been listening to her knows who that has to be! Please give your allegiance to her now."

There was a wild murmuring. The Twice Lost General looked up, somehow fervent and embarrassed at the same time—and, Luce suddenly saw, afraid that the name spoken next *wouldn't* be hers. The blue gleam of her heart-shaped face was like neon reflecting on a rainy street.

Luce took a deep breath. She felt proud and sad and exhilarated and wonderfully free. "General Imani . . . you'll lead the Twice Lost?"

Imani was smiling so vibrantly that Luce ached to see it.

"Oh, you just *know* I will, Luce."

* * *

Luce couldn't sleep. Instead she rocked in Catarina's old hammock, watching the far dark hills. The space under the factory was low enough that she couldn't see much of the bay, only a stripe of moon-banded water crossed occasionally by the container ships that were once again making their way out to sea—but she could *feel* the water stretching all the way to the horizon. Her thoughts pulsed with the breakers far beyond the bridge, crested with slow-rising whales. And if she concentrated she could feel something of the land as well: the college girls in spangled dresses tilting on their platform shoes as they emerged drunk from nightclubs, the candy wrappers gusting through the streets, Dorian asleep in a hotel bed. The night was just as beautiful on land as it was on the sea. A few nights from now she could be curled with Dorian on a sofa, watching a movie and talking about their plans for the future. She thought of his warm smell, his warmer hands stroking her cheeks.

Nausicaa hadn't come home, and Luce wasn't surprised. Her friend was staying away on purpose. Giving Luce room to decide on her own, but also unwilling to face the pain of losing her to the human world.

As dawn sent a spire of smoky amethyst light across the bay Luce felt something else: the certainty that her father was wide awake too. That he was sitting under those bunkers with a cup of takeout coffee in his hand, waiting patiently for her to appear. Luce slipped silently from her hammock and gazed at the sleeping mermaids around her, wishing them goodbye with her eyes.

Fifteen minutes later she found him just where she'd known he would be. It was the same spot where Ben Ellison had brought him when he was mad and vacant. He smiled calmly as he saw her head break through the surface. "Hi there, baby doll. Don't know why, but I figured you'd be showing up soon."

Apart from the two of them the shore was deserted. Without the continual allurement of mermaid song thrumming from under the bridge the crowds had finally gone home to sleep. "It's a good time," Luce whispered. "It's finally quiet. How are you *feeling* now?"

She could see for herself that he was more or less fine, though. He brushed the question away. "We've gotta talk." His cinnamon eyes had a troubled look.

"I know," Luce said. "I saw you yesterday, and I know you saw me. But I guess . . ."

"I wasn't ready to talk to you yet. I had to think it over. About this business of you girls turning human again. You know Dorian's got it all figured out, right? He's already calling people he knows from the Twice Lost Humans, trying to get me a job in Chicago. He's a couple days late getting back to school, and he's planning on you enrolling with him. I've been telling him to slow down."

Luce felt a cold fluttering as she pulled in a long breath. "I'm ready to do it. He can go ahead and plan. I mean, as long as *you* don't mind moving to Chicago."

"Why?" His eyes were hard. It wasn't like him, Luce thought. He almost seemed angry. "Why are you choosing this?"

Luce couldn't lie to him. "I think . . . you might need me to take care of you. That's a big enough reason."

He stood up abruptly, his hands squeezing into fists, and twisted a little while he stared off at the hills. He was definitely angry, but Luce wasn't sure why. The dawn had brightened now and thousands of gleaming copper shards jangled on the water. Then he gave a drawn-out sigh and bent over the rocks to ruffle her hair. "That's just what I was afraid you were thinking, baby doll. Sweet of you and everything. But I don't accept."

"But—"

"I am the parent here, Lucette. It's one thing if you wanna be human again because you're in love with Dorian. He's a good kid, smart enough for you, loves you like crazy. Okay, I'd be down with that. And it's fine if you need me to take care of *you*. That's what I've been hoping for, that I could finally do right by you and help you grow up. Then I started realizing: maybe you've already done that. I've been out of the picture too long, and you've gone and grown up without me."

"You couldn't help being out of the picture! Dad, so much *happened* . . ." Luce had never been able to stand hearing her father blame himself for anything. She still couldn't.

"Got nothing to do with it, if I could help it or not. Lucette, I might not have been much of a dad, but I'm enough of one to *want* you to go beyond me. Go further in yourself than I ever could. You know there are people saying it's got to be a lie about you being my daughter, because there's no way the great mermaid hero could've come from a schmuck like me? How do you think that makes me feel?"

The idea of anyone saying that enraged her. "Horrible."

"No." His hand was still tangled in her short hair, but his gaze was confrontational and fierce. "It makes me feel so proud I want to scream."

Luce felt as if her eyes were melting. Tears flooded her vision, crystalline and wild. "Maybe I could still make you proud. If I was human."

"I don't doubt you would, doll." His voice was softening and he brushed the tears from her lashes with his thumbs. "Don't do it for me, is all I'm saying. If you give up what you really want because of me it'll hurt me worse than I can stand. But if you don't *know* what you want, then, you know, there's no reason why you have to decide yet."

From here Luce could see the open ocean. Not too far in the distance there was a small patch where the light vaporized, blending into eternity; where the waves pitched to a rhythm that was somehow beyond the here and now.

He followed her gaze. "That's kind of what I thought." He paused. "So Dorian's too late?"

"I still love him," Luce said. "I love him a lot." She was searching her own heart, trying to understand what she was feeling. "But it's like he thinks turning me human again would *fix* me."

She was surprised to hear the tone of complaint in her voice. Now *she* was the one who sounded angry.

"I can see that," Andrew Korchak agreed. He grinned. "He does kind of talk that way. And why fix it when it ain't broken?"

"Maybe I am broken, but it's not *because* I'm a mermaid. It's because of things I've done, and I can't take them back by just having a different body!"

"You've done a lot more good than harm, Lucette." He was still stroking her hair. "But I guess I can understand you feeling that way. I mean, God knows I've been there!" He nodded toward the deepening ocean. "You feel like this is where you belong now, don't you?"

It's not that I belong in the sea. I am the sea. My voice is the sea.

"What about Seb?" Luce asked. "Seb Grassley. Our ambassador."

"Ben Ellison's starting up a program for ex-mermaids. You know I got poor old Ben fired from the FBI, mouthing off the way I did? Anyhow Ben said he was giving Seb a job. Offered me one, too, but somehow—I don't think that's what I'm going to be doing next. Don't you worry, though. We'll be okay." He paused. "I left Dorian a note to get down here as soon as he wakes up. I figured, one way or the other, you'd have something to say to him."

"I do."

Luce sang to her father for the last time, smoothing the remaining traces of damage from his mind. As it turned out they didn't have to wait too long. The sun was just gleaming above the distant hills when they heard the rhythm of running steps and Dorian came darting through the bunker at her father's back. Luce fell silent and stared at him, suddenly pierced by doubt. His bronze-blond hair flurried in the breeze, and his ochre eyes showed such passionate intelligence that Luce's heart skipped to see it. She still adored him, in fact. More than she'd realized.

Andrew Korchak got up and climbed a nearby staircase, giving them some privacy. He stood half-concealed by the roof's edge, facing the sea. He seemed to be watching the same patch of light Luce had noticed earlier: a place where the waves seemed to beat beyond the confines of time, where the light glimmered all the way to always. *The forever world.*

"Luce!"

No matter how confidently Dorian had been explaining his plans to her father, Luce could see that he was actually worried. He knew the conversation might not go his way. "Hi, Dorian." She caught his hand as he scrambled onto the rock above her. "I . . ." She didn't know if she could say it; she didn't even know if she *would* say it. "I wanted to say goodbye."

"Don't, Luce. *Don't* say that." Dorian paused. "You know how much I love you now, right? I've done everything I can think of to get you to forgive me. I really—"

"That's not why. I forgive you and I . . . I love you more now than I *ever* have. I wish everything was different. But you need a human girlfriend."

"You *can* be now. Luce, we can be together forever. We *should.*"

He was crying, and Luce knew that she would give anything to comfort him. Anything except for who she truly was.

"Dorian . . . it doesn't matter if I *could* be human again. I'm not. I mean, that's not who I really am."

She glanced over her shoulder again. A figure emerged from that wavering blot of light. Luce knew it was Nausicaa. She turned to wave at someone Luce couldn't see and then dived.

"What am I supposed to *do*, Luce?"

"Kiss me. Then get up and walk away." She smiled at him through the tears that blurred her vision. "And tell Zoe I said hi."

Dorian was in the water with her now. Tears merged where their cheeks touched, and Luce kissed his face and mouth again and again. How *soft* his lips were, how sweet each light touch of his hands . . .

Then she pulled away. She had to, *now*, before her heart shattered completely. "Go on, Dorian," Luce whispered. "Go be a hero. I'll remember."

The gold of his eyes was so charged with grief and longing and exultation that it looked almost inhuman as he gazed at her for the last time. Then, like the hero Luce knew he was, he accepted it. He climbed over the rocks and half smiled at her before he straightened himself.

And turned away.

From the darkness of the bunker Luce heard his voice breaking out in a drawn-out, wordless cry. It faded gradually until it sounded like the last faint shimmer of a song.

Luce was staring again at that velvety patch of glow. *Everywhere* and *always*, a million bits of winking focus blurring through one another. Now there were two figures silhouetted in front of it: girls, visible from the shoulders up. They were waiting.

Her father saw them too from his vantage up on the roof. Luce remembered again exactly why she loved her father so deeply when she caught sight of his expression. She could tell he understood, and he was smiling down at her with such pride that her tears quickened all over again.

Nausicaa broke through the surface just beside her. "Luce! I told you before, we have an invitation. And if you wish . . ."

She saw the answer in Luce's eyes and fell silent. As Nausicaa held out her hand the only sound was the rushing waves. The song of the waves rolled all the way to forever, and Luce pressed Nausicaa's fingers in her own.

They didn't have far to go.

ACKNOWLEDGMENTS

I am especially grateful to my much-loved friends Tera Freedman and Jenny Lemper, both of whom took me on scouting expeditions around San Francisco Bay to locate suitable mermaid habitats. (Tera brought me to the encampment at Islais Creek, and Jenny showed me Mare Island.) The sailors hanging out at the Bay View Boat Club offered dubious information ("There's a pod of whales out there, and they dance on their tails in the moonlight!") but charming company. The Monterey Bay Aquarium was both thrilling and extremely helpful in forming a mermaid's-eye-view of the area. And my wonderful husband, Todd Polenberg, first suggested that a blockade of the Golden Gate might be an effective strategy for mermaids in trouble.

* * *

In addition to the sources already mentioned in the acknowledgments for *Waking Storms*, I am indebted to Wendy Williams's book *Kraken* for giving me an entirely new appreciation of squids.